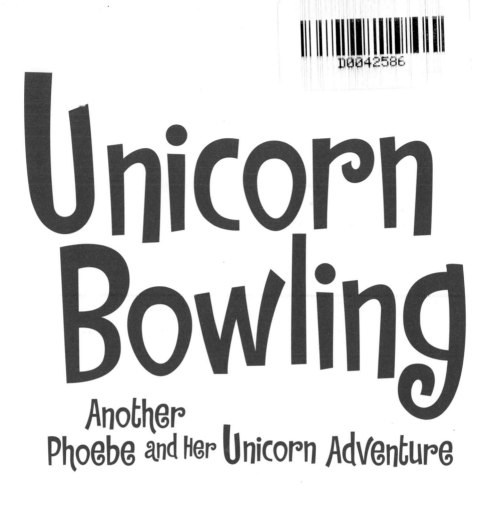

Unicorn Bowling

Another Phoebe and Her Unicorn Adventure

Dana Simpson

Andrews McMeel
PUBLISHING®

Hey, kids!

Check out the glossary starting on page 172
if you come across words you don't know.

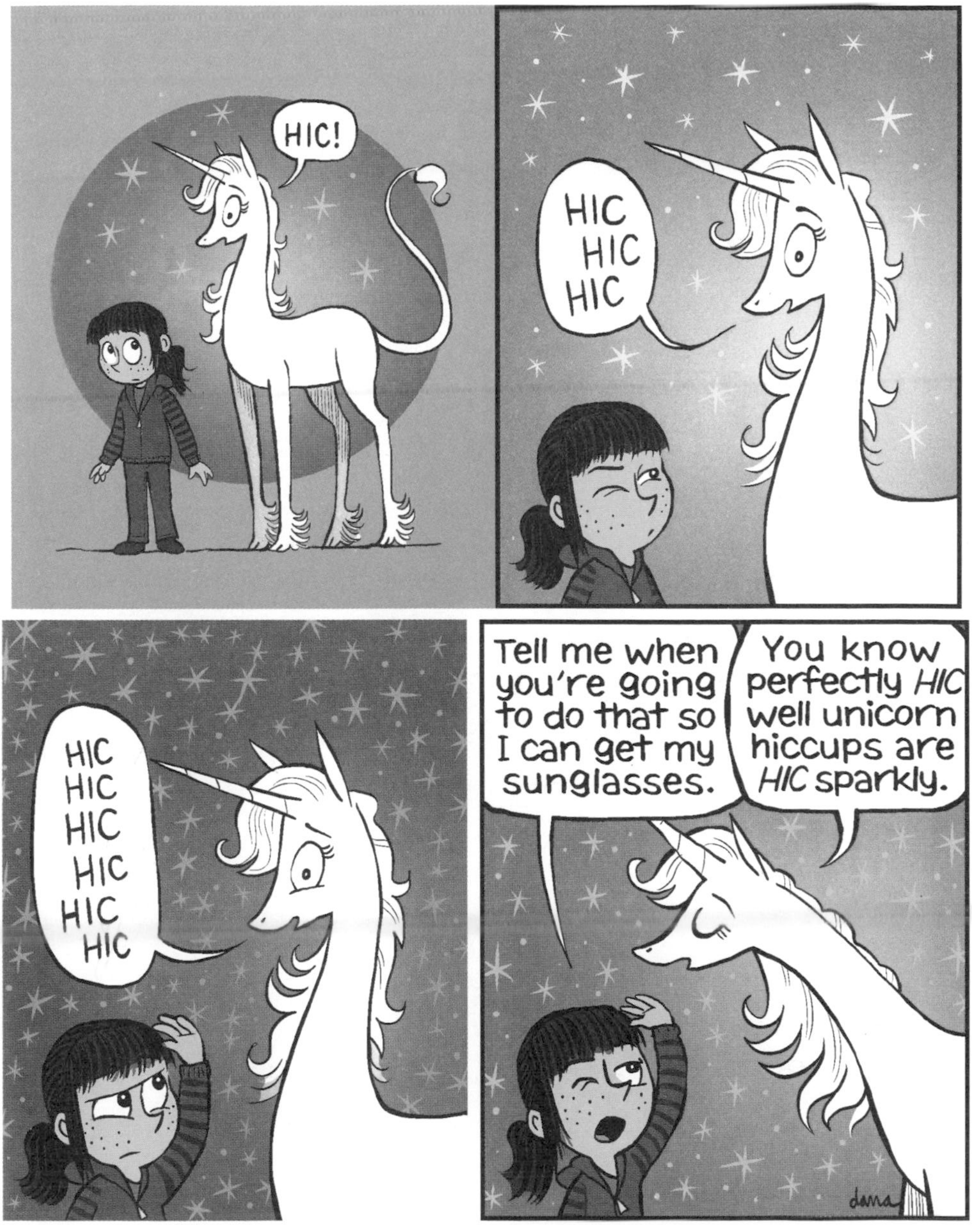
HIC!
HIC HIC HIC
HIC HIC HIC HIC HIC HIC
Tell me when you're going to do that so I can get my sunglasses.
You know perfectly *HIC* well unicorn hiccups are *HIC* sparkly.
dana

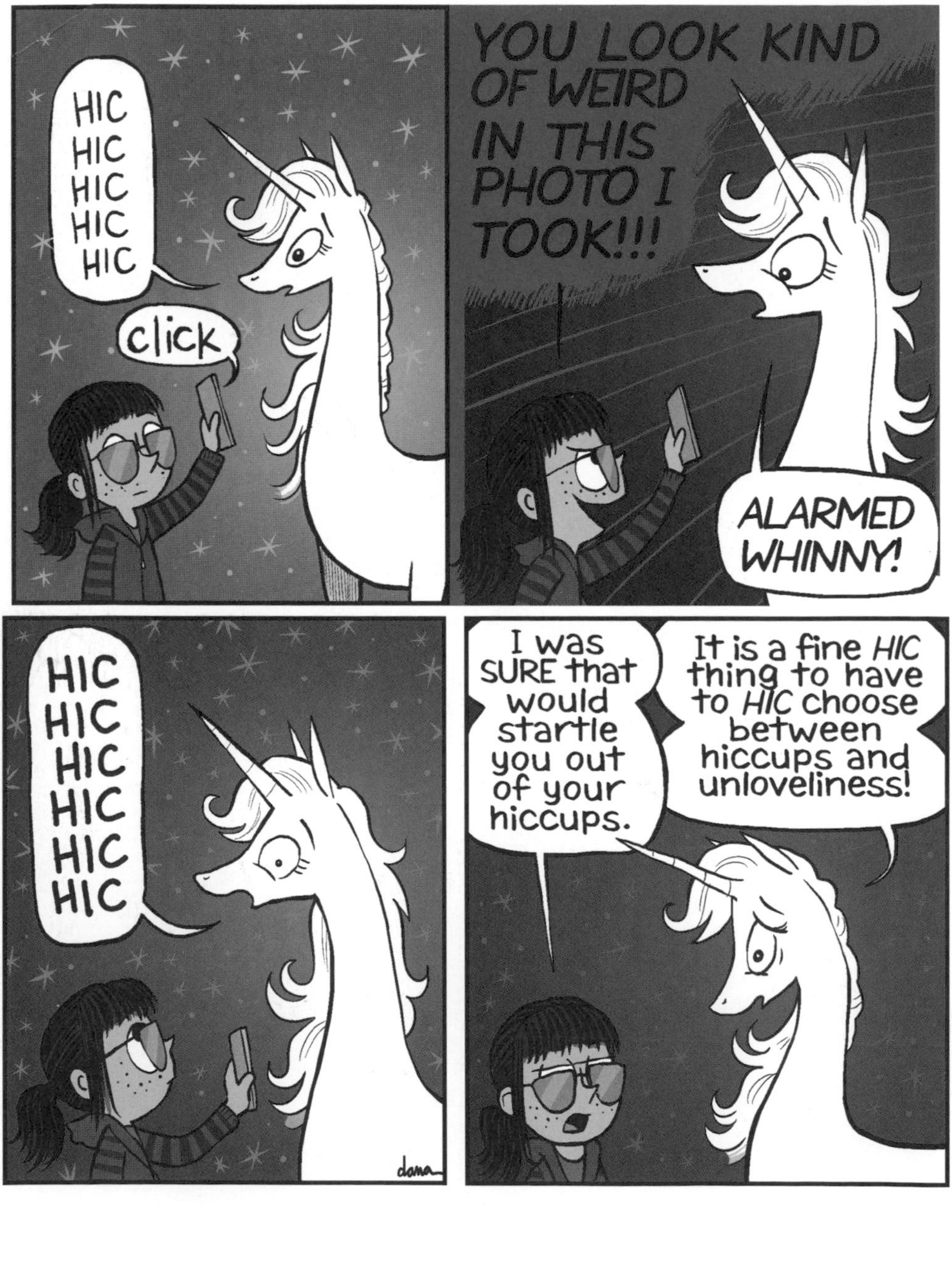
HIC HIC HIC HIC HIC
click
YOU LOOK KIND OF WEIRD IN THIS PHOTO I TOOK!!!
ALARMED WHINNY!
HIC HIC HIC HIC HIC HIC
I was SURE that would startle you out of your hiccups.
It is a fine HIC thing to have to HIC choose between hiccups and unloveliness!
dana

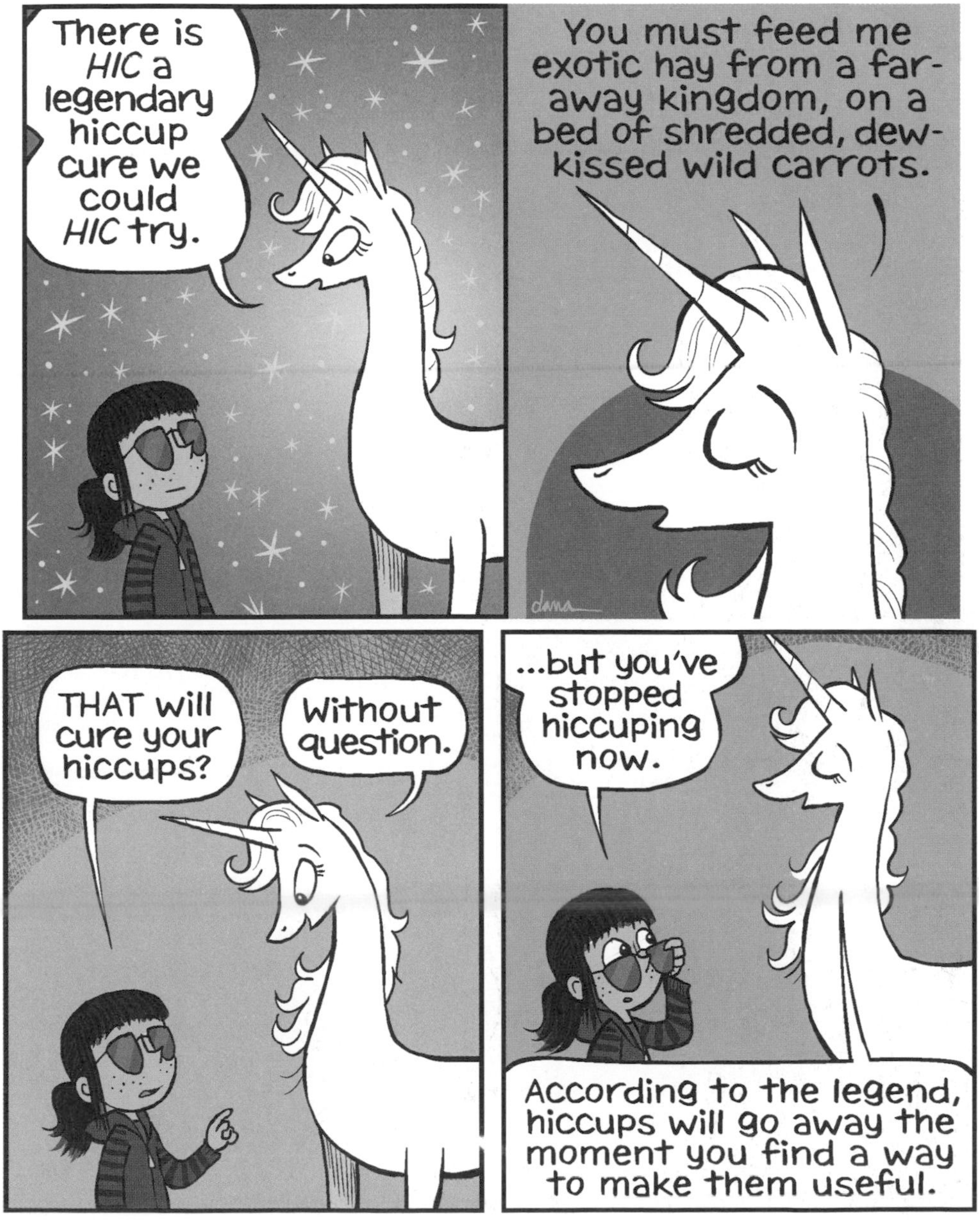

There is HIC a legendary hiccup cure we could HIC try.
You must feed me exotic hay from a far-away kingdom, on a bed of shredded, dew-kissed wild carrots.
dana
THAT will cure your hiccups?
Without question.
...but you've stopped hiccuping now.
According to the legend, hiccups will go away the moment you find a way to make them useful.

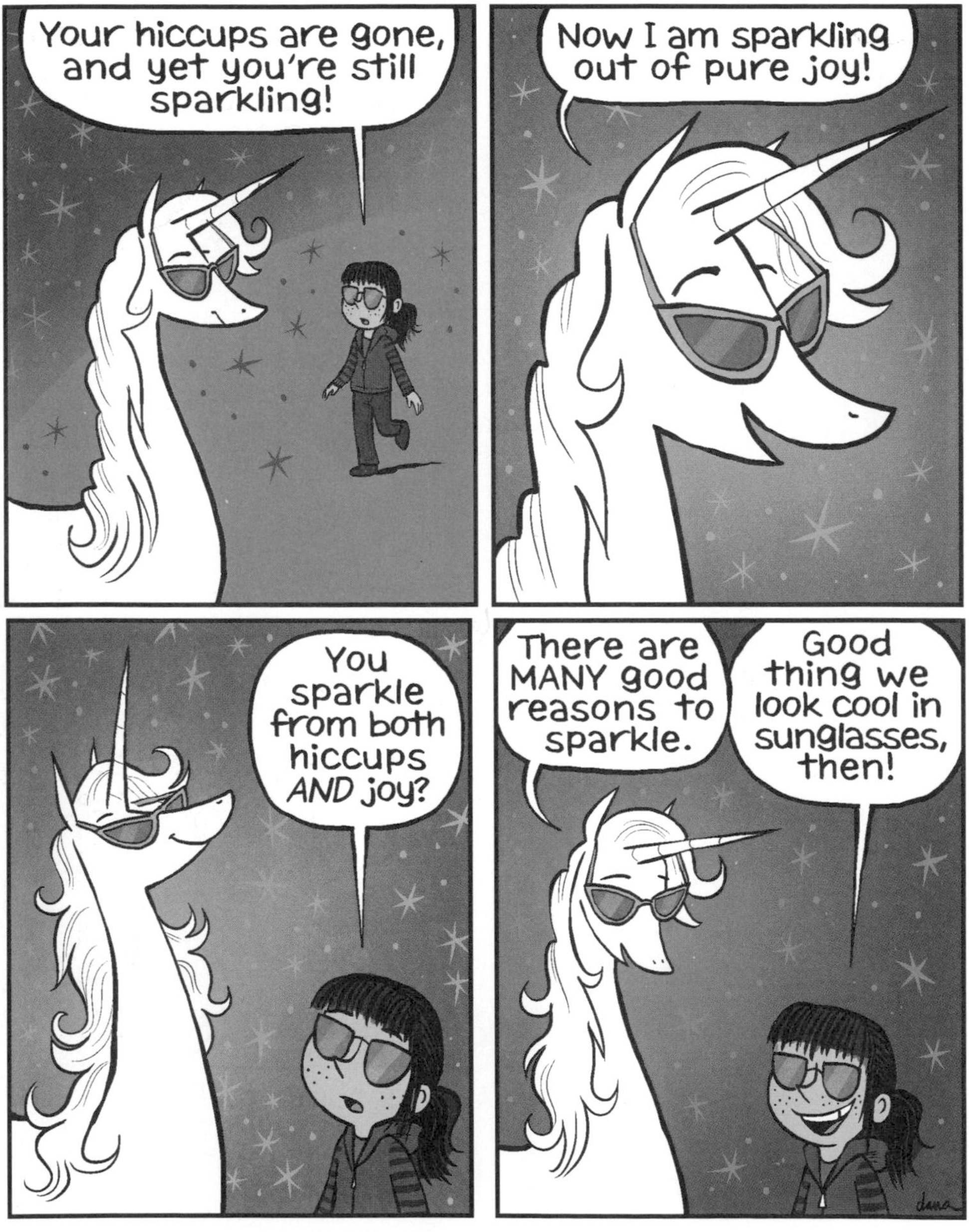
Your hiccups are gone, and yet you're still sparkling!
Now I am sparkling out of pure joy!
You sparkle from both hiccups *AND* joy?
There are MANY good reasons to sparkle.
Good thing we look cool in sunglasses, then!

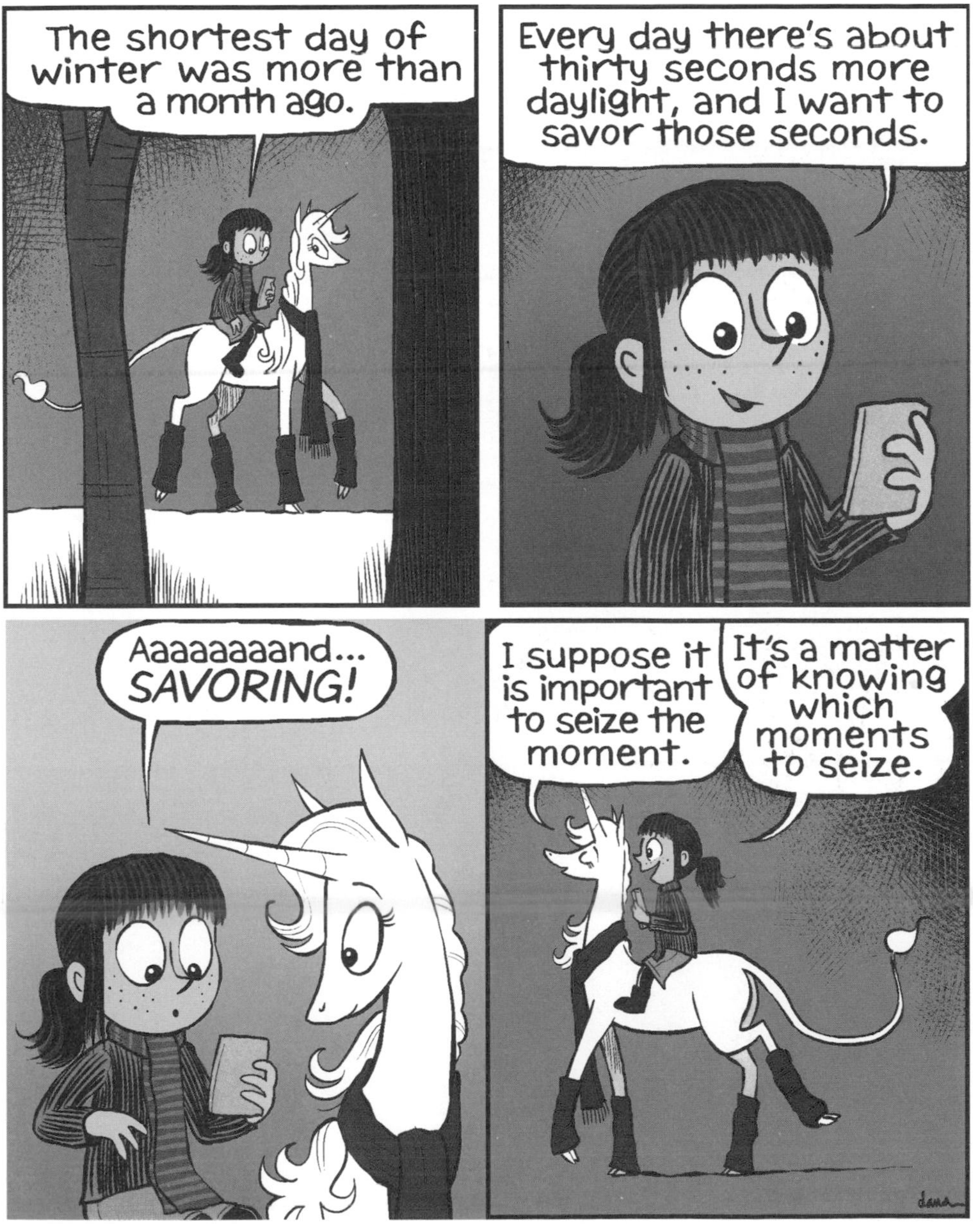
The shortest day of winter was more than a month ago.
Every day there's about thirty seconds more daylight, and I want to savor those seconds.
Aaaaaaaand... *SAVORING!*
I suppose it is important to seize the moment.
It's a matter of knowing which moments to seize.
dana

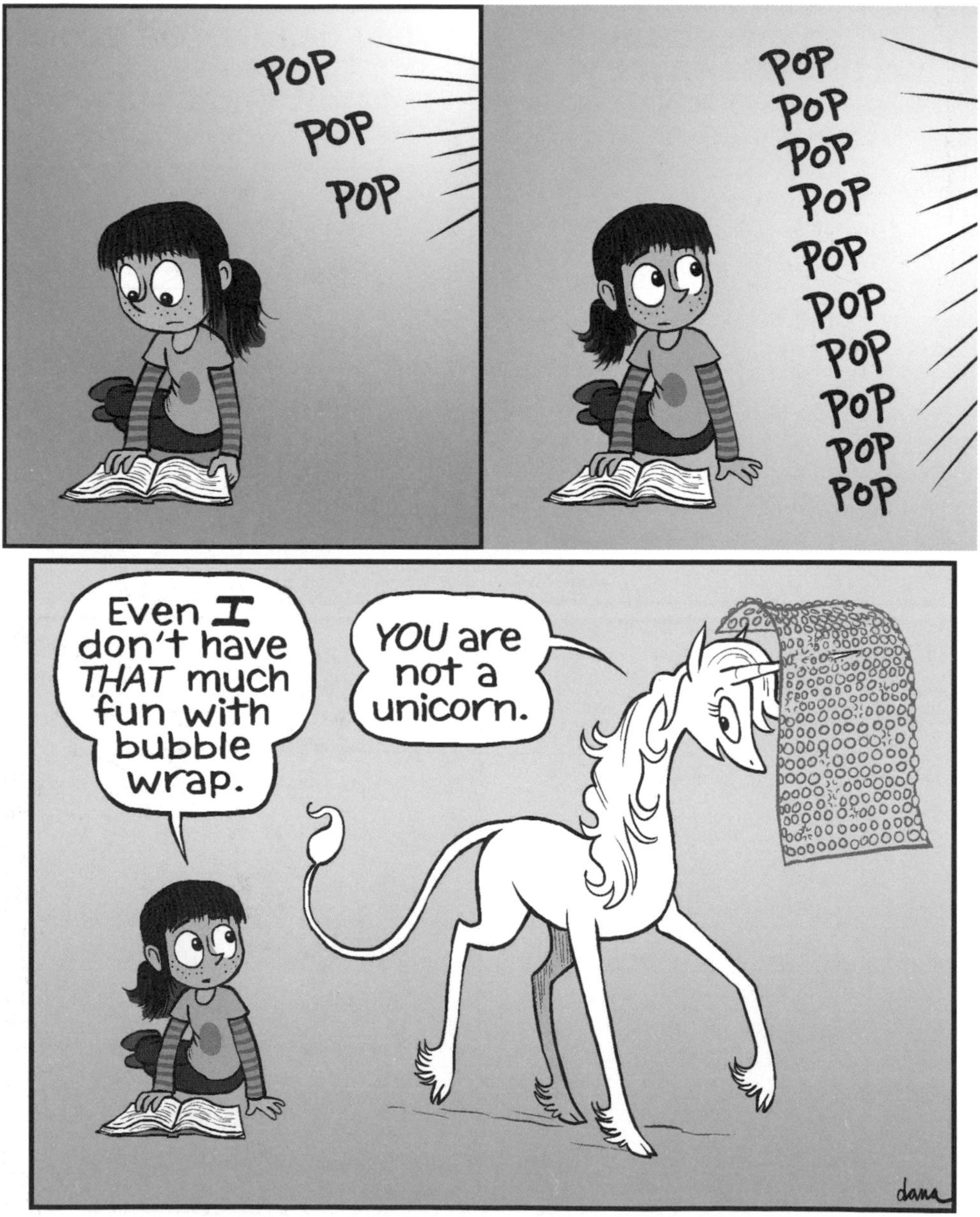
POP
POP
POP
POP
POP
POP
POP
POP
POP
POP
POP
POP
POP
Even I don't have THAT much fun with bubble wrap.
YOU are not a unicorn.
dana

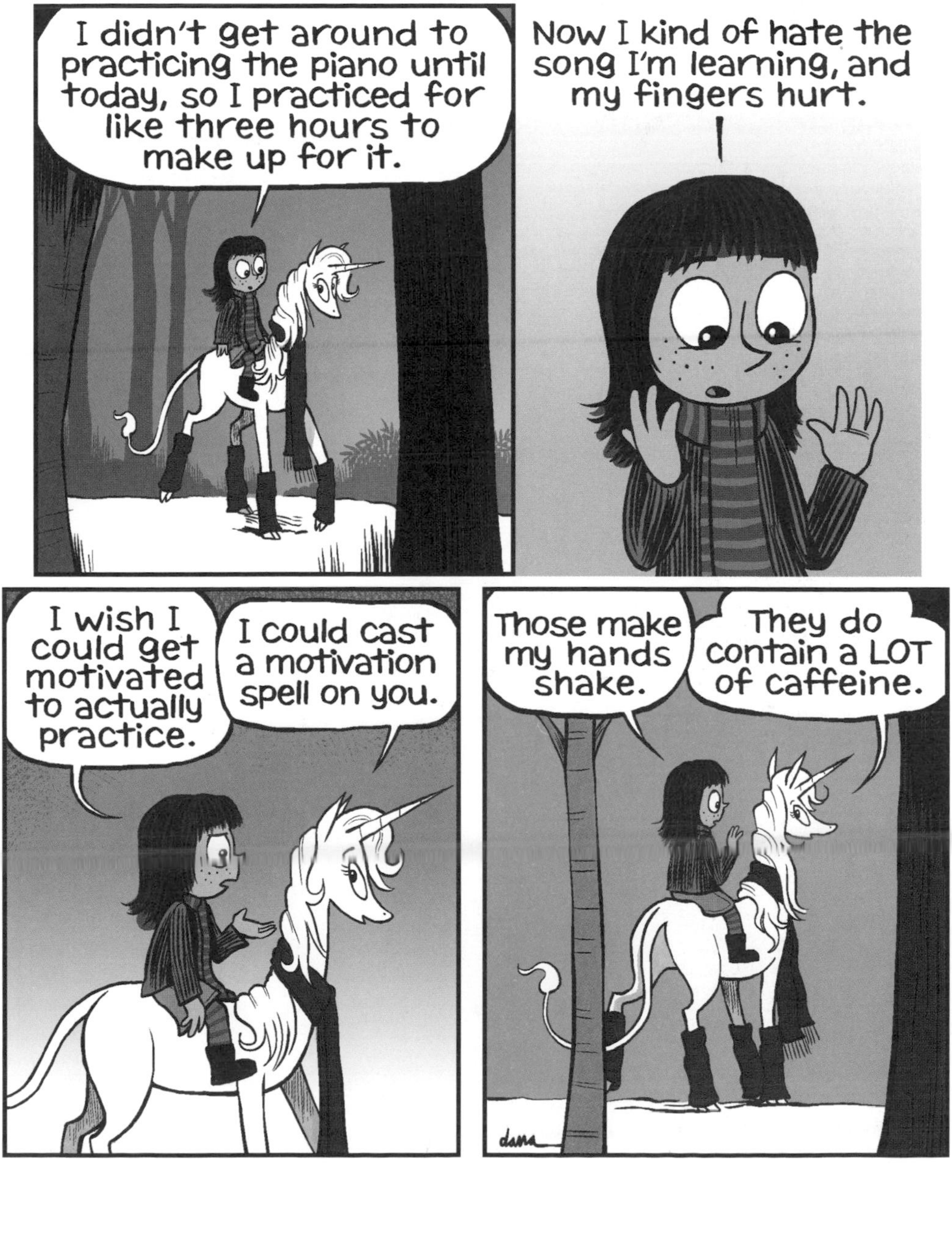
I didn't get around to practicing the piano until today, so I practiced for like three hours to make up for it.
Now I kind of hate the song I'm learning, and my fingers hurt.
I wish I could get motivated to actually practice.
I could cast a motivation spell on you.
Those make my hands shake.
They do contain a LOT of caffeine.
dana

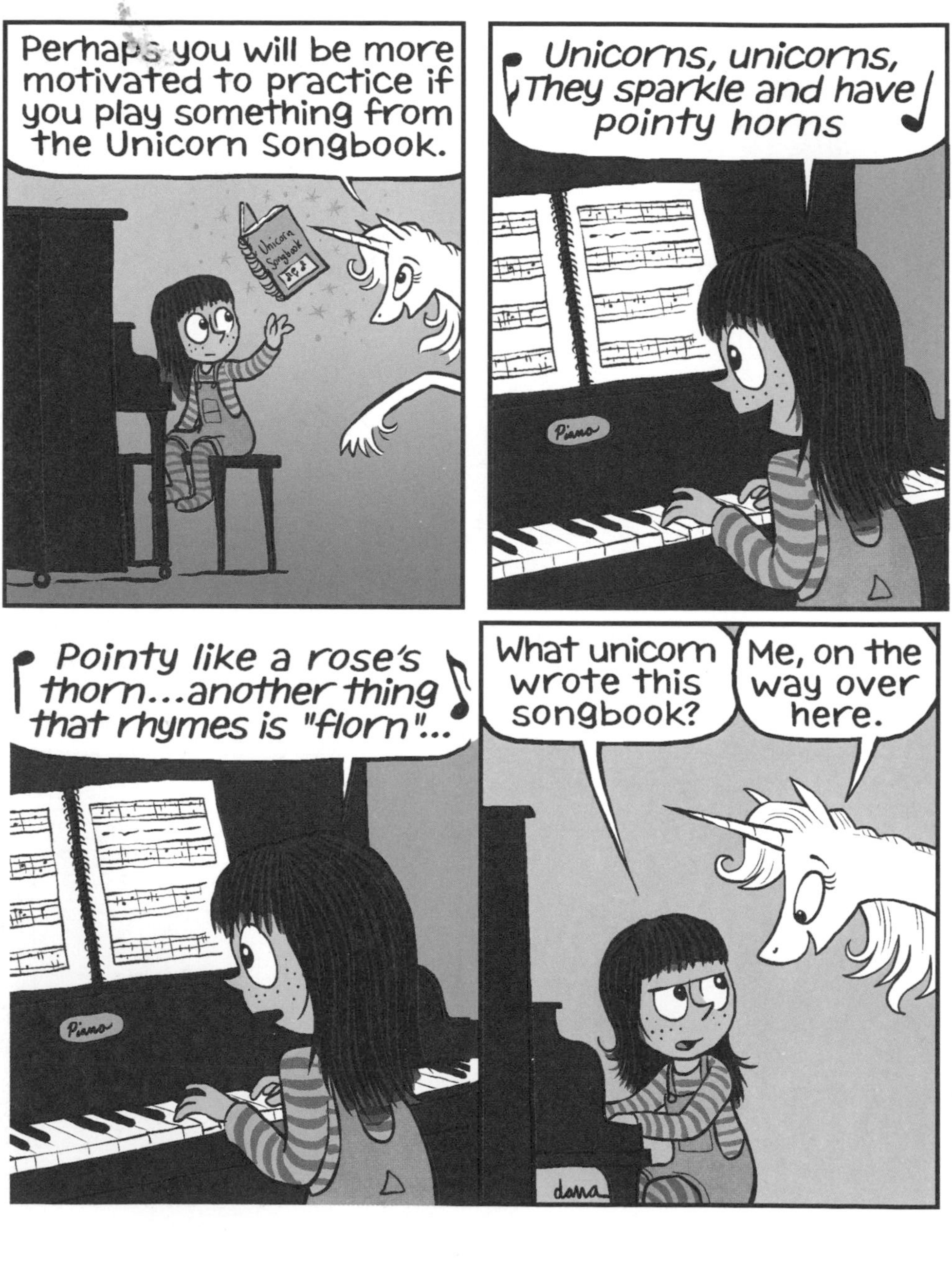
Perhaps you will be more motivated to practice if you play something from the Unicorn Songbook.
Unicorn Songbook
Unicorns, unicorns, They sparkle and have pointy horns
Piano
Pointy like a rose's thorn...another thing that rhymes is "florn"...
Piano
What unicorn wrote this songbook?
Me, on the way over here.
dana

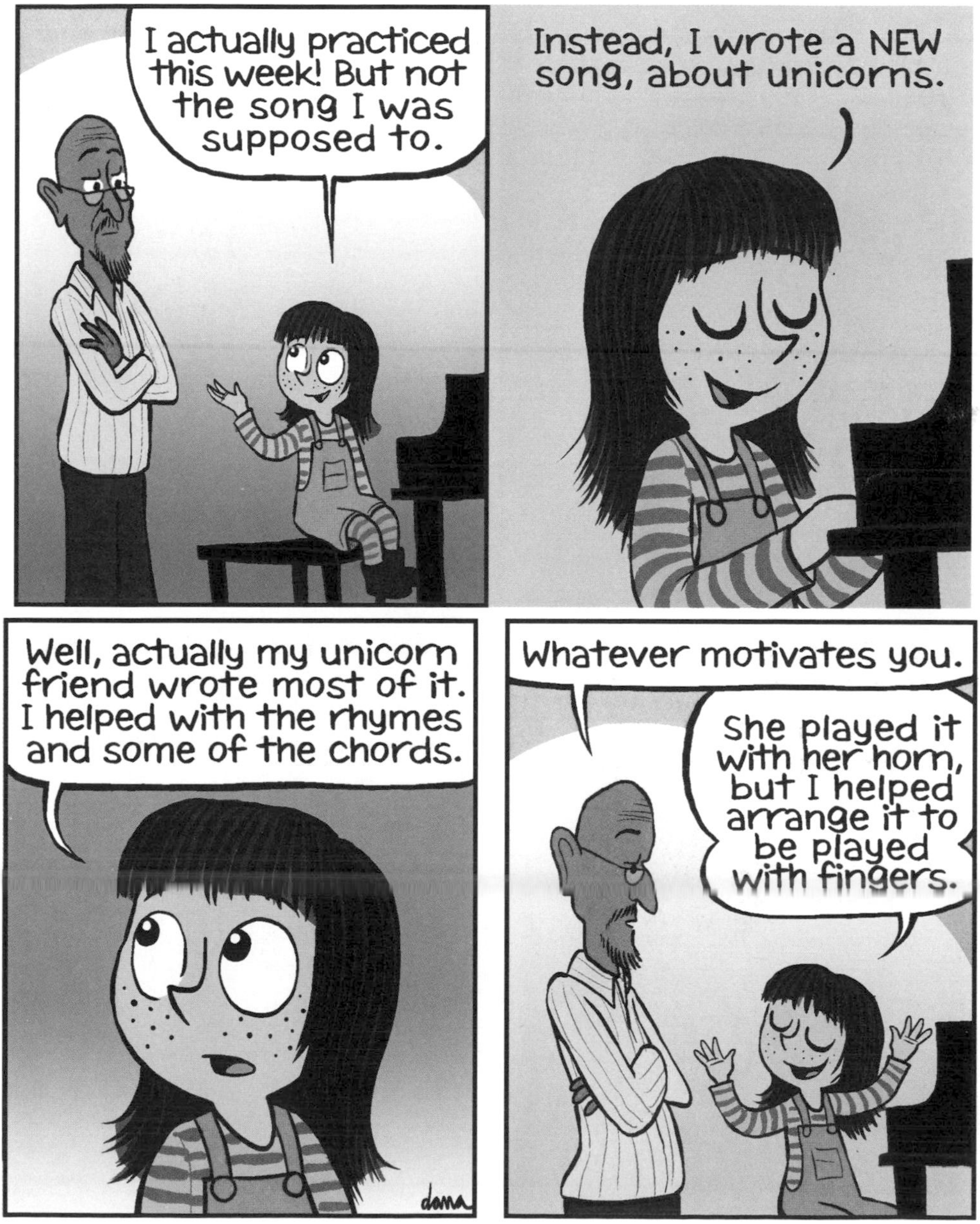
I actually practiced this week! But not the song I was supposed to.
Instead, I wrote a NEW song, about unicorns.
Well, actually my unicorn friend wrote most of it. I helped with the rhymes and some of the chords.
Whatever motivates you.
She played it with her horn, but I helped arrange it to be played with fingers.
dana

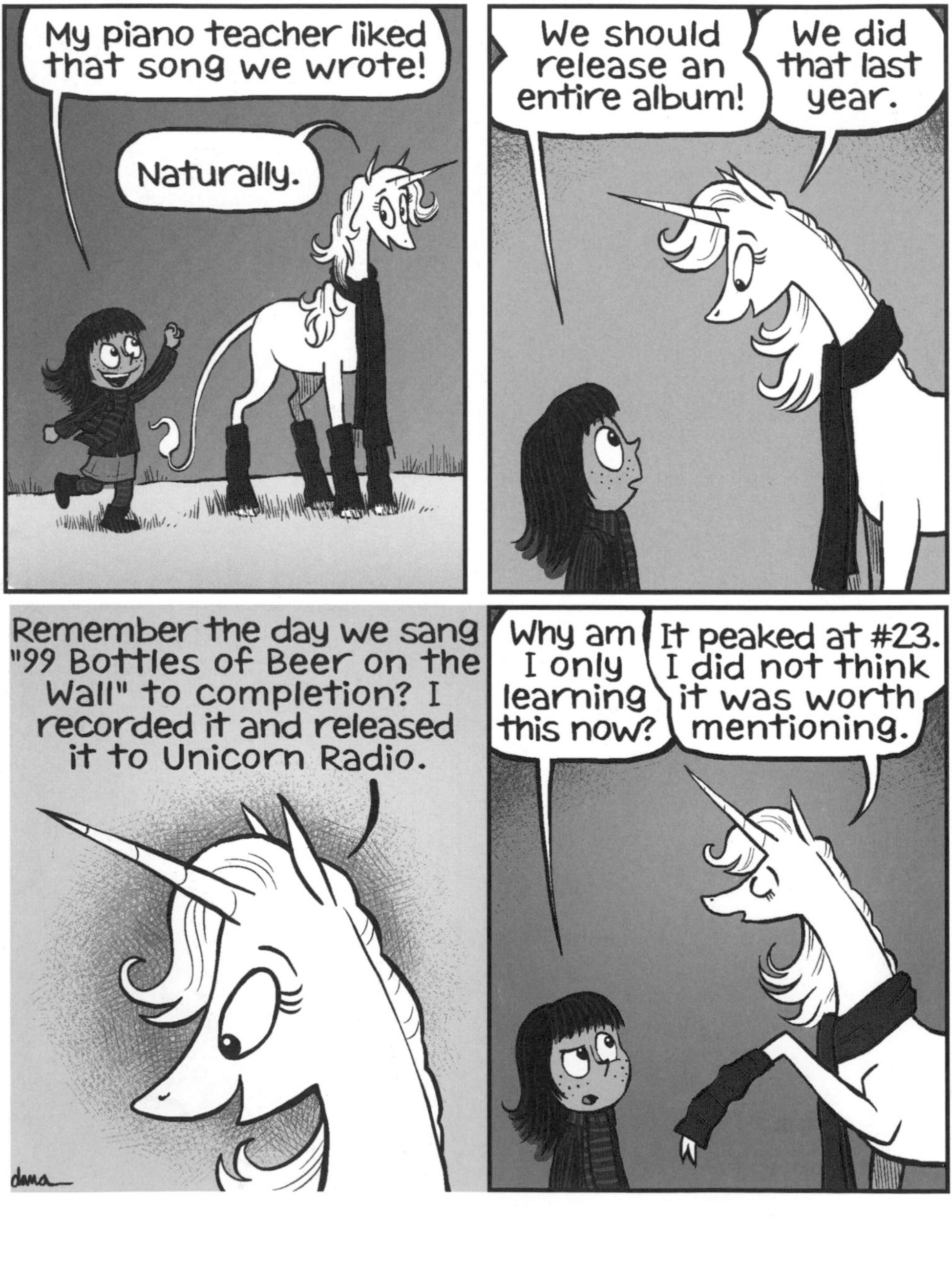
My piano teacher liked that song we wrote!
Naturally.
We should release an entire album!
We did that last year.
Remember the day we sang "99 Bottles of Beer on the Wall" to completion? I recorded it and released it to Unicorn Radio.
Why am I only learning this now?
It peaked at #23. I did not think it was worth mentioning.
dana

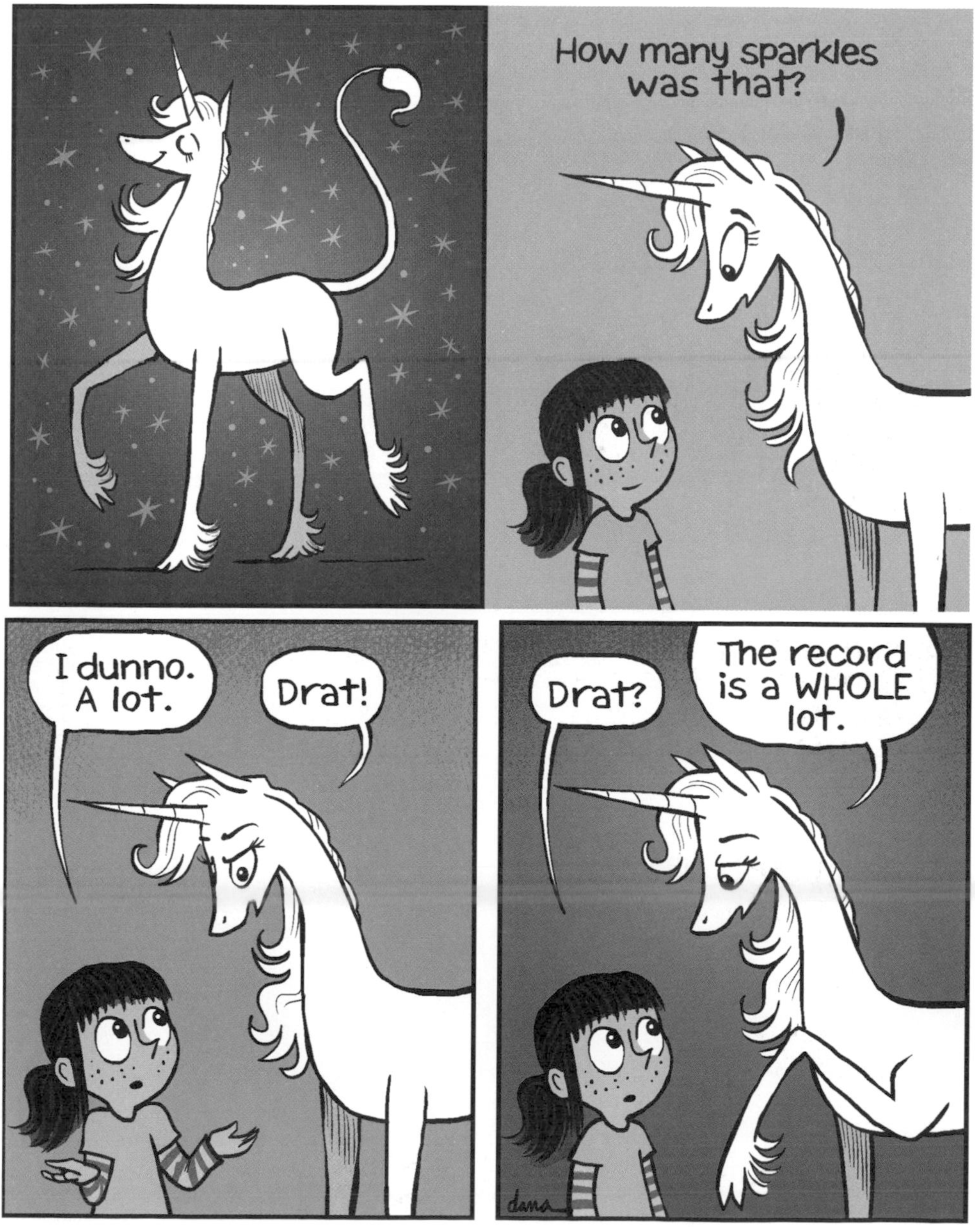
How many sparkles was that?
I dunno. A lot.
Drat!
Drat?
The record is a WHOLE lot.
dana

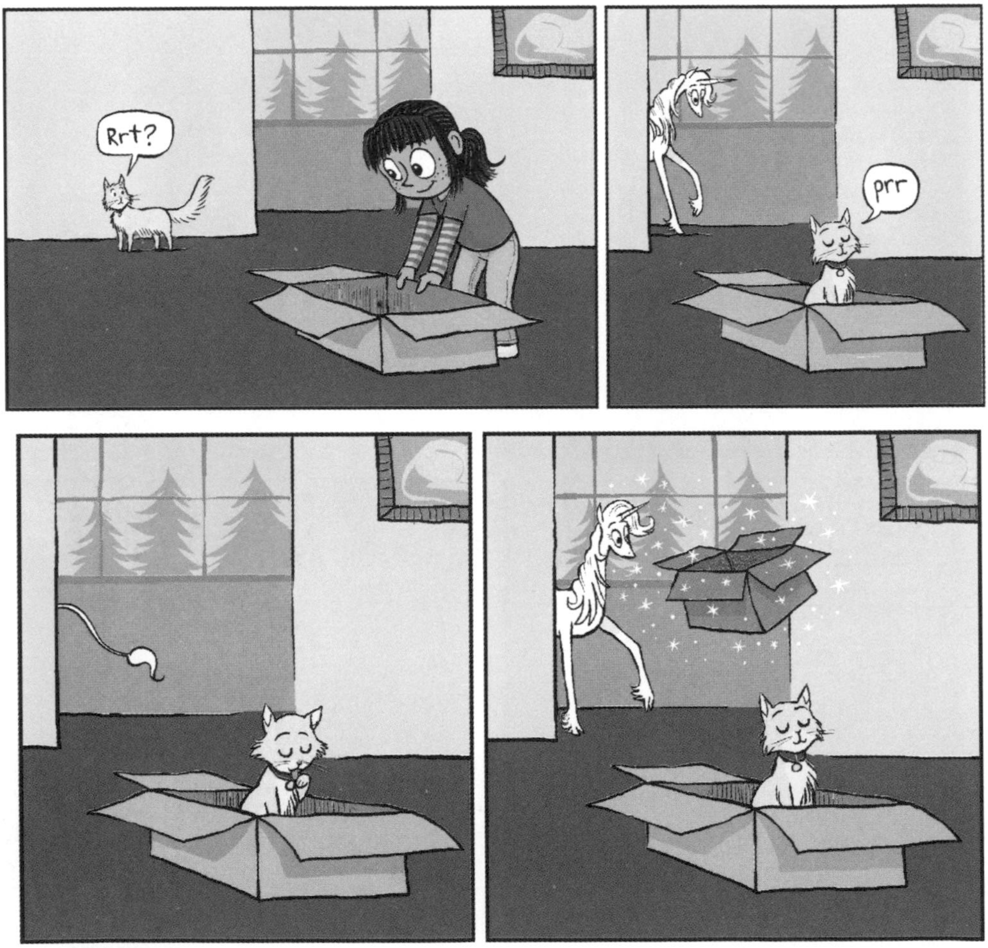
Rrt?
prr

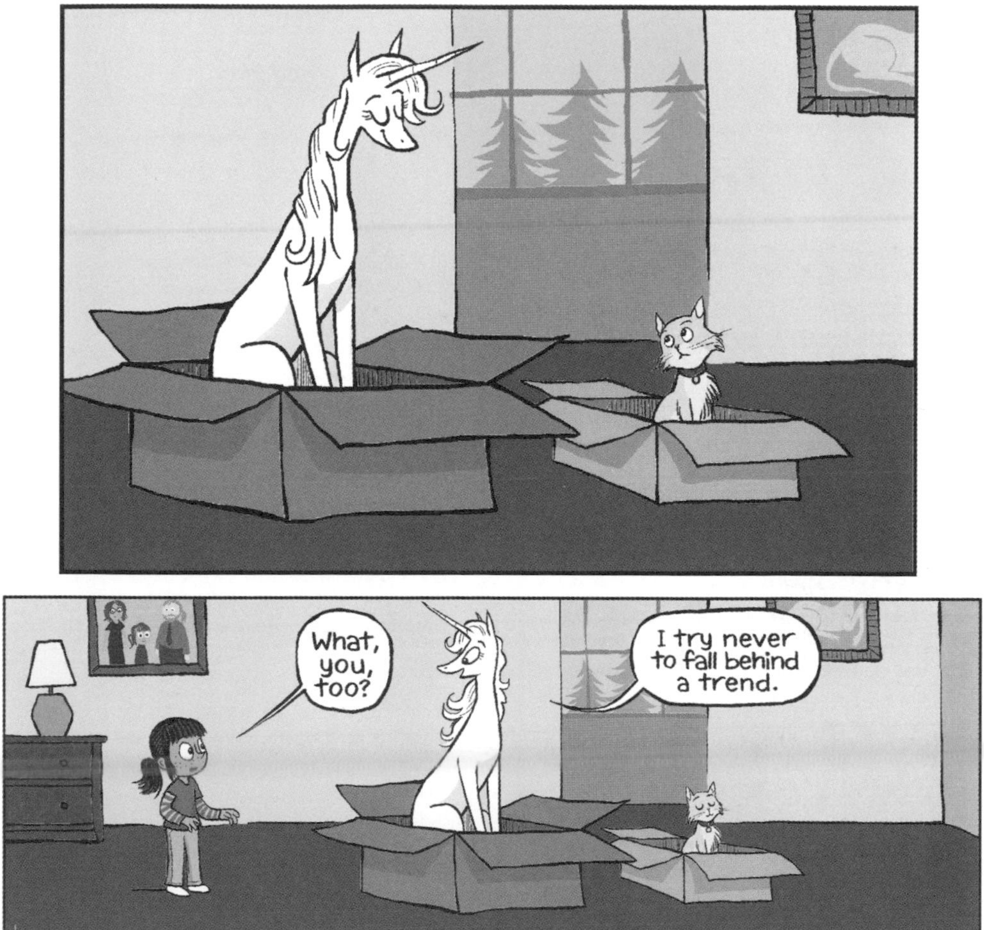
What, you, too?
I try never to fall behind a trend.

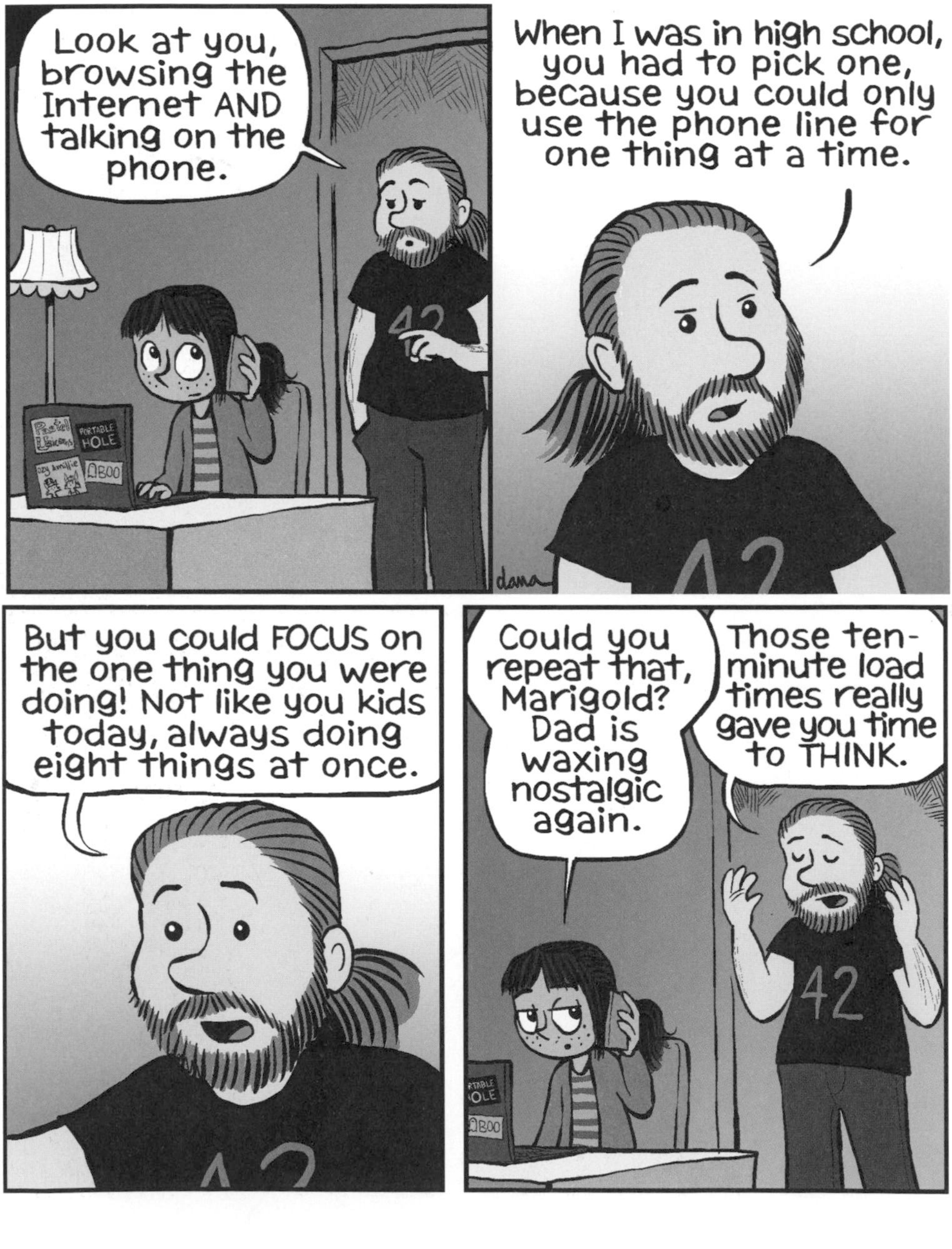
Look at you, browsing the Internet AND talking on the phone.
When I was in high school, you had to pick one, because you could only use the phone line for one thing at a time.
But you could FOCUS on the one thing you were doing! Not like you kids today, always doing eight things at once.
Could you repeat that, Marigold? Dad is waxing nostalgic again.
Those ten-minute load times really gave you time to THINK.

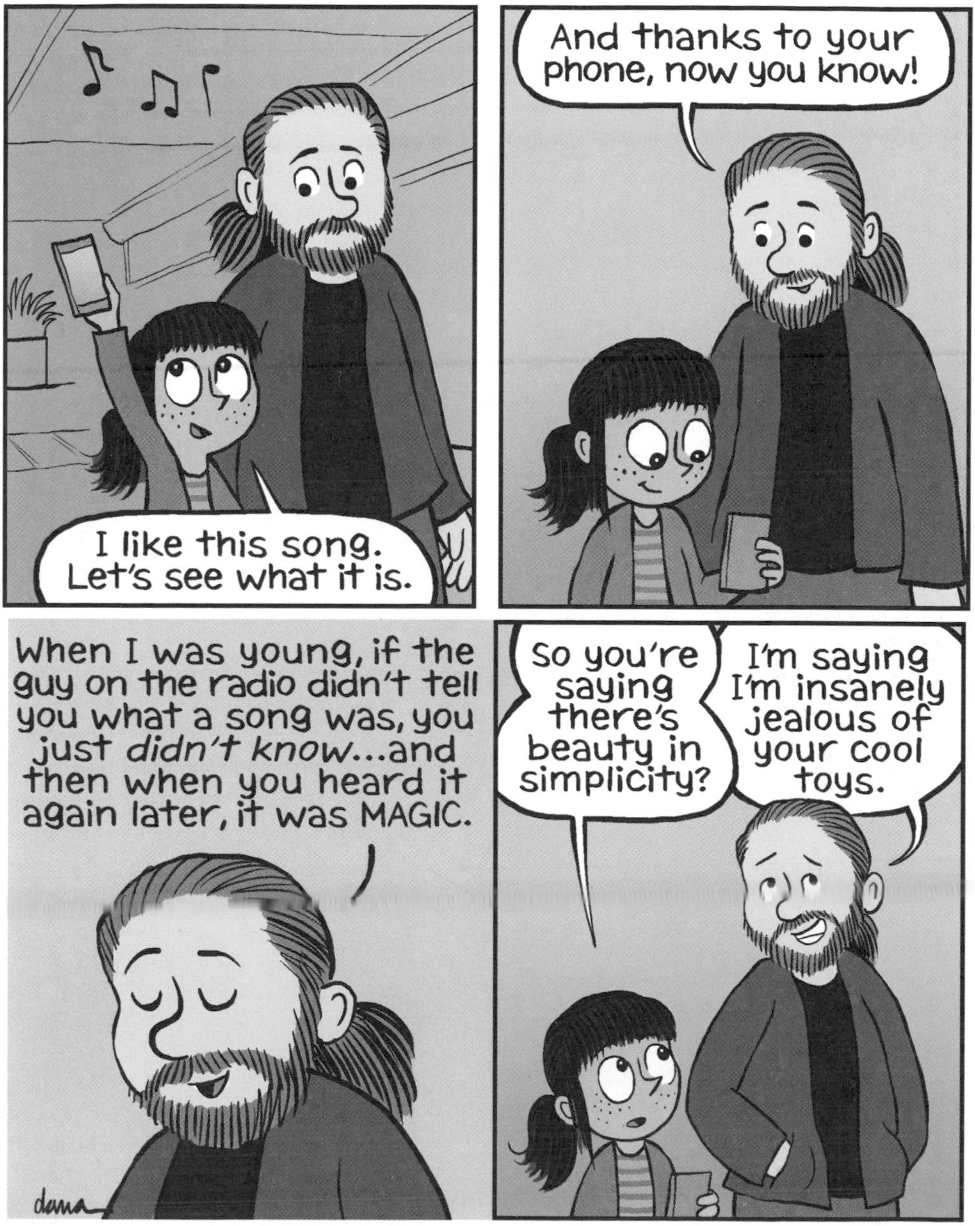
I like this song. Let's see what it is.
And thanks to your phone, now you know!
When I was young, if the guy on the radio didn't tell you what a song was, you just *didn't know*...and then when you heard it again later, it was MAGIC.
So you're saying there's beauty in simplicity?
I'm saying I'm insanely jealous of your cool toys.
dana

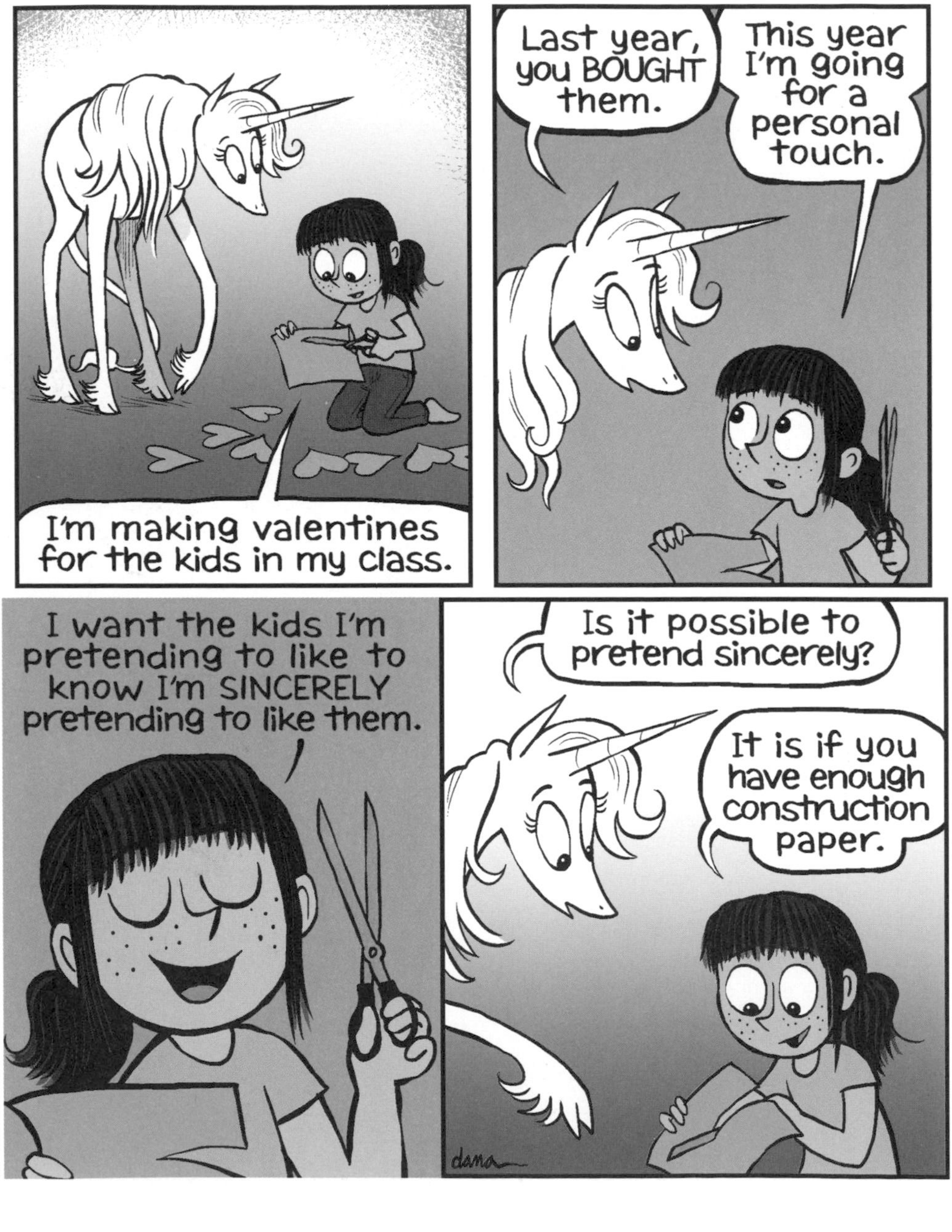
I'm making valentines for the kids in my class.
Last year, you BOUGHT them.
This year I'm going for a personal touch.
I want the kids I'm pretending to like to know I'm SINCERELY pretending to like them.
Is it possible to pretend sincerely?
It is if you have enough construction paper.
dana

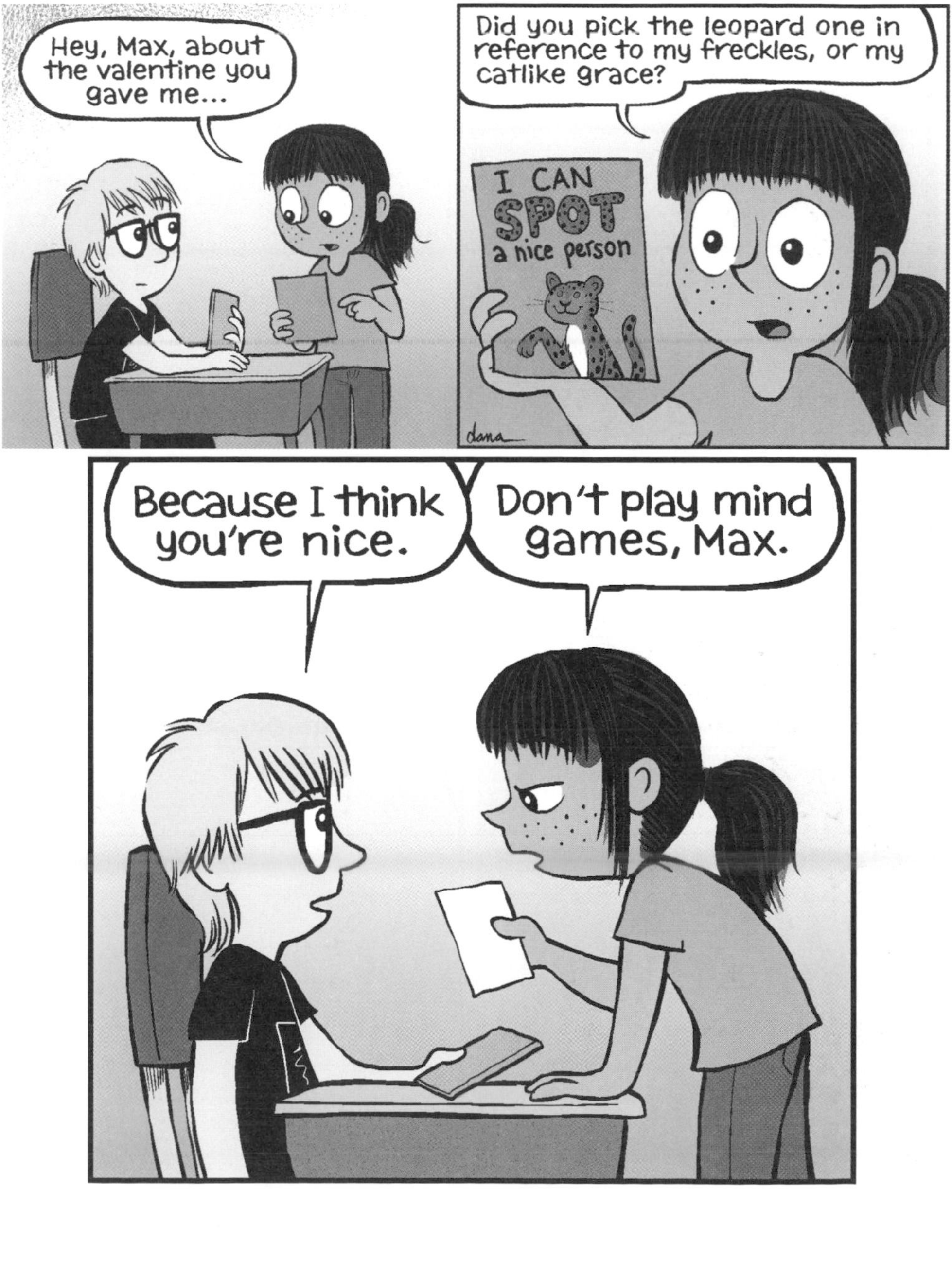
Hey, Max, about the valentine you gave me...
Did you pick the leopard one in reference to my freckles, or my catlike grace?
I CAN SPOT a nice person
dana
Because I think you're nice.
Don't play mind games, Max.

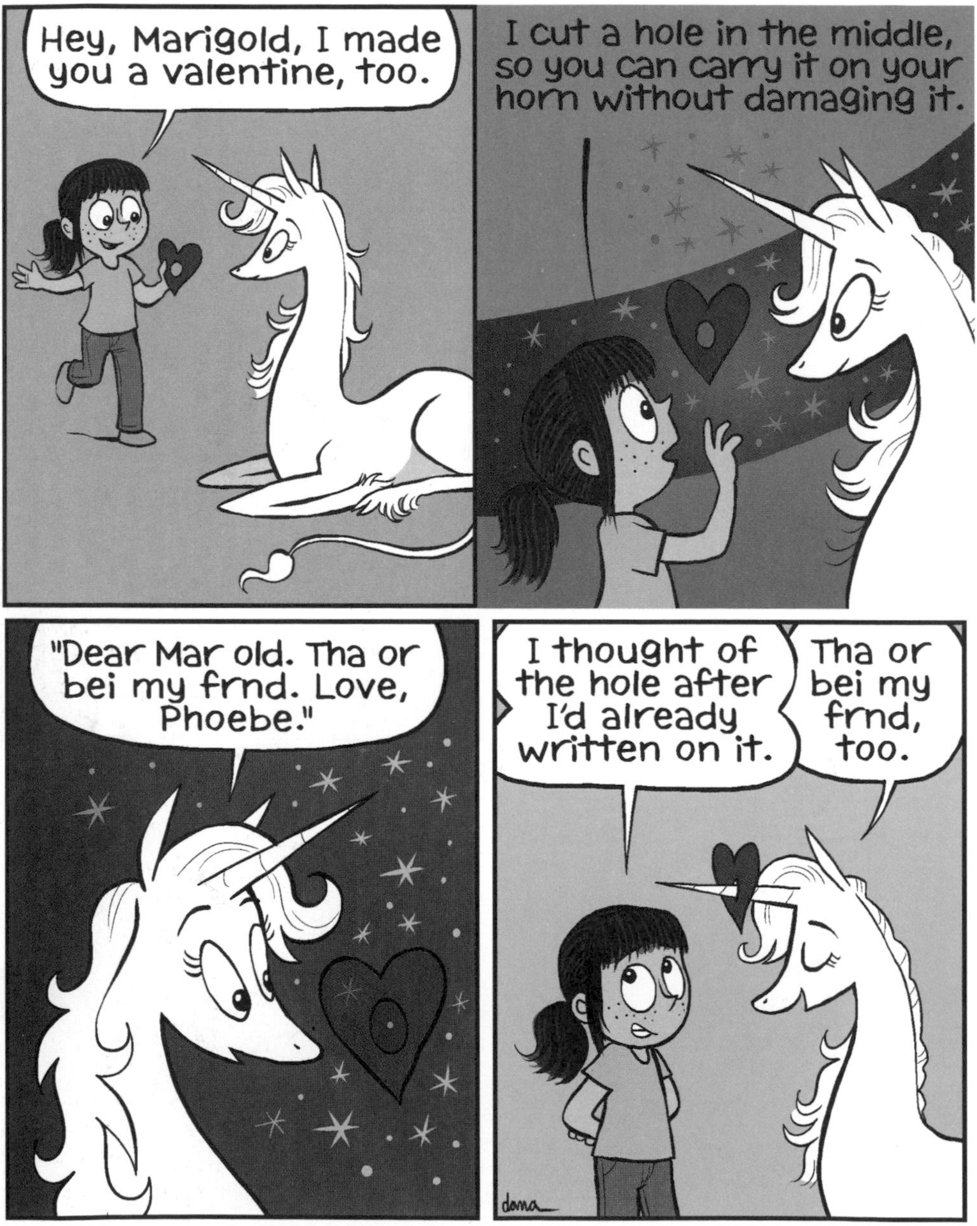
Hey, Marigold, I made you a valentine, too.
I cut a hole in the middle, so you can carry it on your horn without damaging it.
"Dear Mar old. Tha or bei my frnd. Love, Phoebe."
I thought of the hole after I'd already written on it.
Tha or bei my frnd, too.
dana

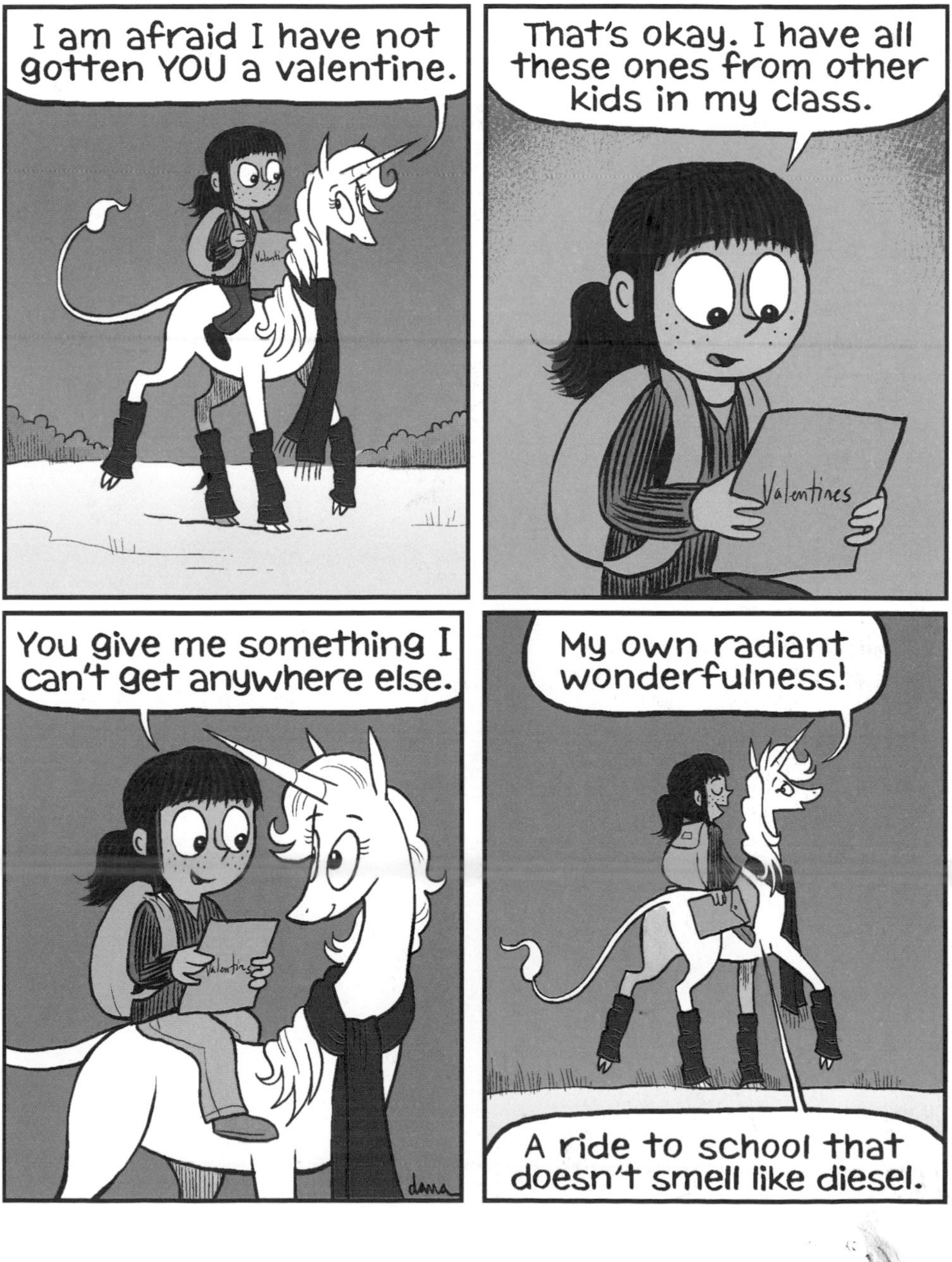
I am afraid I have not gotten YOU a valentine.
Valentines
That's okay. I have all these ones from other kids in my class.
Valentines
You give me something I can't get anywhere else.
Valentines
dana
My own radiant wonderfulness!
A ride to school that doesn't smell like diesel.

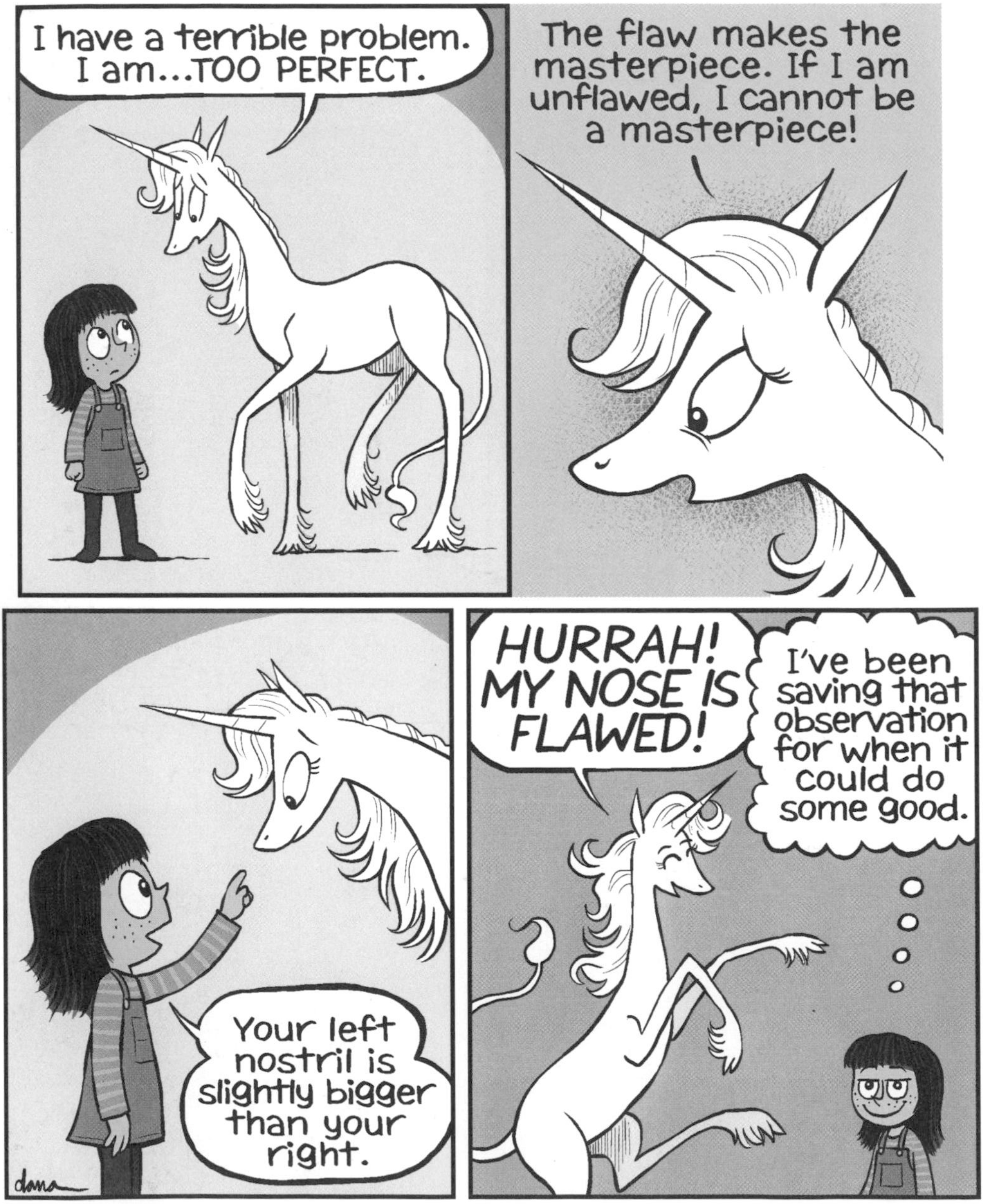

I have a terrible problem. I am...TOO PERFECT.
The flaw makes the masterpiece. If I am unflawed, I cannot be a masterpiece!
Your left nostril is slightly bigger than your right.
dana
HURRAH! MY NOSE IS FLAWED!
I've been saving that observation for when it could do some good.

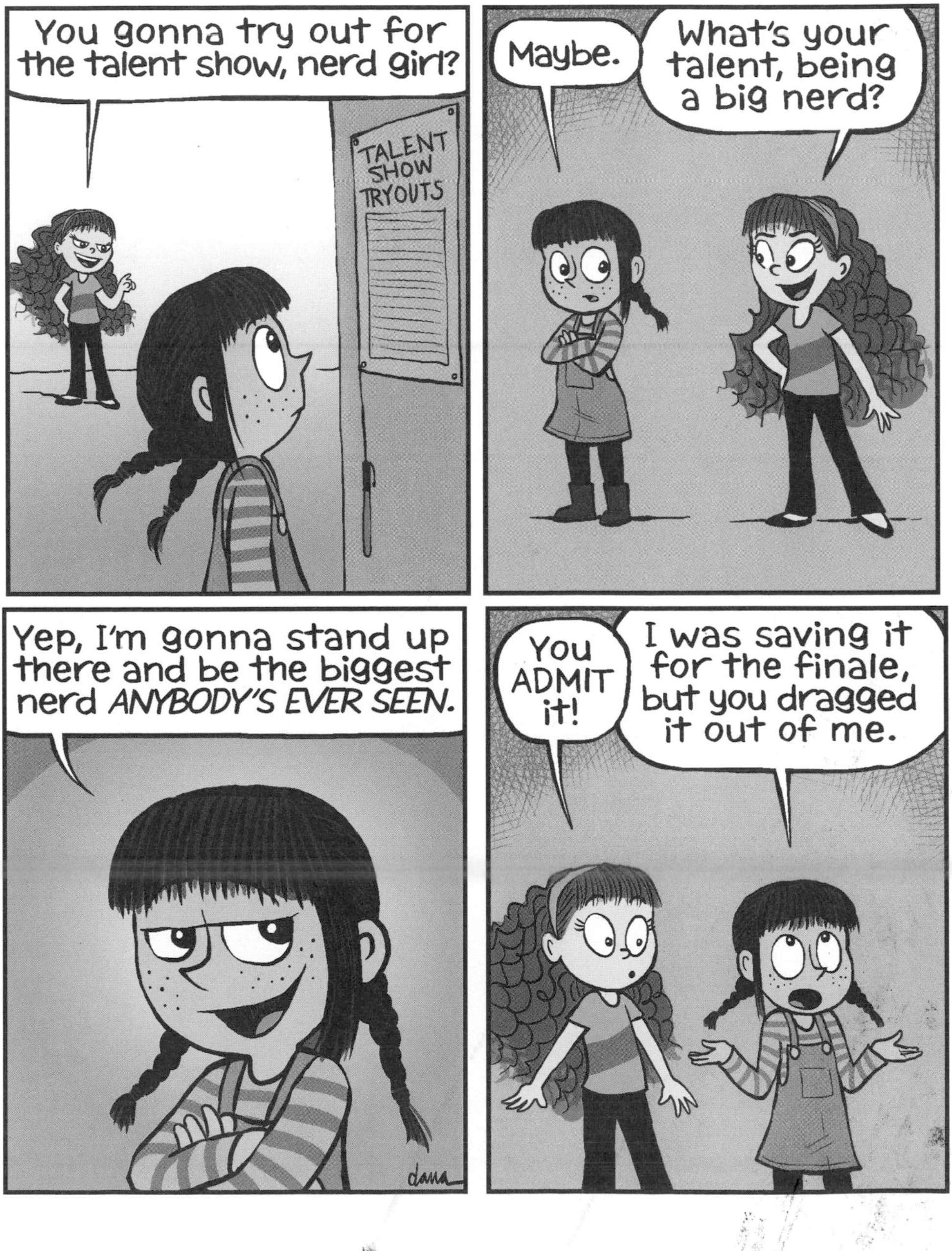
You gonna try out for the talent show, nerd girl?
TALENT SHOW TRYOUTS
Maybe.
What's your talent, being a big nerd?
Yep, I'm gonna stand up there and be the biggest nerd *ANYBODY'S EVER SEEN.*
dana
You ADMIT it!
I was saving it for the finale, but you dragged it out of me.

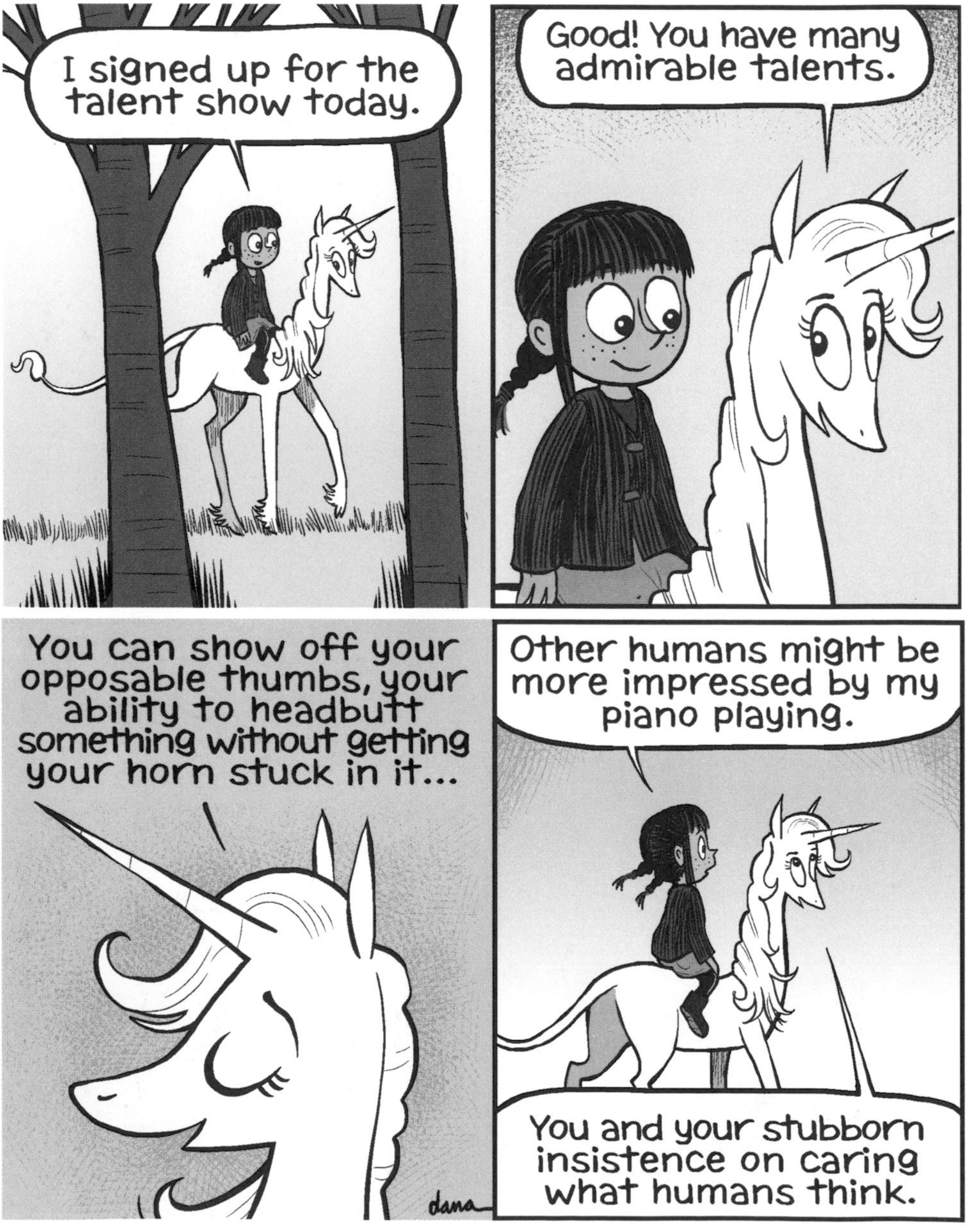
I signed up for the talent show today.
Good! You have many admirable talents.
You can show off your opposable thumbs, your ability to headbutt something without getting your horn stuck in it...
dana
Other humans might be more impressed by my piano playing.
You and your stubborn insistence on caring what humans think.

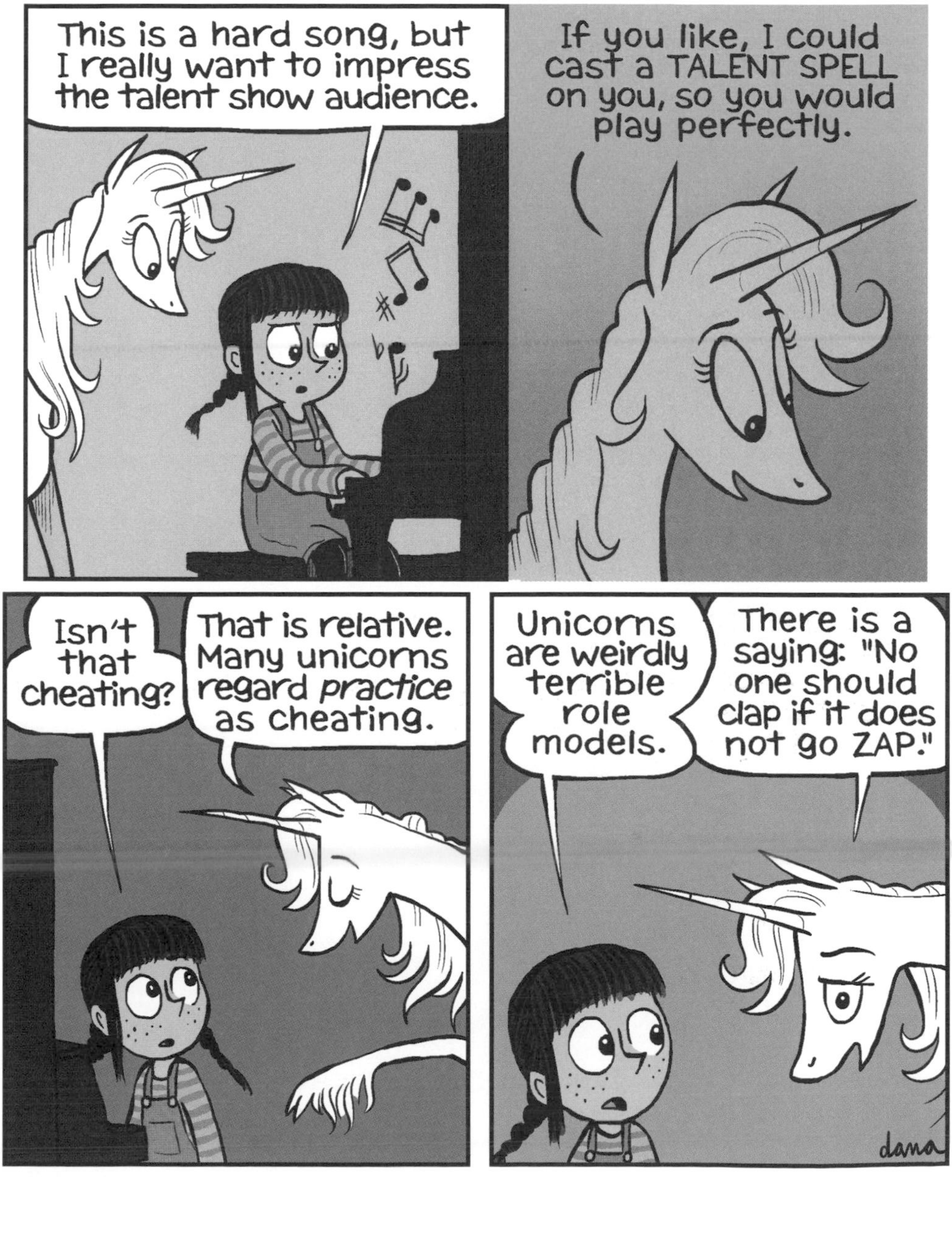
This is a hard song, but I really want to impress the talent show audience.
If you like, I could cast a TALENT SPELL on you, so you would play perfectly.
Isn't that cheating?
That is relative. Many unicorns regard *practice* as cheating.
Unicorns are weirdly terrible role models.
There is a saying: "No one should clap if it does not go ZAP."
dana

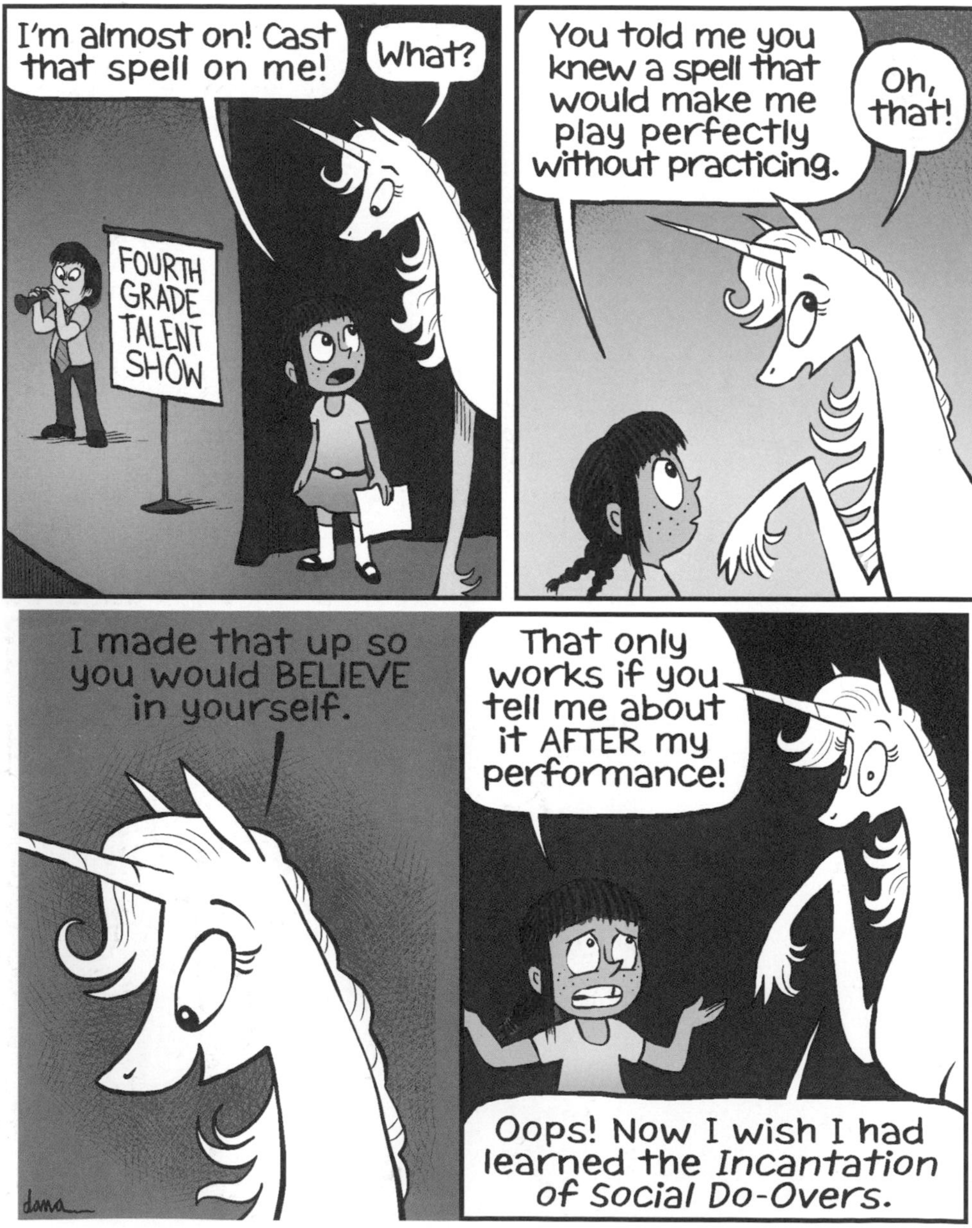

I'm almost on! Cast that spell on me!
What?
FOURTH GRADE TALENT SHOW
You told me you knew a spell that would make me play perfectly without practicing.
Oh, that!
I made that up so you would BELIEVE in yourself.
That only works if you tell me about it AFTER my performance!
Oops! Now I wish I had learned the *Incantation of Social Do-Overs*.
dana

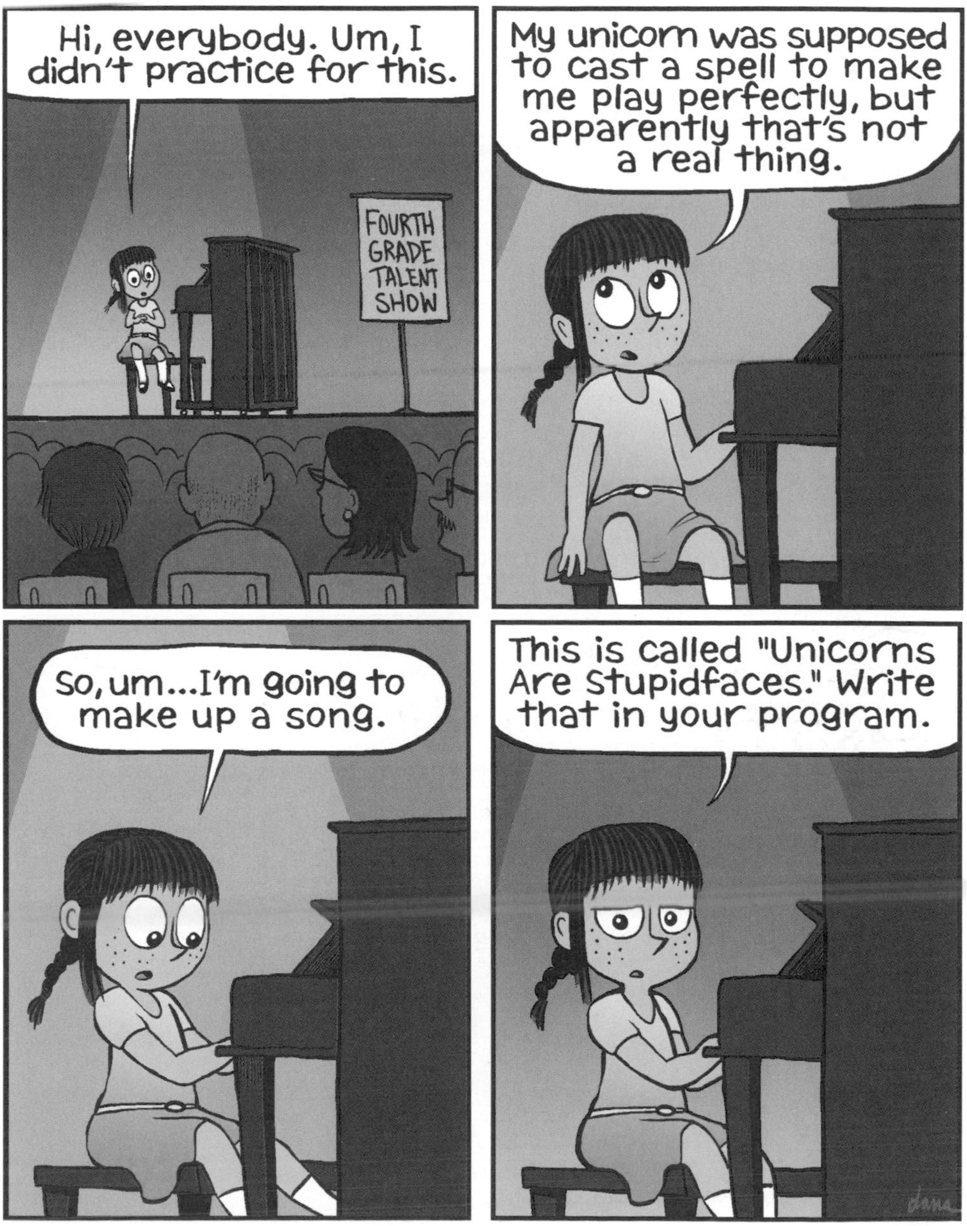
Hi, everybody. Um, I didn't practice for this.
FOURTH GRADE TALENT SHOW
My unicorn was supposed to cast a spell to make me play perfectly, but apparently that's not a real thing.
So, um...I'm going to make up a song.
This is called "Unicorns Are Stupidfaces." Write that in your program.
dana

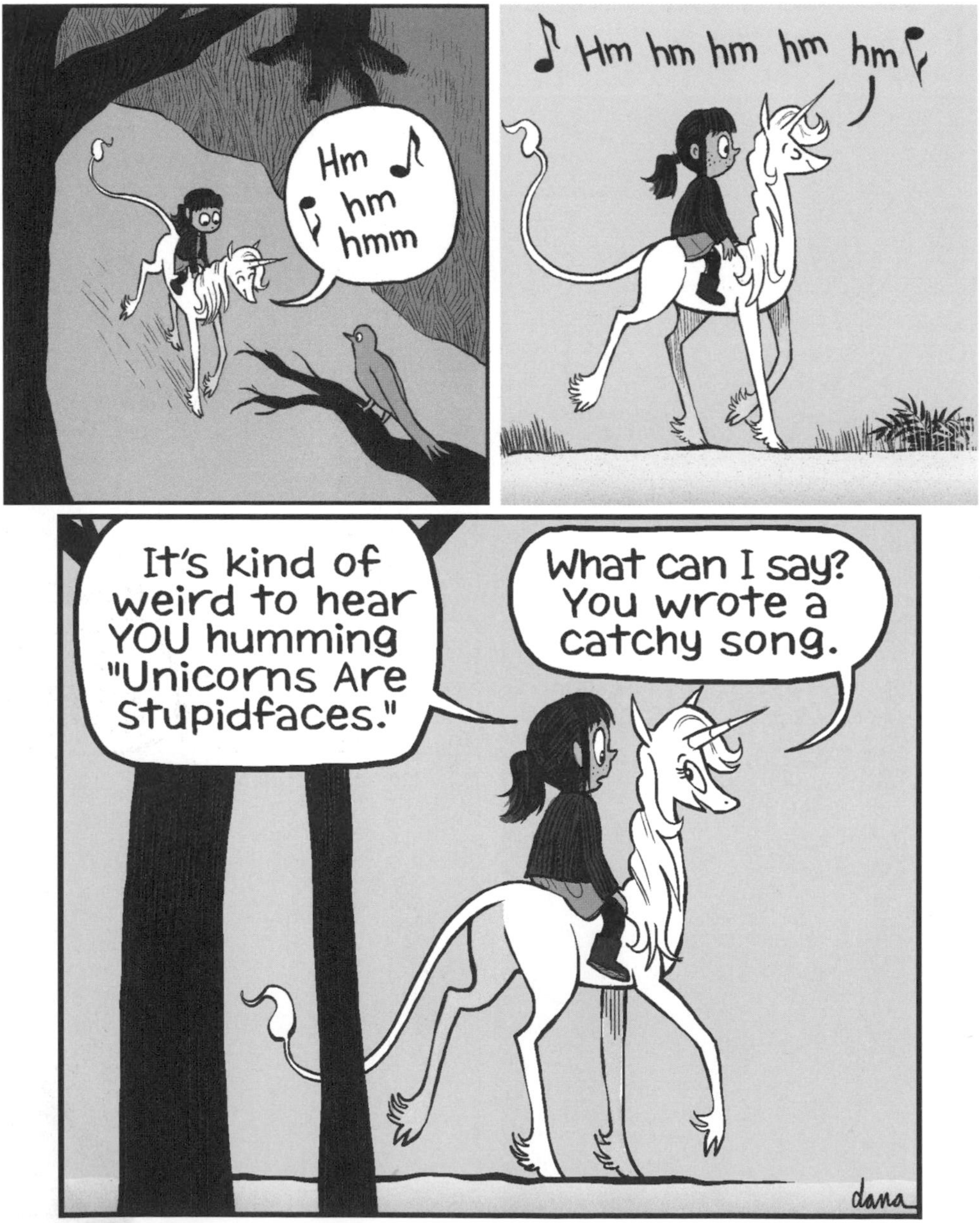
Hm hm hmm
Hm hm hm hm hm
It's kind of weird to hear YOU humming "Unicorns Are Stupidfaces."
What can I say? You wrote a catchy song.
dana

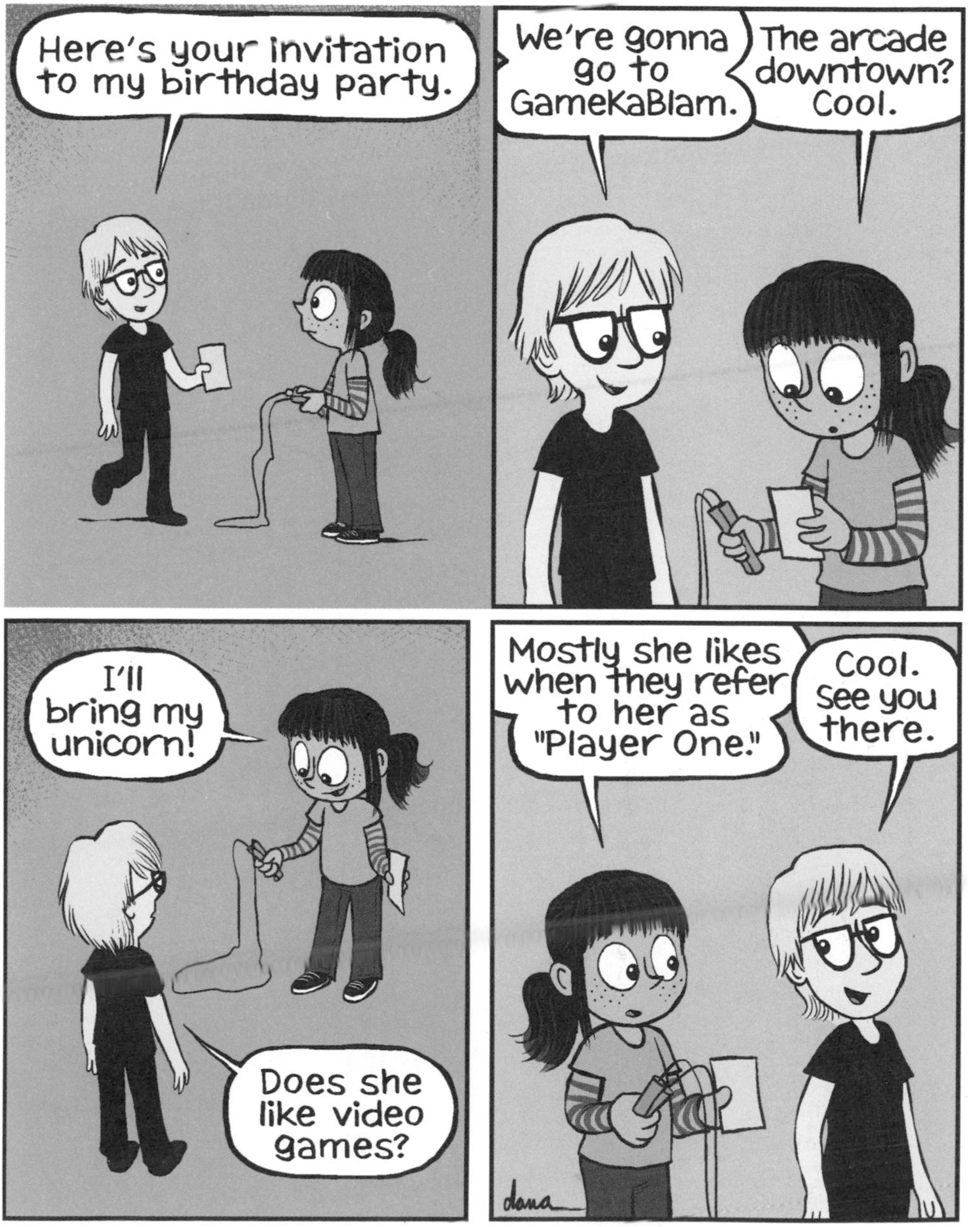
Here's your invitation to my birthday party.
We're gonna go to GameKaBlam.
The arcade downtown? Cool.
I'll bring my unicorn!
Does she like video games?
Mostly she likes when they refer to her as "Player One."
Cool. See you there.
dana

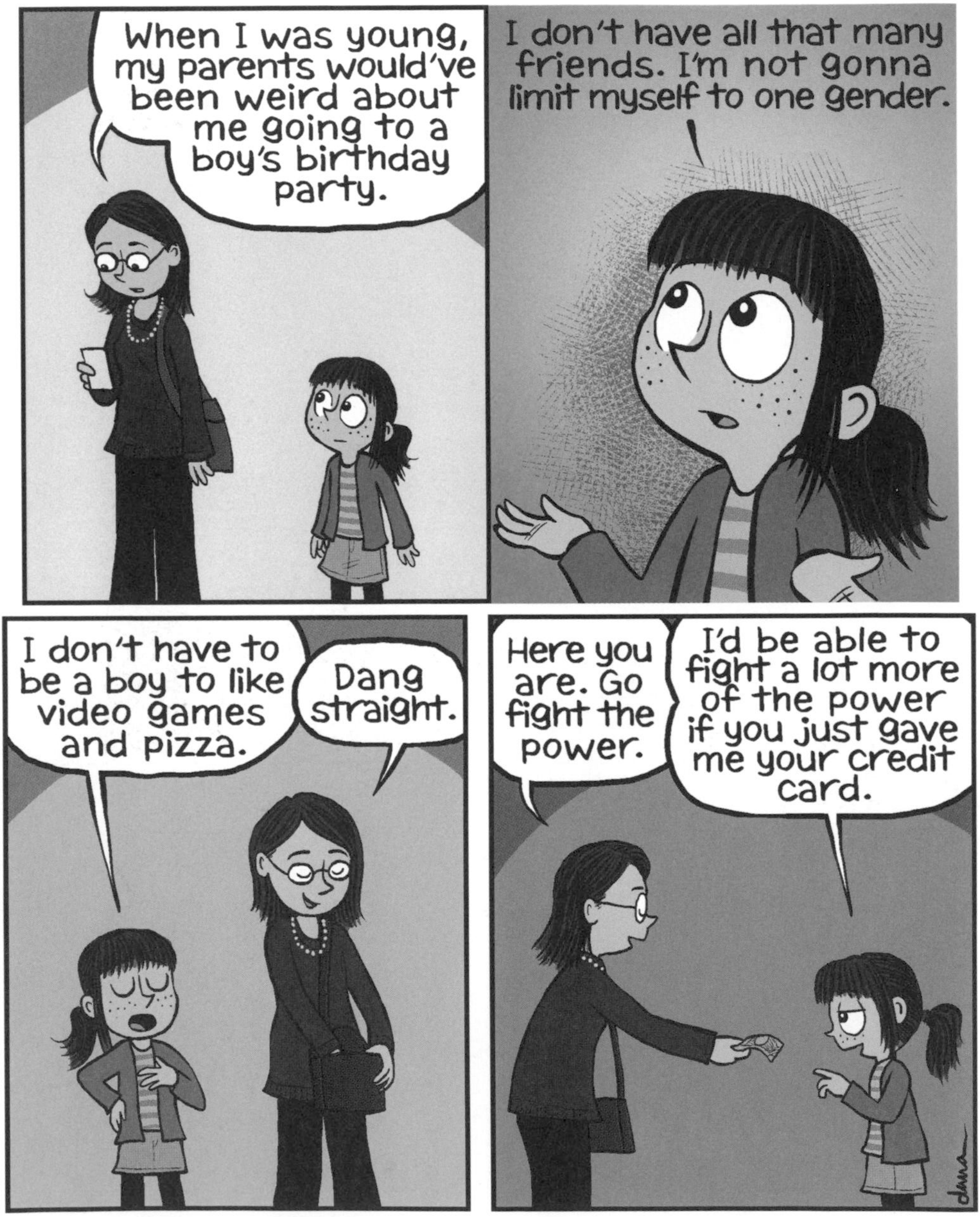
When I was young, my parents would've been weird about me going to a boy's birthday party.
I don't have all that many friends. I'm not gonna limit myself to one gender.
I don't have to be a boy to like video games and pizza.
Dang straight.
Here you are. Go fight the power.
I'd be able to fight a lot more of the power if you just gave me your credit card.

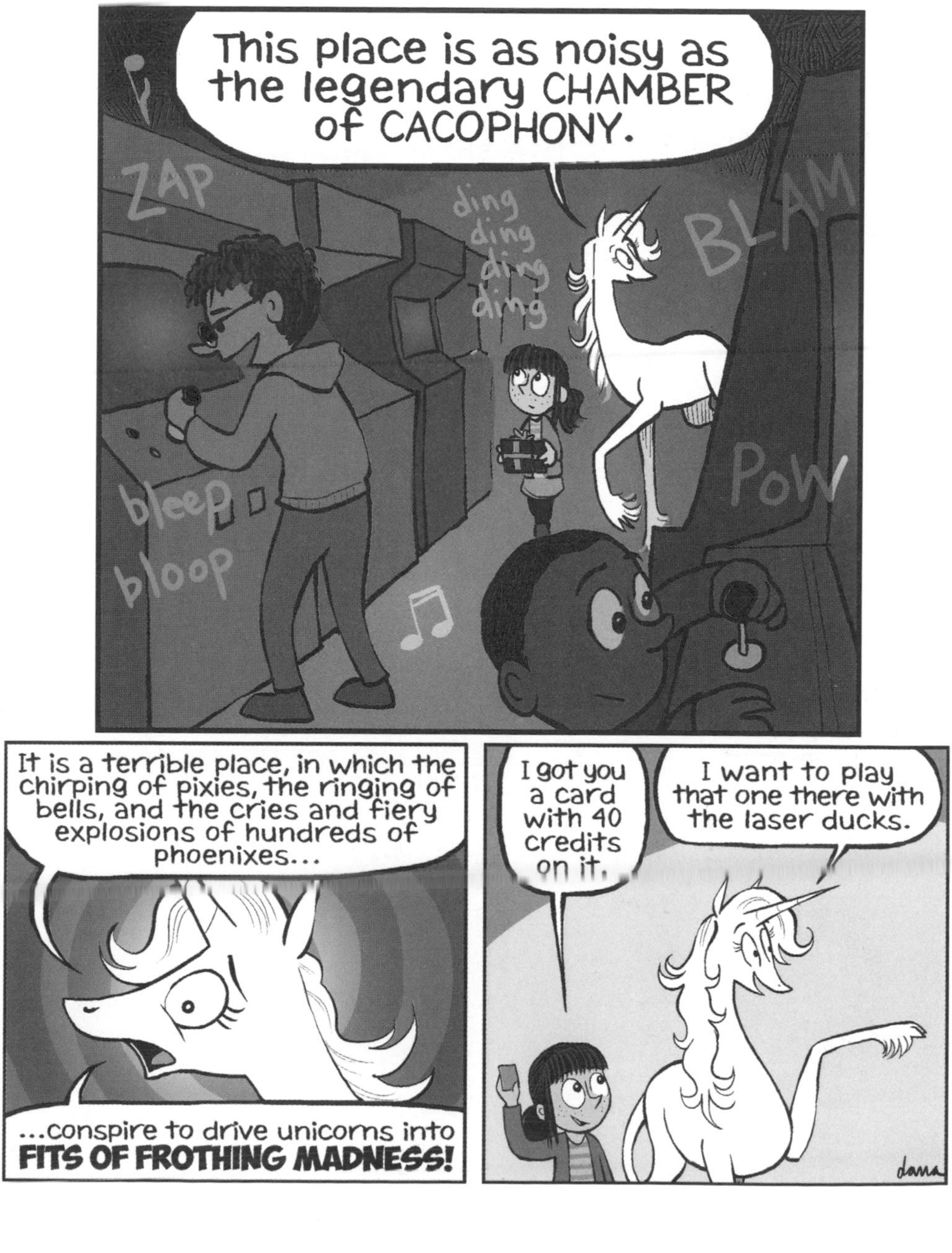
This place is as noisy as the legendary CHAMBER of CACOPHONY.
ZAP
ding ding ding ding
BLAM
bleep bloop
POW
It is a terrible place, in which the chirping of pixies, the ringing of bells, and the cries and fiery explosions of hundreds of phoenixes...
...conspire to drive unicorns into FITS OF FROTHING MADNESS!
I got you a card with 40 credits on it.
I want to play that one there with the laser ducks.
dana

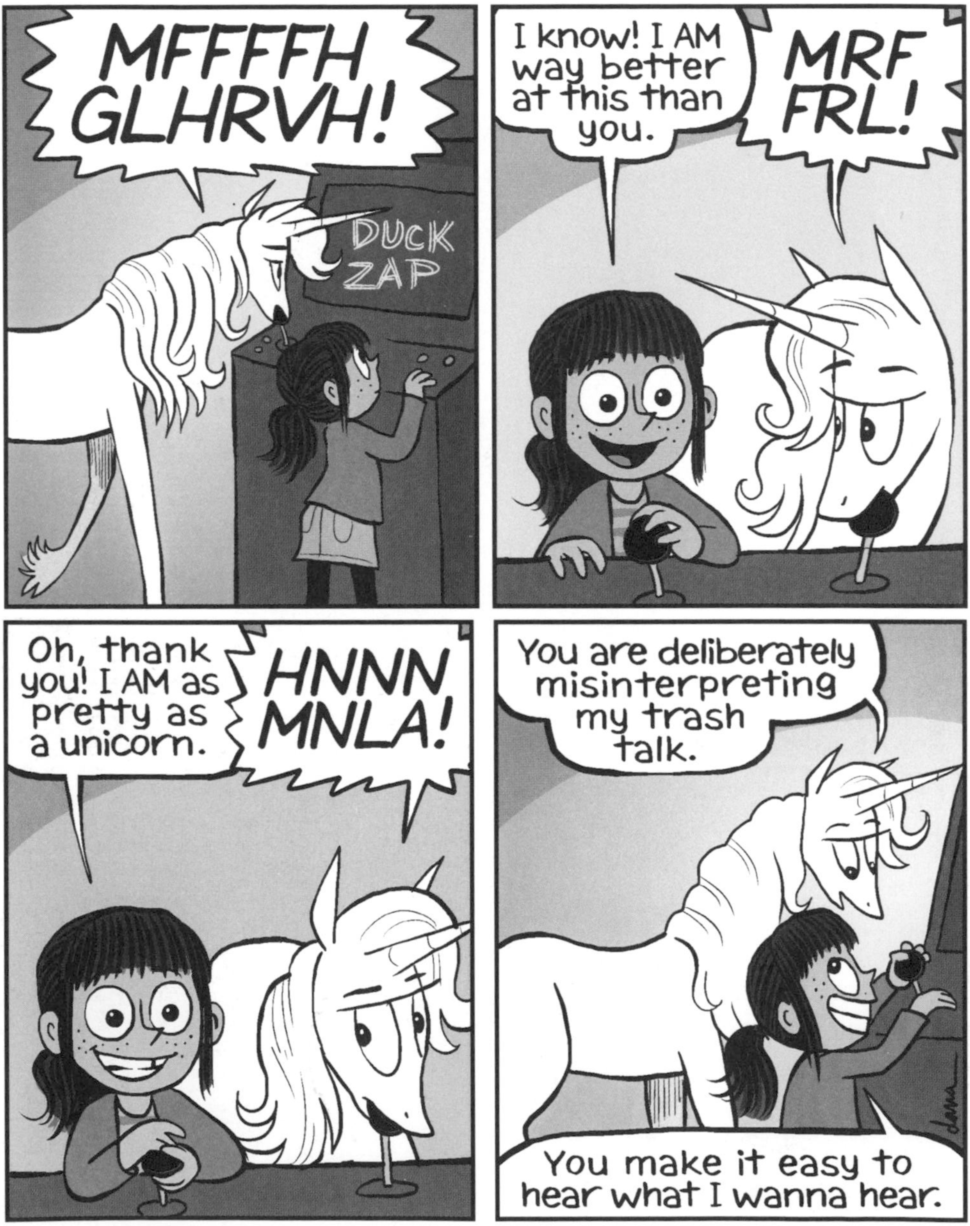
MFFFFH GLHRVH!
DUCK ZAP
I know! I AM way better at this than you.
MRF FRL!
Oh, thank you! I AM as pretty as a unicorn.
HNNN MNLA!
You are deliberately misinterpreting my trash talk.
You make it easy to hear what I wanna hear.

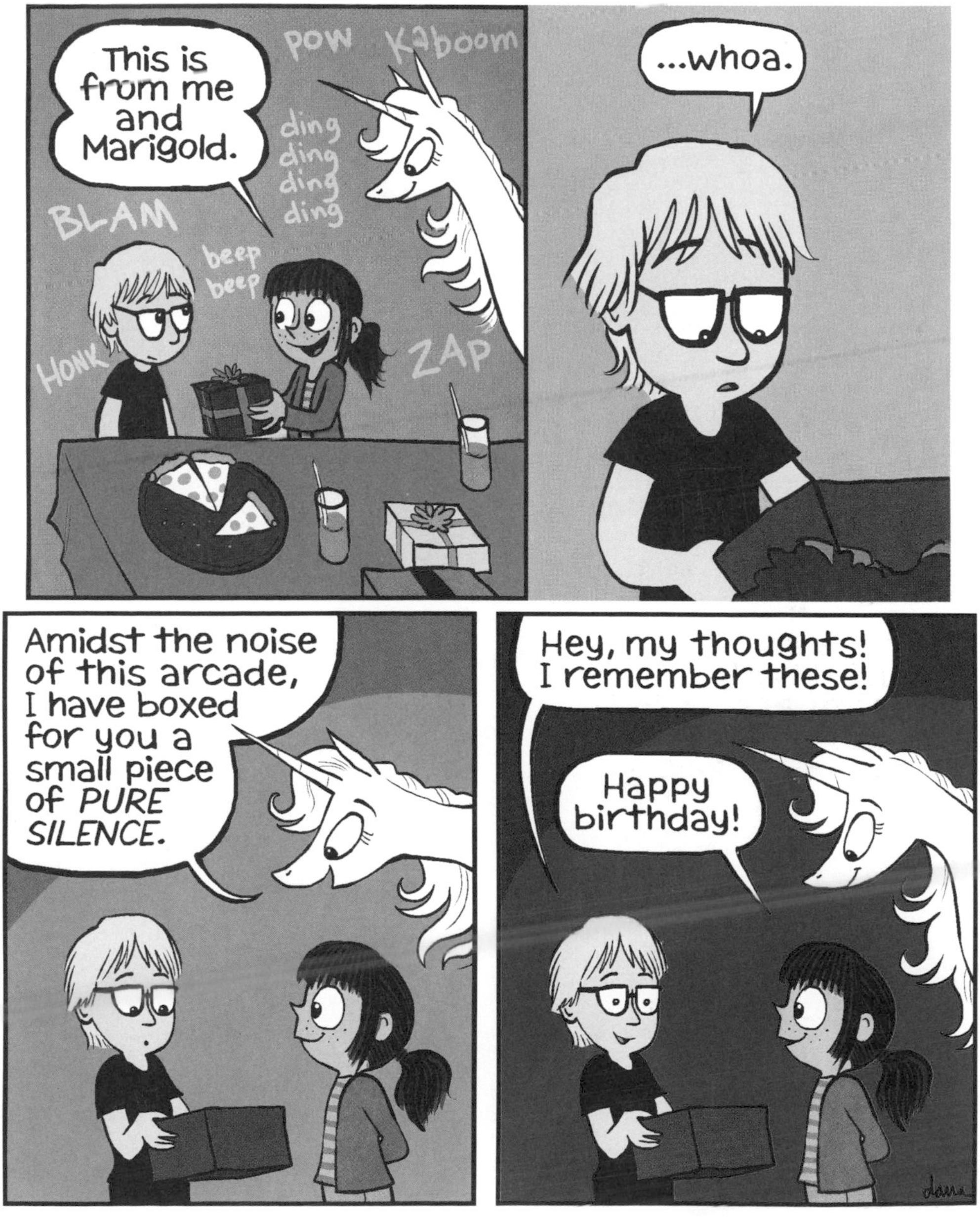
This is from me and Marigold.
POW
Kaboom
ding ding ding ding
BLAM
beep beep
HONK
ZAP
...whoa.
Amidst the noise of this arcade, I have boxed for you a small piece of *PURE SILENCE*.
Hey, my thoughts! I remember these!
Happy birthday!

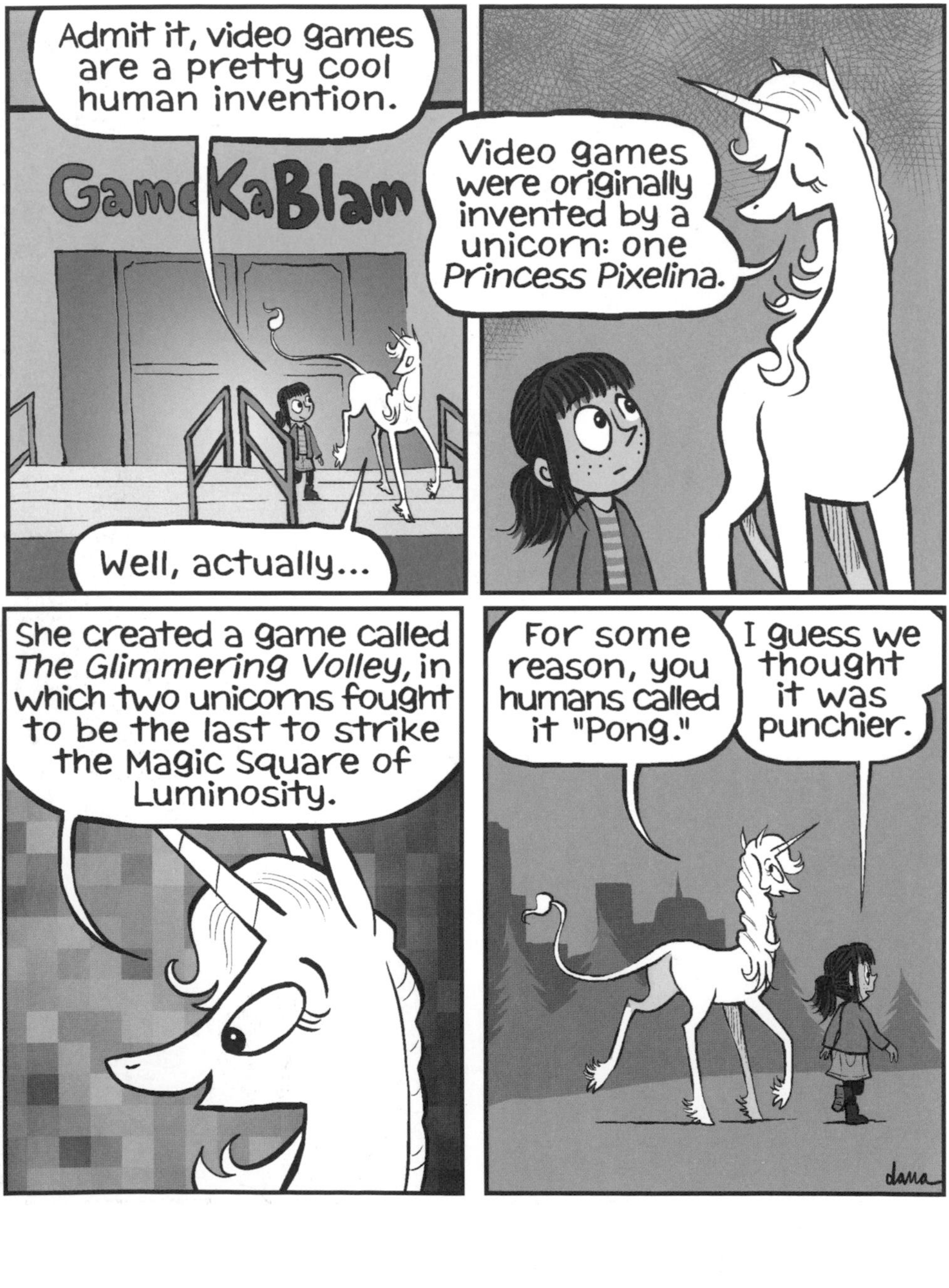
GameKaBlam
Admit it, video games are a pretty cool human invention.
Well, actually...
Video games were originally invented by a unicorn: one *Princess Pixelina.*
She created a game called *The Glimmering Volley,* in which two unicorns fought to be the last to strike the Magic Square of Luminosity.
For some reason, you humans called it "Pong."
I guess we thought it was punchier.
dana

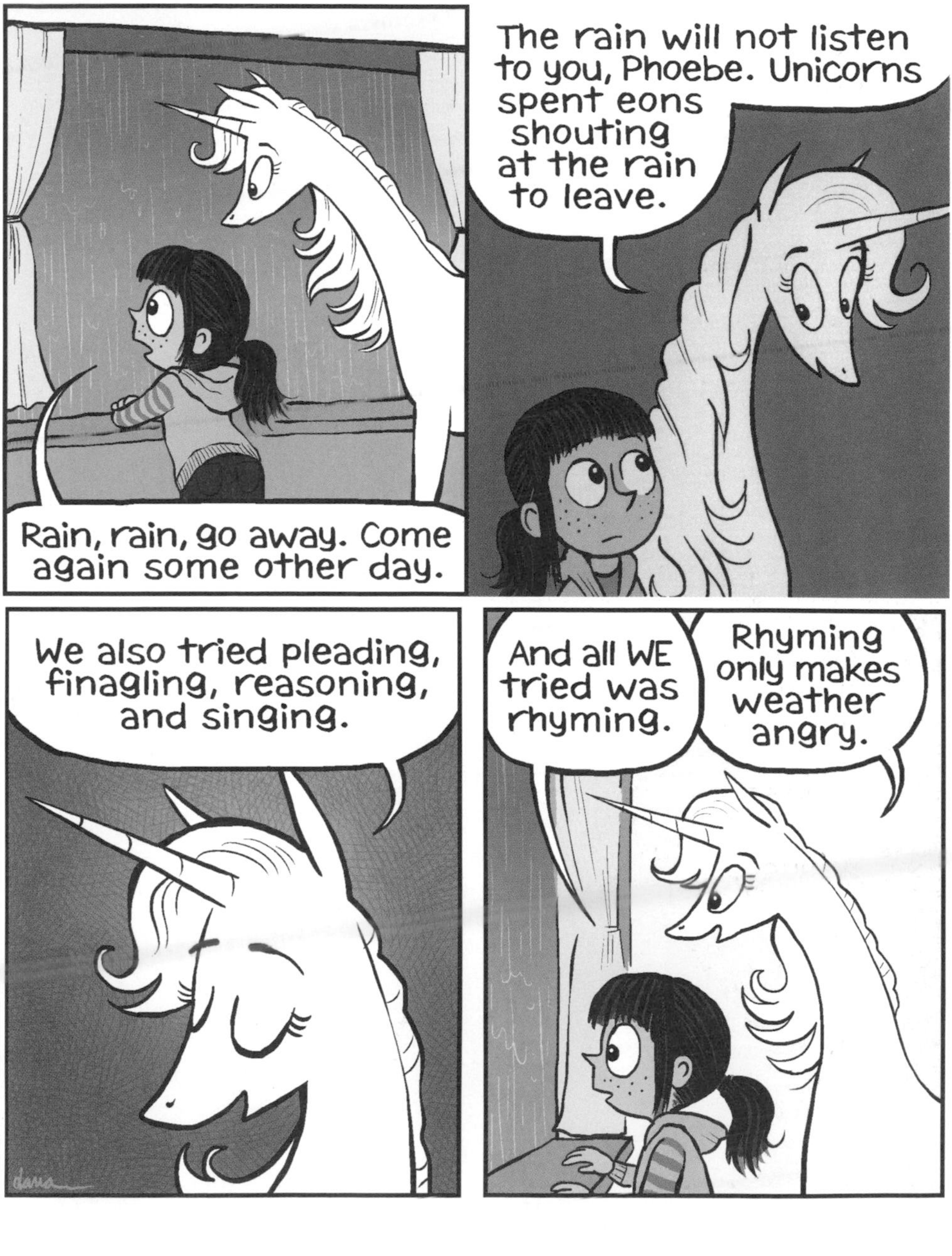
Rain, rain, go away. Come again some other day.
The rain will not listen to you, Phoebe. Unicorns spent eons shouting at the rain to leave.
We also tried pleading, finagling, reasoning, and singing.
And all WE tried was rhyming.
Rhyming only makes weather angry.

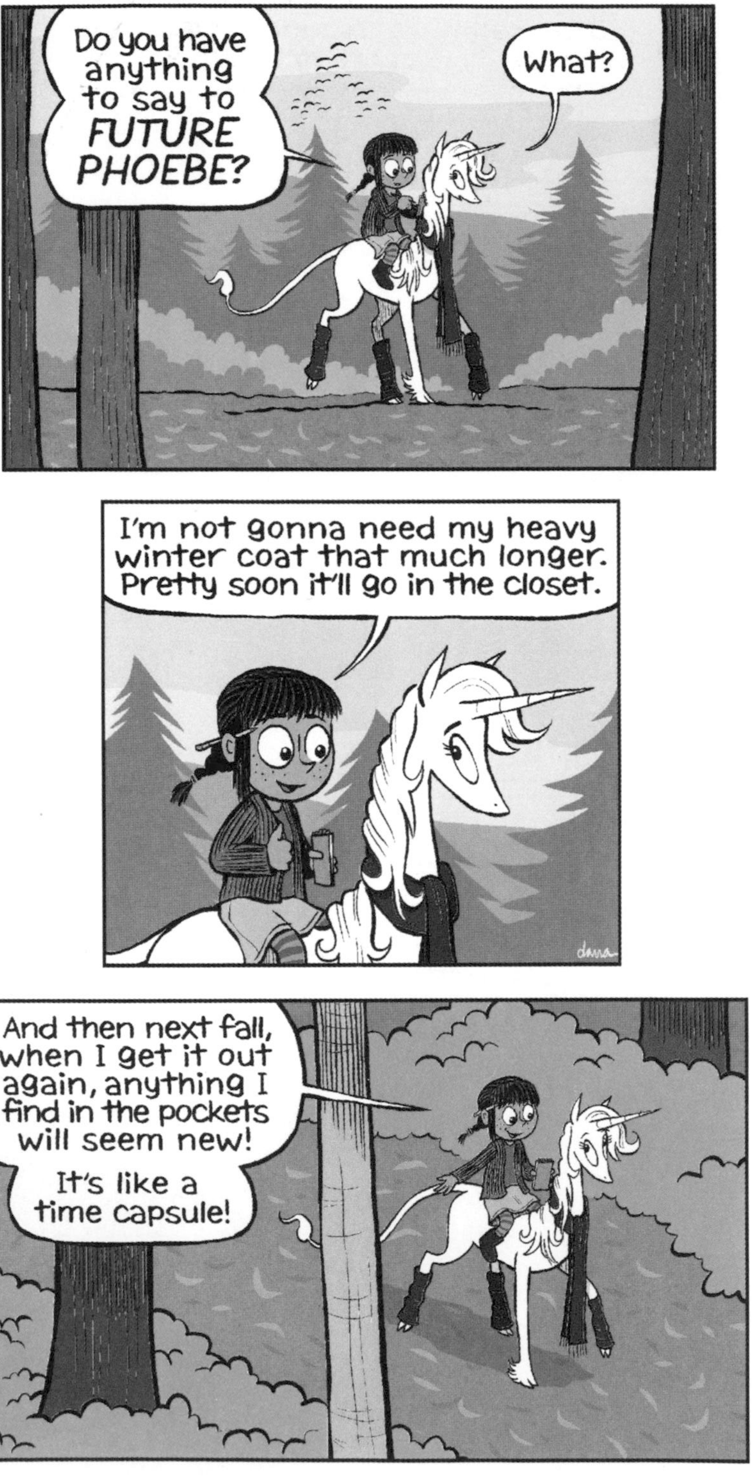
Do you have anything to say to *FUTURE PHOEBE?*
What?
I'm not gonna need my heavy winter coat that much longer. Pretty soon it'll go in the closet.
And then next fall, when I get it out again, anything I find in the pockets will seem new!
It's like a time capsule!

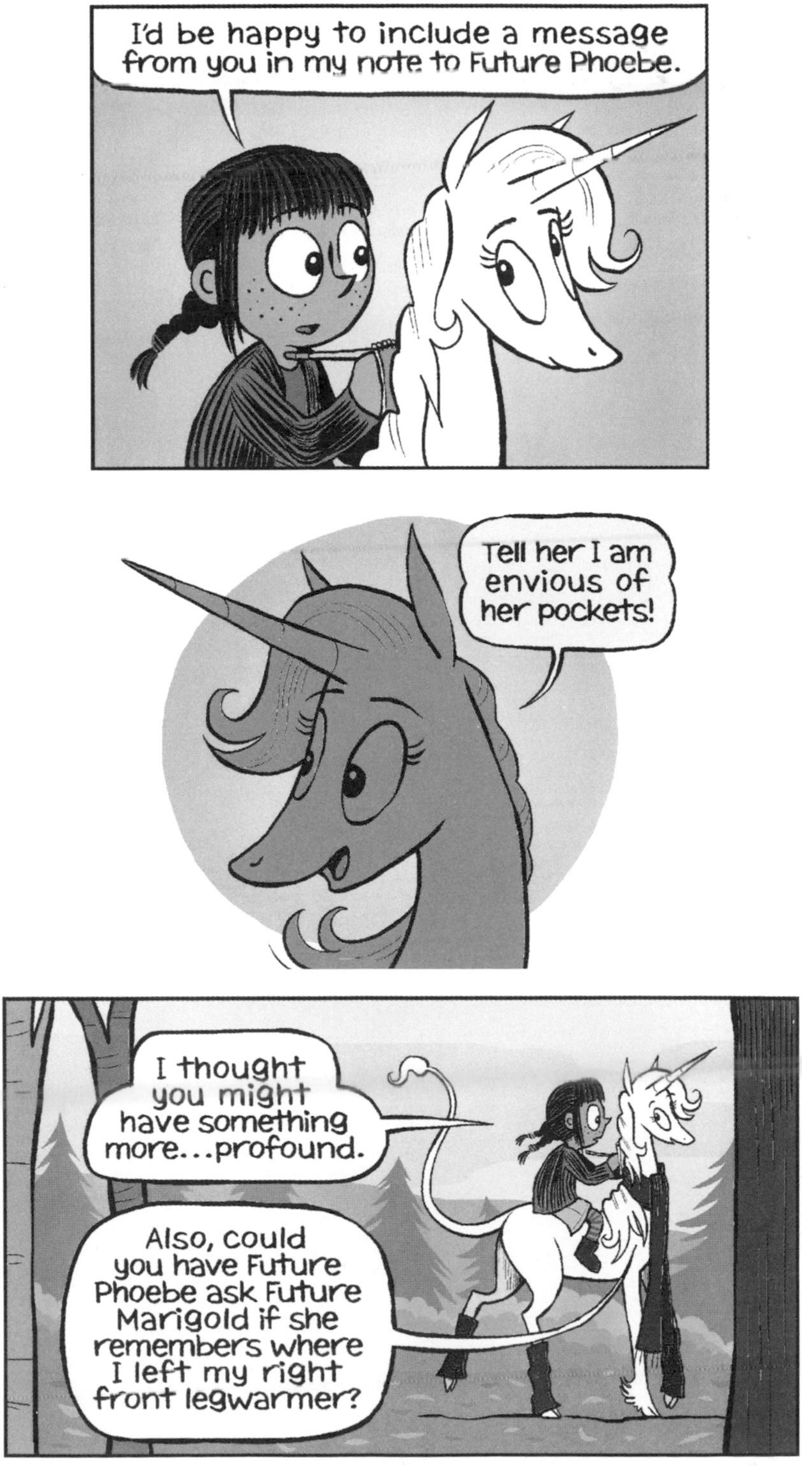
I'd be happy to include a message from you in my note to Future Phoebe.
Tell her I am envious of her pockets!
I thought you might have something more...profound.
Also, could you have Future Phoebe ask Future Marigold if she remembers where I left my right front legwarmer?

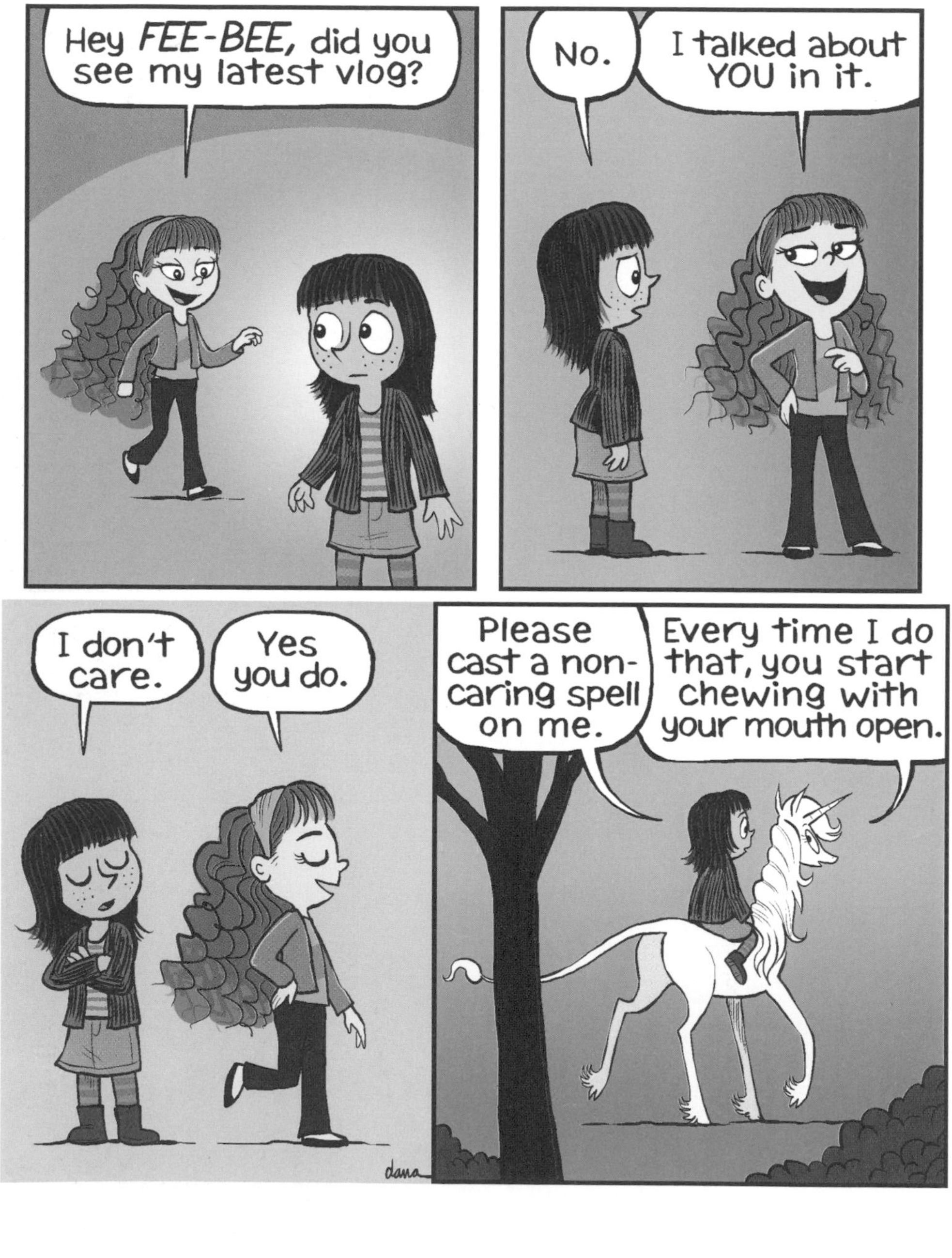
Hey *FEE-BEE,* did you see my latest vlog?
No.
I talked about YOU in it.
I don't care.
Yes you do.
Please cast a non-caring spell on me.
Every time I do that, you start chewing with your mouth open.
dana

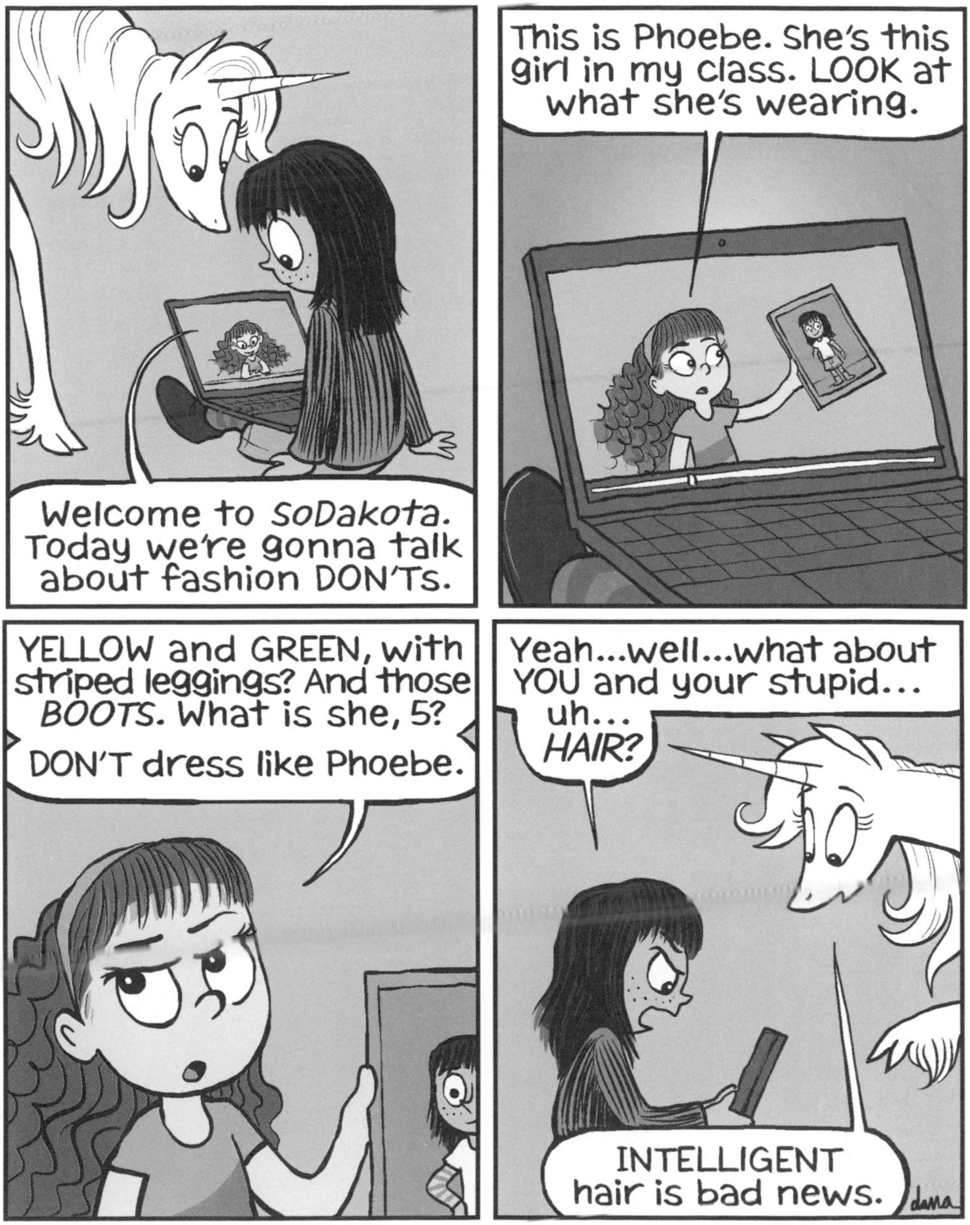
Welcome to SoDakota. Today we're gonna talk about fashion DON'Ts.
This is Phoebe. She's this girl in my class. LOOK at what she's wearing.
YELLOW and GREEN, with striped leggings? And those BOOTS. What is she, 5?
DON'T dress like Phoebe.
Yeah...well...what about YOU and your stupid...
uh... HAIR?
INTELLIGENT hair is bad news.
dana

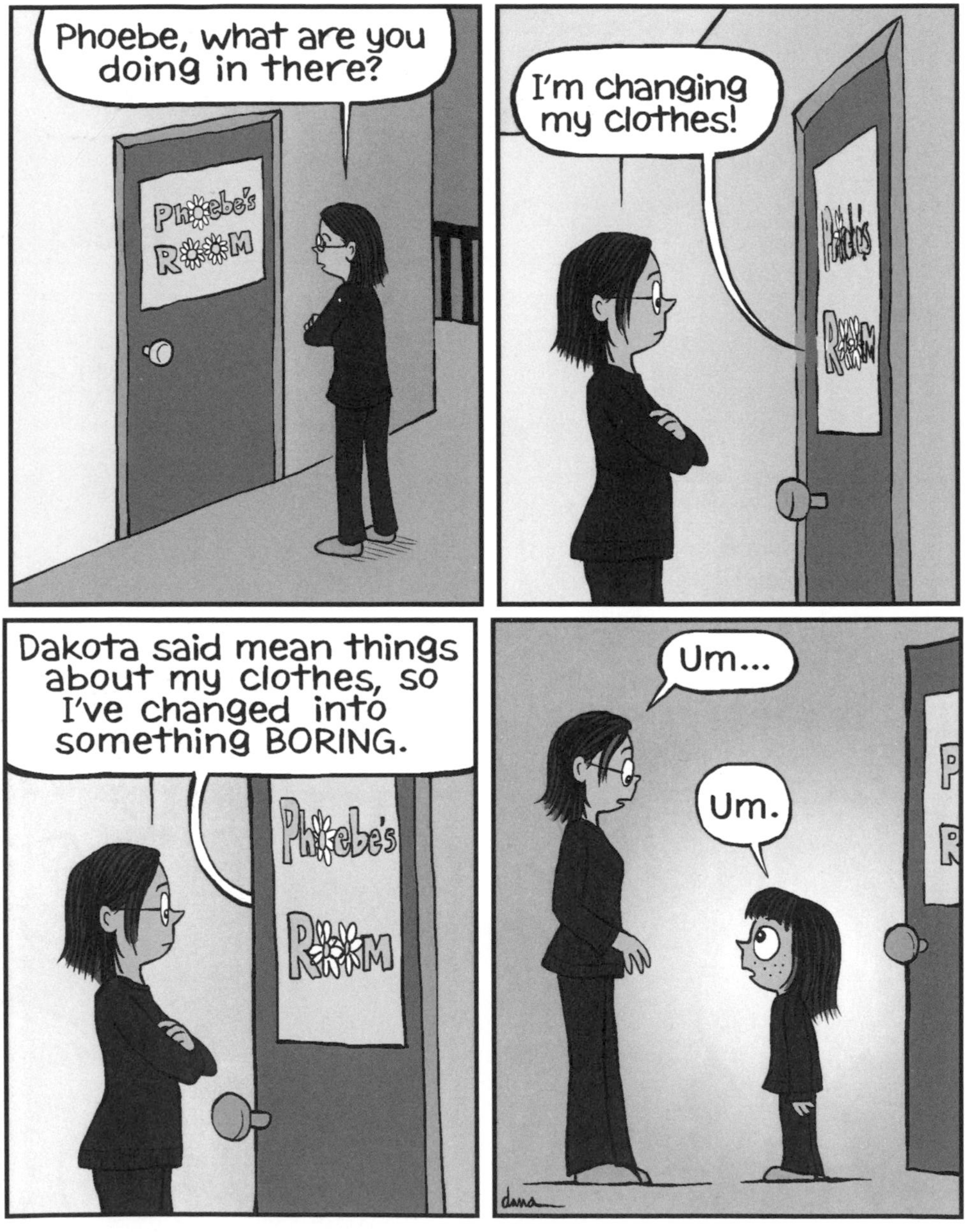
Phoebe, what are you doing in there?
Phoebe's Room
I'm changing my clothes!
Dakota said mean things about my clothes, so I've changed into something BORING.
Phoebe's Room
Um...
Um.
dana

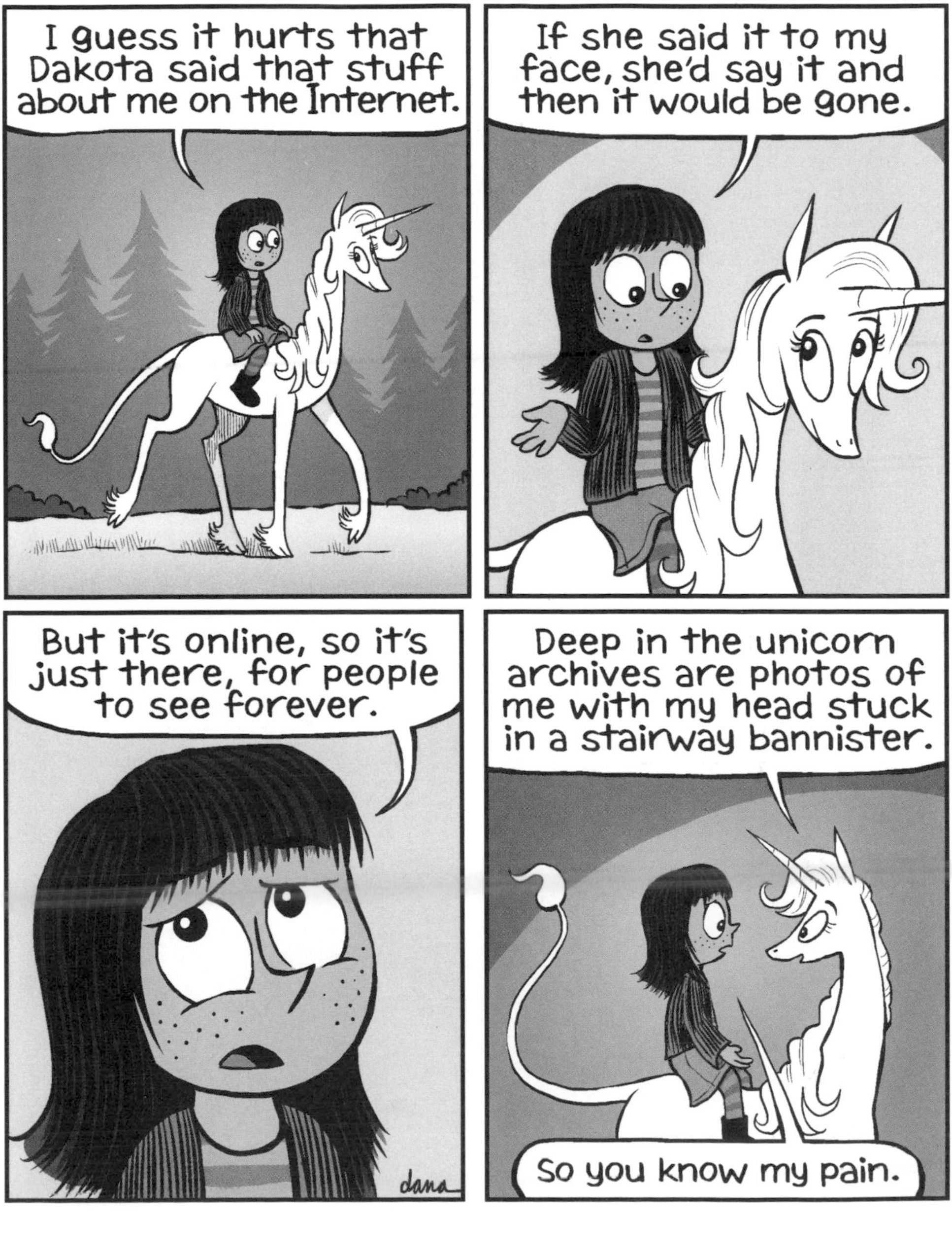
I guess it hurts that Dakota said that stuff about me on the Internet.
If she said it to my face, she'd say it and then it would be gone.
But it's online, so it's just there, for people to see forever.
dana
Deep in the unicorn archives are photos of me with my head stuck in a stairway bannister.
So you know my pain.

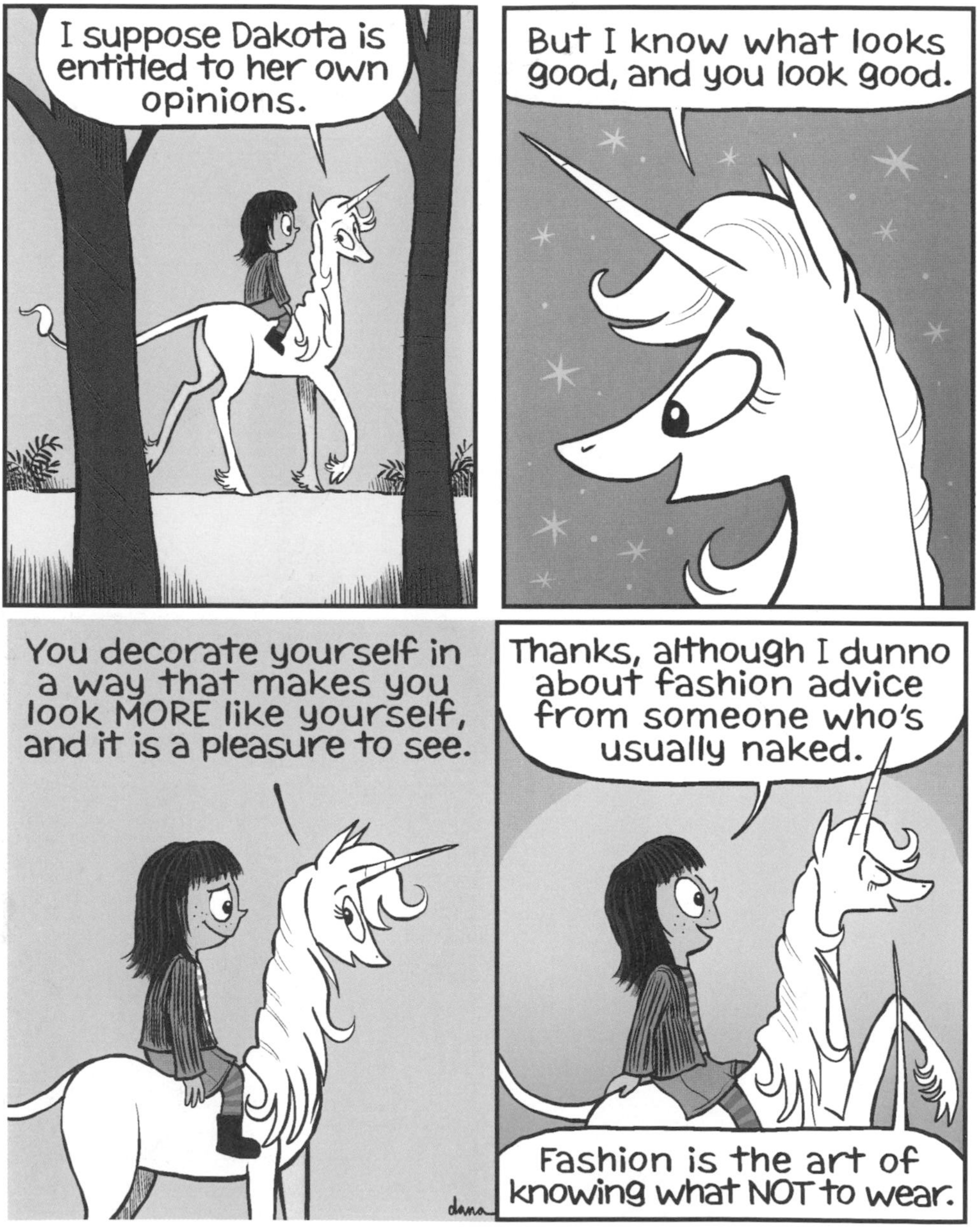
I suppose Dakota is entitled to her own opinions.
But I know what looks good, and you look good.
You decorate yourself in a way that makes you look MORE like yourself, and it is a pleasure to see.
Thanks, although I dunno about fashion advice from someone who's usually naked.
Fashion is the art of knowing what NOT to wear.
dana

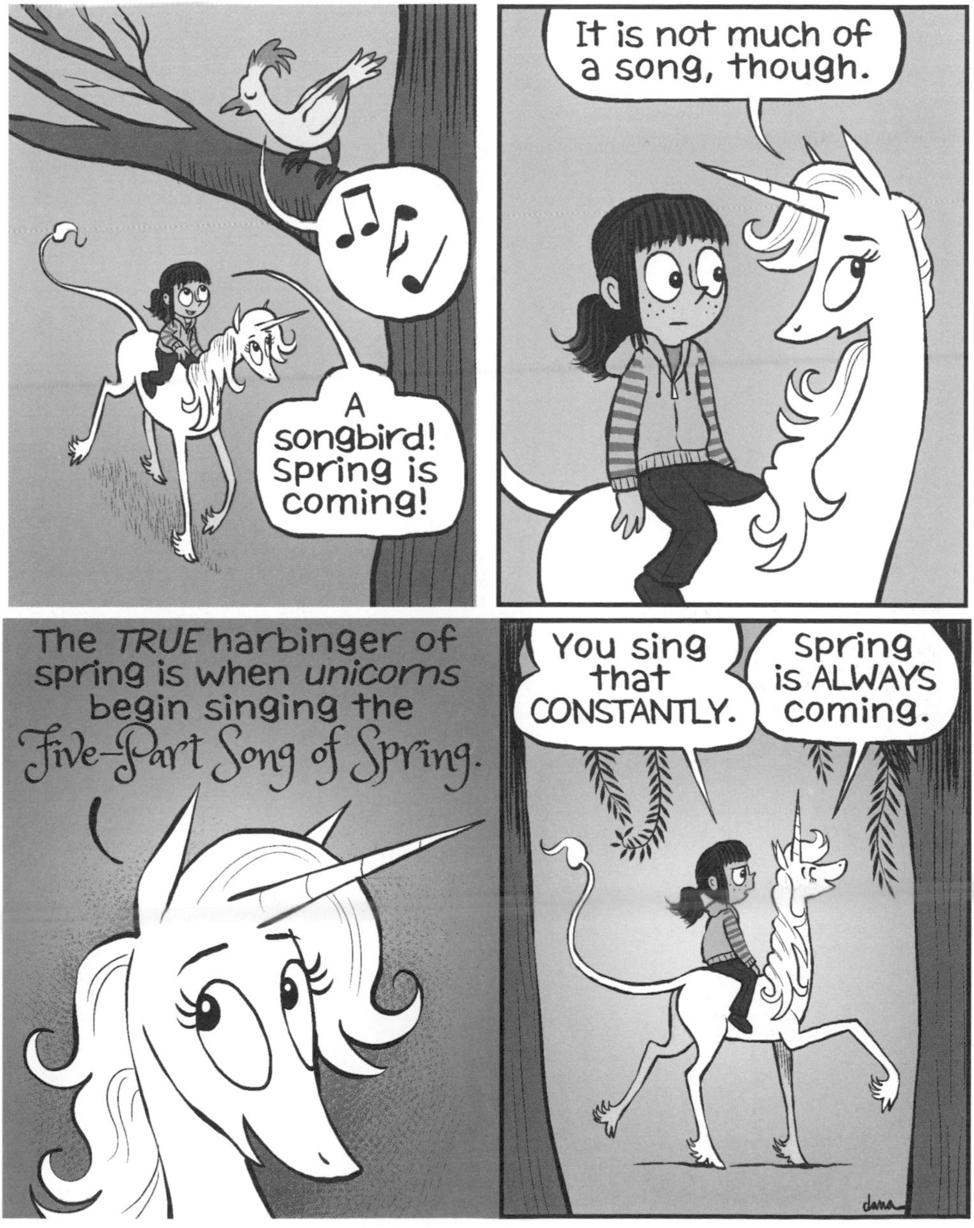
A songbird! Spring is coming!
It is not much of a song, though.
The *TRUE* harbinger of spring is when *unicorns* begin singing the Five-Part Song of Spring.
You sing that CONSTANTLY.
Spring is ALWAYS coming.
dana

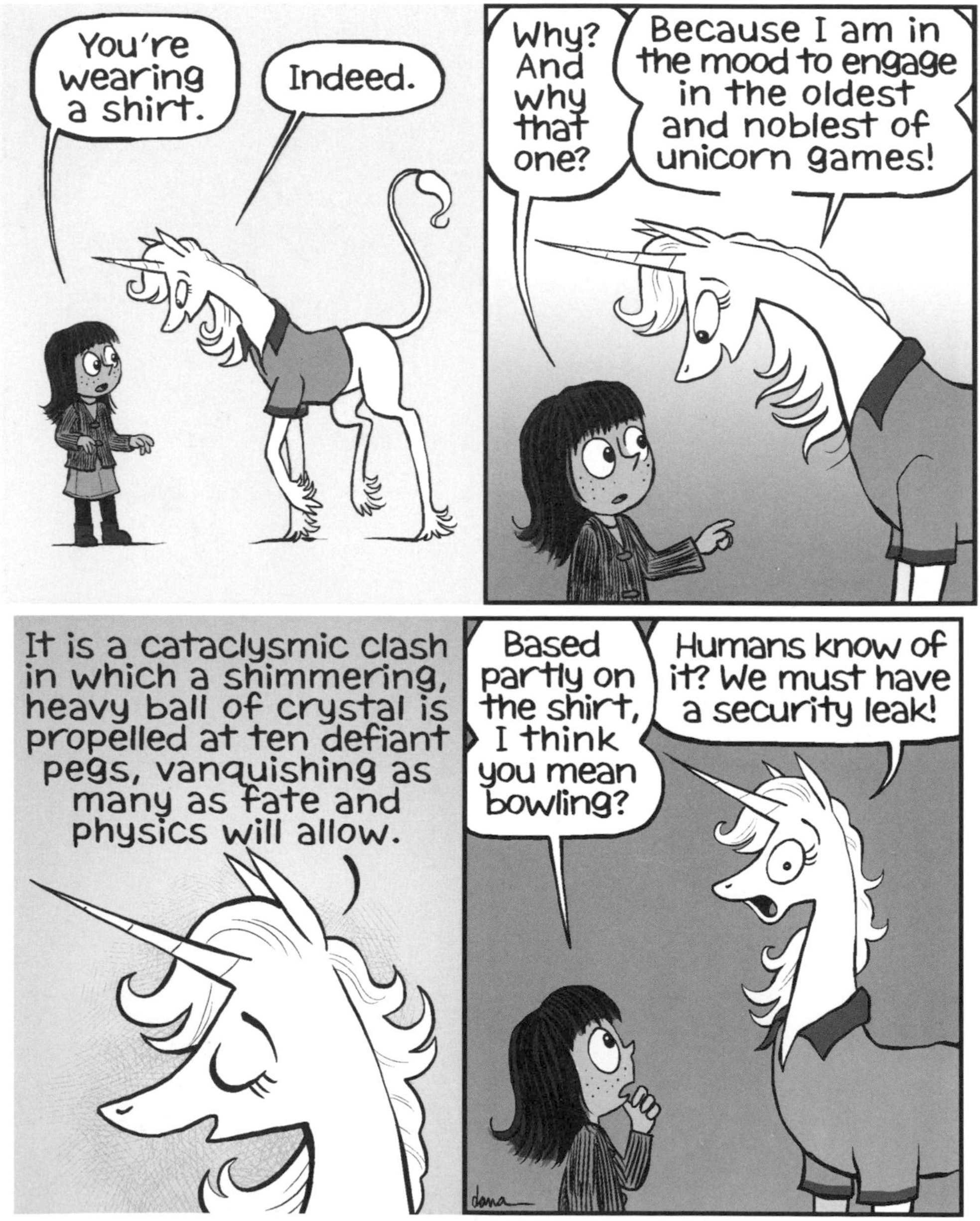
You're wearing a shirt.
Indeed.
Why? And why that one?
Because I am in the mood to engage in the oldest and noblest of unicorn games!
It is a cataclysmic clash in which a shimmering, heavy ball of crystal is propelled at ten defiant pegs, vanquishing as many as fate and physics will allow.
Based partly on the shirt, I think you mean bowling?
Humans know of it? We must have a security leak!
dana

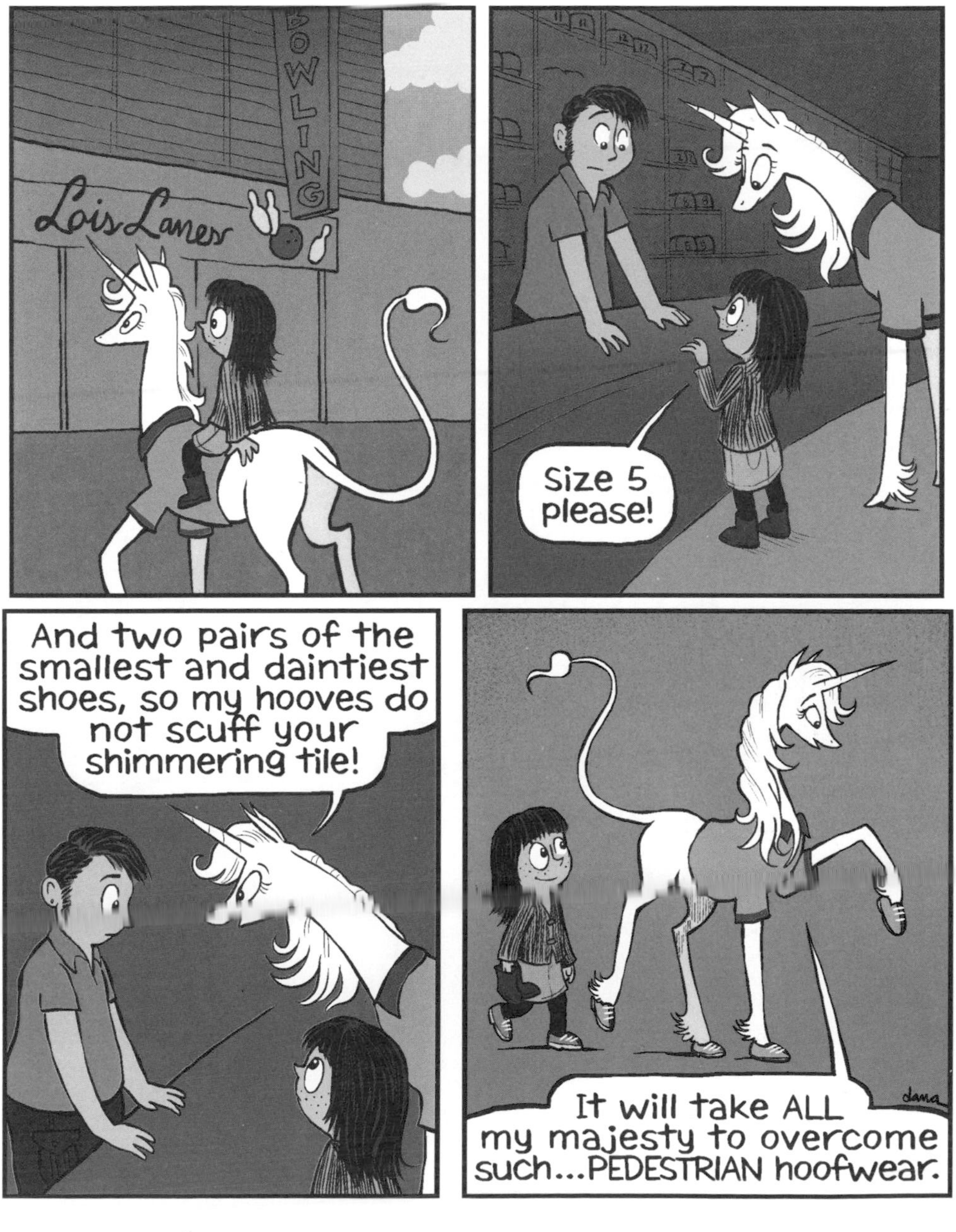
BOWLING
Lois Lanes
Size 5 please!
And two pairs of the smallest and daintiest shoes, so my hooves do not scuff your shimmering tile!
It will take ALL my majesty to overcome such...PEDESTRIAN hoofwear.
dana

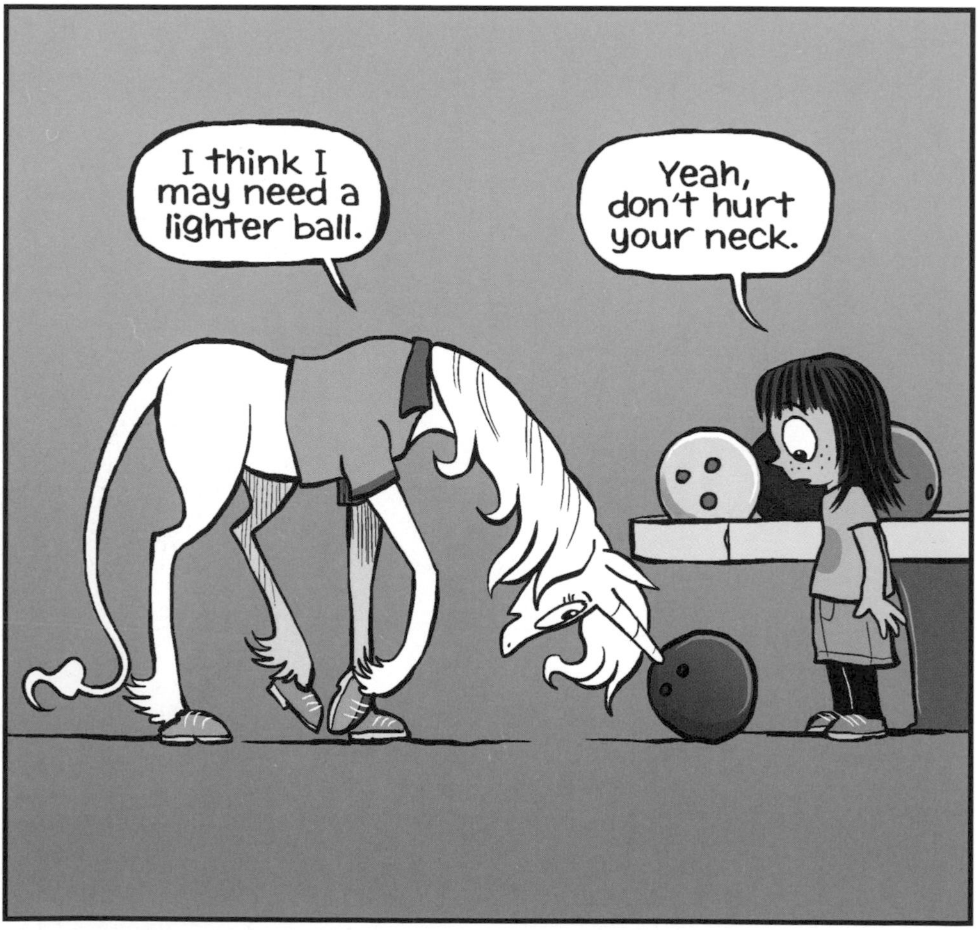
I think I may need a lighter ball.
Yeah, don't hurt your neck.

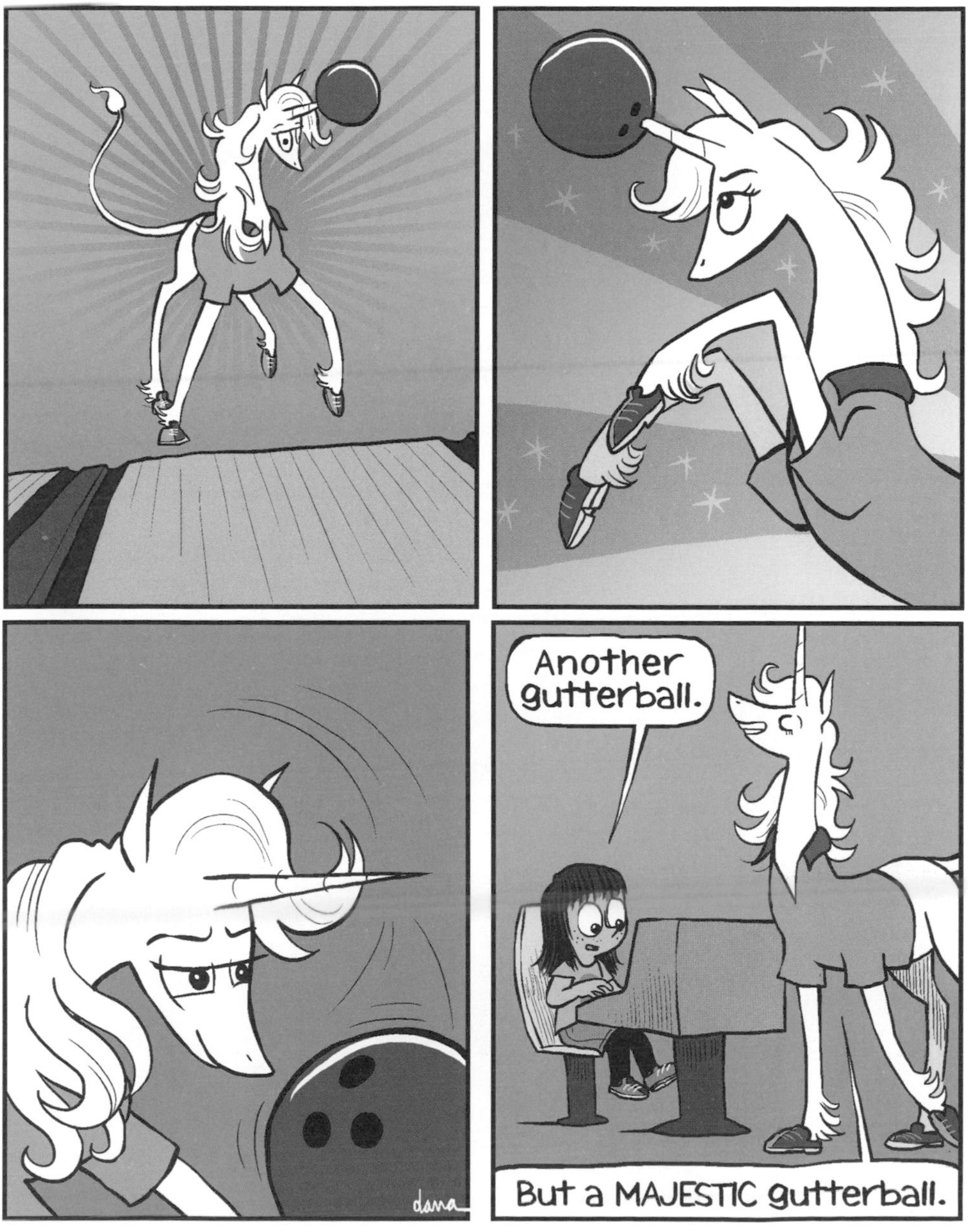
Another gutterball.
But a MAJESTIC gutterball.
dana

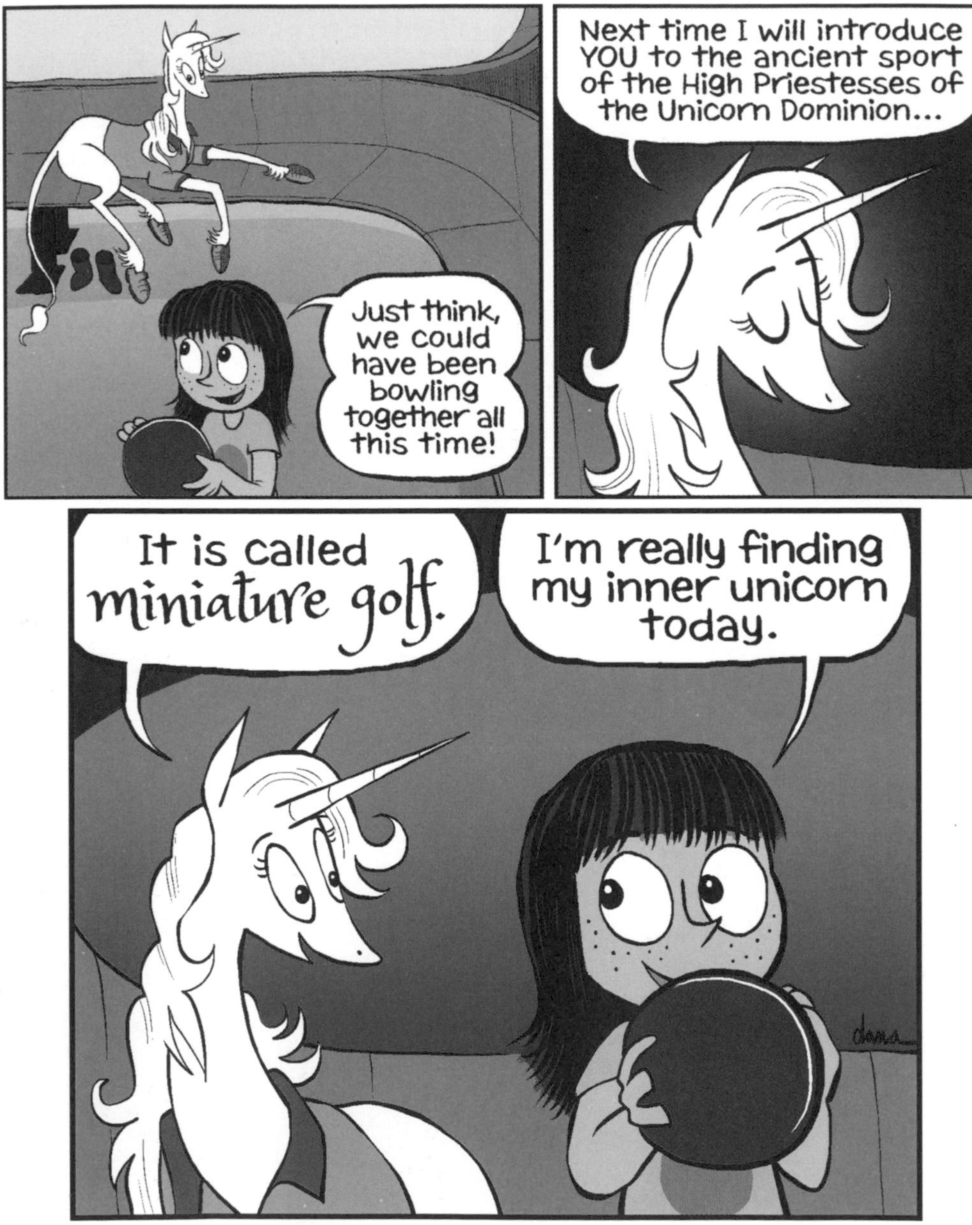
Just think, we could have been bowling together all this time!
Next time I will introduce YOU to the ancient sport of the High Priestesses of the Unicorn Dominion...
It is called miniature golf.
I'm really finding my inner unicorn today.
dana

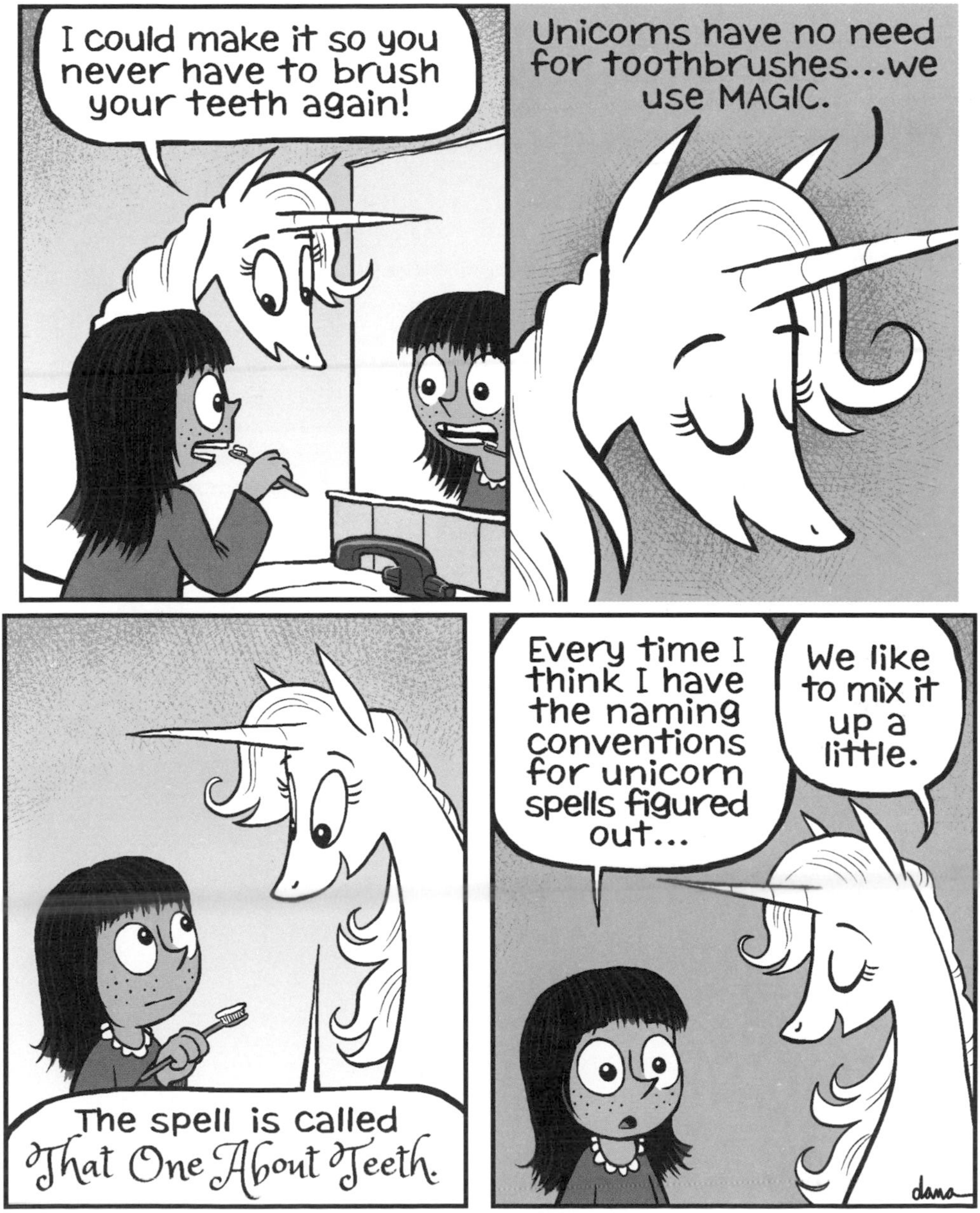

I could make it so you never have to brush your teeth again!
Unicorns have no need for toothbrushes...we use MAGIC.
The spell is called That One About Teeth.
Every time I think I have the naming conventions for unicorn spells figured out...
We like to mix it up a little.
dana

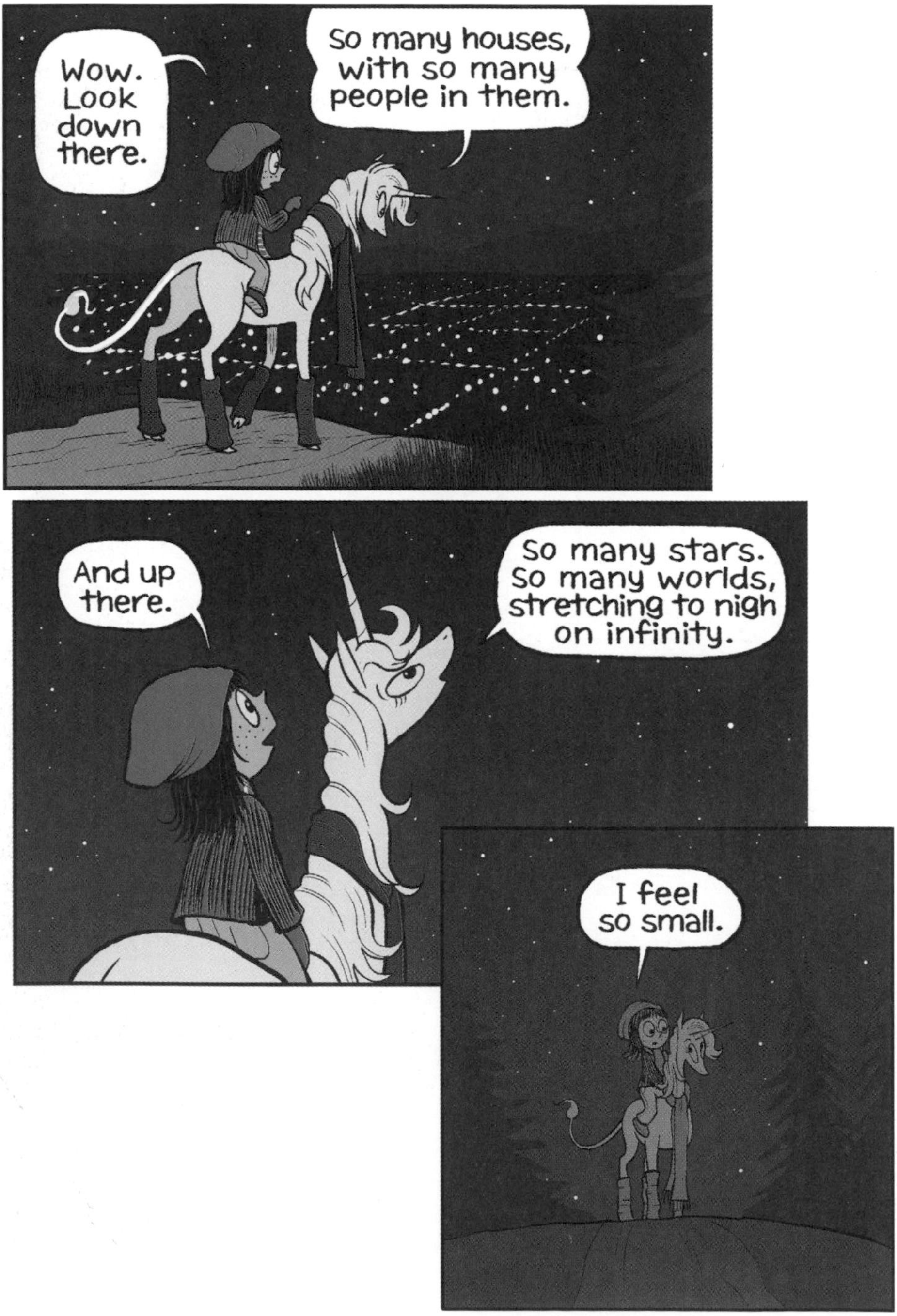
Wow. Look down there.
So many houses, with so many people in them.
And up there.
So many stars. So many worlds, stretching to nigh on infinity.
I feel so small.

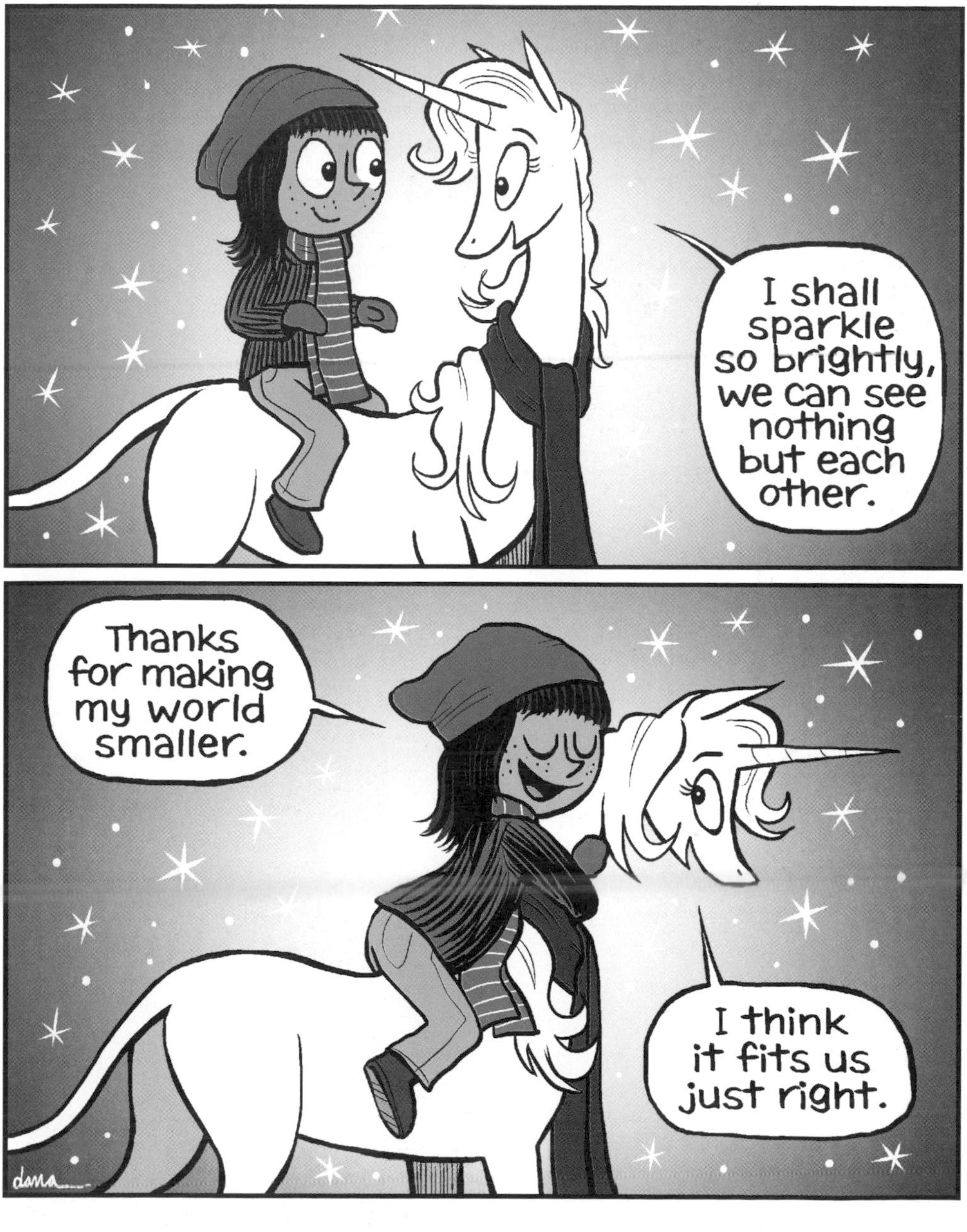
I shall sparkle so brightly, we can see nothing but each other.
Thanks for making my world smaller.
I think it fits us just right.
dana

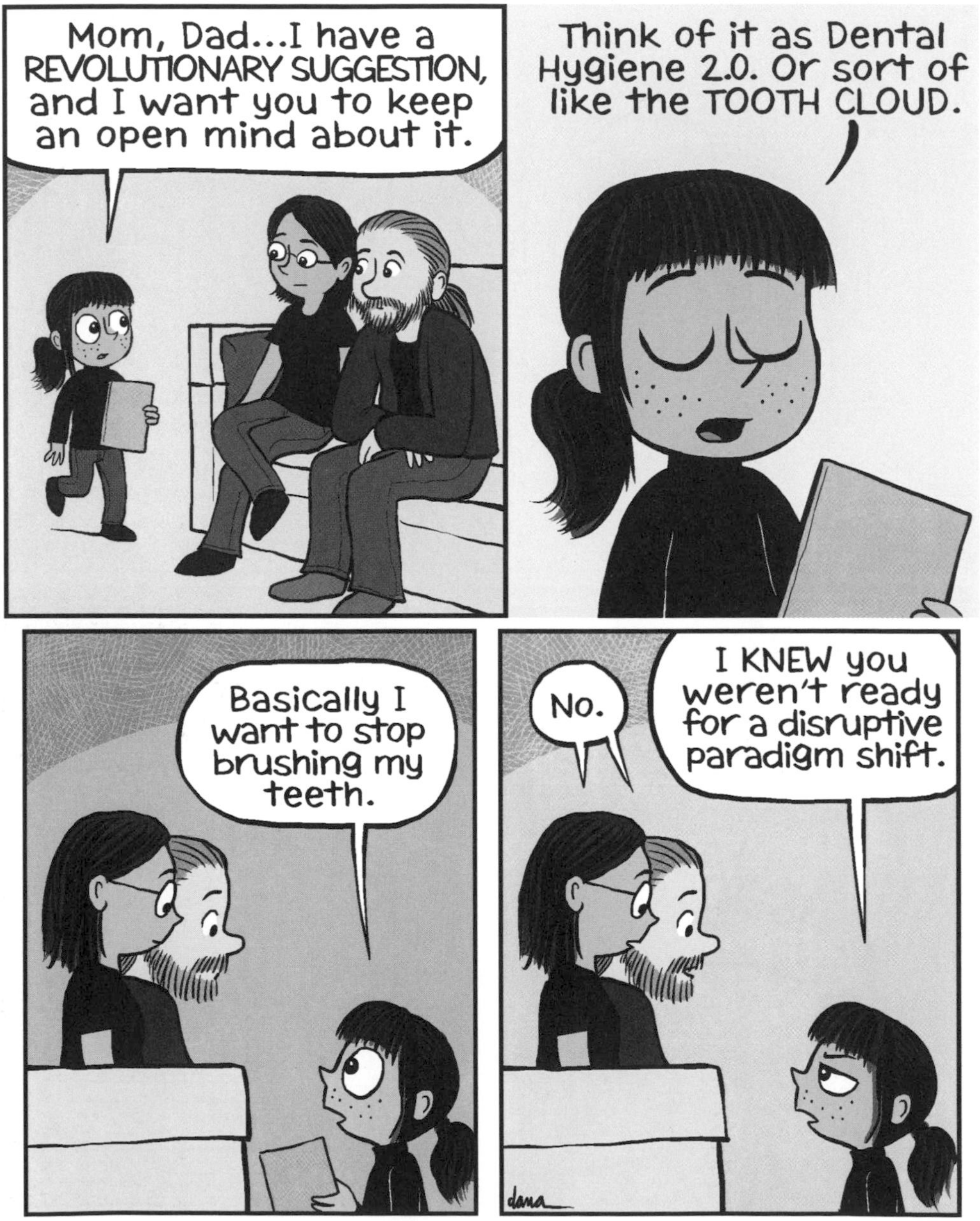
Mom, Dad...I have a REVOLUTIONARY SUGGESTION, and I want you to keep an open mind about it.
Think of it as Dental Hygiene 2.0. Or sort of like the TOOTH CLOUD.
Basically I want to stop brushing my teeth.
No.
I KNEW you weren't ready for a disruptive paradigm shift.
dana

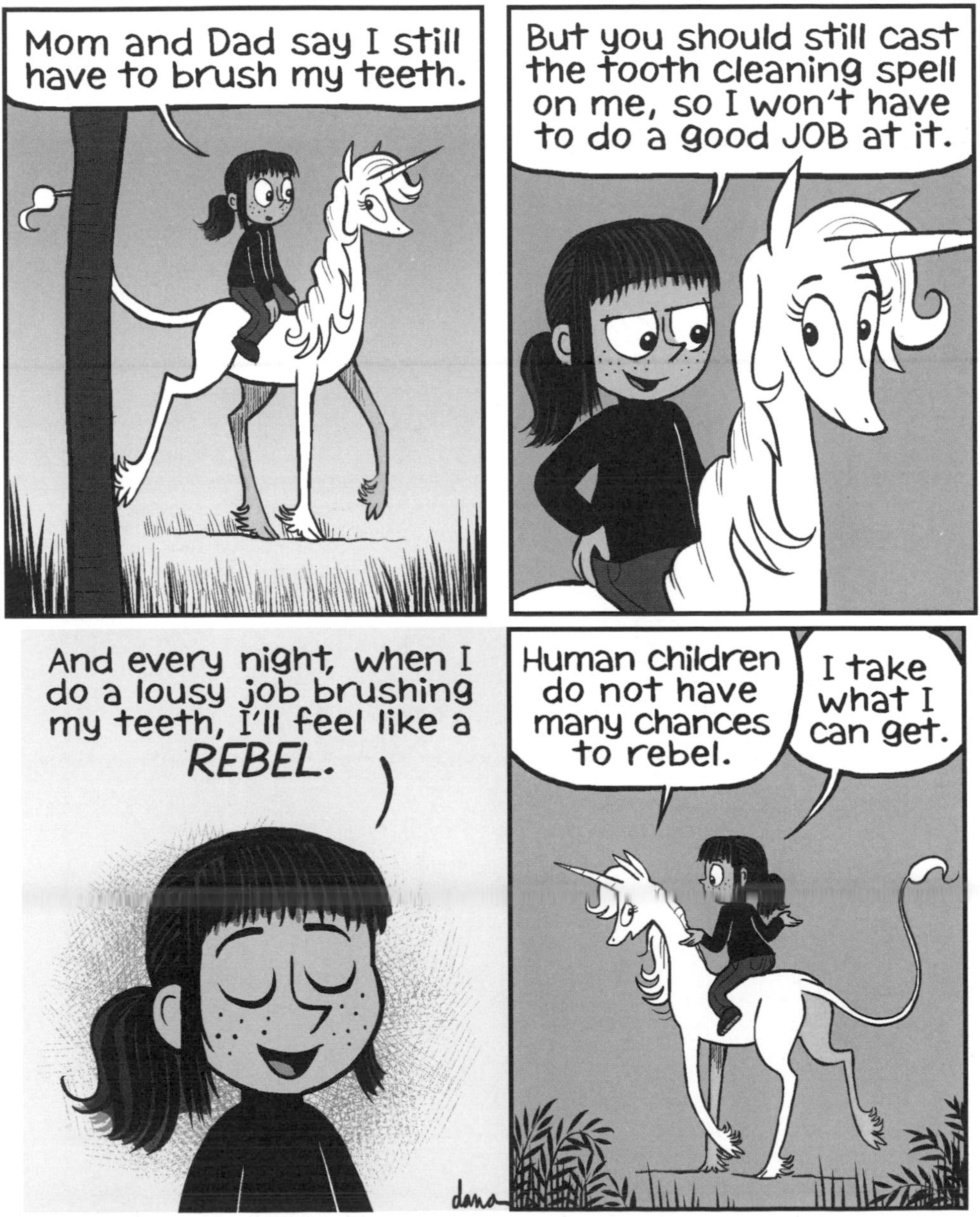
Mom and Dad say I still have to brush my teeth.
But you should still cast the tooth cleaning spell on me, so I won't have to do a good JOB at it.
And every night, when I do a lousy job brushing my teeth, I'll feel like a REBEL.
Human children do not have many chances to rebel.
I take what I can get.
dana

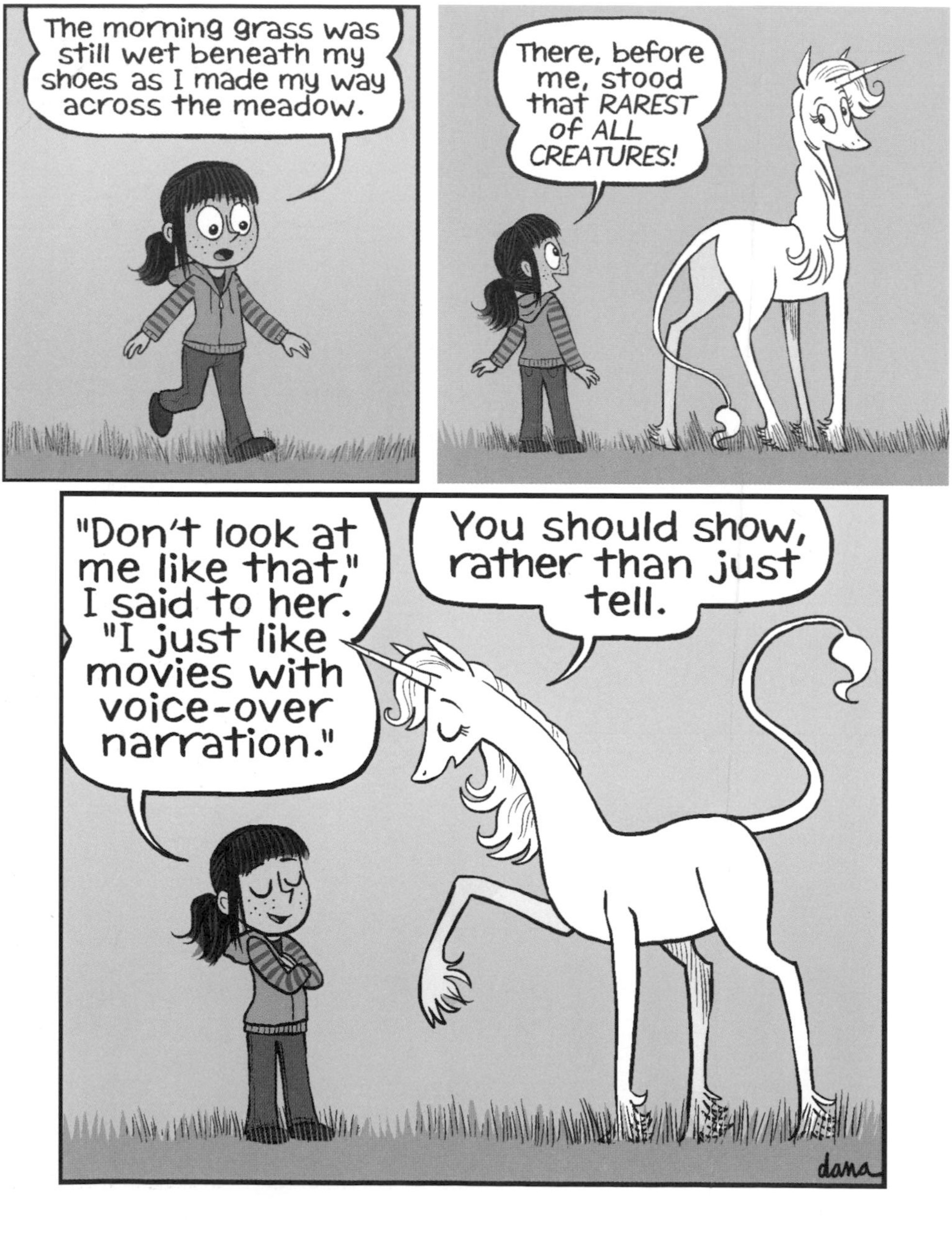
The morning grass was still wet beneath my shoes as I made my way across the meadow.
There, before me, stood that RAREST of ALL CREATURES!
"Don't look at me like that," I said to her. "I just like movies with voice-over narration."
You should show, rather than just tell.
dana

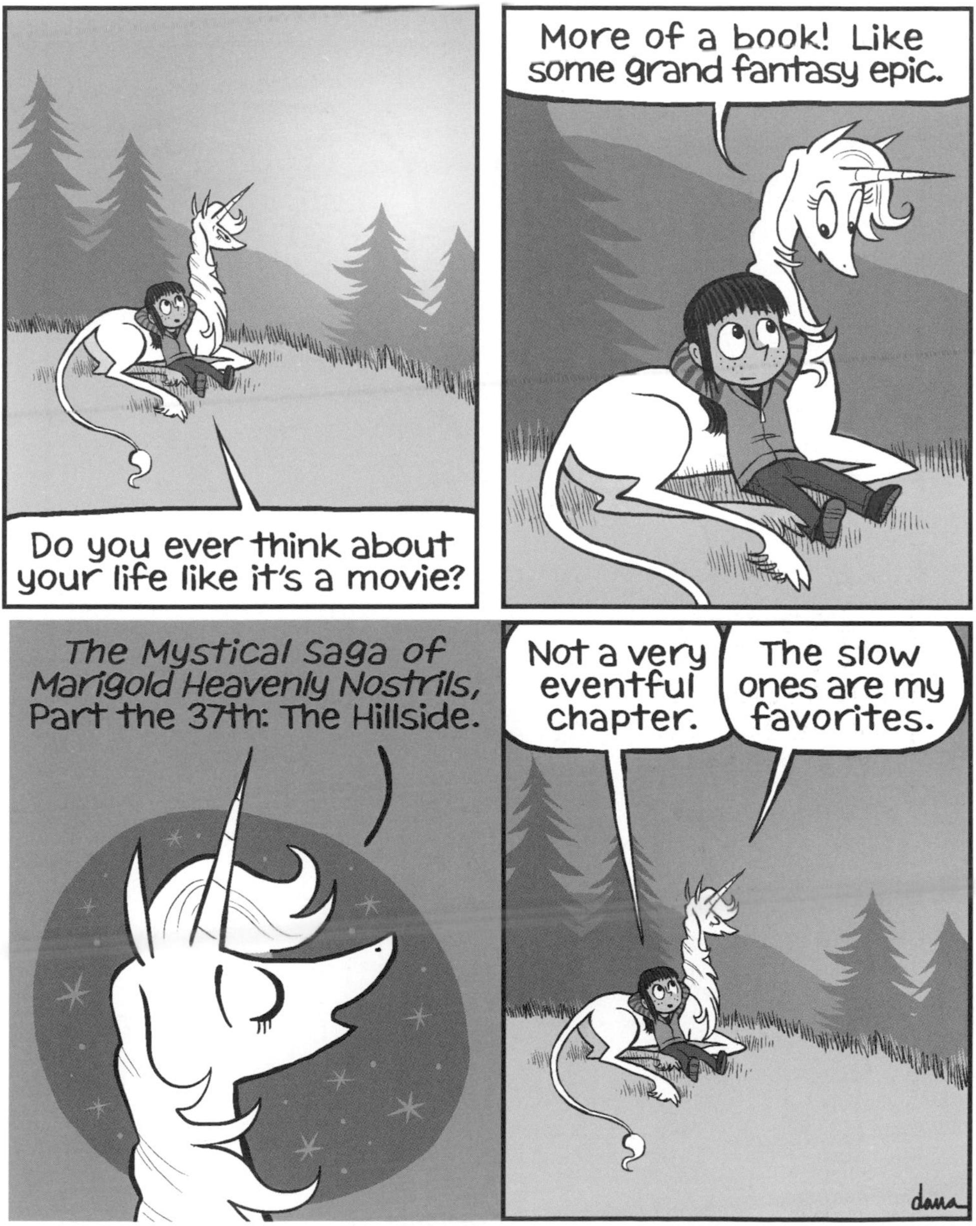
Do you ever think about your life like it's a movie?
More of a book! Like some grand fantasy epic.
The Mystical Saga of Marigold Heavenly Nostrils, Part the 37th: The Hillside.
Not a very eventful chapter.
The slow ones are my favorites.
dana

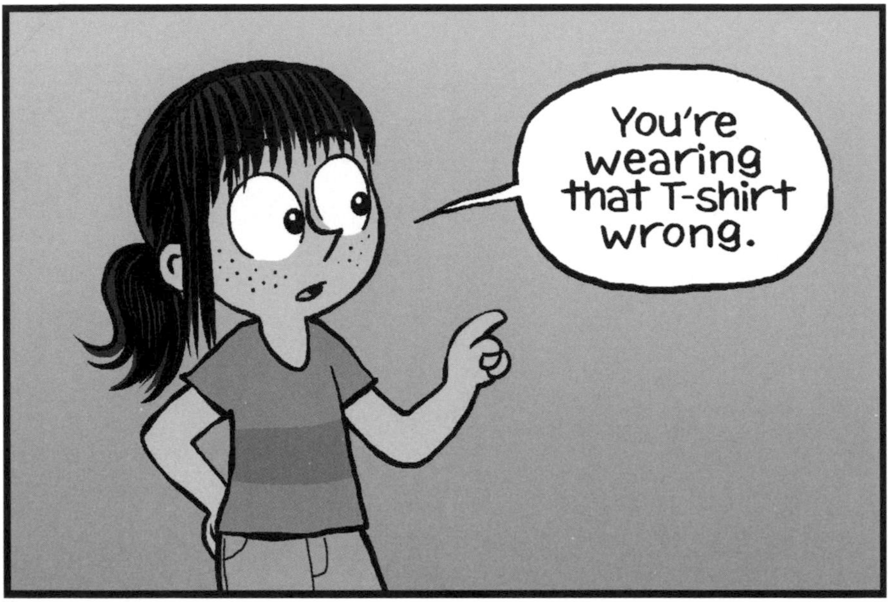
You're wearing that T-shirt wrong.

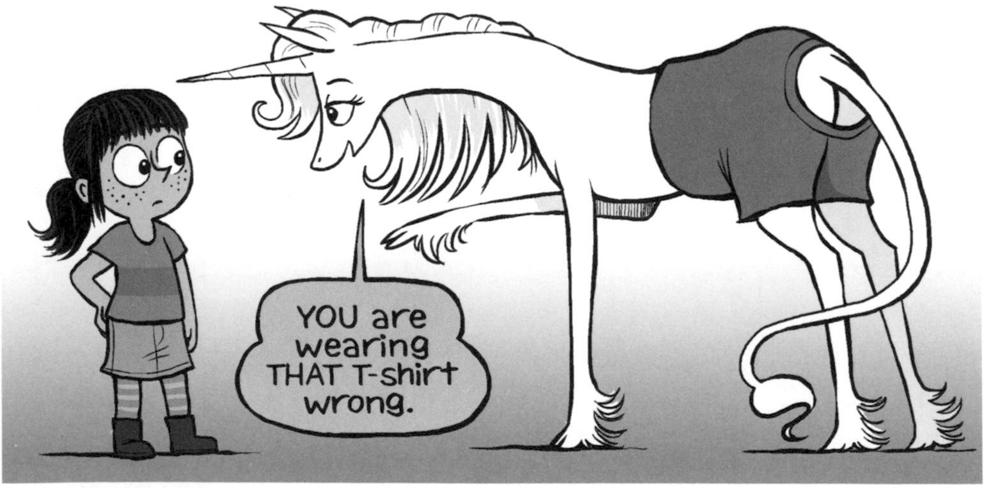
YOU are wearing THAT T-shirt wrong.

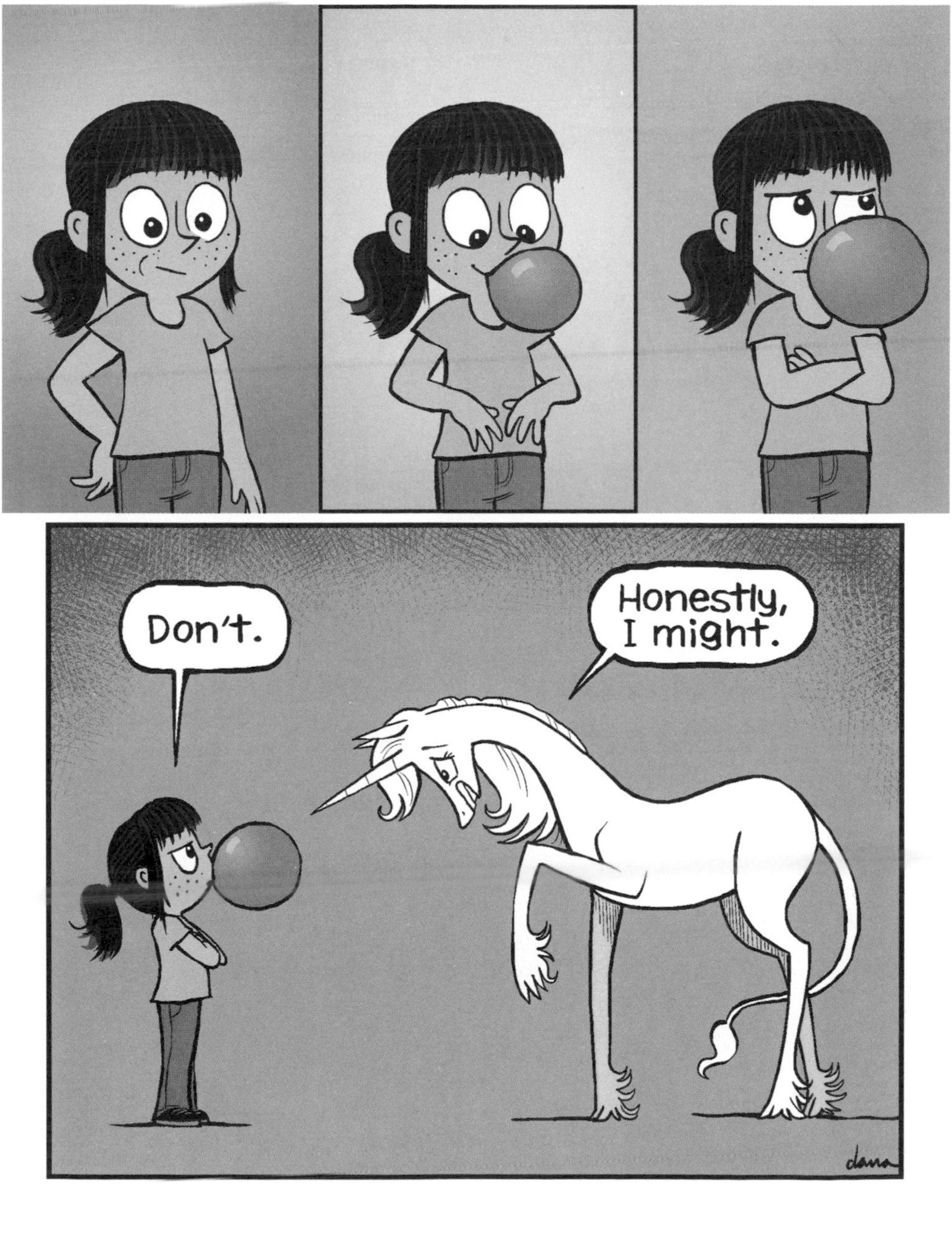
Don't.
Honestly, I might.
dana

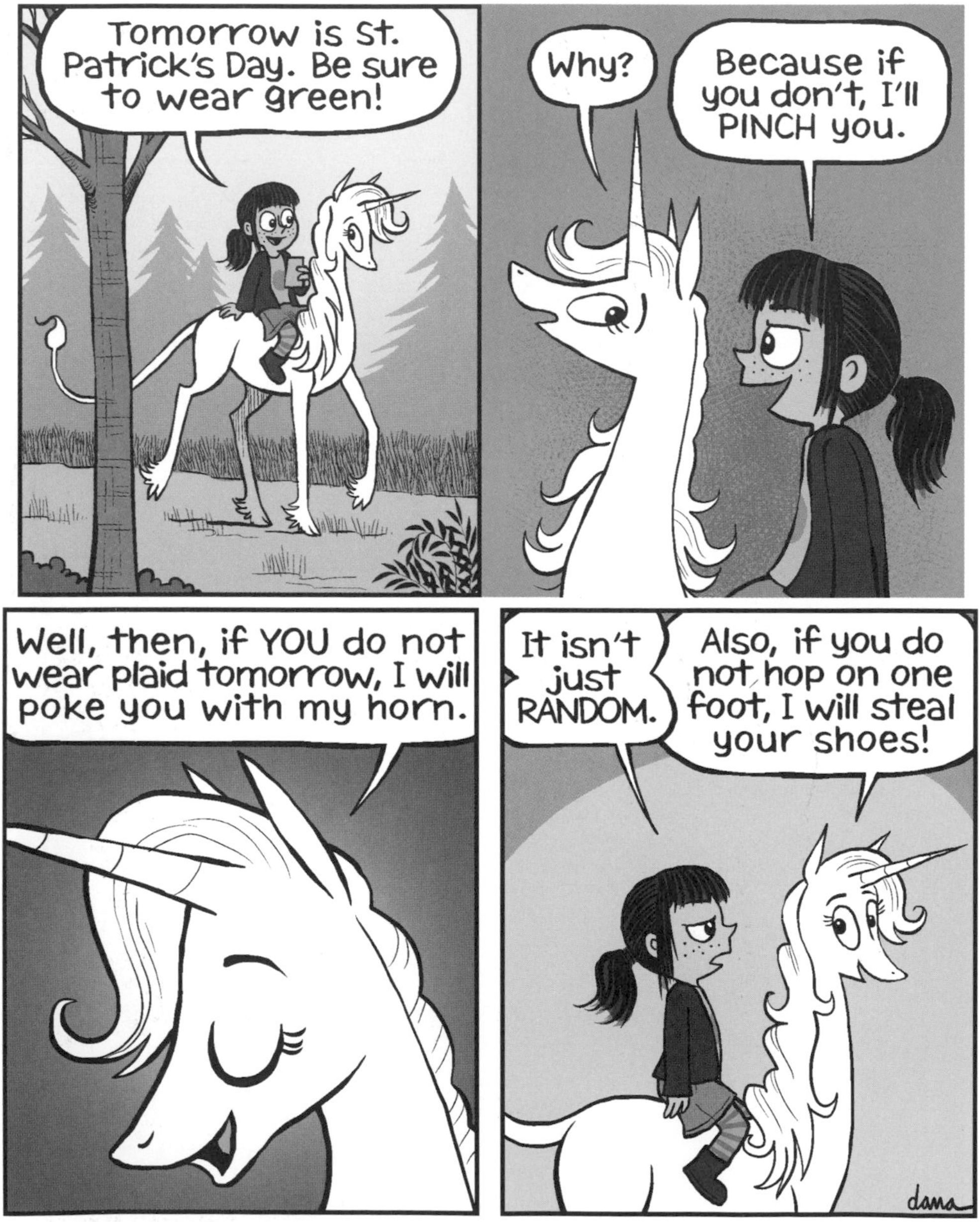
Tomorrow is St. Patrick's Day. Be sure to wear green!
Why?
Because if you don't, I'll PINCH you.
Well, then, if YOU do not wear plaid tomorrow, I will poke you with my horn.
It isn't just RANDOM.
Also, if you do not hop on one foot, I will steal your shoes!
dana

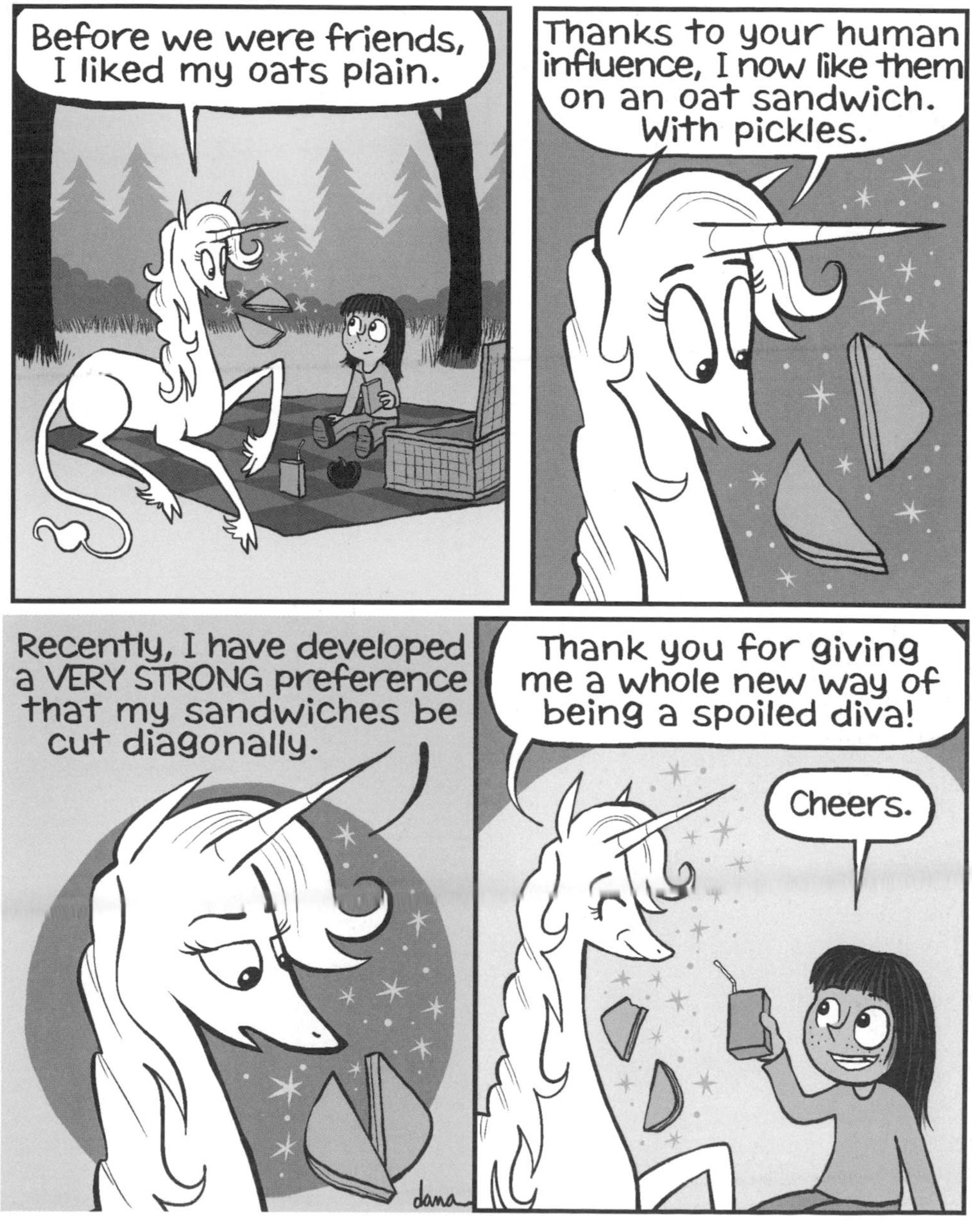
Before we were friends, I liked my oats plain.
Thanks to your human influence, I now like them on an oat sandwich. With pickles.
Recently, I have developed a VERY STRONG preference that my sandwiches be cut diagonally.
Thank you for giving me a whole new way of being a spoiled diva!
Cheers.
dana

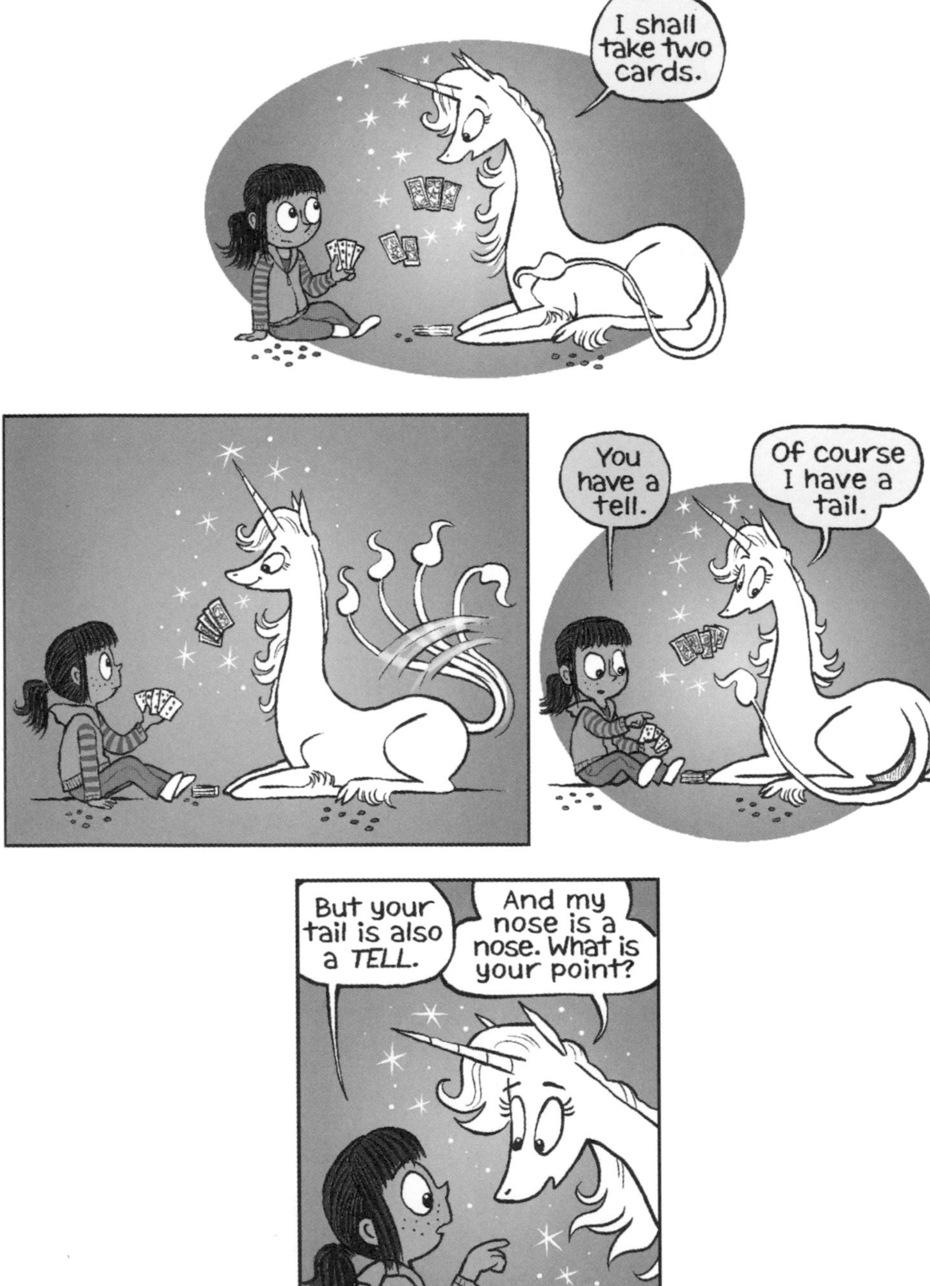
I shall take two cards.
You have a tell.
Of course I have a tail.
But your tail is also a TELL.
And my nose is a nose. What is your point?

Your TELL is how I know what kind of cards you have.
You cannot read my mind via my tail! My brain is at the other end entirely.
FOLD.
Drat! I had good cards!
Yeah, something told me that.
You are just jealous of my tail.
dana

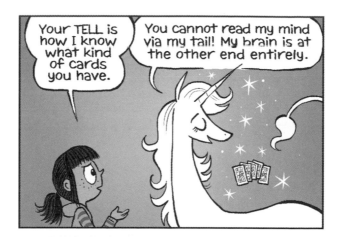

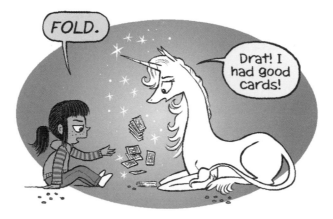

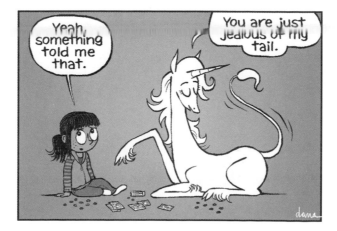

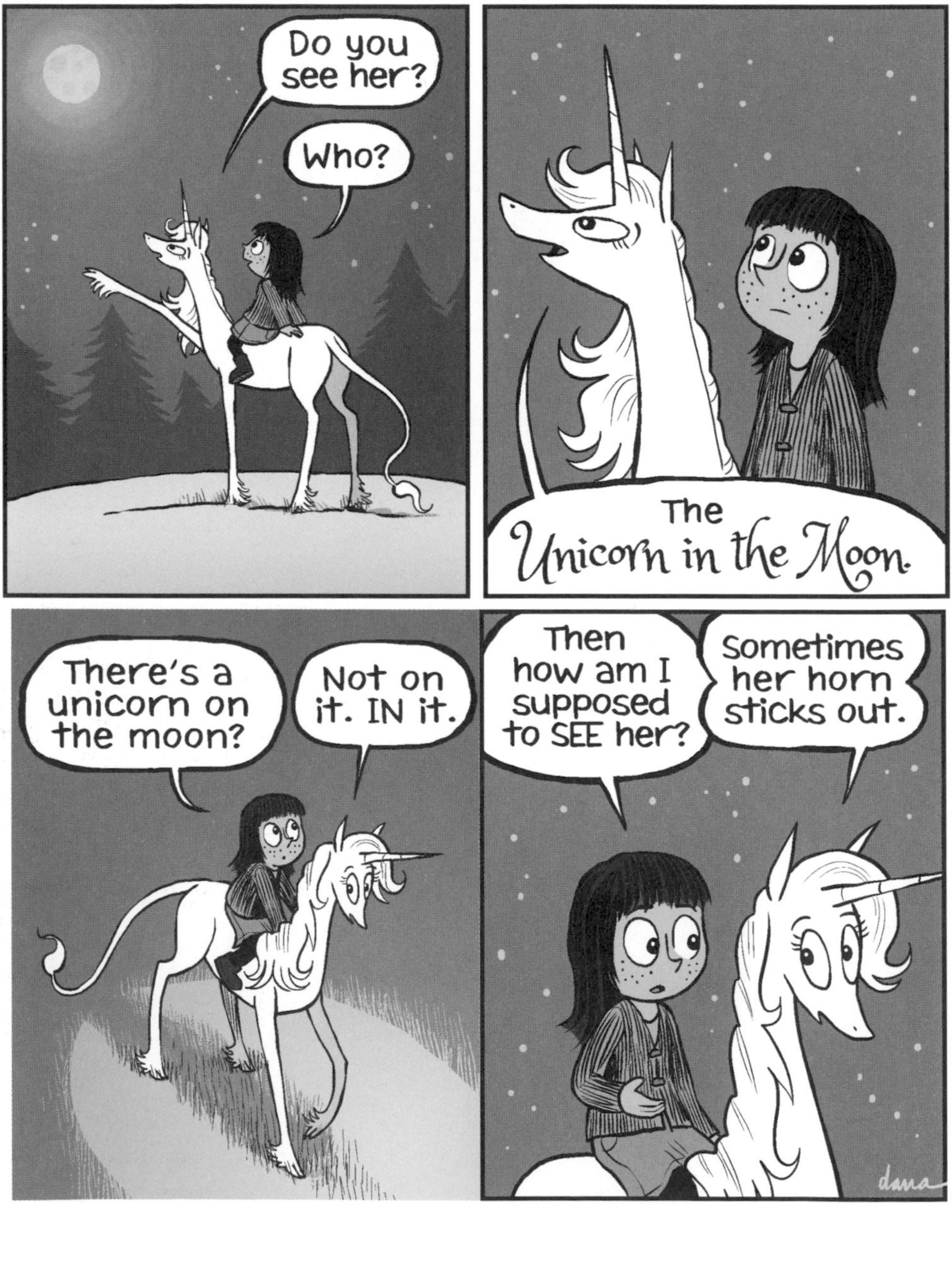
Do you see her?
Who?
The Unicorn in the Moon.
There's a unicorn on the moon?
Not on it. IN it.
Then how am I supposed to SEE her?
Sometimes her horn sticks out.
dana

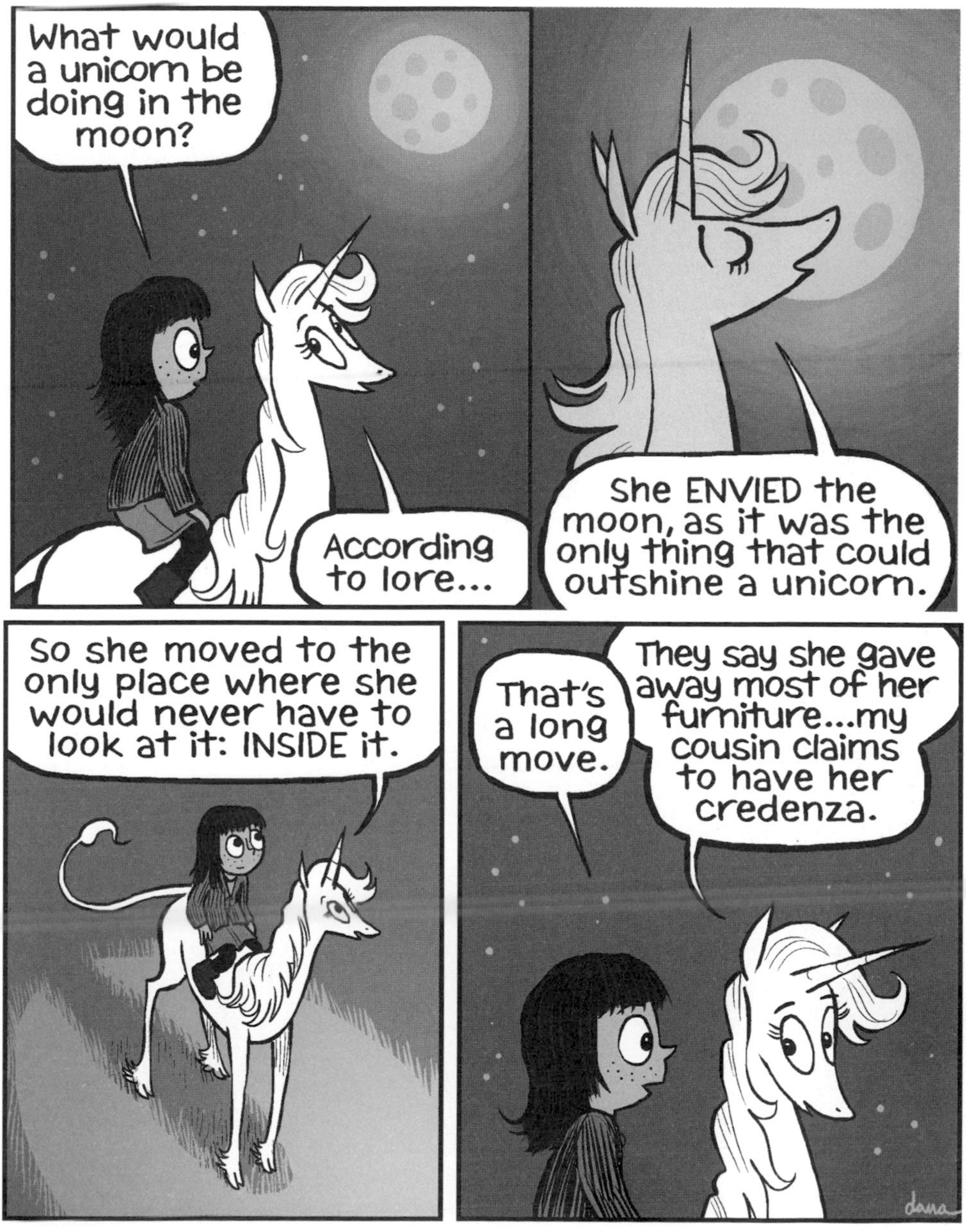
What would a unicorn be doing in the moon?
According to lore...
She ENVIED the moon, as it was the only thing that could outshine a unicorn.
So she moved to the only place where she would never have to look at it: INSIDE it.
That's a long move.
They say she gave away most of her furniture...my cousin claims to have her credenza.
dana

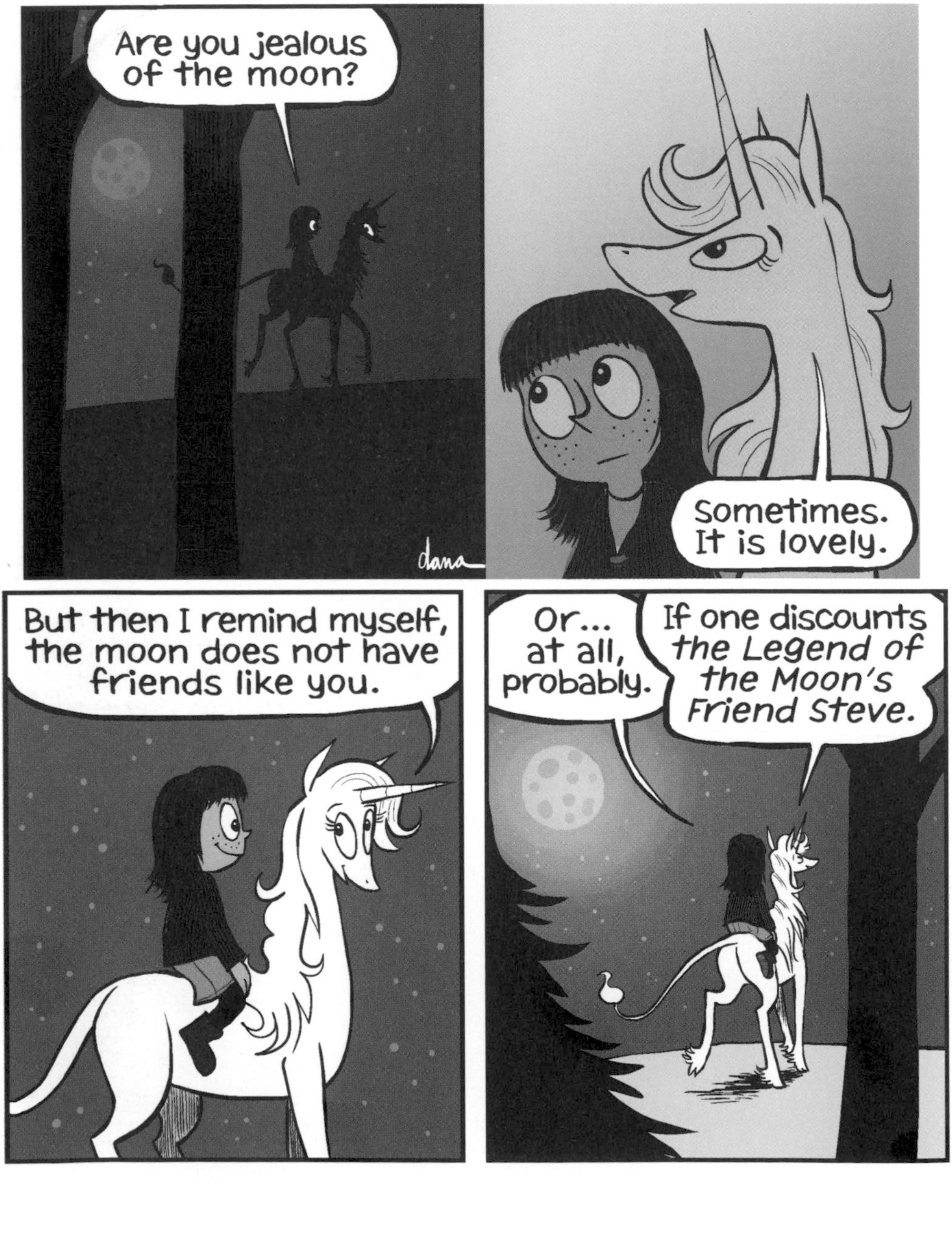
Are you jealous of the moon?
Sometimes. It is lovely.
dana
But then I remind myself, the moon does not have friends like you.
Or... at all, probably.
If one discounts *the Legend of the Moon's Friend Steve.*

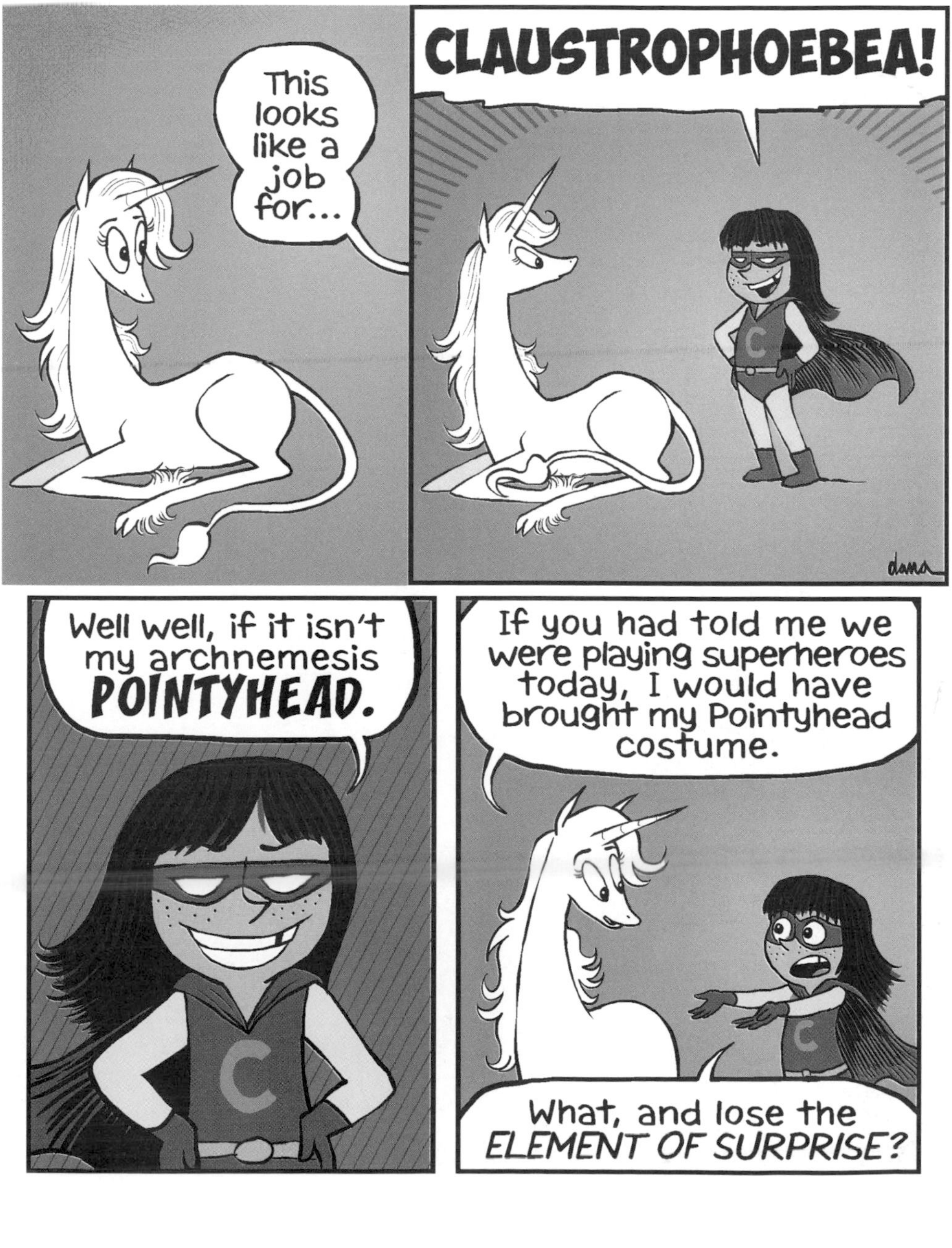
This looks like a job for...
CLAUSTROPHOEBEA!
Well well, if it isn't my archnemesis POINTYHEAD.
If you had told me we were playing superheroes today, I would have brought my Pointyhead costume.
What, and lose the ELEMENT OF SURPRISE?

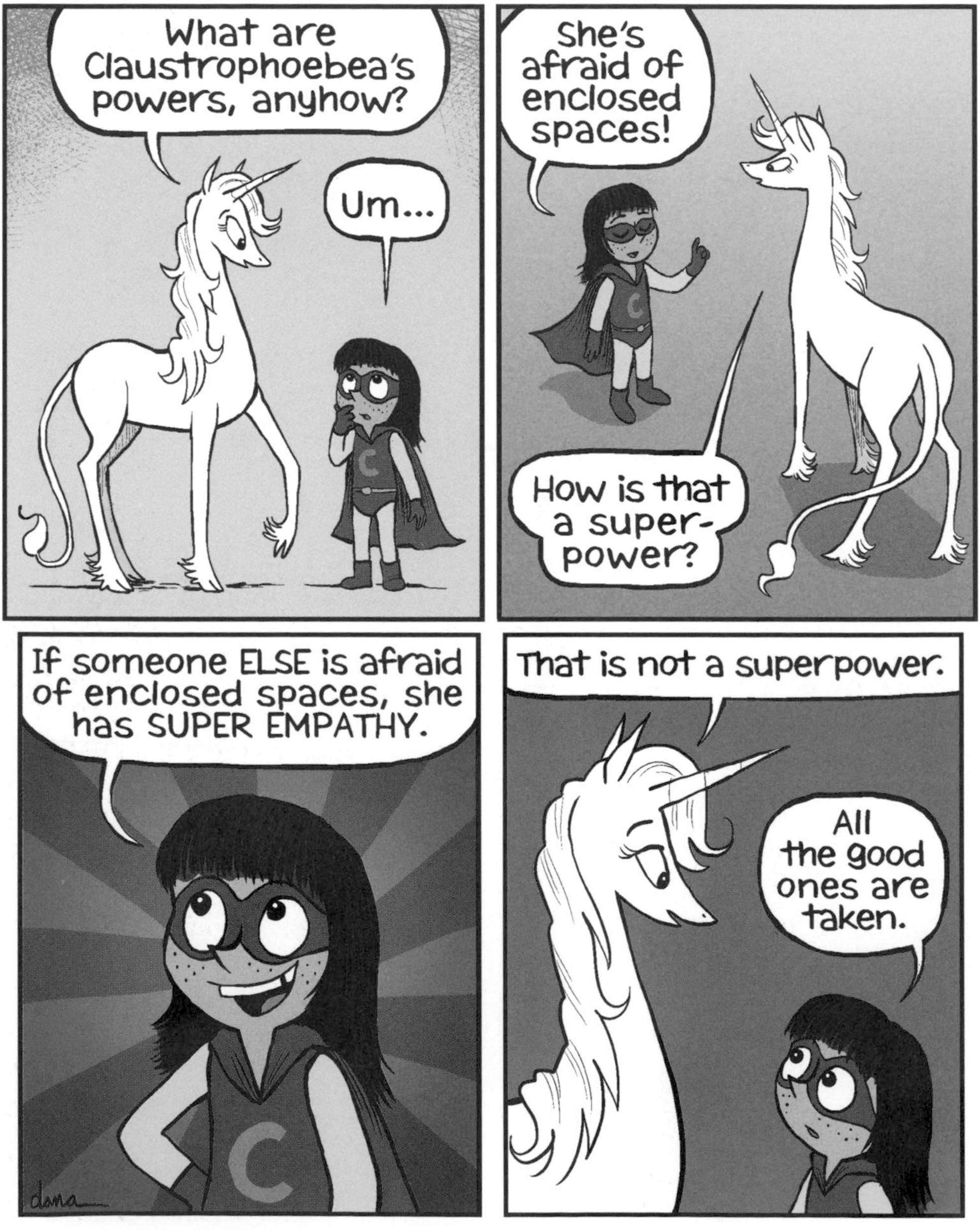
What are Claustrophoebea's powers, anyhow?
Um...
She's afraid of enclosed spaces!
How is that a super-power?
If someone ELSE is afraid of enclosed spaces, she has SUPER EMPATHY.
That is not a superpower.
All the good ones are taken.
dana

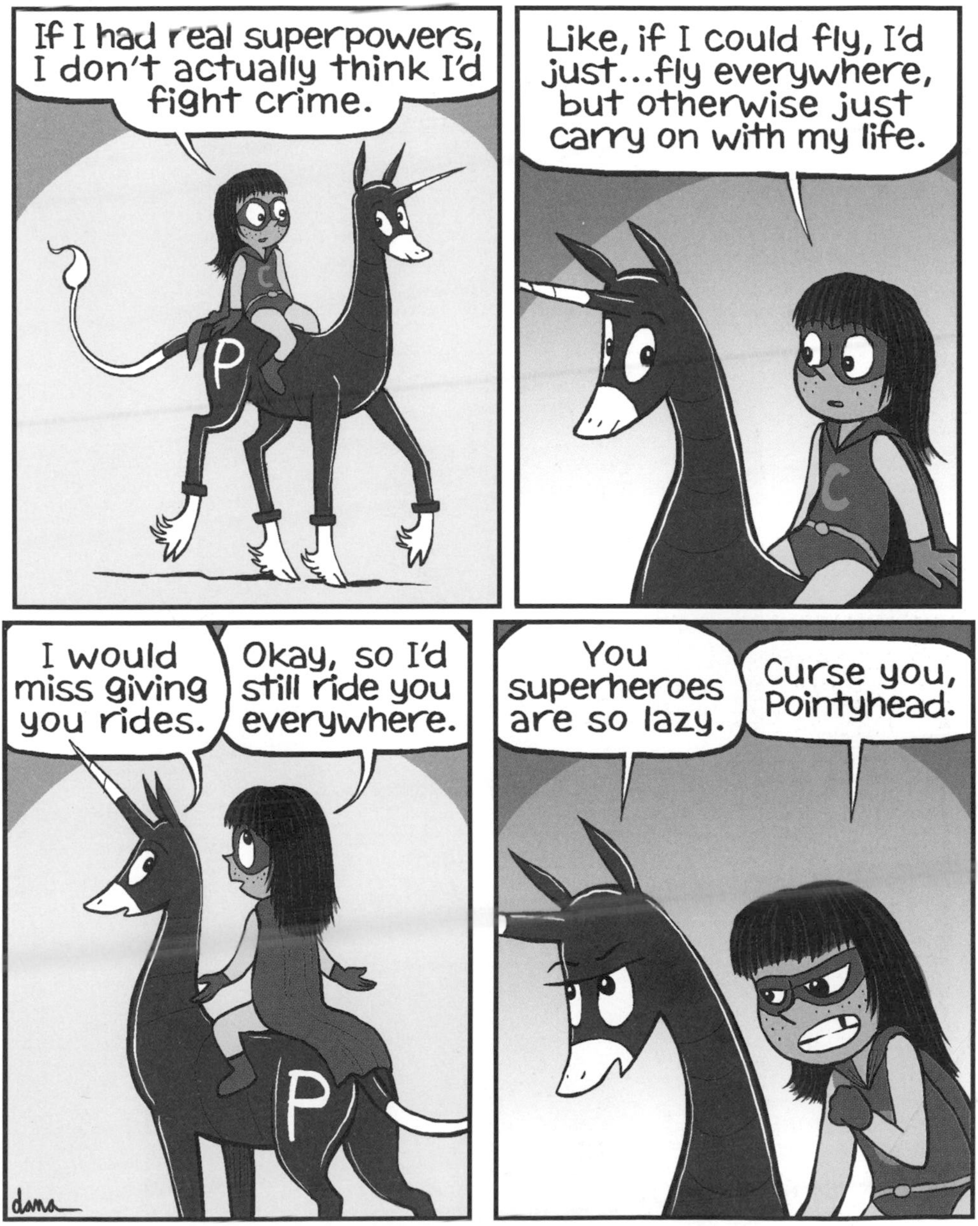
If I had real superpowers, I don't actually think I'd fight crime.
Like, if I could fly, I'd just...fly everywhere, but otherwise just carry on with my life.
I would miss giving you rides.
Okay, so I'd still ride you everywhere.
You superheroes are so lazy.
Curse you, Pointyhead.
dana

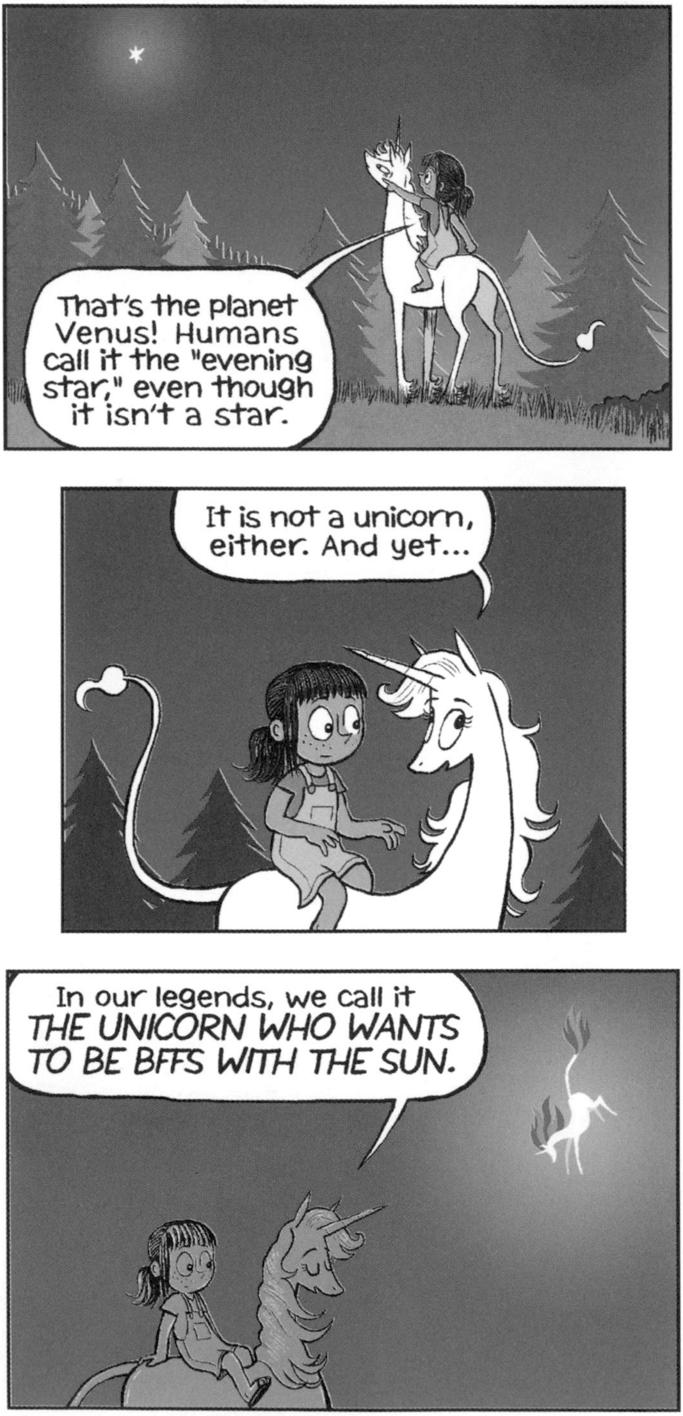
That's the planet Venus! Humans call it the "evening star," even though it isn't a star.
It is not a unicorn, either. And yet...
In our legends, we call it *THE UNICORN WHO WANTS TO BE BFFS WITH THE SUN.*

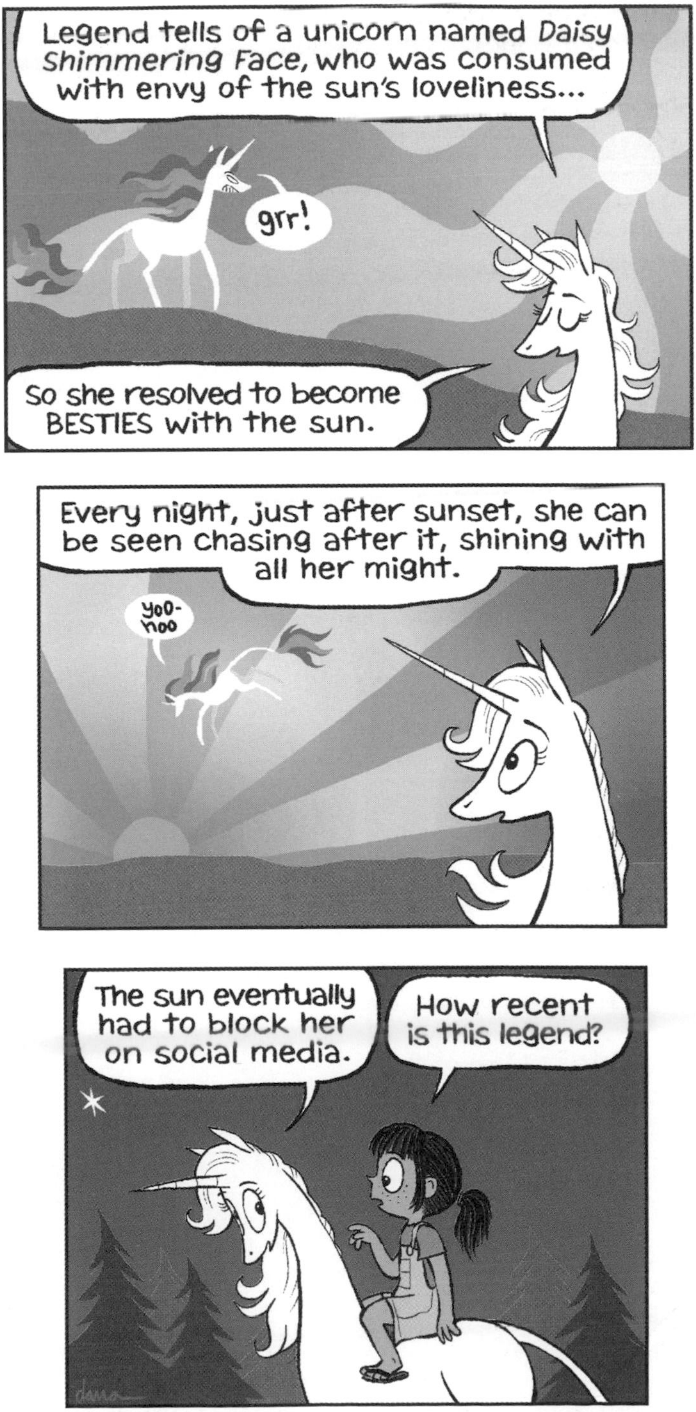
Legend tells of a unicorn named Daisy Shimmering Face, who was consumed with envy of the sun's loveliness...
grr!
So she resolved to become BESTIES with the sun.
Every night, just after sunset, she can be seen chasing after it, shining with all her might.
yoo-hoo
The sun eventually had to block her on social media.
How recent is this legend?

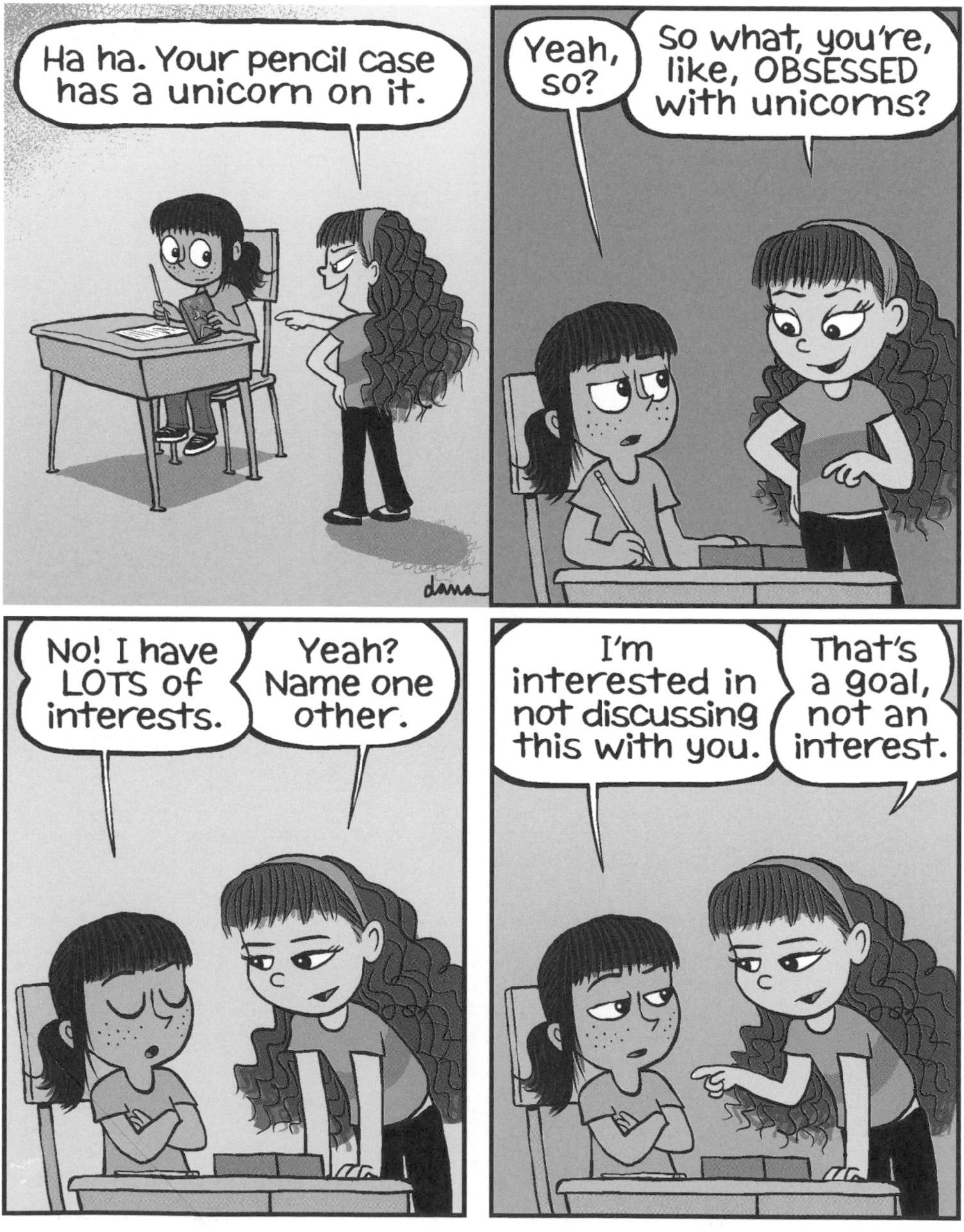
Ha ha. Your pencil case has a unicorn on it.
Yeah, so?
So what, you're, like, OBSESSED with unicorns?
No! I have LOTS of interests.
Yeah? Name one other.
I'm interested in not discussing this with you.
That's a goal, not an interest.

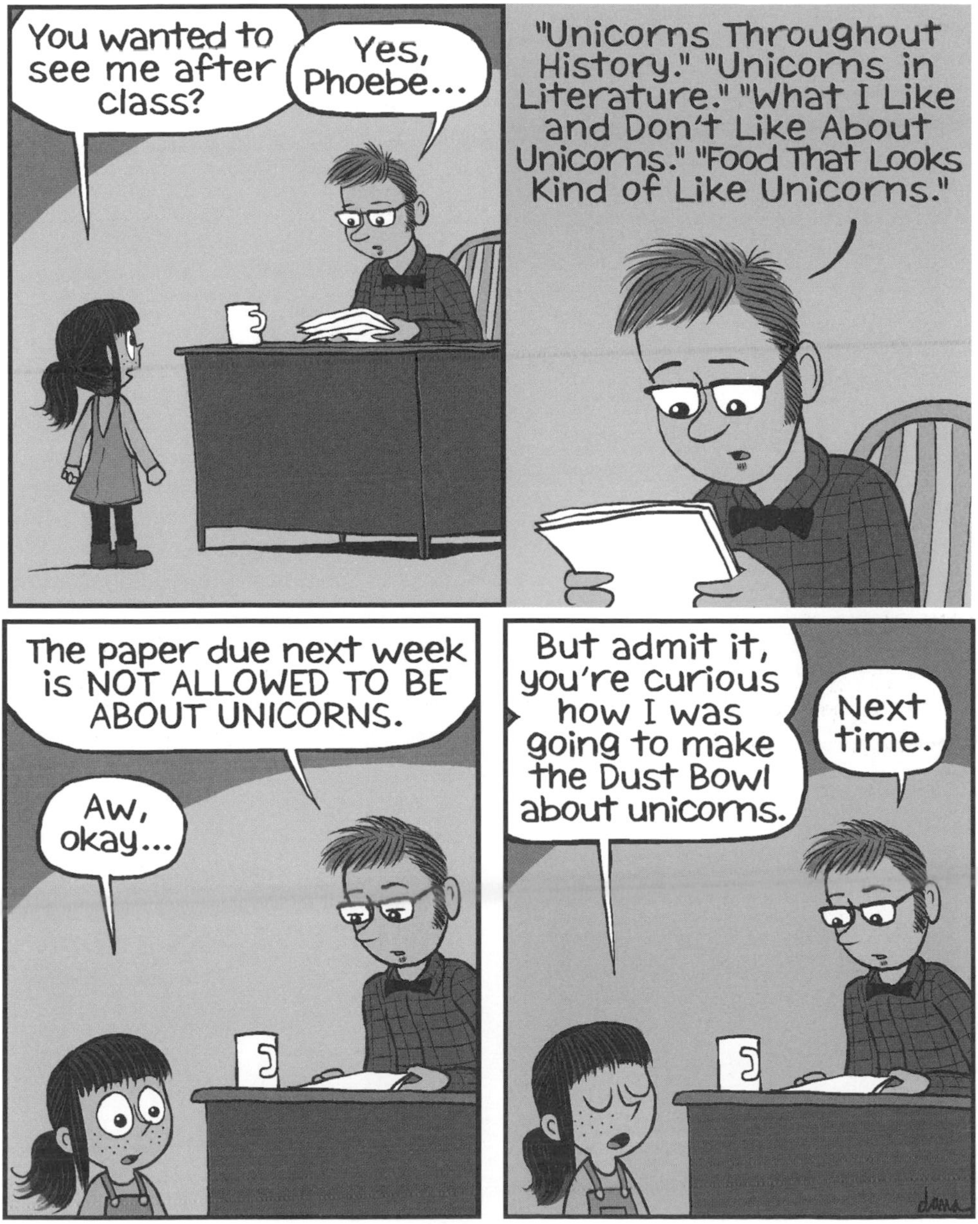
You wanted to see me after class?
Yes, Phoebe...
"Unicorns Throughout History." "Unicorns in Literature." "What I Like and Don't Like About Unicorns." "Food That Looks Kind of Like Unicorns."
The paper due next week is NOT ALLOWED TO BE ABOUT UNICORNS.
Aw, okay...
But admit it, you're curious how I was going to make the Dust Bowl about unicorns.
Next time.

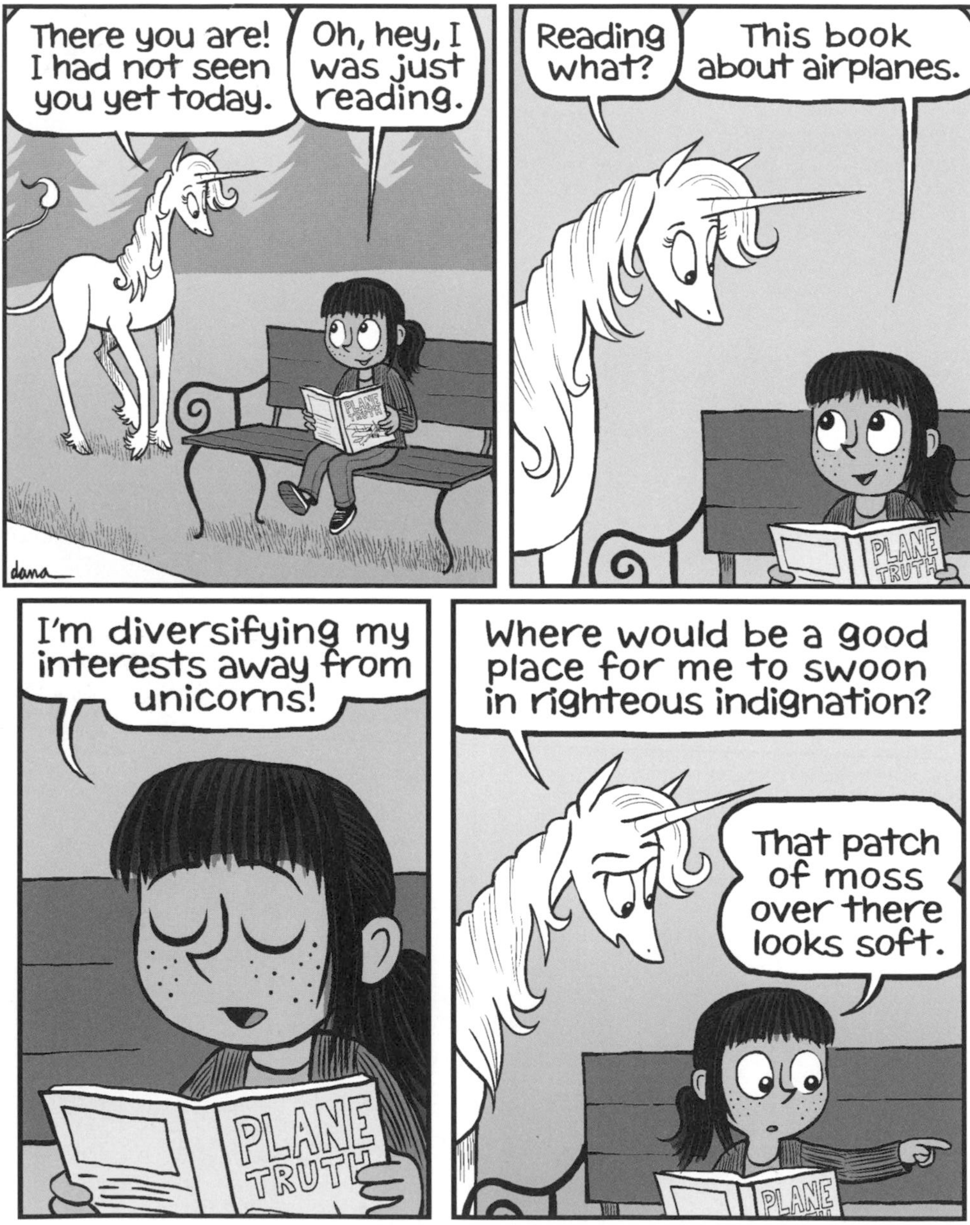

There you are! I had not seen you yet today.
Oh, hey, I was just reading.
PLANE TRUTH
dana
Reading what?
This book about airplanes.
PLANE TRUTH
I'm diversifying my interests away from unicorns!
PLANE TRUTH
Where would be a good place for me to swoon in righteous indignation?
That patch of moss over there looks soft.
PLANE

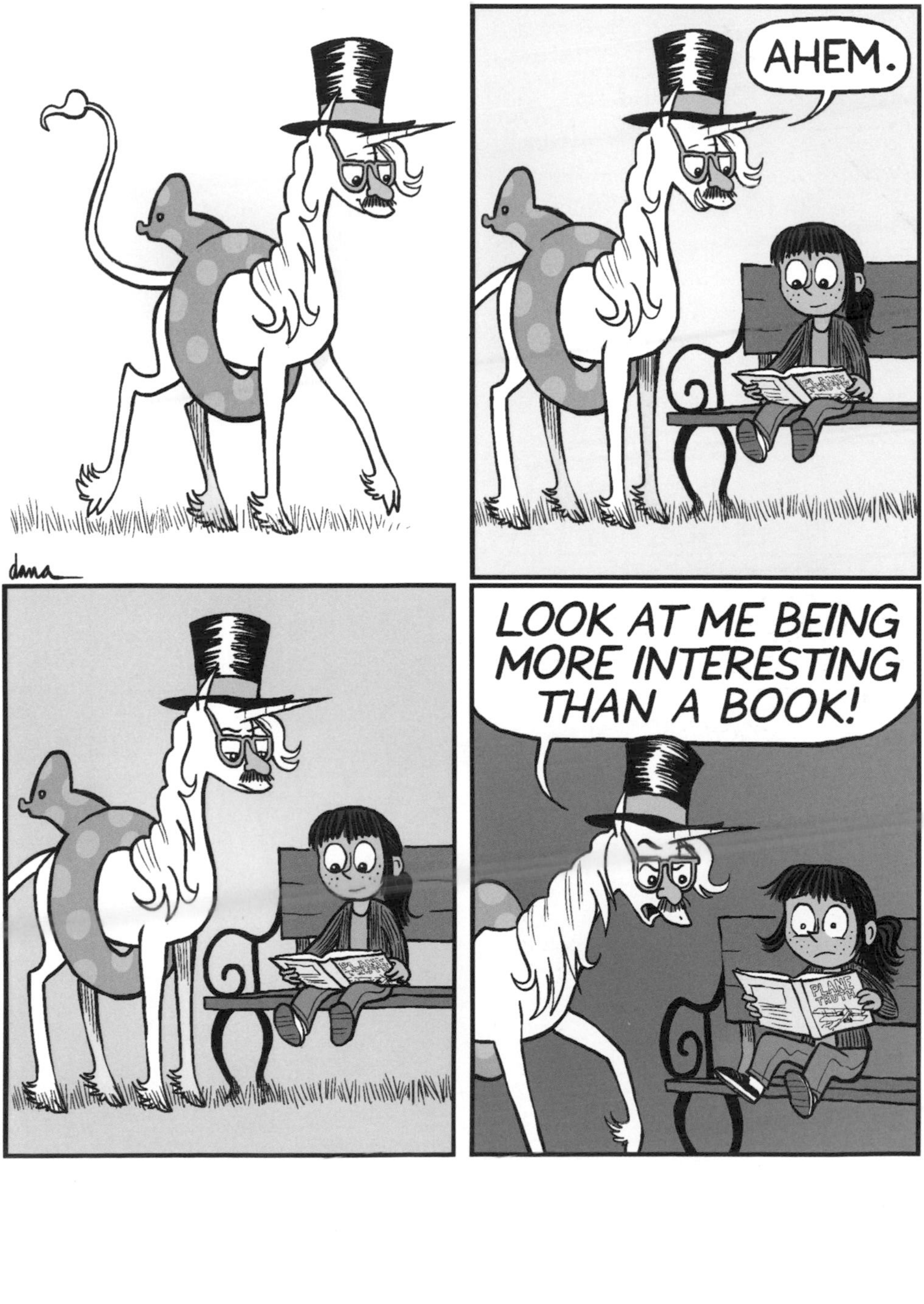
dana
AHEM.
LOOK AT ME BEING MORE INTERESTING THAN A BOOK!
PLANE TRUTH

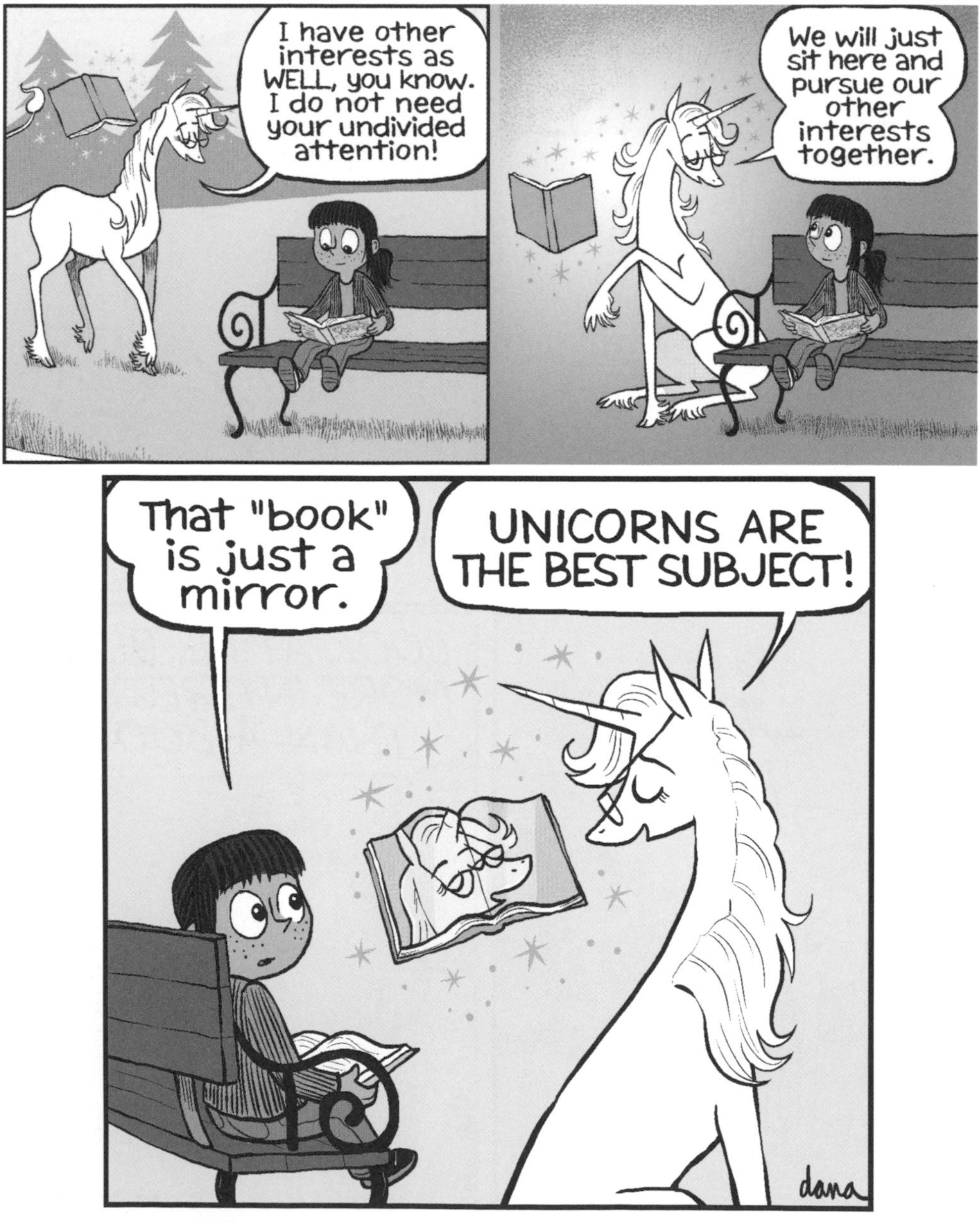
I have other interests as WELL, you know. I do not need your undivided attention!
We will just sit here and pursue our other interests together.
That "book" is just a mirror.
UNICORNS ARE THE BEST SUBJECT!
dana

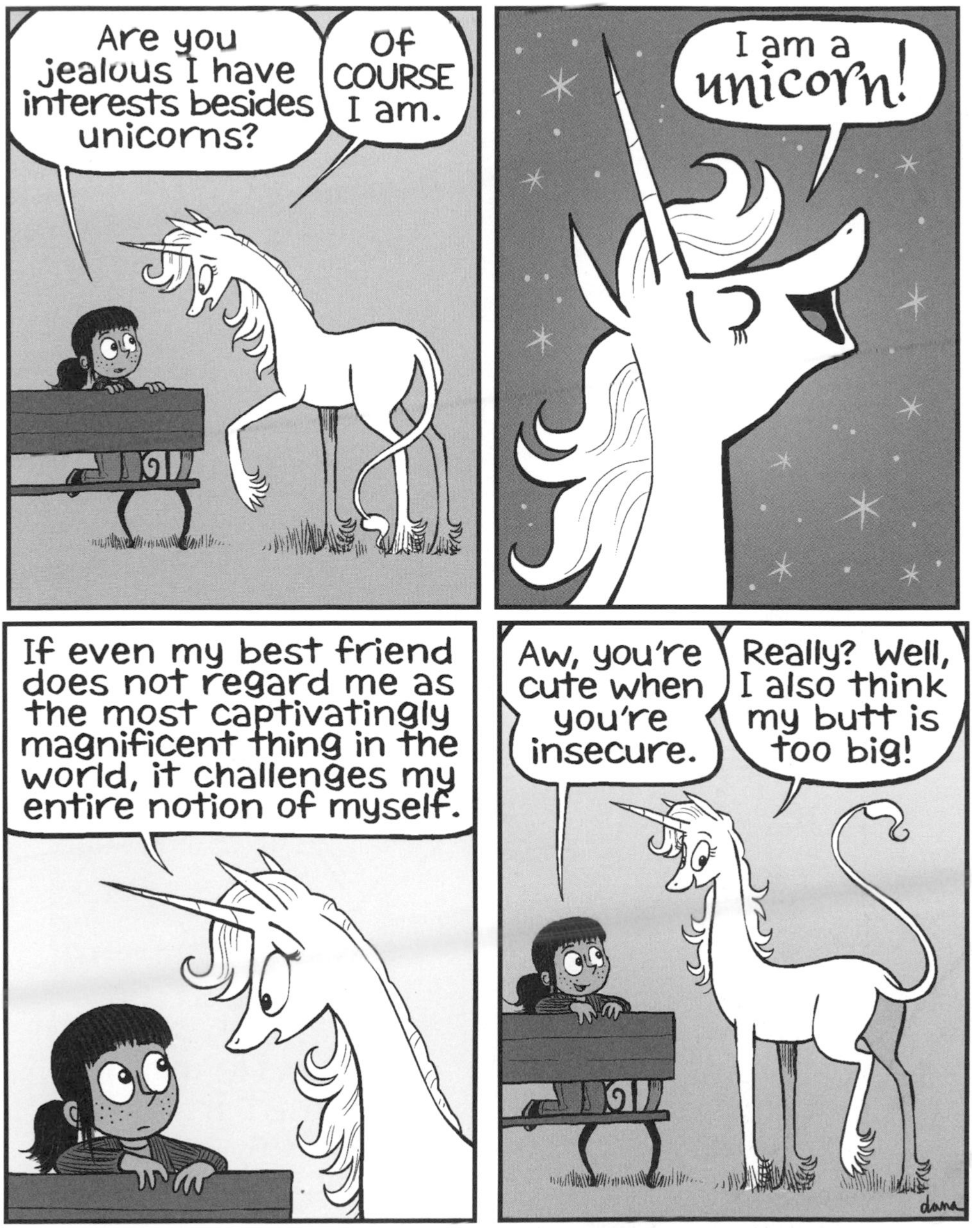
Are you jealous I have interests besides unicorns?
Of COURSE I am.
I am a unicorn!
If even my best friend does not regard me as the most captivatingly magnificent thing in the world, it challenges my entire notion of myself.
Aw, you're cute when you're insecure.
Really? Well, I also think my butt is too big!
dana

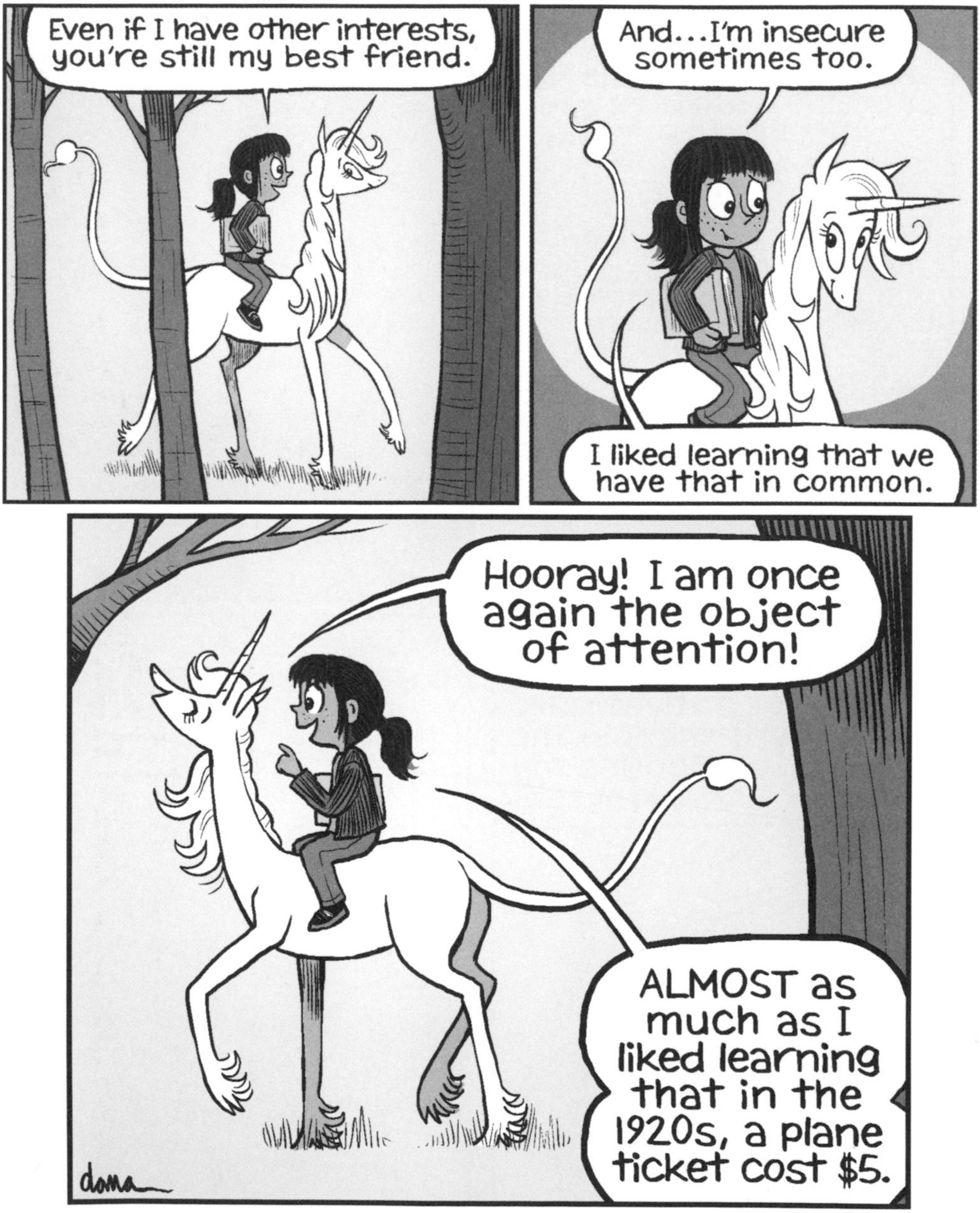
Even if I have other interests, you're still my best friend.
And...I'm insecure sometimes too.
I liked learning that we have that in common.
Hooray! I am once again the object of attention!
ALMOST as much as I liked learning that in the 1920s, a plane ticket cost $5.
dana

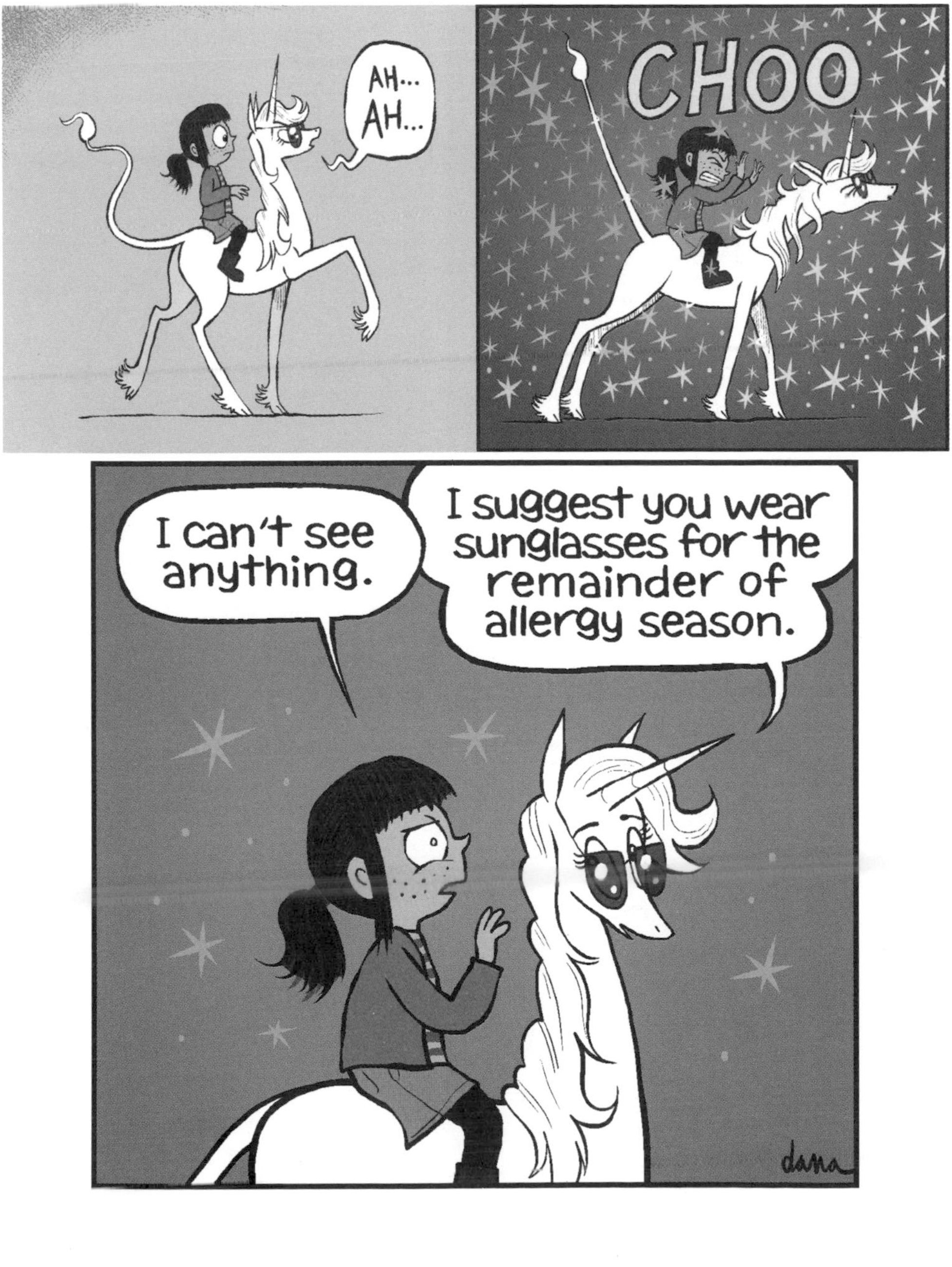
AH... AH...
CHOO
I can't see anything.
I suggest you wear sunglasses for the remainder of allergy season.
dana

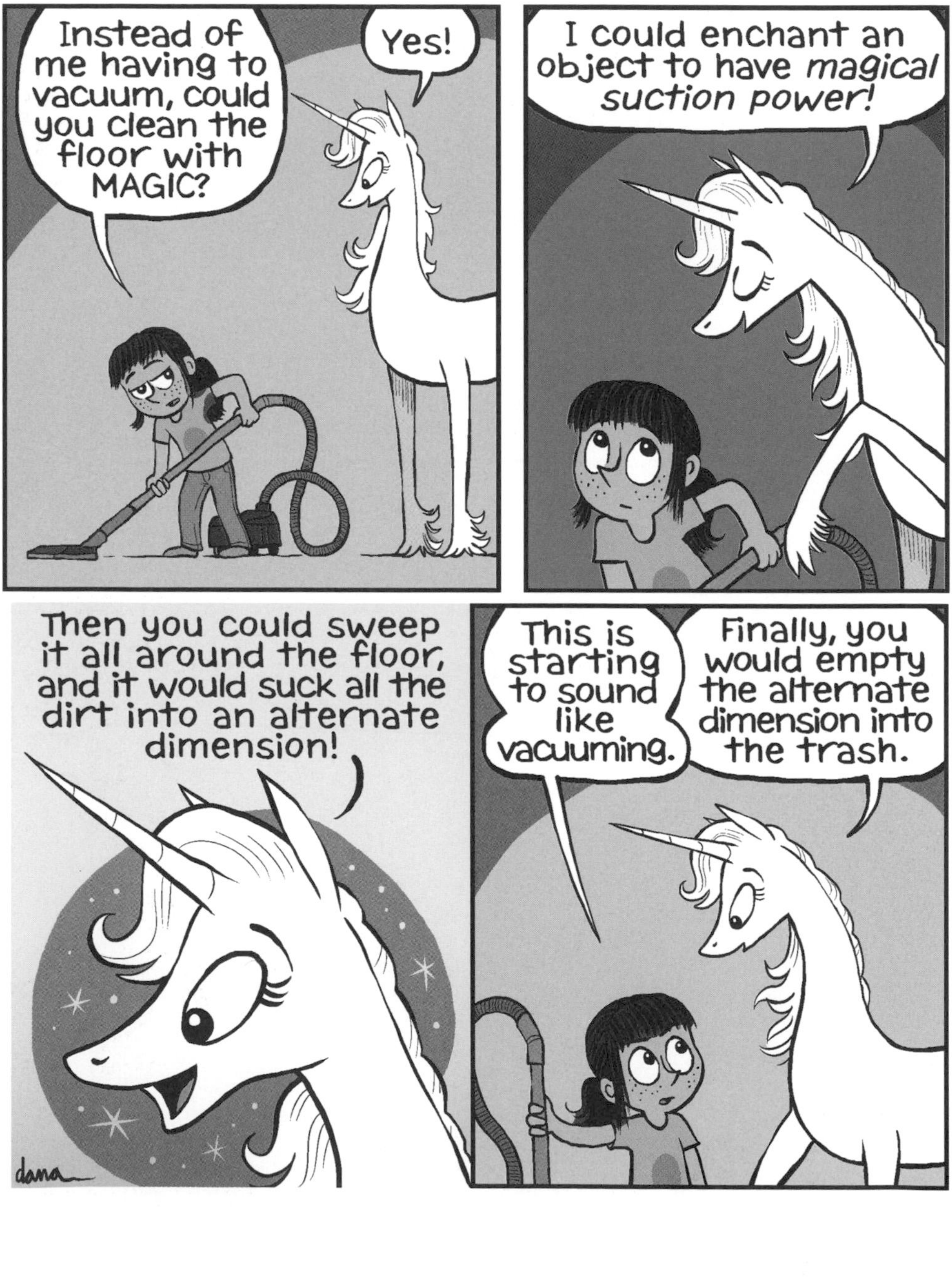
Instead of me having to vacuum, could you clean the floor with MAGIC?
Yes!
I could enchant an object to have *magical suction power!*
Then you could sweep it all around the floor, and it would suck all the dirt into an alternate dimension!
This is starting to sound like vacuuming.
Finally, you would empty the alternate dimension into the trash.
dana

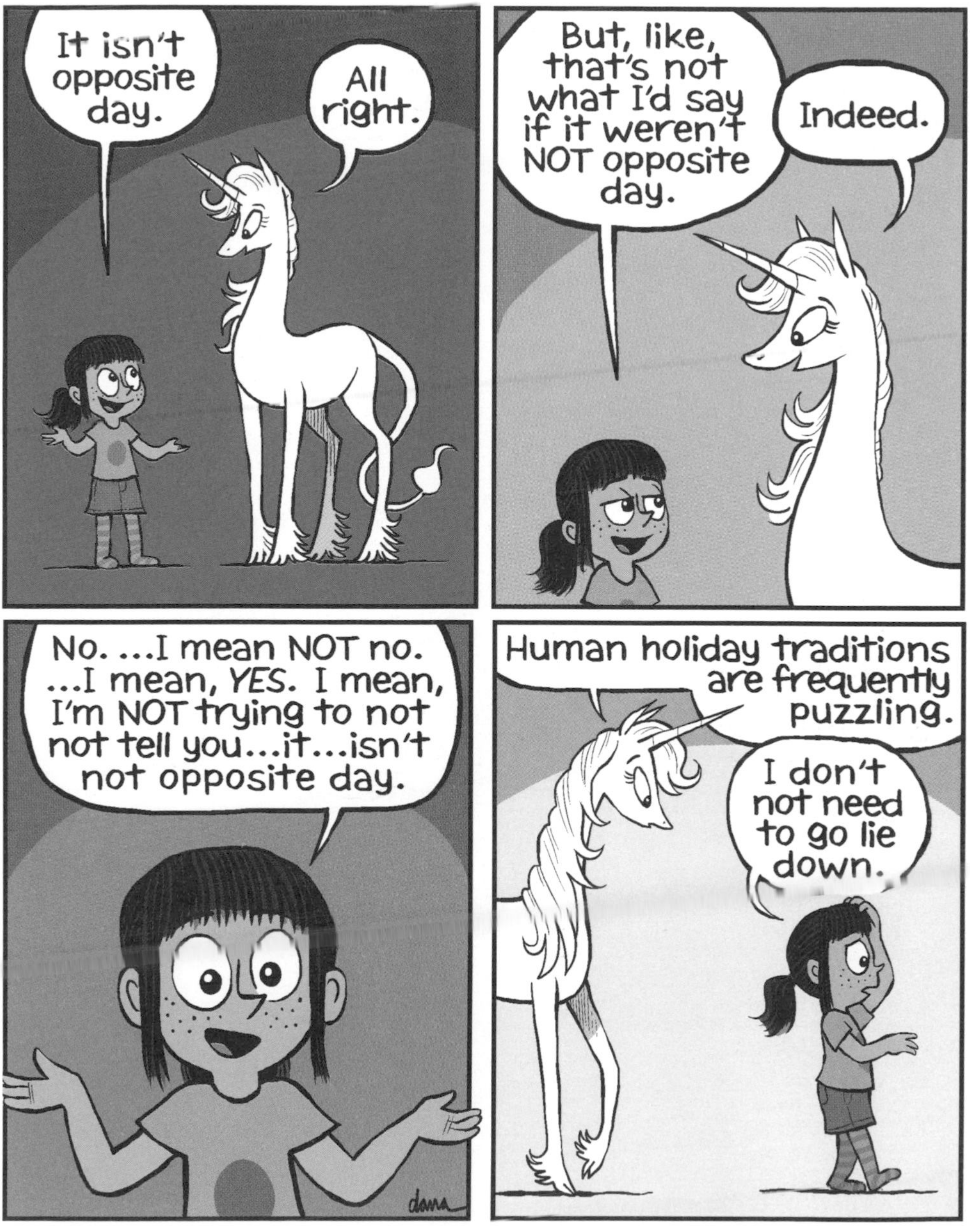

It isn't opposite day.
All right.
But, like, that's not what I'd say if it weren't NOT opposite day.
Indeed.
No. ...I mean NOT no. ...I mean, *YES*. I mean, I'm NOT trying to not not tell you...it...isn't not opposite day.
Human holiday traditions are frequently puzzling.
I don't not need to go lie down.
dana

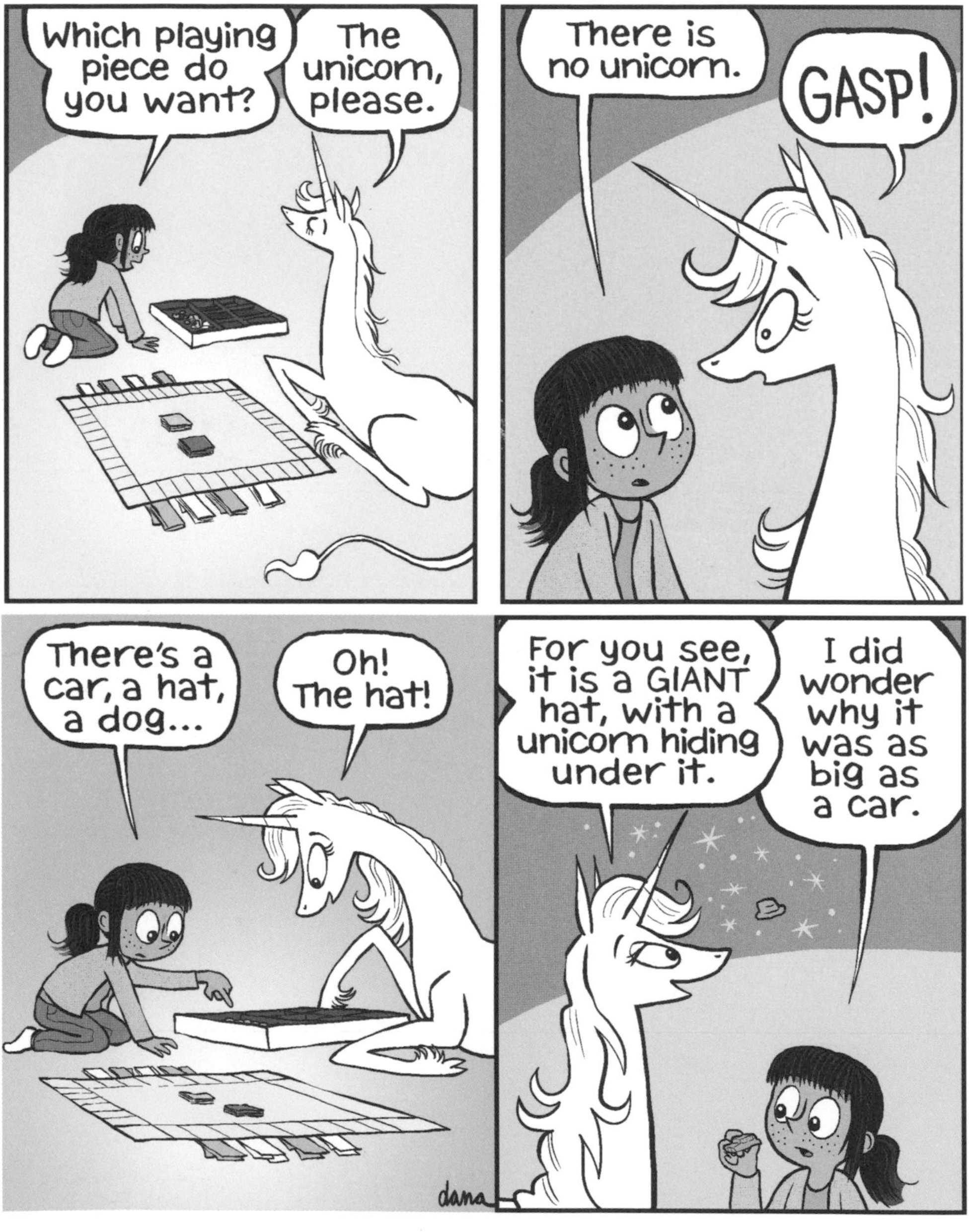
Which playing piece do you want?
The unicorn, please.
There is no unicorn.
GASP!
There's a car, a hat, a dog...
Oh! The hat!
For you see, it is a GIANT hat, with a unicorn hiding under it.
I did wonder why it was as big as a car.
dana

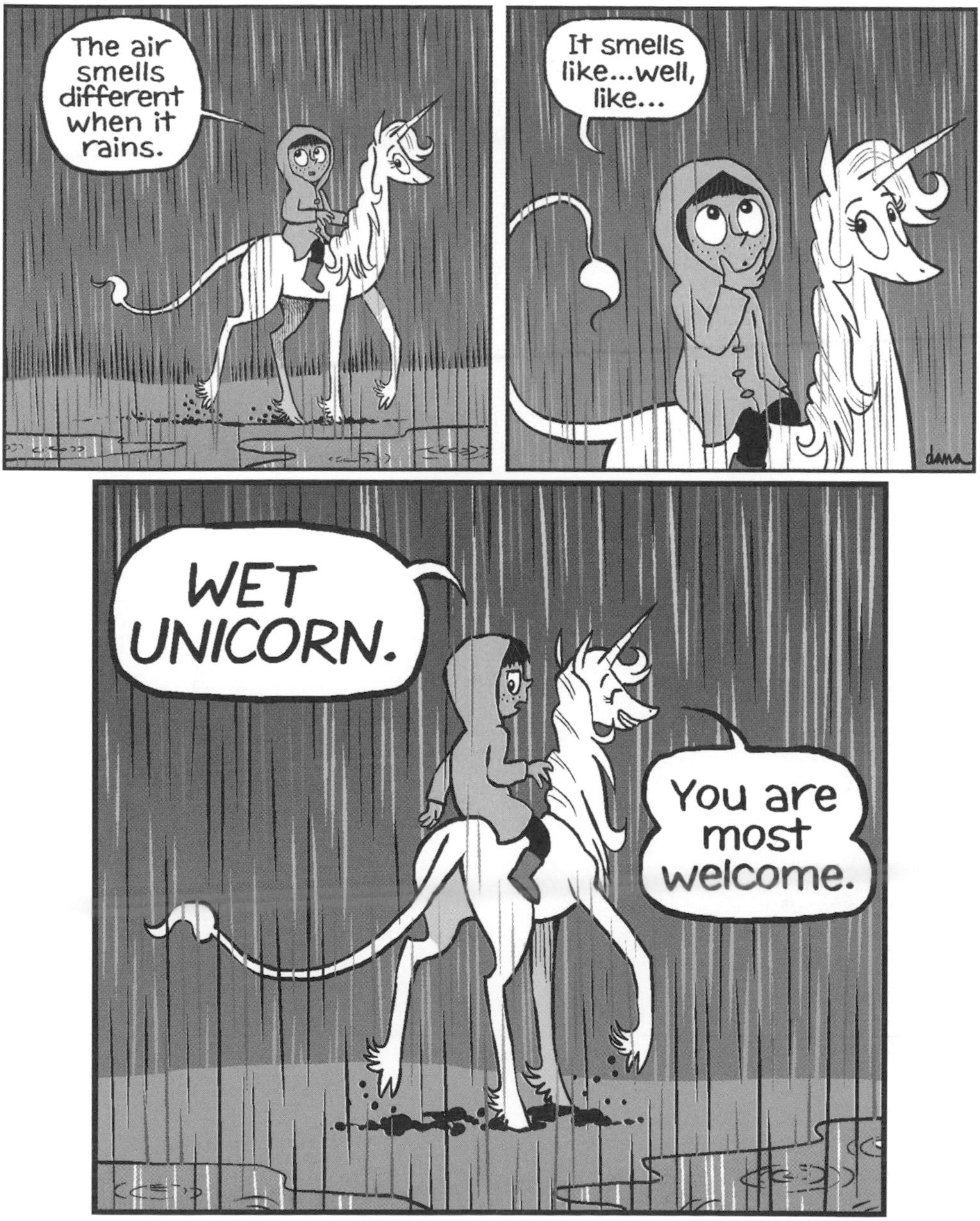
The air smells different when it rains.
It smells like...well, like...
dana
WET UNICORN.
You are most welcome.

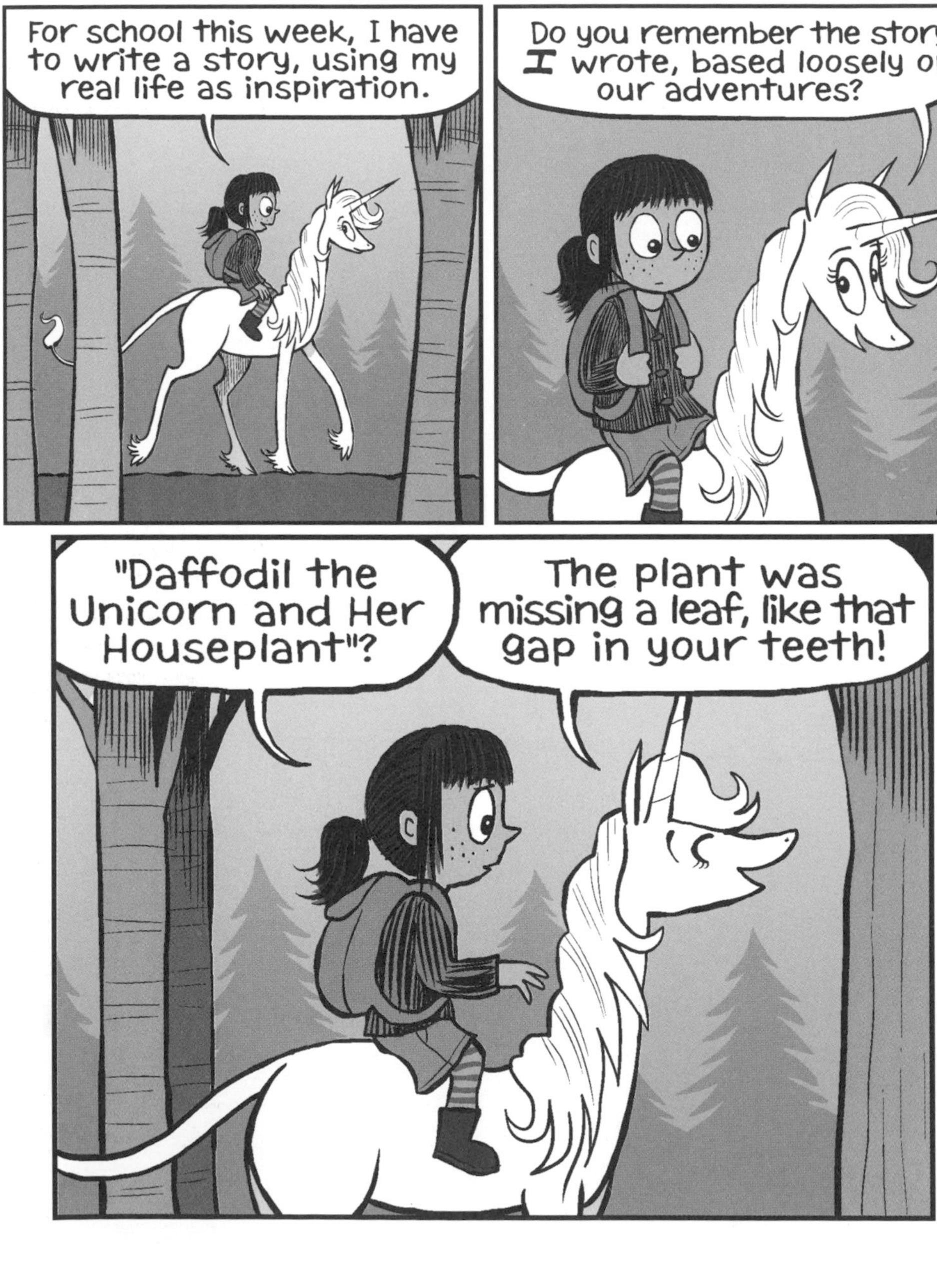
For school this week, I have to write a story, using my real life as inspiration.
Do you remember the story I wrote, based loosely on our adventures?
dana
"Daffodil the Unicorn and Her Houseplant"?
The plant was missing a leaf, like that gap in your teeth!

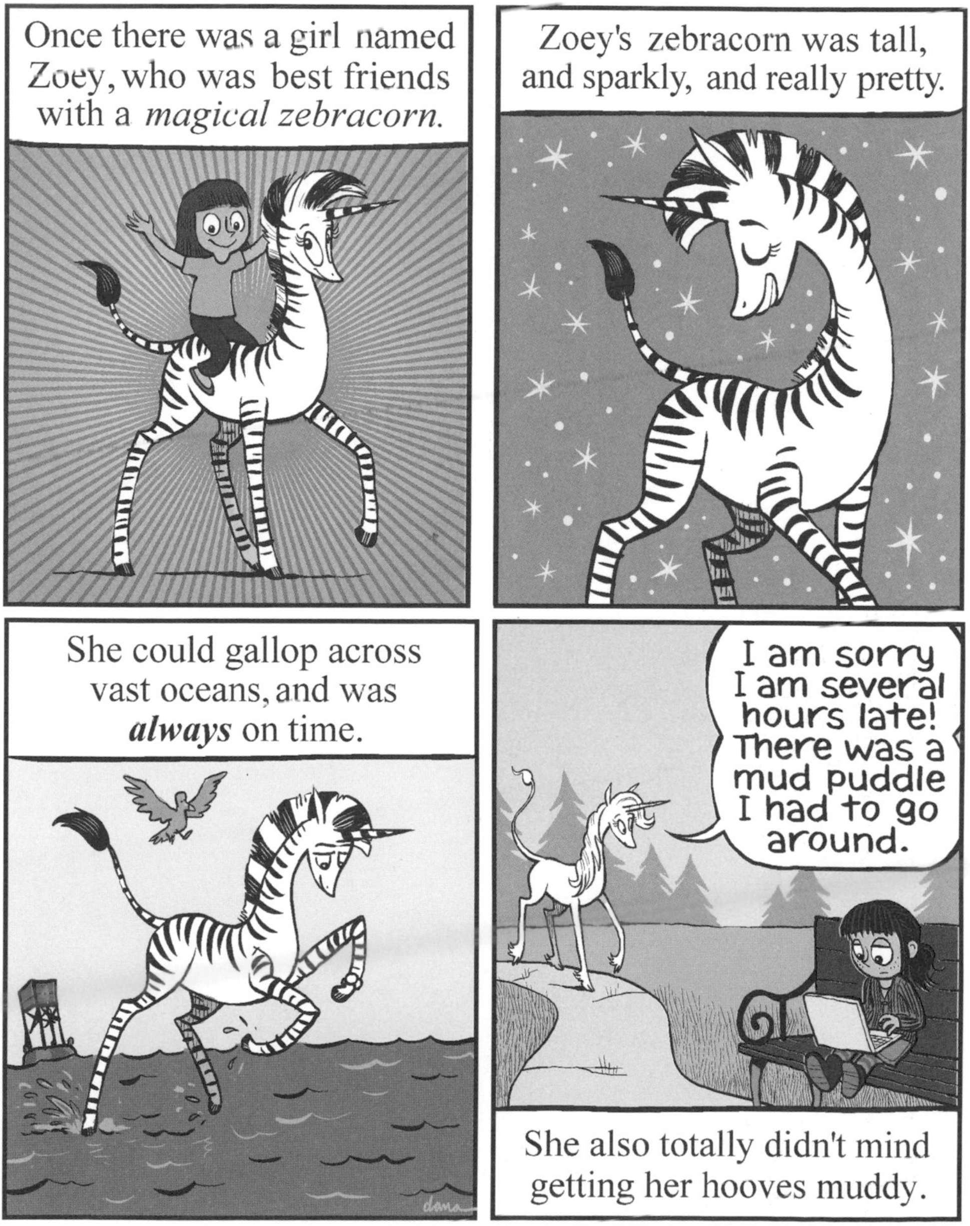
Once there was a girl named Zoey, who was best friends with a *magical zebracorn.*
Zoey's zebracorn was tall, and sparkly, and really pretty.
She could gallop across vast oceans, and was ***always*** on time.
I am sorry I am several hours late! There was a mud puddle I had to go around.
She also totally didn't mind getting her hooves muddy.

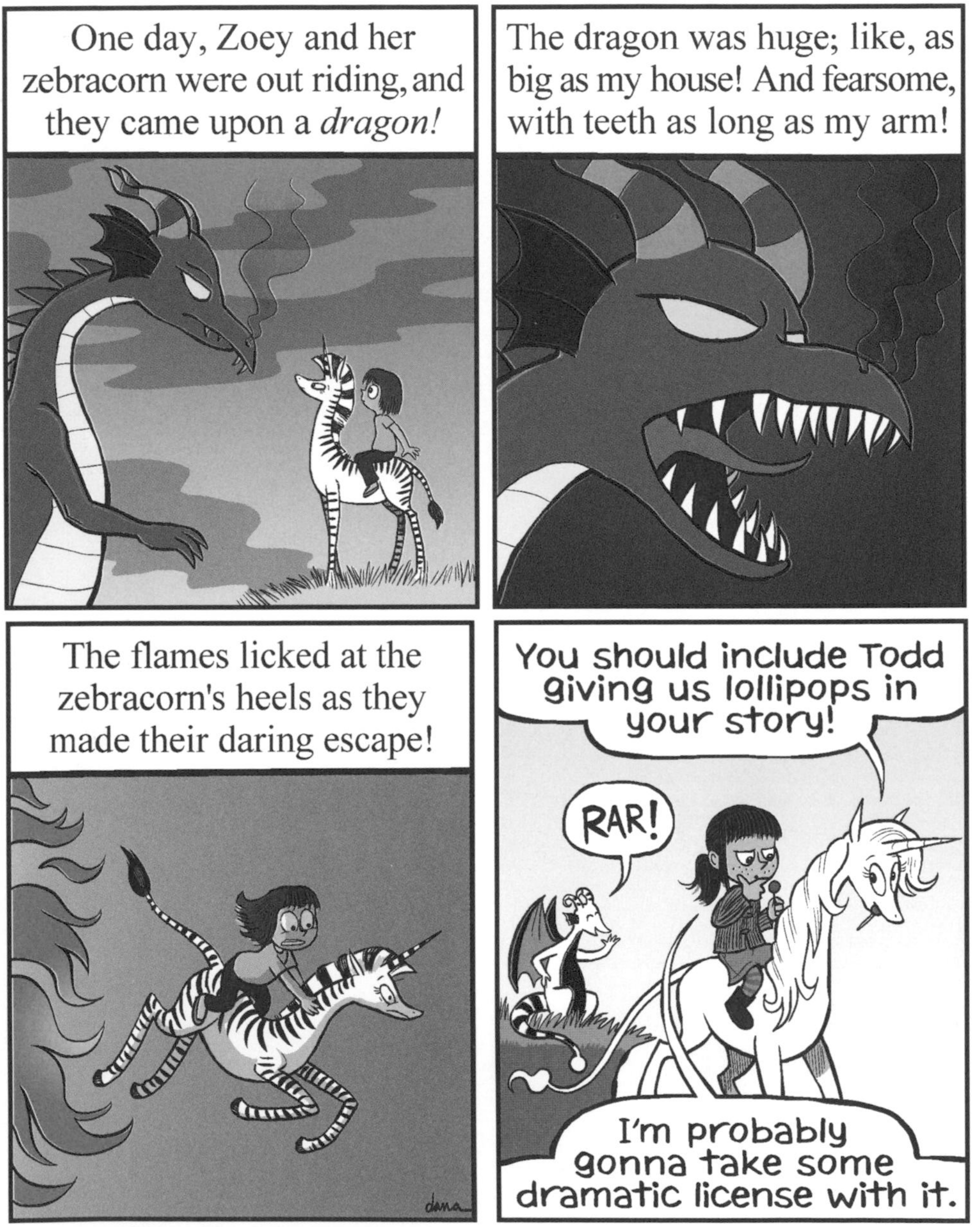
One day, Zoey and her zebracorn were out riding, and they came upon a *dragon!*
The dragon was huge; like, as big as my house! And fearsome, with teeth as long as my arm!
The flames licked at the zebracorn's heels as they made their daring escape!
You should include Todd giving us lollipops in your story!
RAR!
I'm probably gonna take some dramatic license with it.

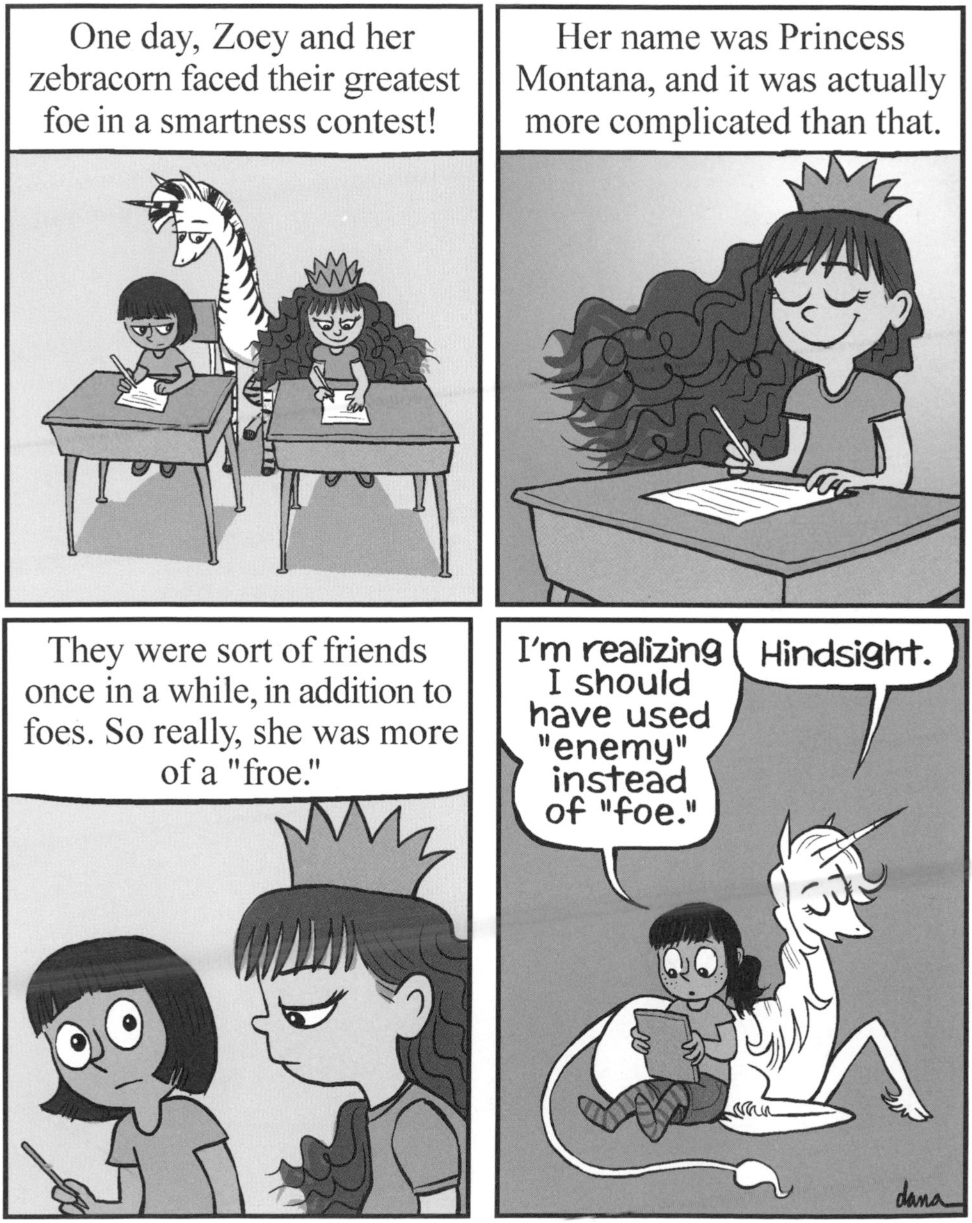
One day, Zoey and her zebracorn faced their greatest foe in a smartness contest!
Her name was Princess Montana, and it was actually more complicated than that.
They were sort of friends once in a while, in addition to foes. So really, she was more of a "froe."
I'm realizing I should have used "enemy" instead of "foe."
Hindsight.
dana

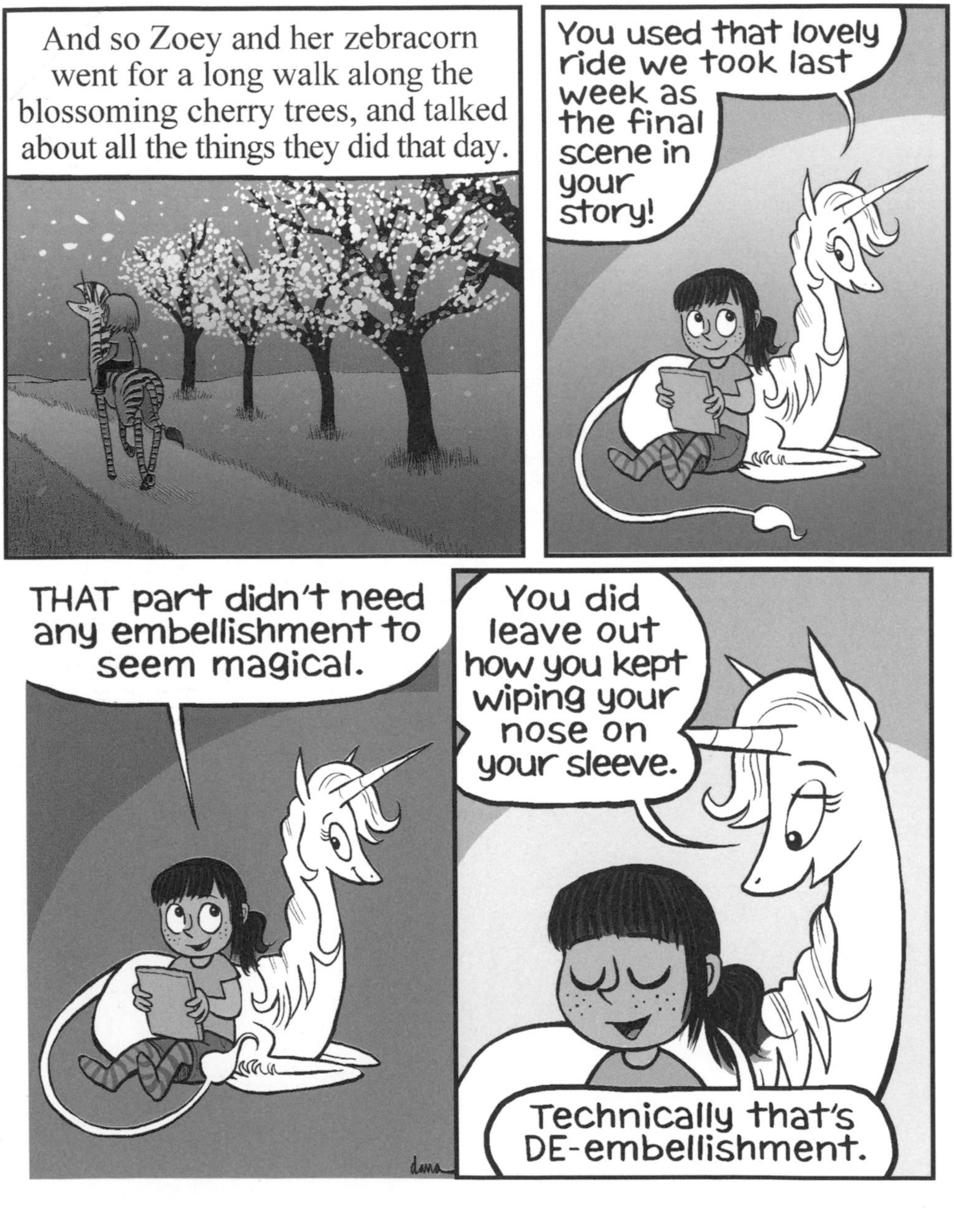

And so Zoey and her zebracorn went for a long walk along the blossoming cherry trees, and talked about all the things they did that day.
You used that lovely ride we took last week as the final scene in your story!
THAT part didn't need any embellishment to seem magical.
You did leave out how you kept wiping your nose on your sleeve.
Technically that's DE-embellishment.

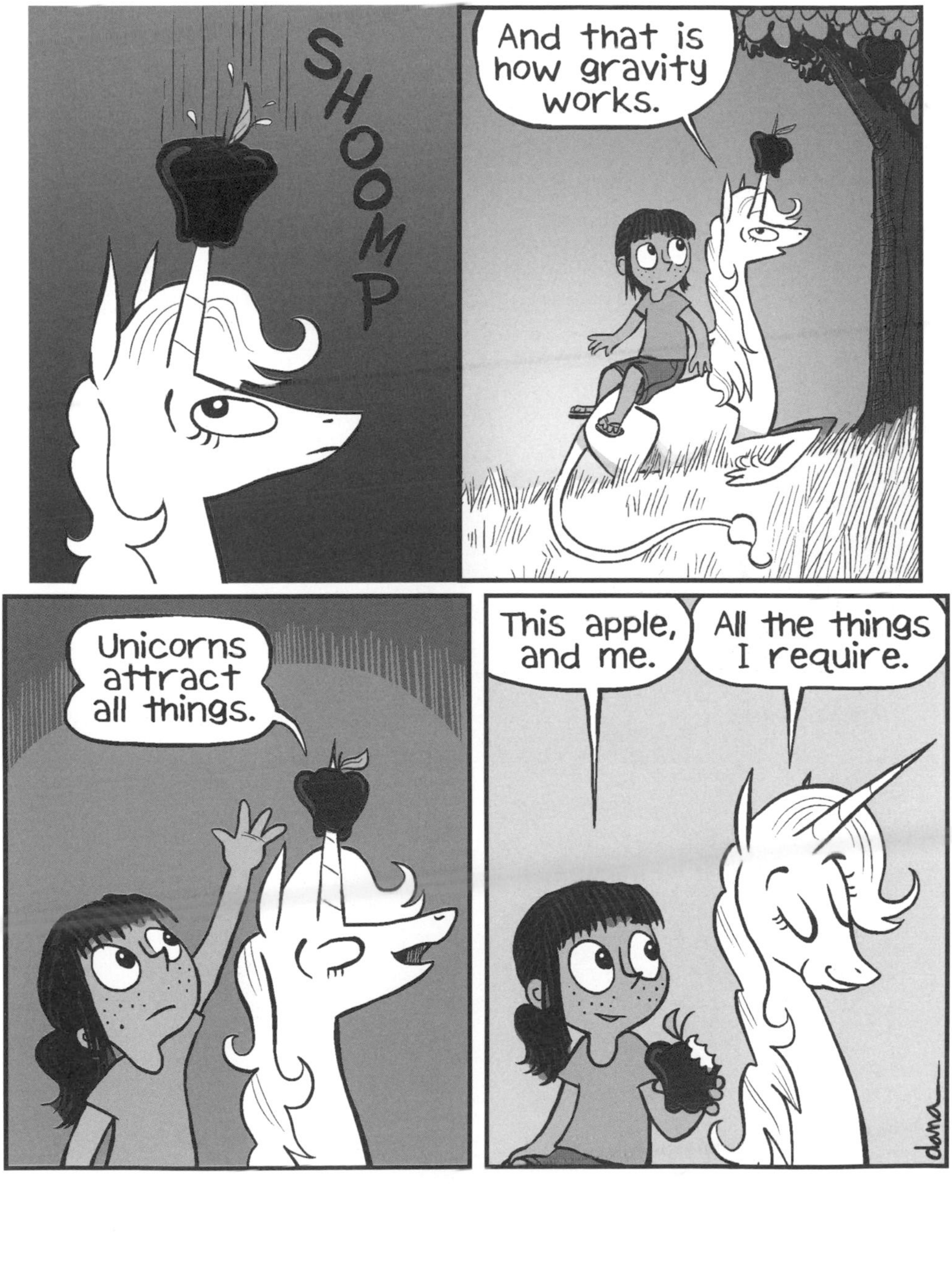
SHOOMP
And that is how gravity works.
Unicorns attract all things.
This apple, and me.
All the things I require.
dana

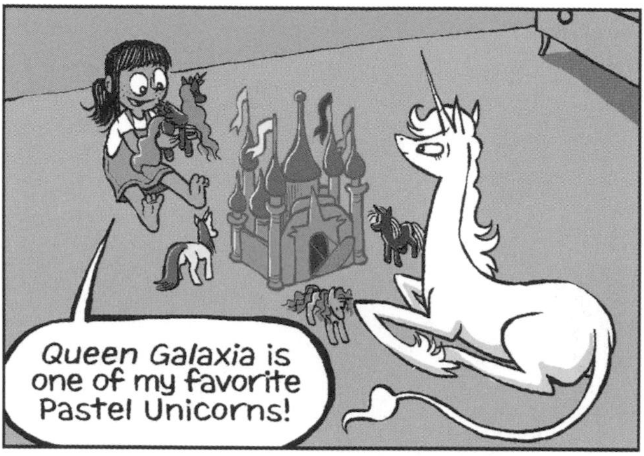
Queen Galaxia is one of my favorite Pastel Unicorns!

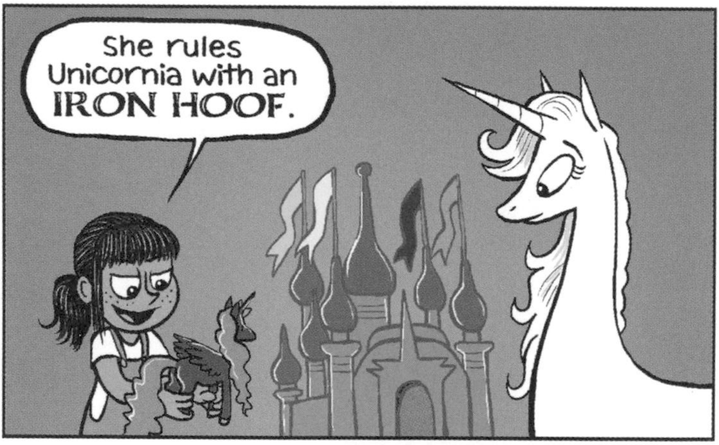
She rules Unicornia with an IRON HOOF.

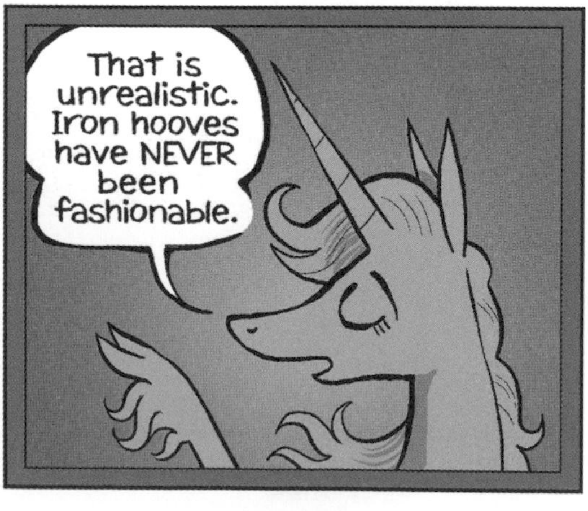
That is unrealistic. Iron hooves have NEVER been fashionable.

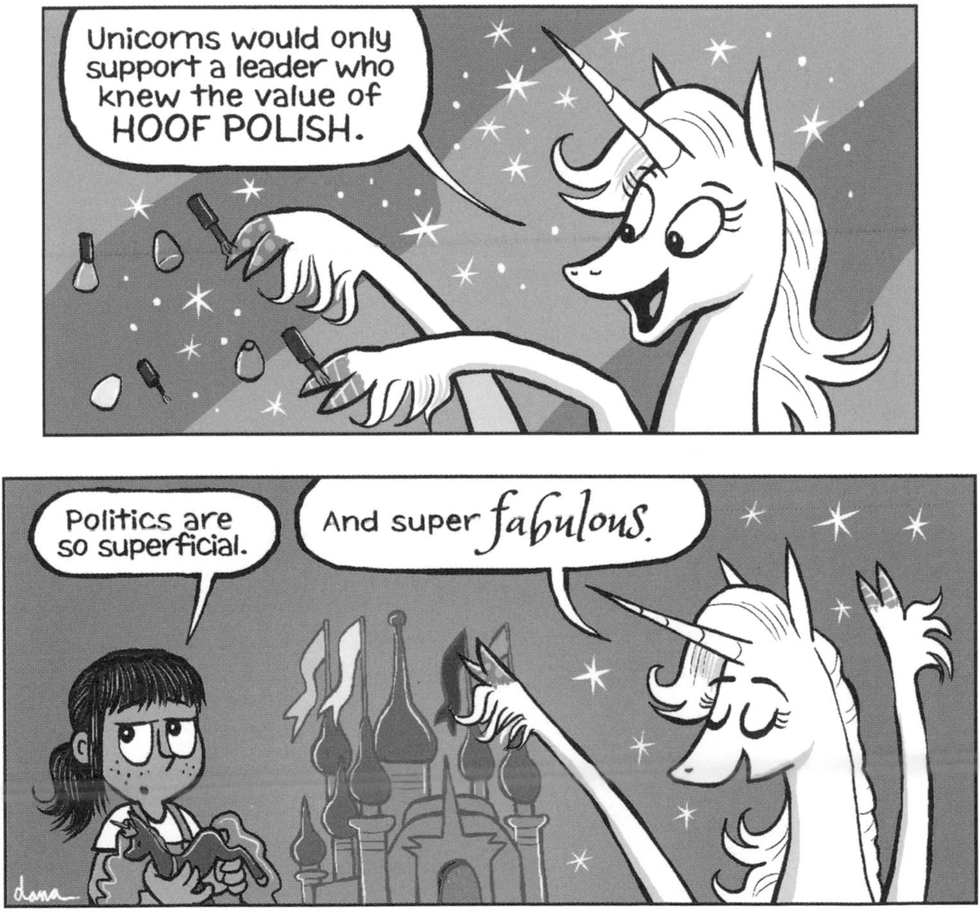
Unicorns would only support a leader who knew the value of HOOF POLISH.
Politics are so superficial.
And super fabulous.
dana

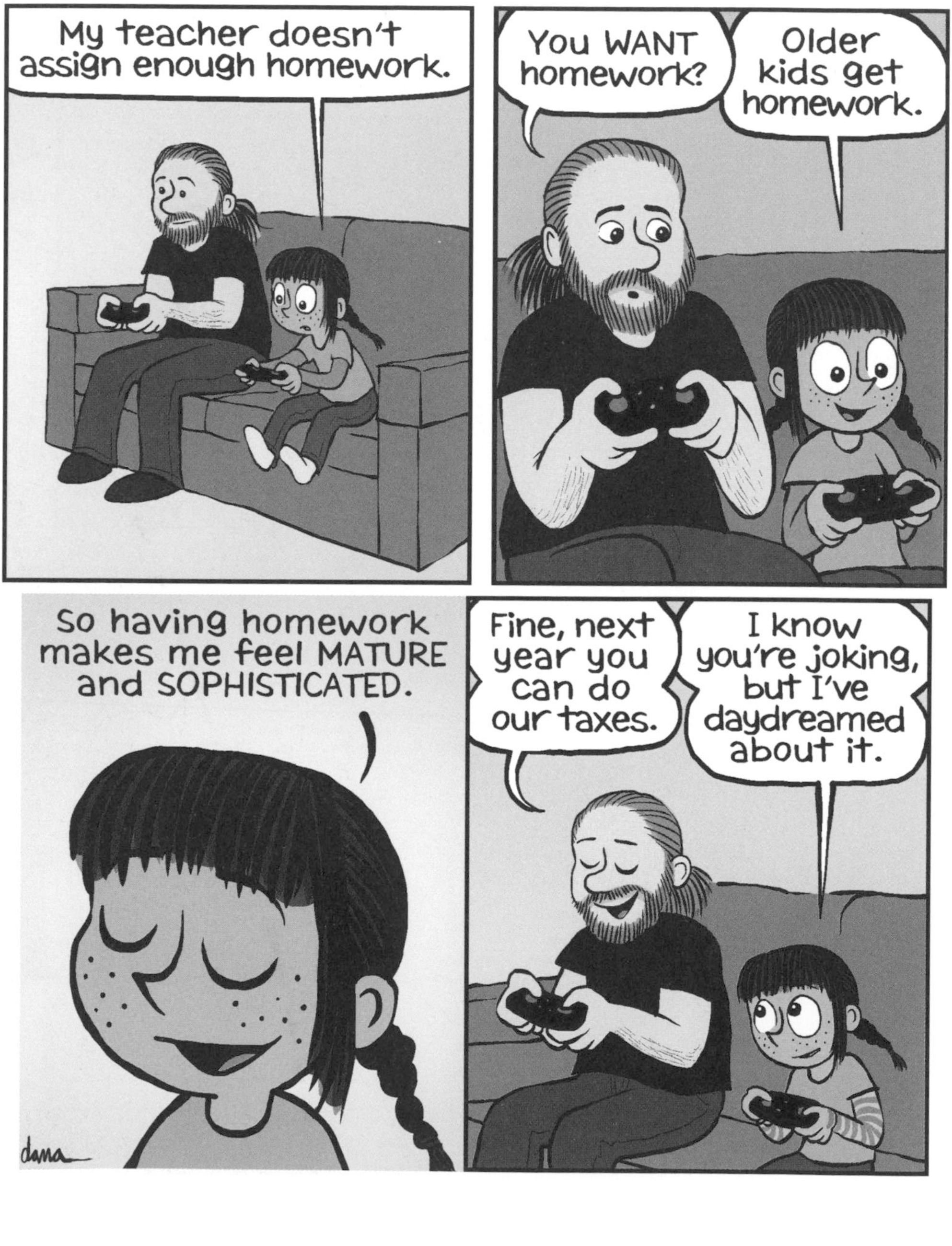

My teacher doesn't assign enough homework.
You WANT homework?
Older kids get homework.
So having homework makes me feel MATURE and SOPHISTICATED.
Fine, next year you can do our taxes.
I know you're joking, but I've daydreamed about it.
dana

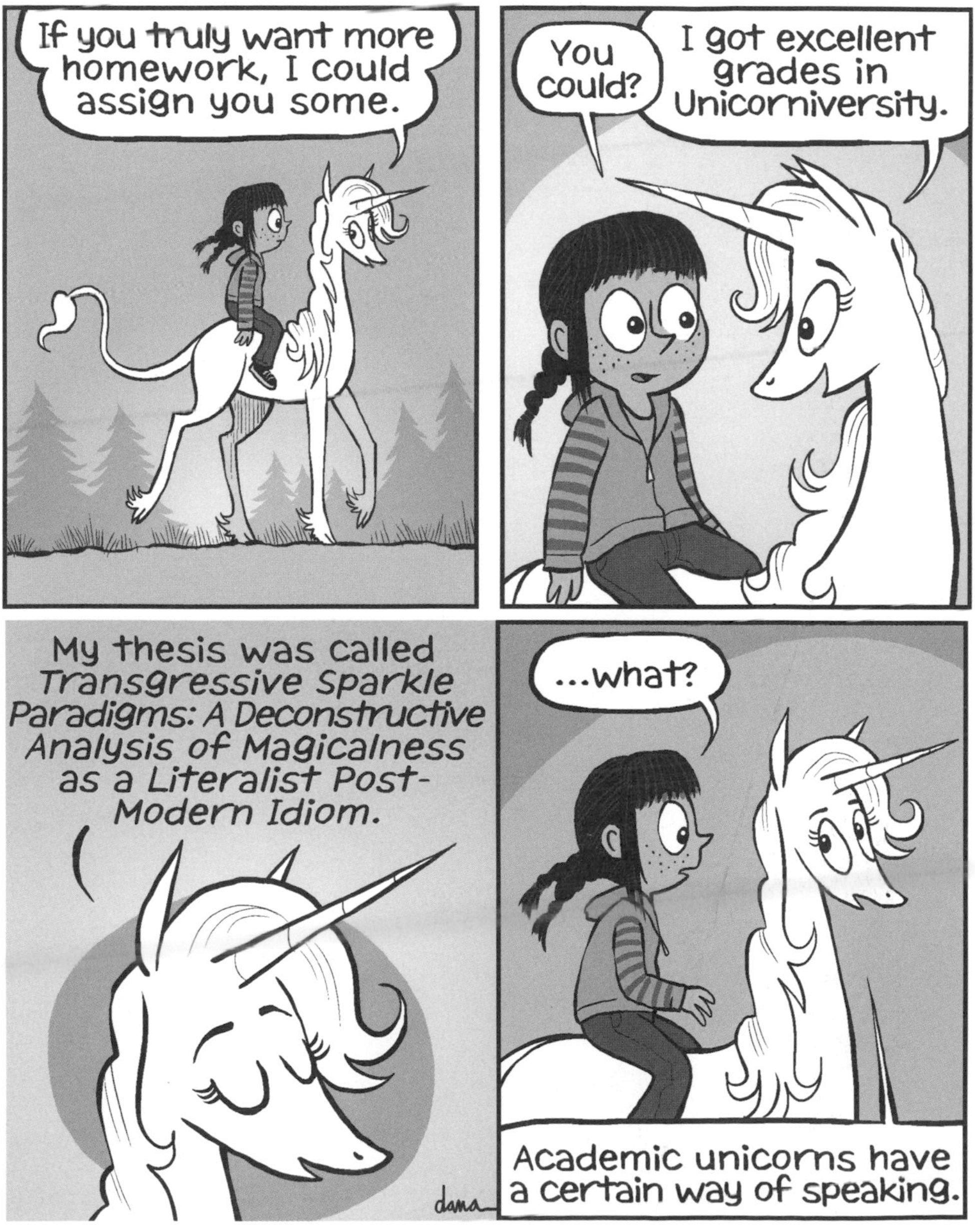
If you truly want more homework, I could assign you some.
You could?
I got excellent grades in Unicorniversity.
My thesis was called *Transgressive Sparkle Paradigms: A Deconstructive Analysis of Magicalness as a Literalist Post-Modern Idiom.*
...what?
Academic unicorns have a certain way of speaking.
dana

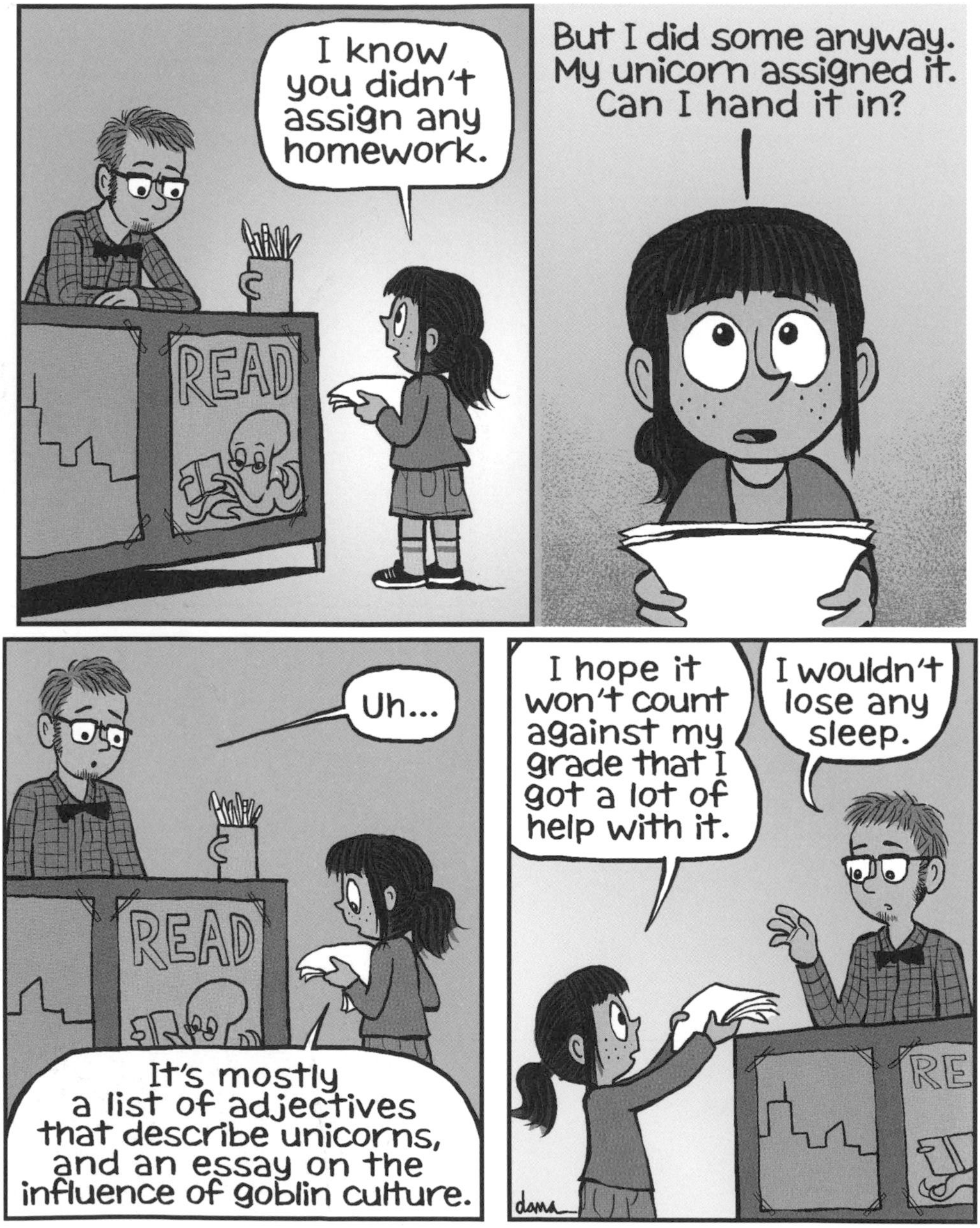
I know you didn't assign any homework.
But I did some anyway. My unicorn assigned it. Can I hand it in?
READ
Uh...
It's mostly a list of adjectives that describe unicorns, and an essay on the influence of goblin culture.
READ
I hope it won't count against my grade that I got a lot of help with it.
I wouldn't lose any sleep.
RE
dana

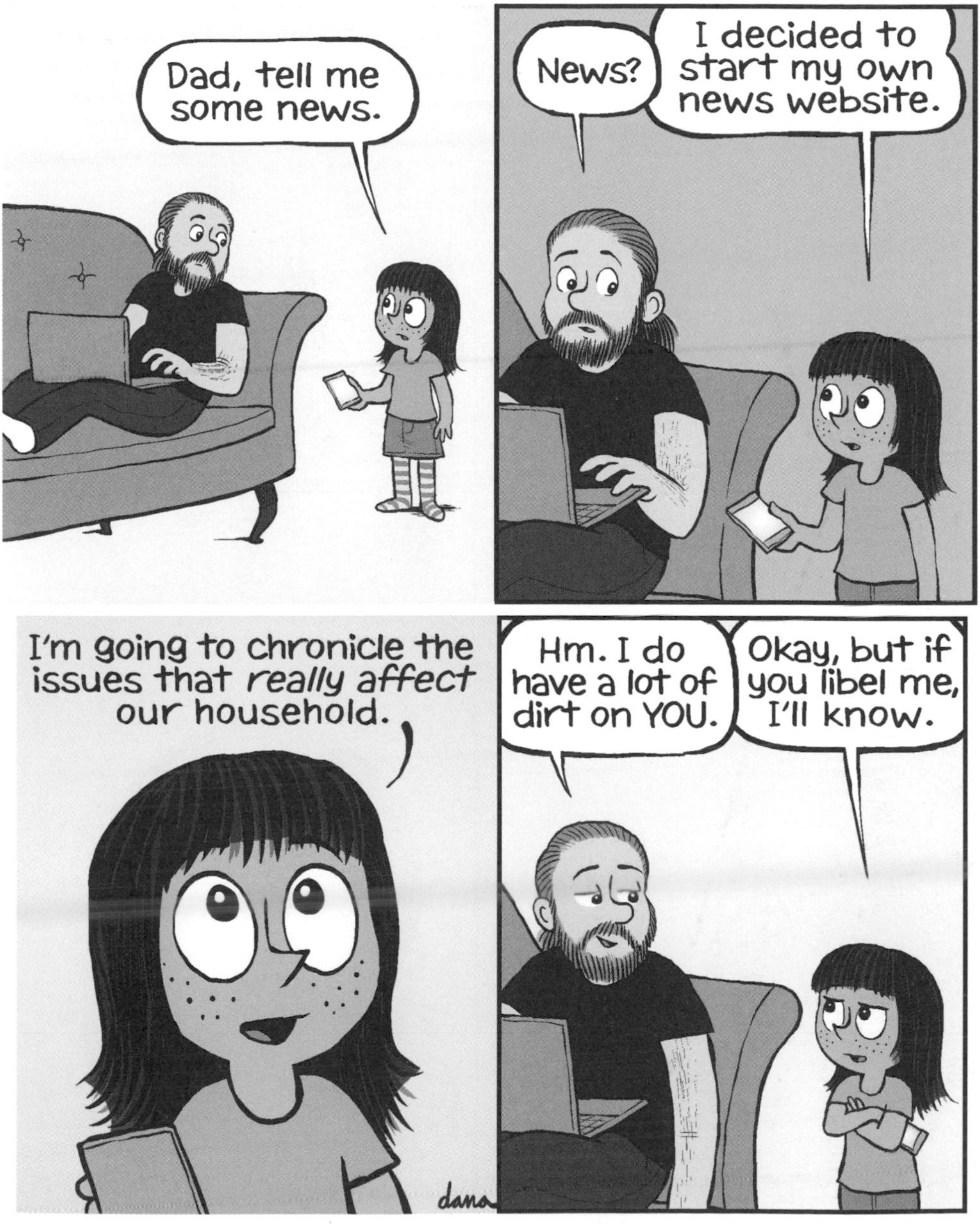
Dad, tell me some news.
News?
I decided to start my own news website.
I'm going to chronicle the issues that *really affect* our household.
Hm. I do have a lot of dirt on YOU.
Okay, but if you libel me, I'll know.
dana

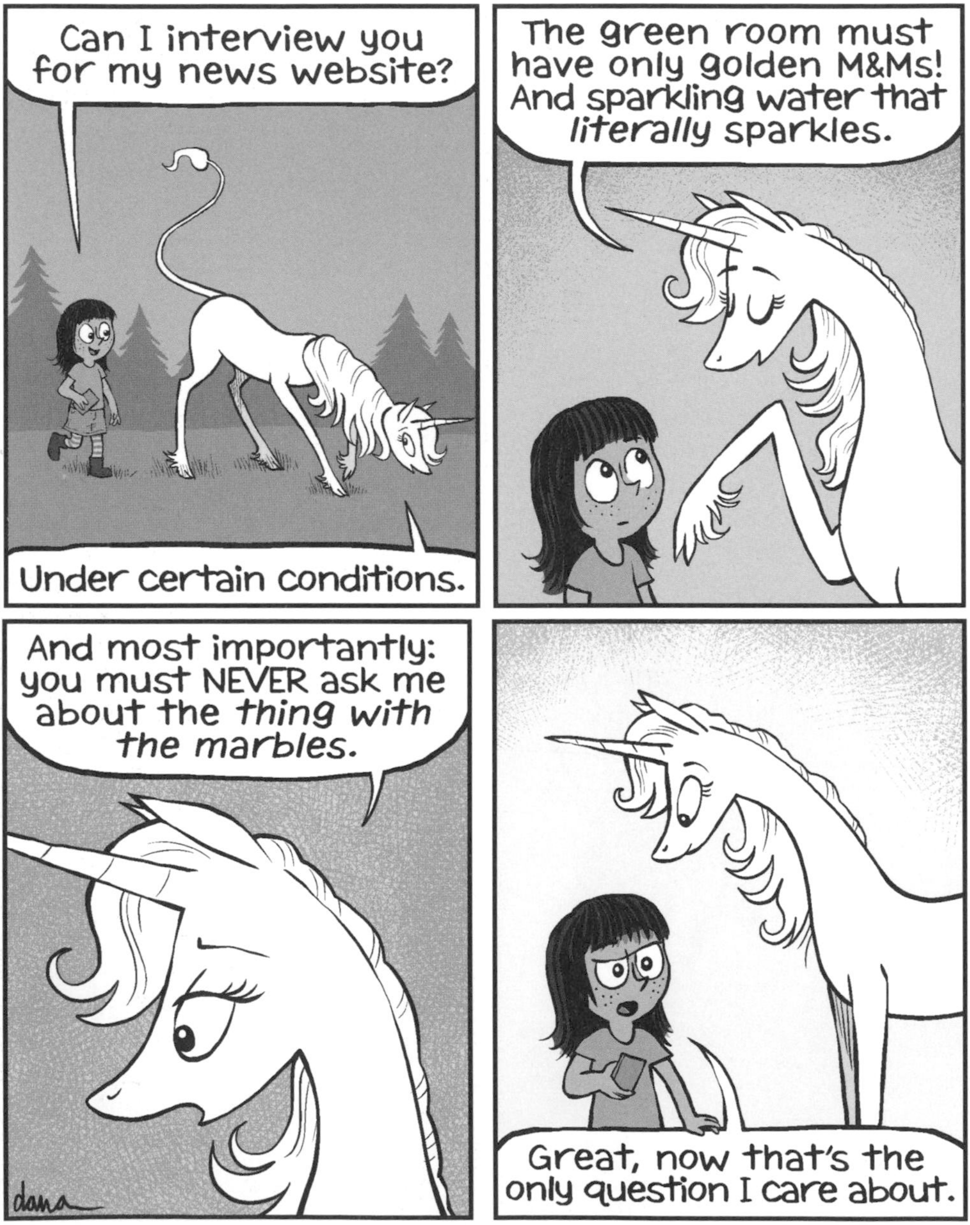
Can I interview you for my news website?
Under certain conditions.
The green room must have only golden M&Ms! And sparkling water that *literally* sparkles.
And most importantly: you must NEVER ask me about the *thing with the marbles.*
dana
Great, now that's the only question I care about.

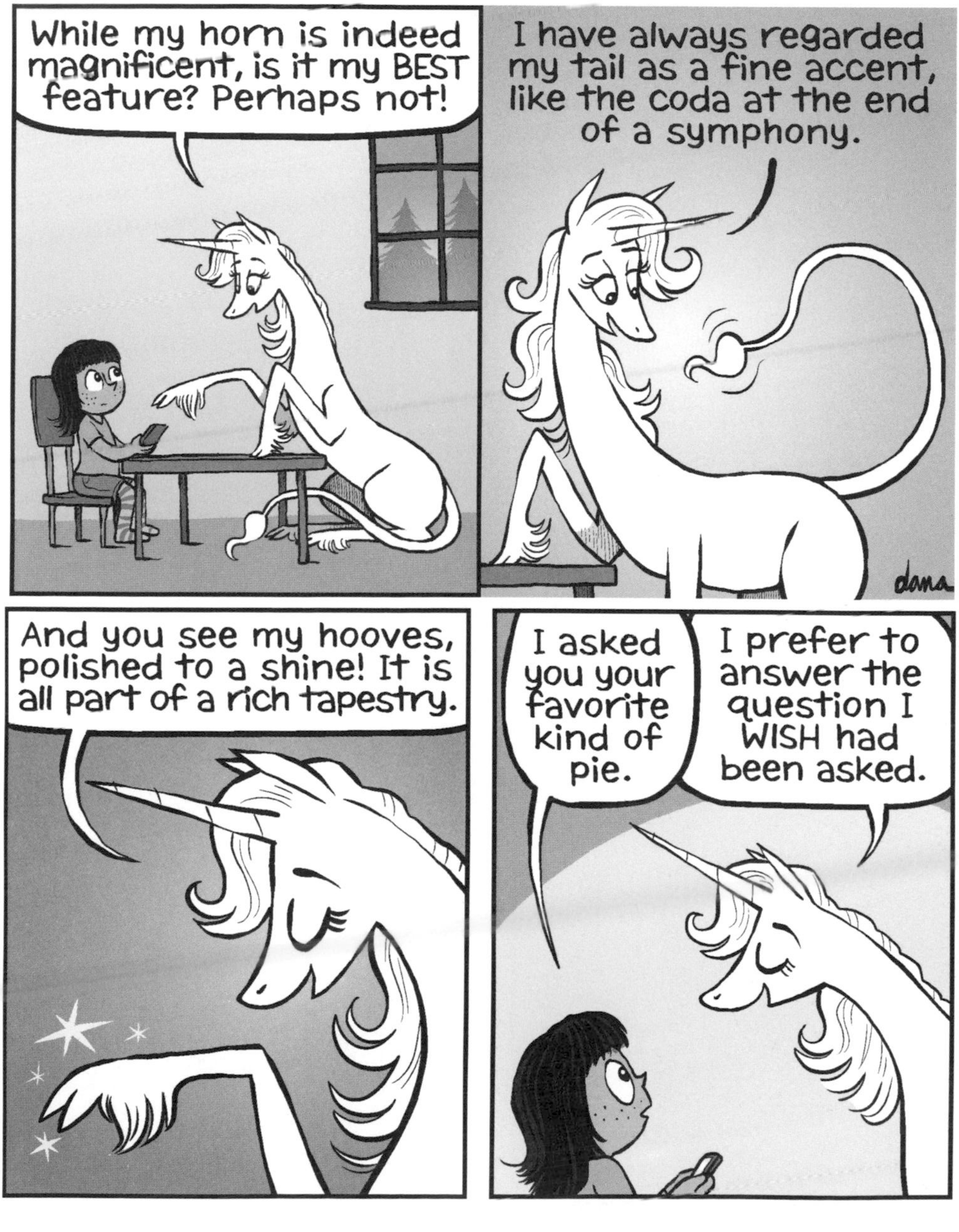
While my horn is indeed magnificent, is it my BEST feature? Perhaps not!
I have always regarded my tail as a fine accent, like the coda at the end of a symphony.
dana
And you see my hooves, polished to a shine! It is all part of a rich tapestry.
I asked you your favorite kind of pie.
I prefer to answer the question I WISH had been asked.

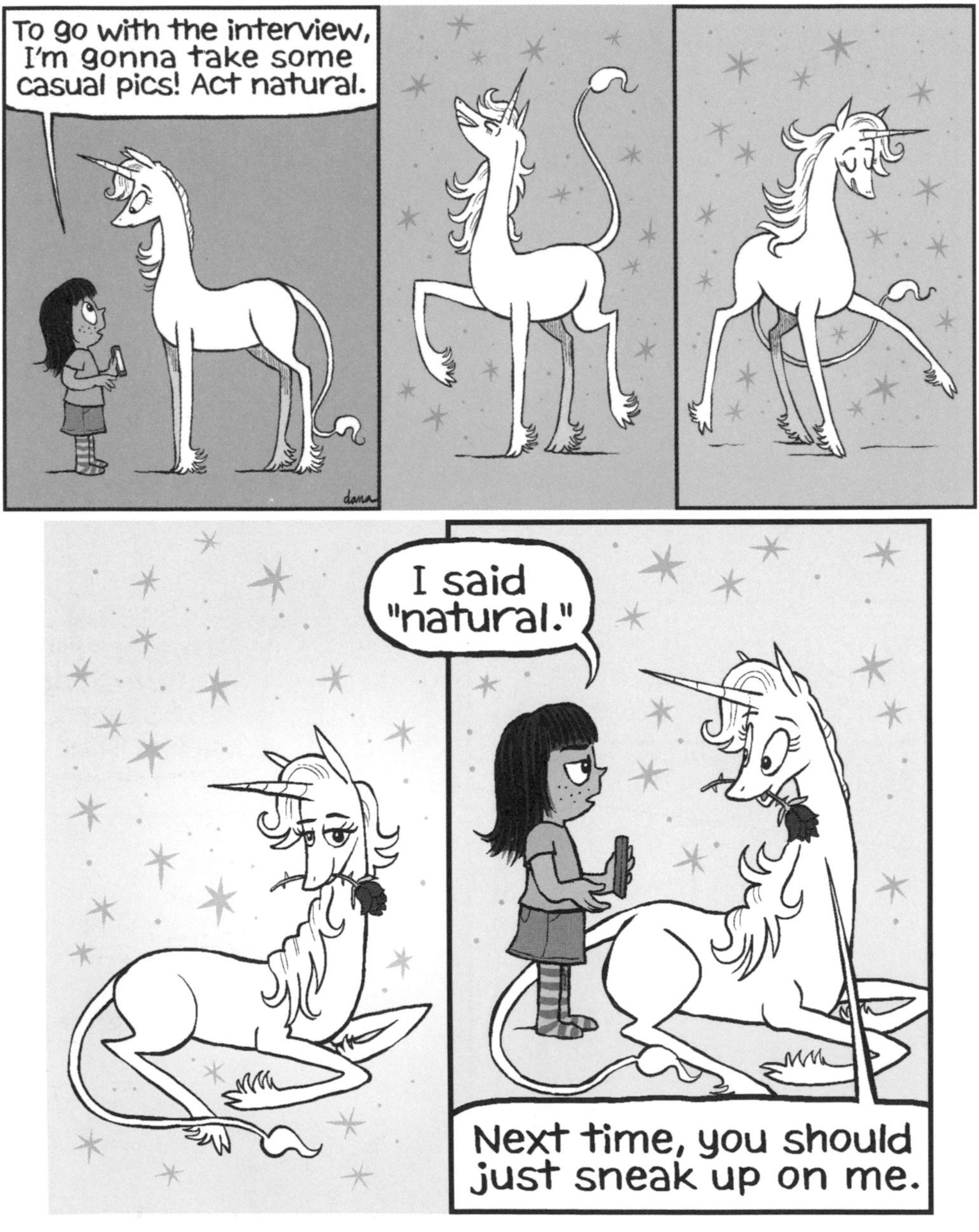
To go with the interview, I'm gonna take some casual pics! Act natural.
dana
I said "natural."
Next time, you should just sneak up on me.

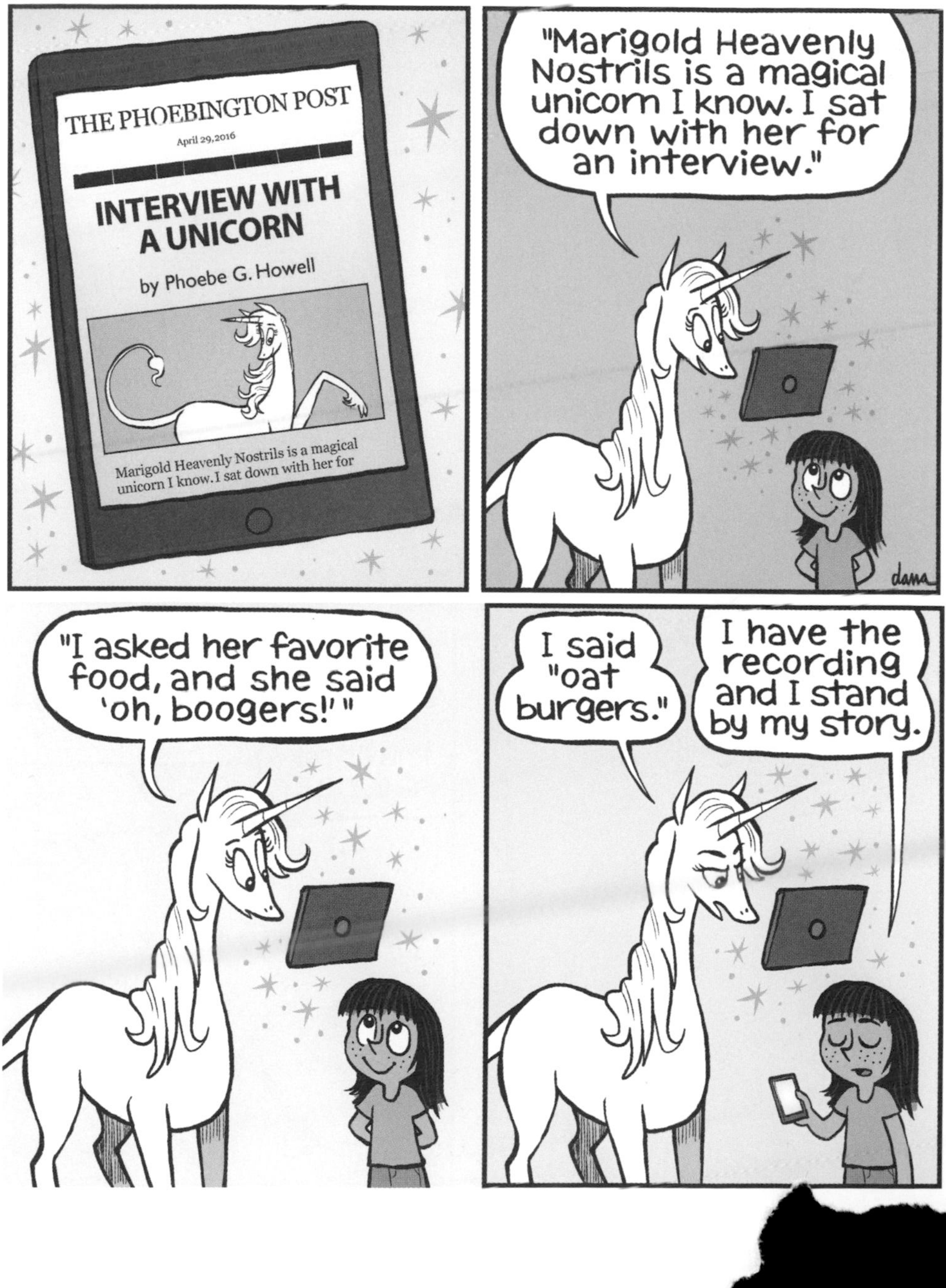
THE PHOEBINGTON POST
April 29,2016
INTERVIEW WITH A UNICORN
by Phoebe G. Howell
Marigold Heavenly Nostrils is a magical unicorn I know. I sat down with her for
"Marigold Heavenly Nostrils is a magical unicorn I know. I sat down with her for an interview."
dana
"I asked her favorite food, and she said 'oh, boogers!'"
I said "oat burgers."
I have the recording and I stand by my story.

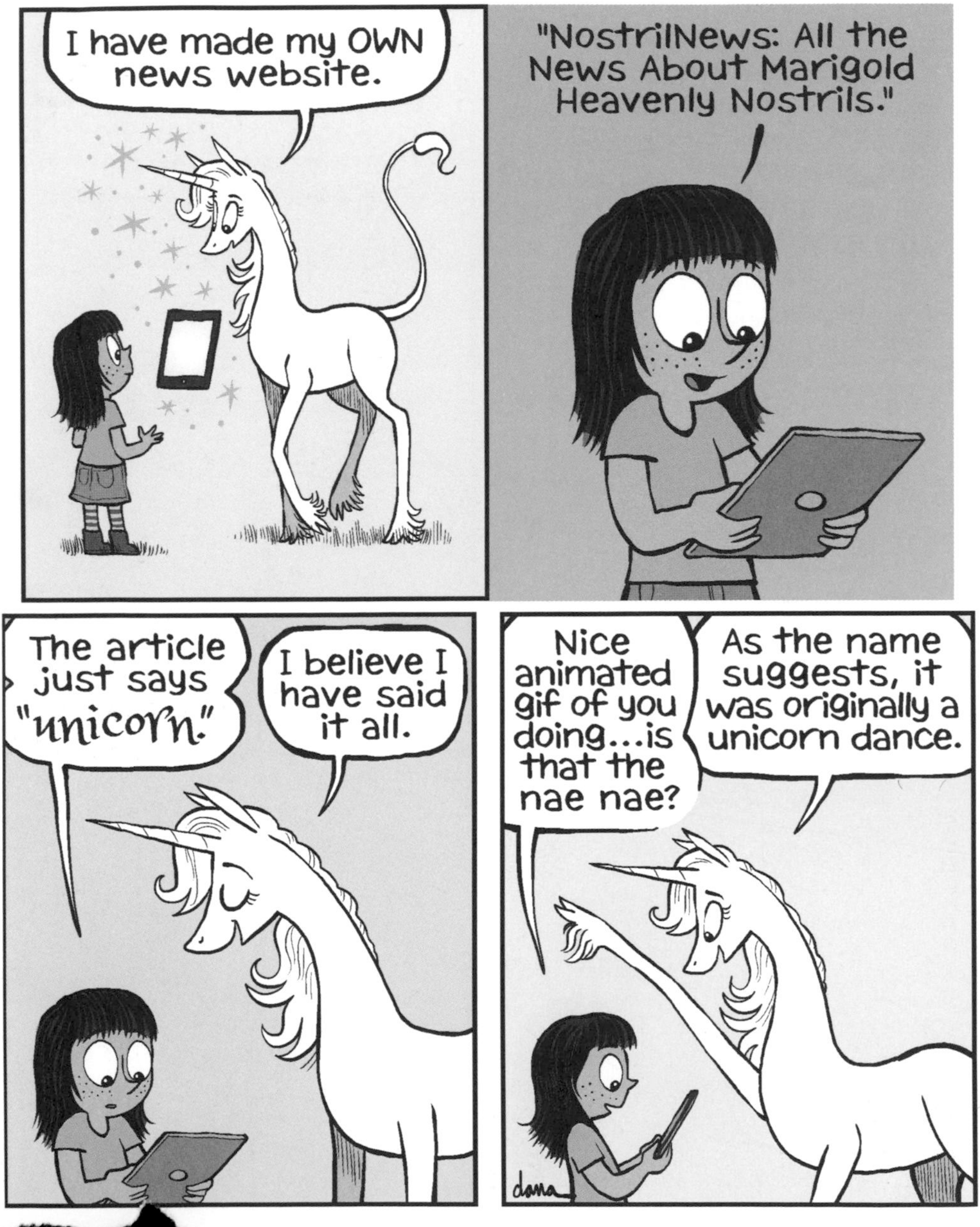
I have made my OWN news website.
"NostrilNews: All the News About Marigold Heavenly Nostrils."
The article just says "unicorn."
I believe I have said it all.
Nice animated gif of you doing...is that the nae nae?
As the name suggests, it was originally a unicorn dance.
dana

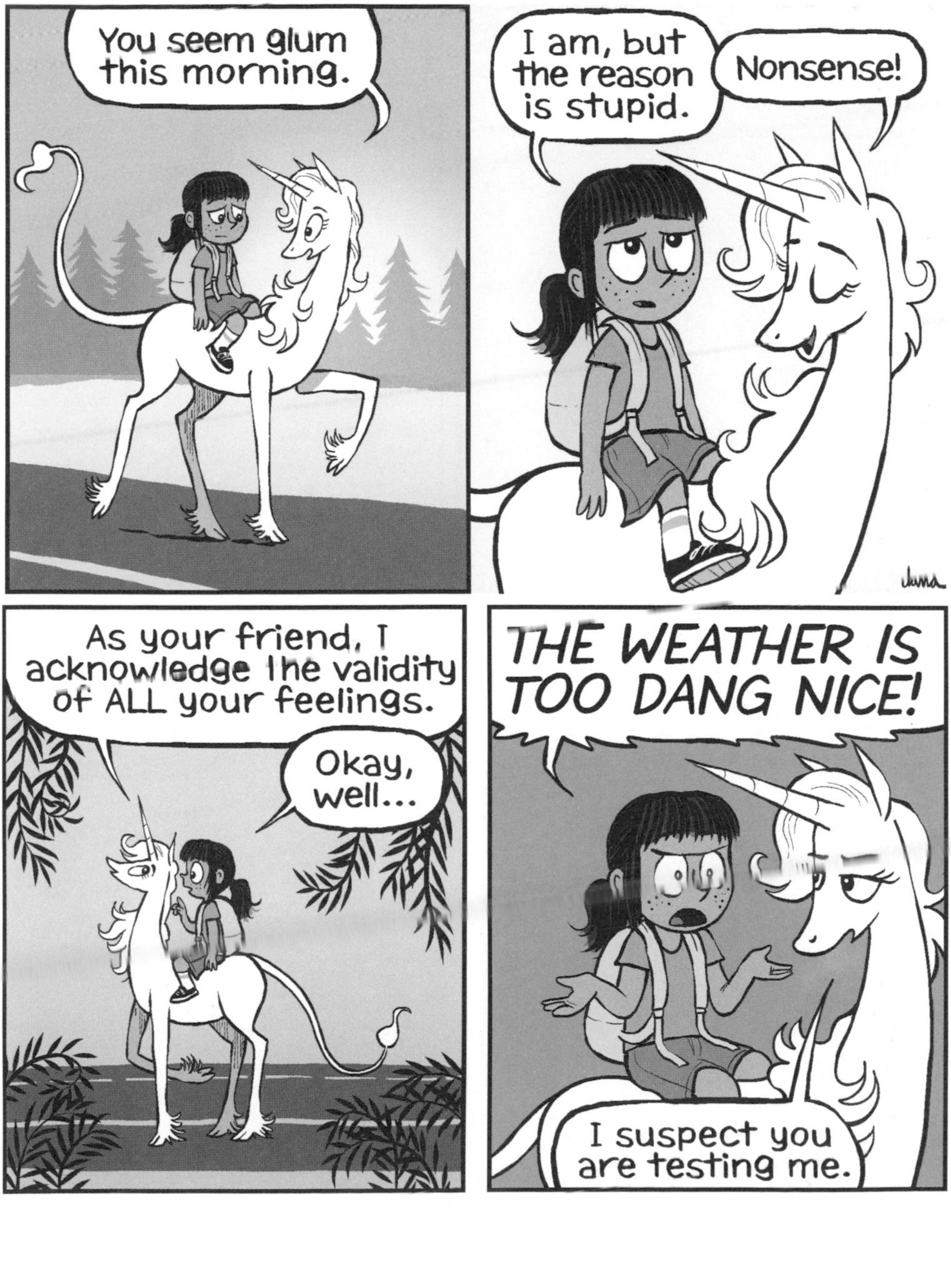
You seem glum this morning.
I am, but the reason is stupid.
Nonsense!
As your friend, I acknowledge the validity of ALL your feelings.
Okay, well...
THE WEATHER IS TOO DANG NICE!
I suspect you are testing me.

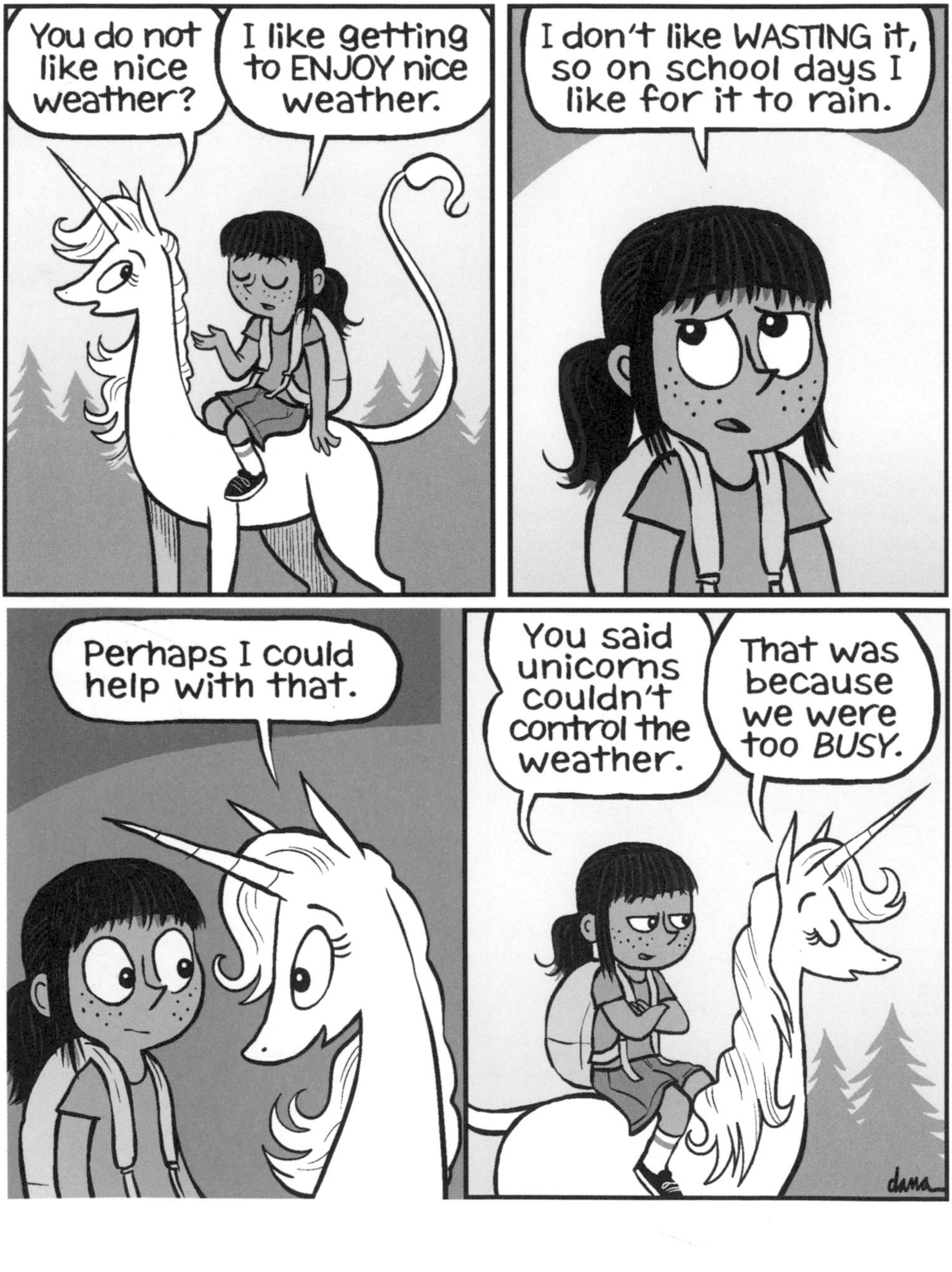

You do not like nice weather?
I like getting to ENJOY nice weather.
I don't like WASTING it, so on school days I like for it to rain.
Perhaps I could help with that.
You said unicorns couldn't control the weather.
That was because we were too *BUSY*.
dana

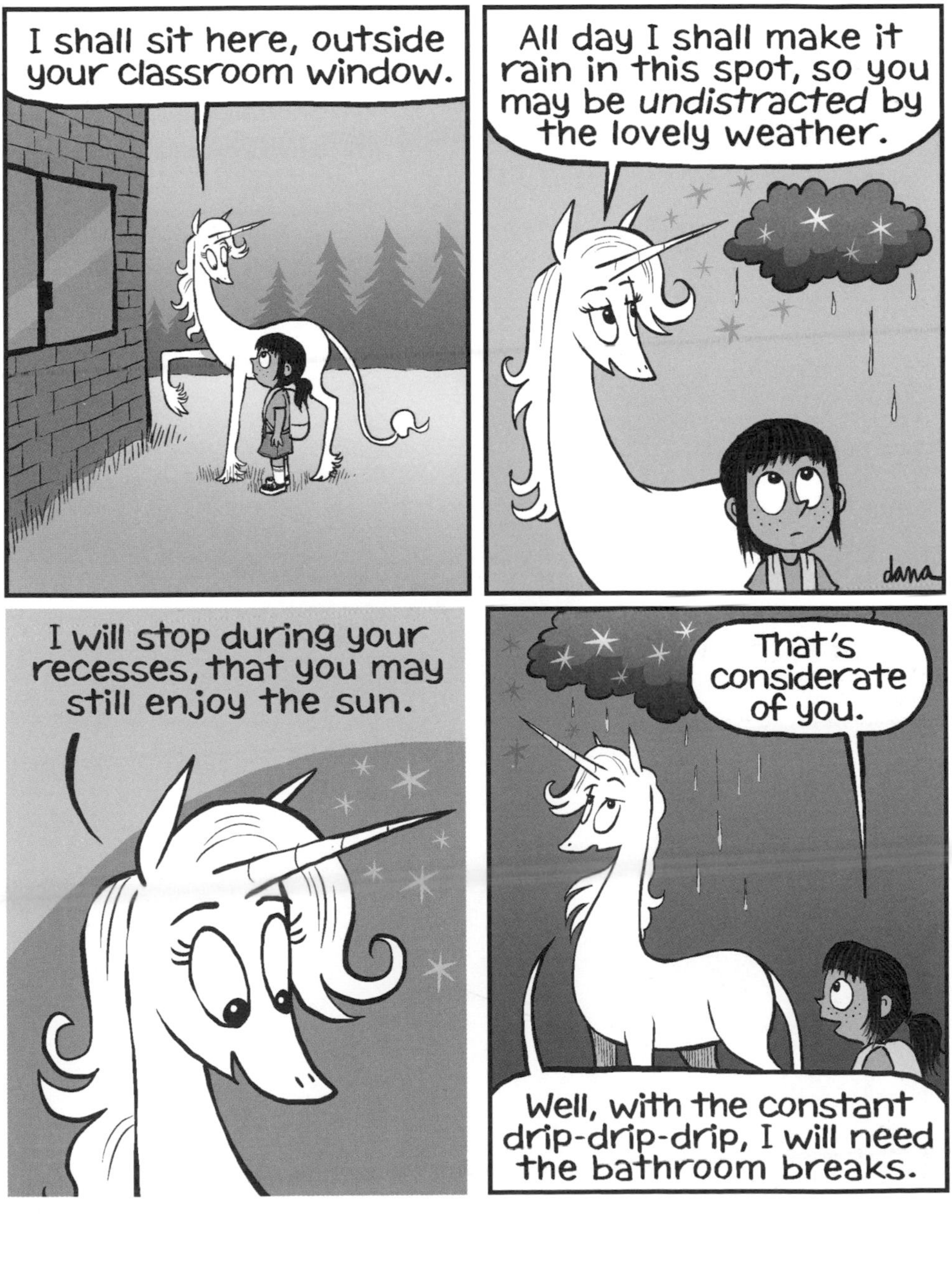
I shall sit here, outside your classroom window.
All day I shall make it rain in this spot, so you may be *undistracted* by the lovely weather.
dana
I will stop during your recesses, that you may still enjoy the sun.
That's considerate of you.
Well, with the constant drip-drip-drip, I will need the bathroom breaks.

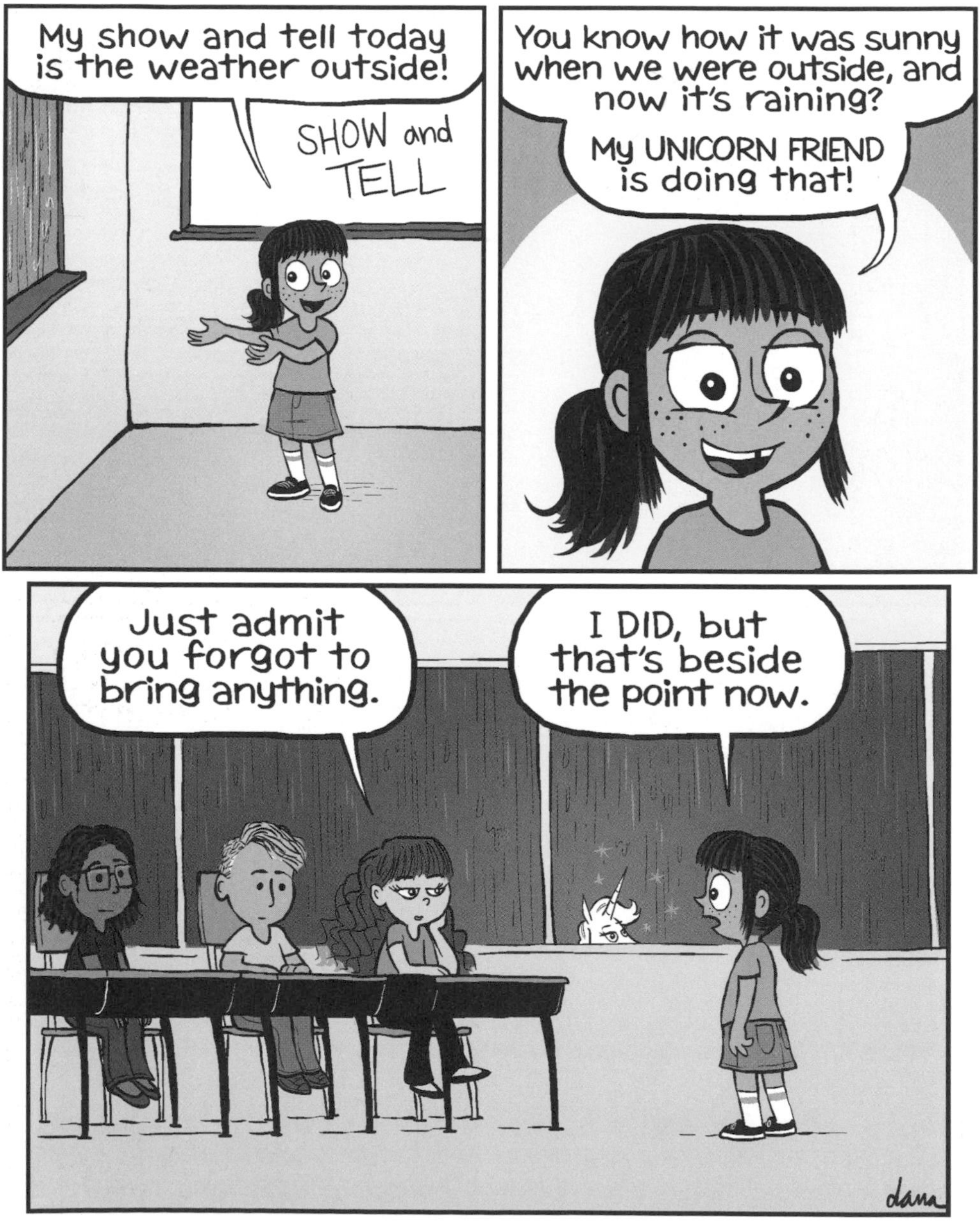
My show and tell today is the weather outside!
SHOW and TELL
You know how it was sunny when we were outside, and now it's raining?
My UNICORN FRIEND is doing that!
Just admit you forgot to bring anything.
I DID, but that's beside the point now.
dana

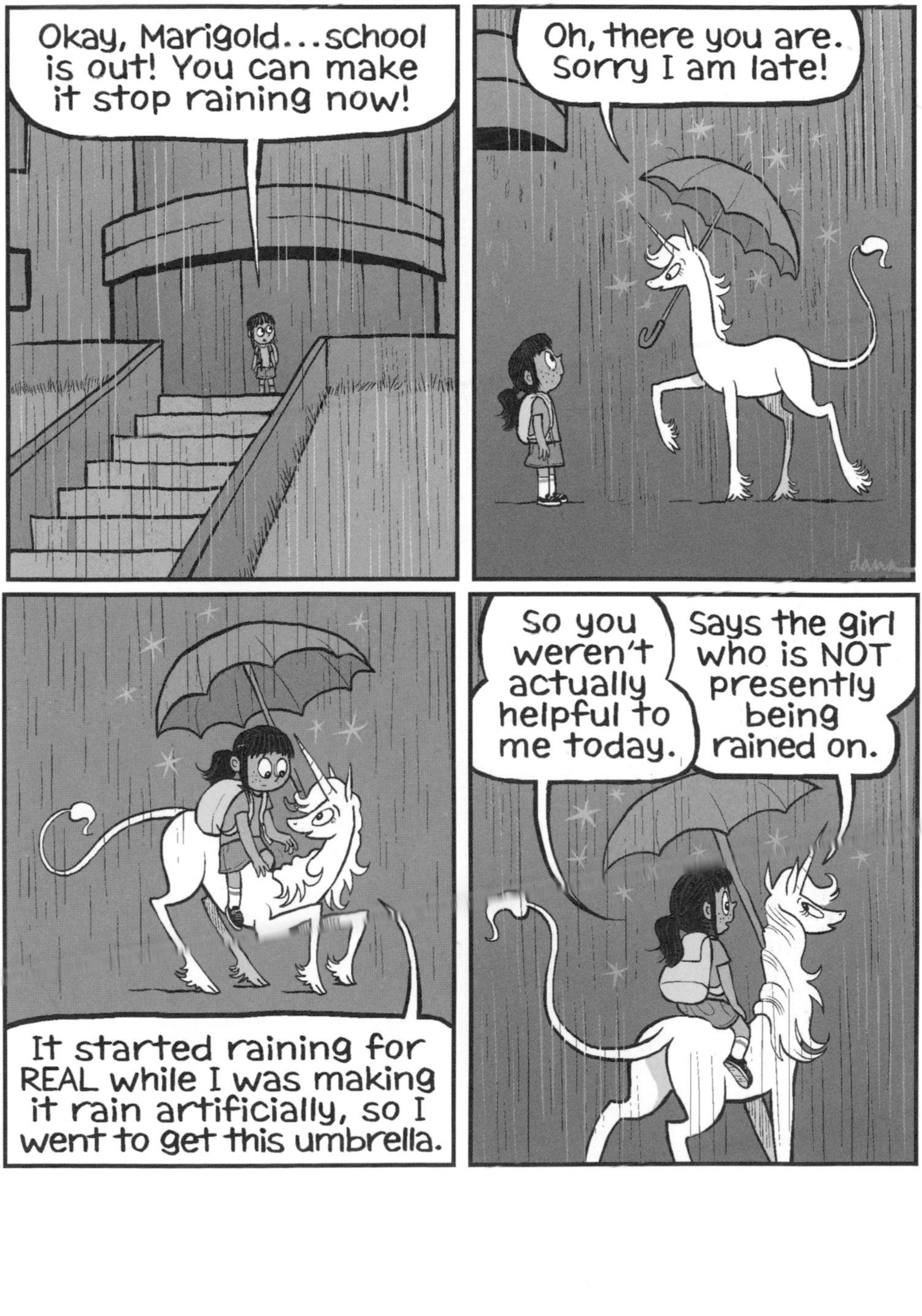
Okay, Marigold...school is out! You can make it stop raining now!
Oh, there you are. Sorry I am late!
It started raining for REAL while I was making it rain artificially, so I went to get this umbrella.
So you weren't actually helpful to me today.
Says the girl who is NOT presently being rained on.

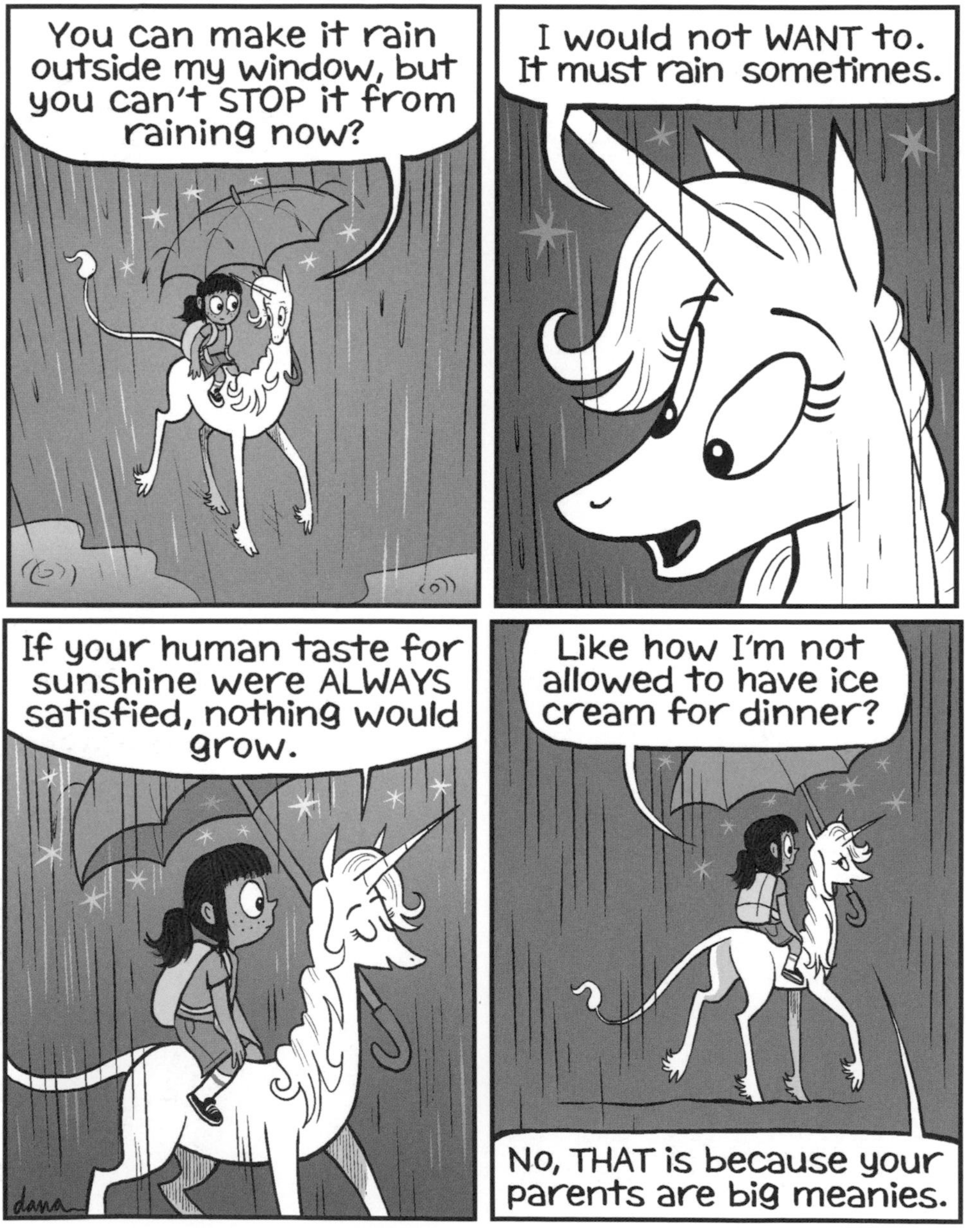
You can make it rain outside my window, but you can't STOP it from raining now?
I would not WANT to. It must rain sometimes.
If your human taste for sunshine were ALWAYS satisfied, nothing would grow.
dana
Like how I'm not allowed to have ice cream for dinner?
No, THAT is because your parents are big meanies.

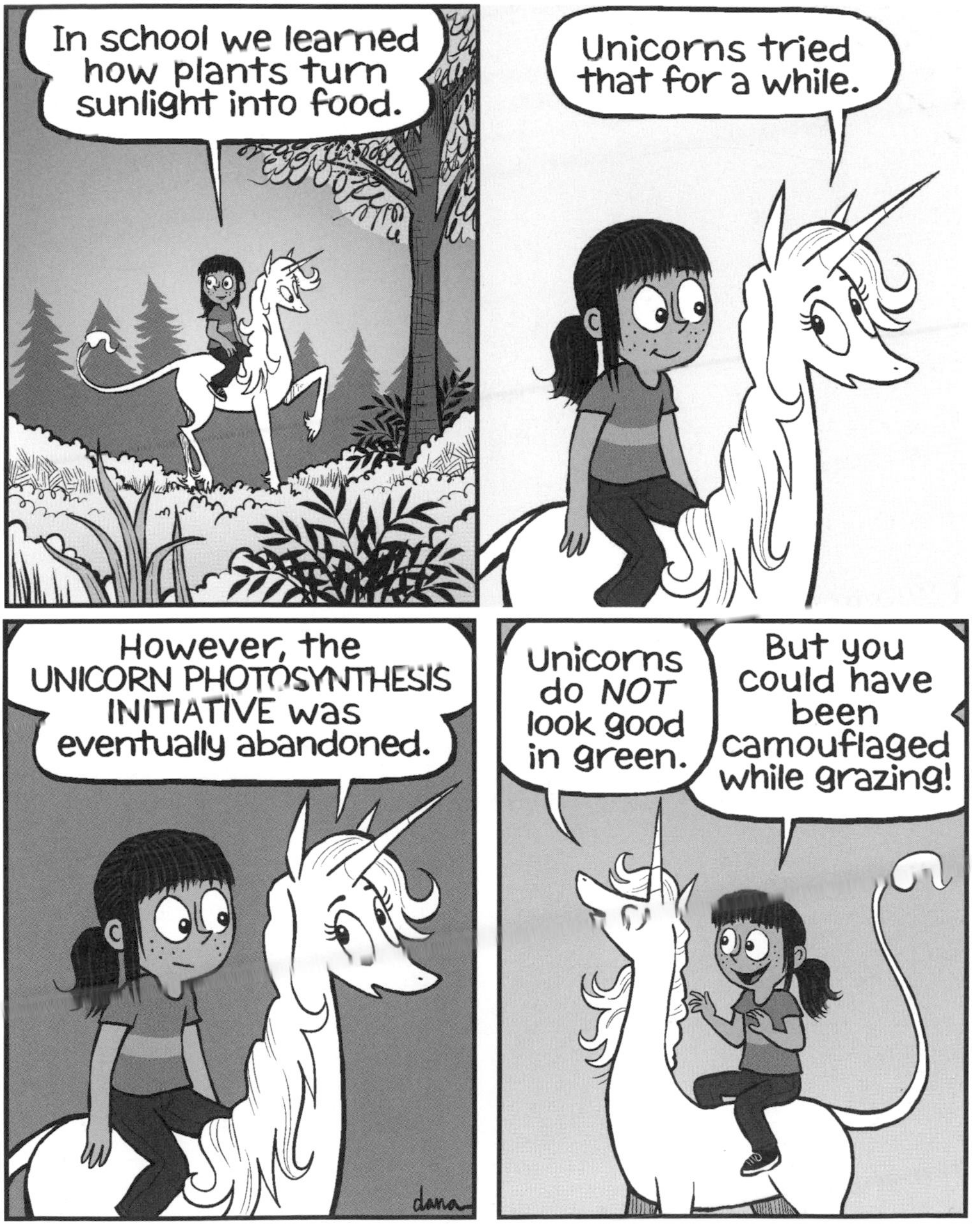
In school we learned how plants turn sunlight into food.
Unicorns tried that for a while.
However, the UNICORN PHOTOSYNTHESIS INITIATIVE was eventually abandoned.
Unicorns do *NOT* look good in green.
But you could have been camouflaged while grazing!
dana

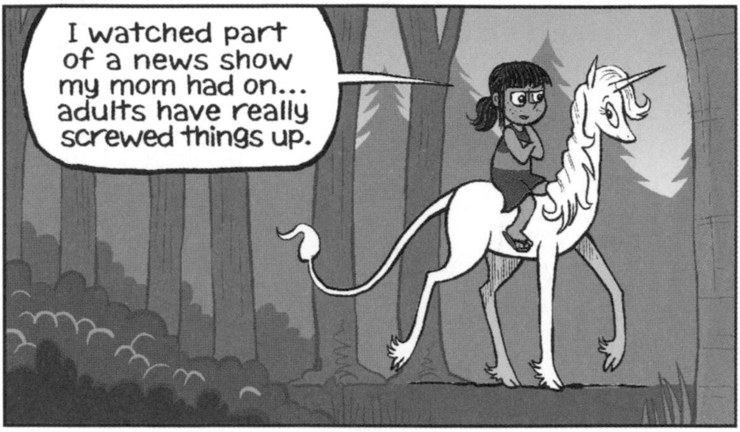
I watched part of a news show my mom had on... adults have really screwed things up.

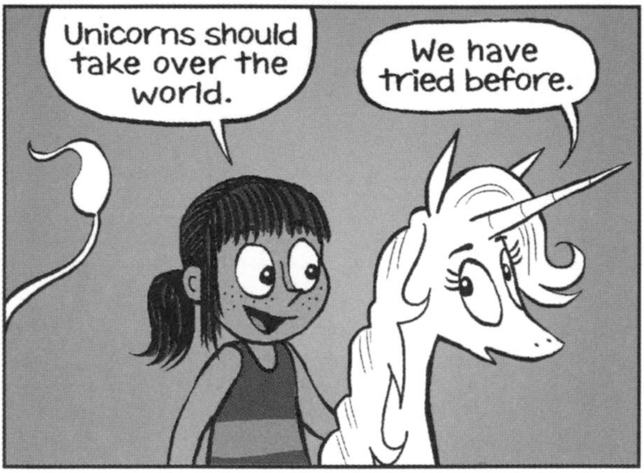
Unicorns should take over the world.
We have tried before.

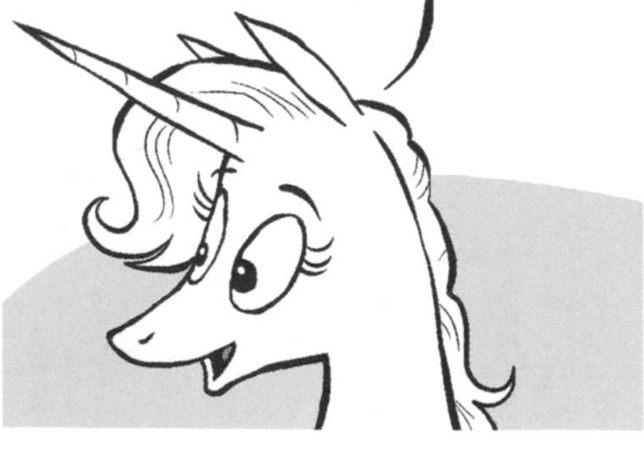
In times of old, we staged a campaign for power, without success.

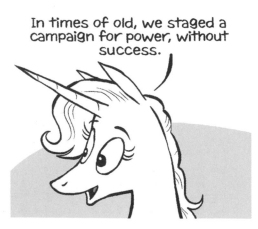

Hello. We would like to rule the world, please.
We dare not lift the *Shield of Boringness*, or our glory would BLIND you.
Trust us. We are magical.
For some reason, we are still not in charge.
dana

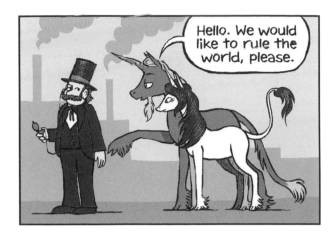

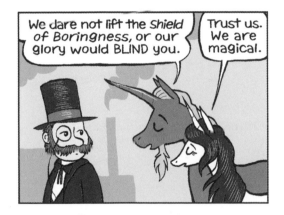

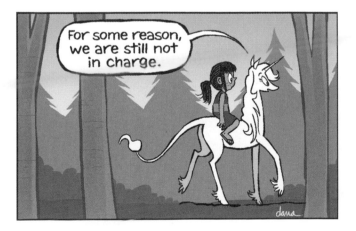

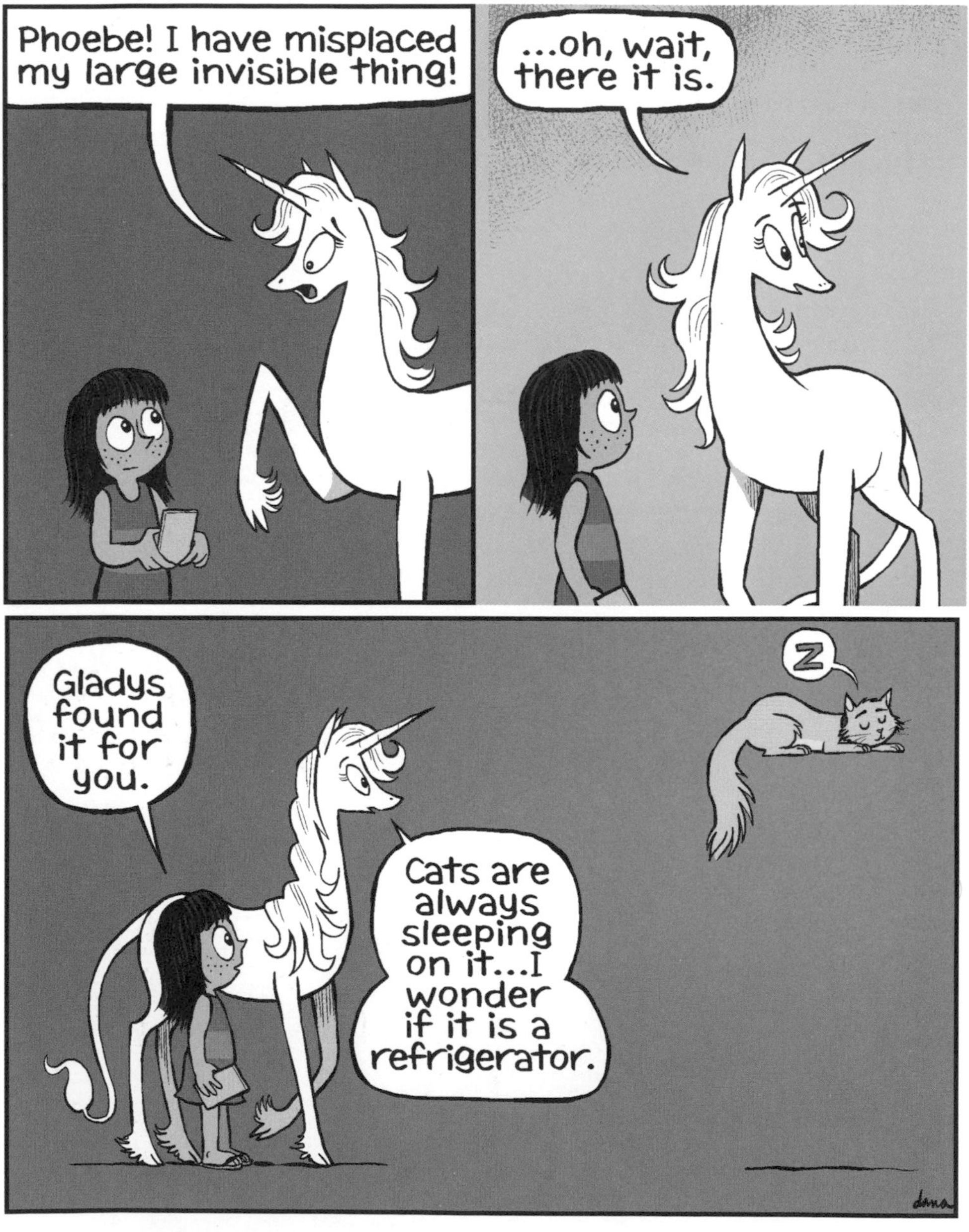
Phoebe! I have misplaced my large invisible thing!
...oh, wait, there it is.
Gladys found it for you.
Cats are always sleeping on it...I wonder if it is a refrigerator.
Z
dana

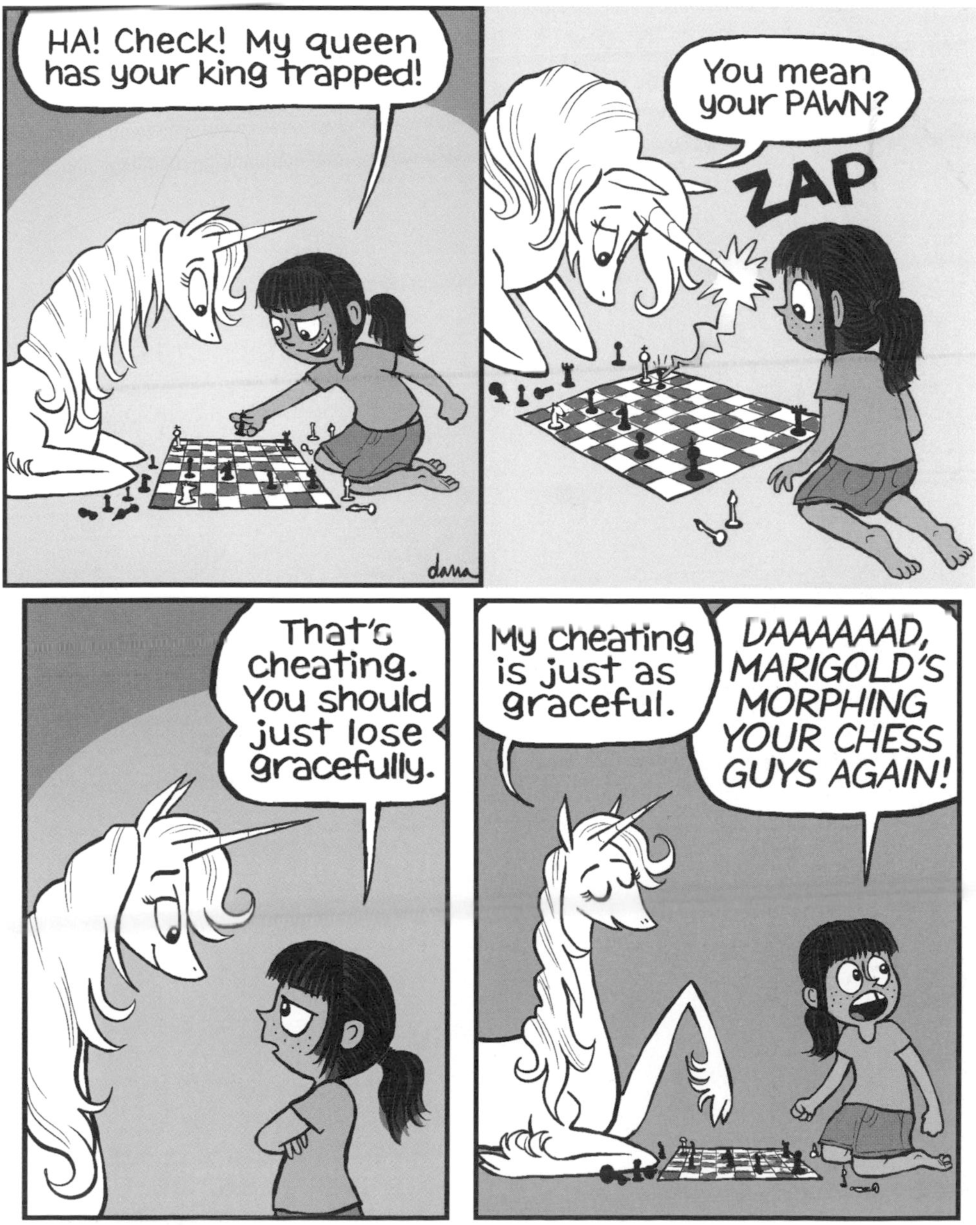
HA! Check! My queen has your king trapped!
dana
You mean your PAWN?
ZAP
That's cheating. You should just lose gracefully.
My cheating is just as graceful.
DAAAAAAD, MARIGOLD'S MORPHING YOUR CHESS GUYS AGAIN!

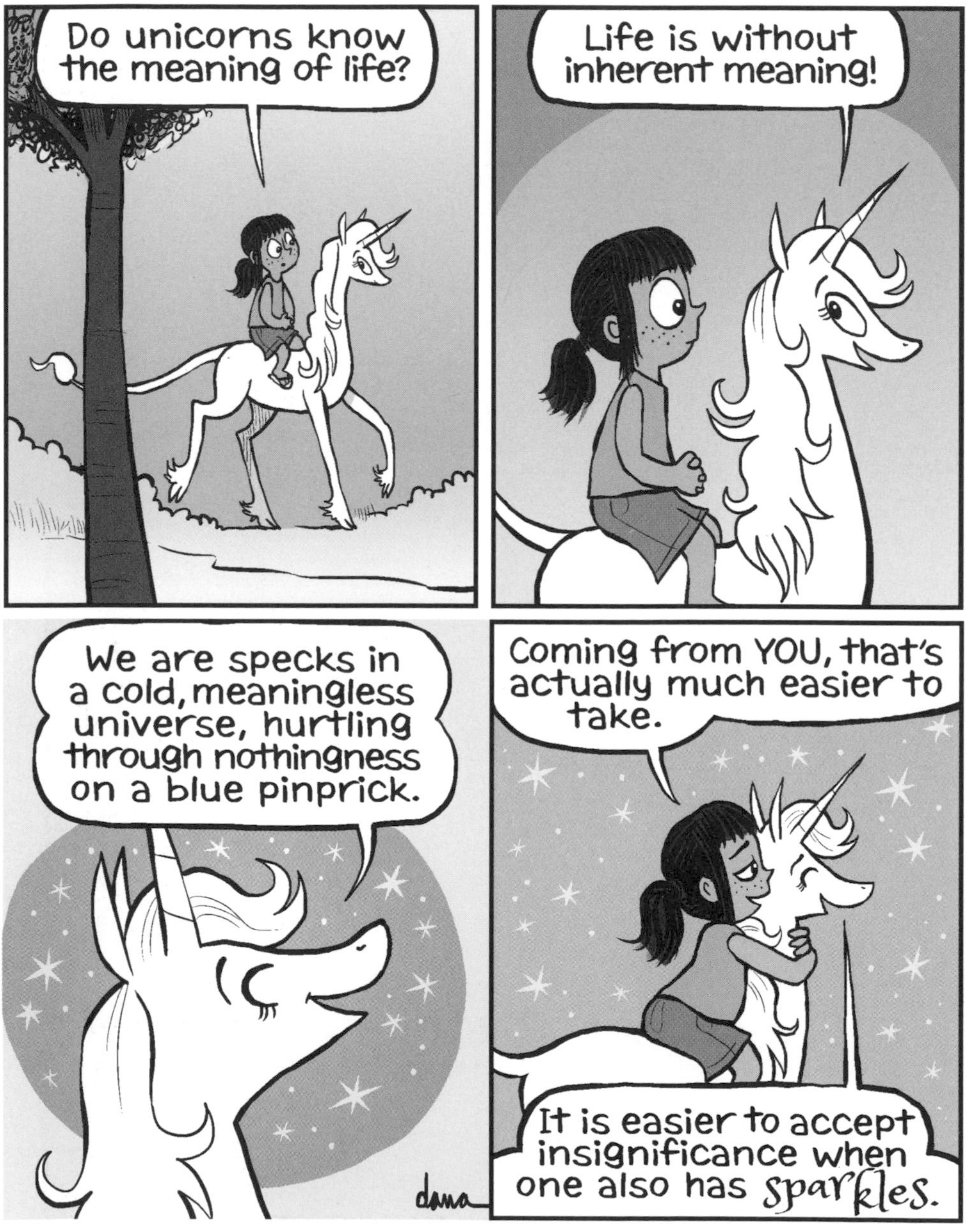
Do unicorns know the meaning of life?
Life is without inherent meaning!
We are specks in a cold, meaningless universe, hurtling through nothingness on a blue pinprick.
Coming from YOU, that's actually much easier to take.
It is easier to accept insignificance when one also has sparkles.
dana

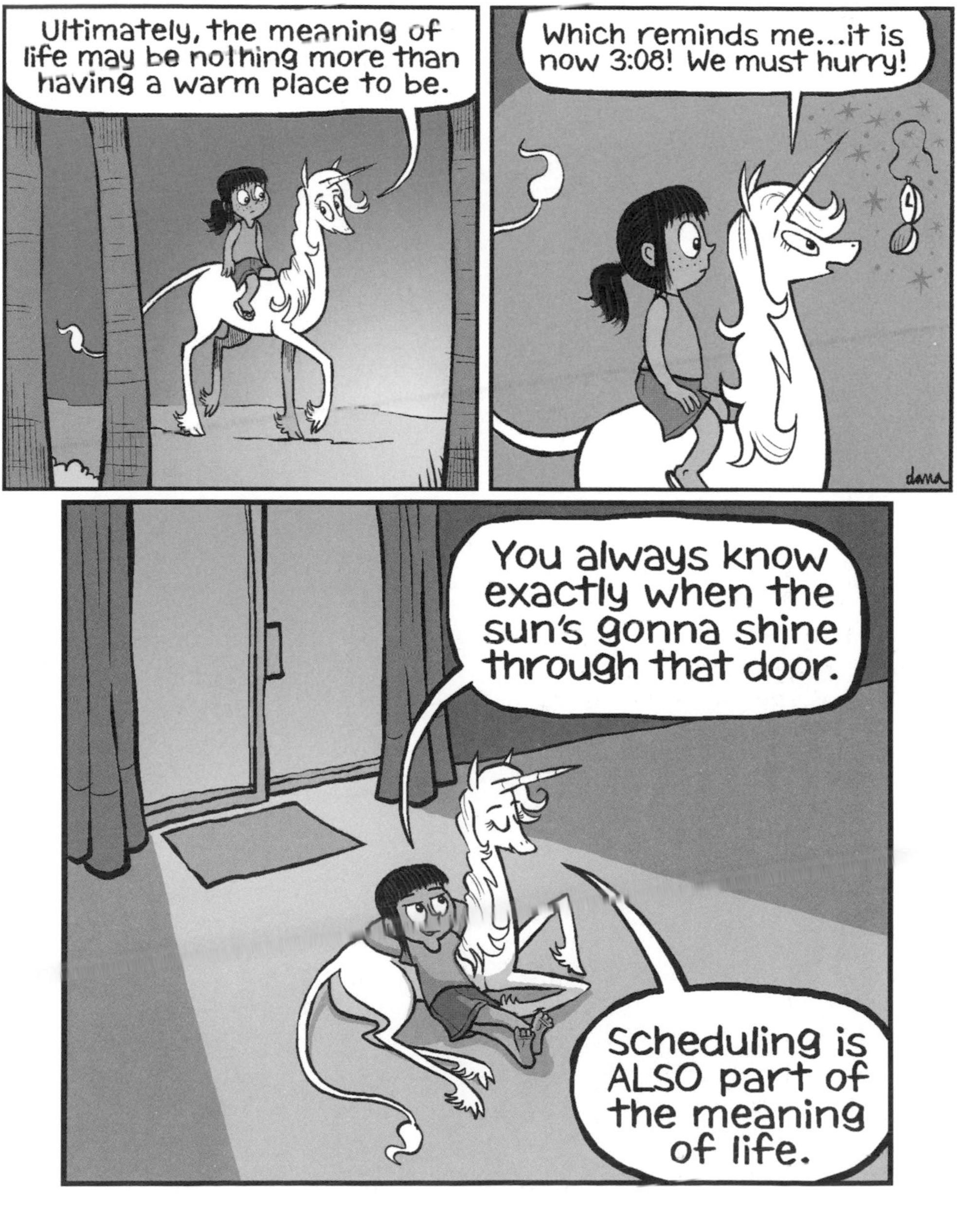
Ultimately, the meaning of life may be nothing more than having a warm place to be.
Which reminds me...it is now 3:08! We must hurry!
dana
You always know exactly when the sun's gonna shine through that door.
Scheduling is ALSO part of the meaning of life.

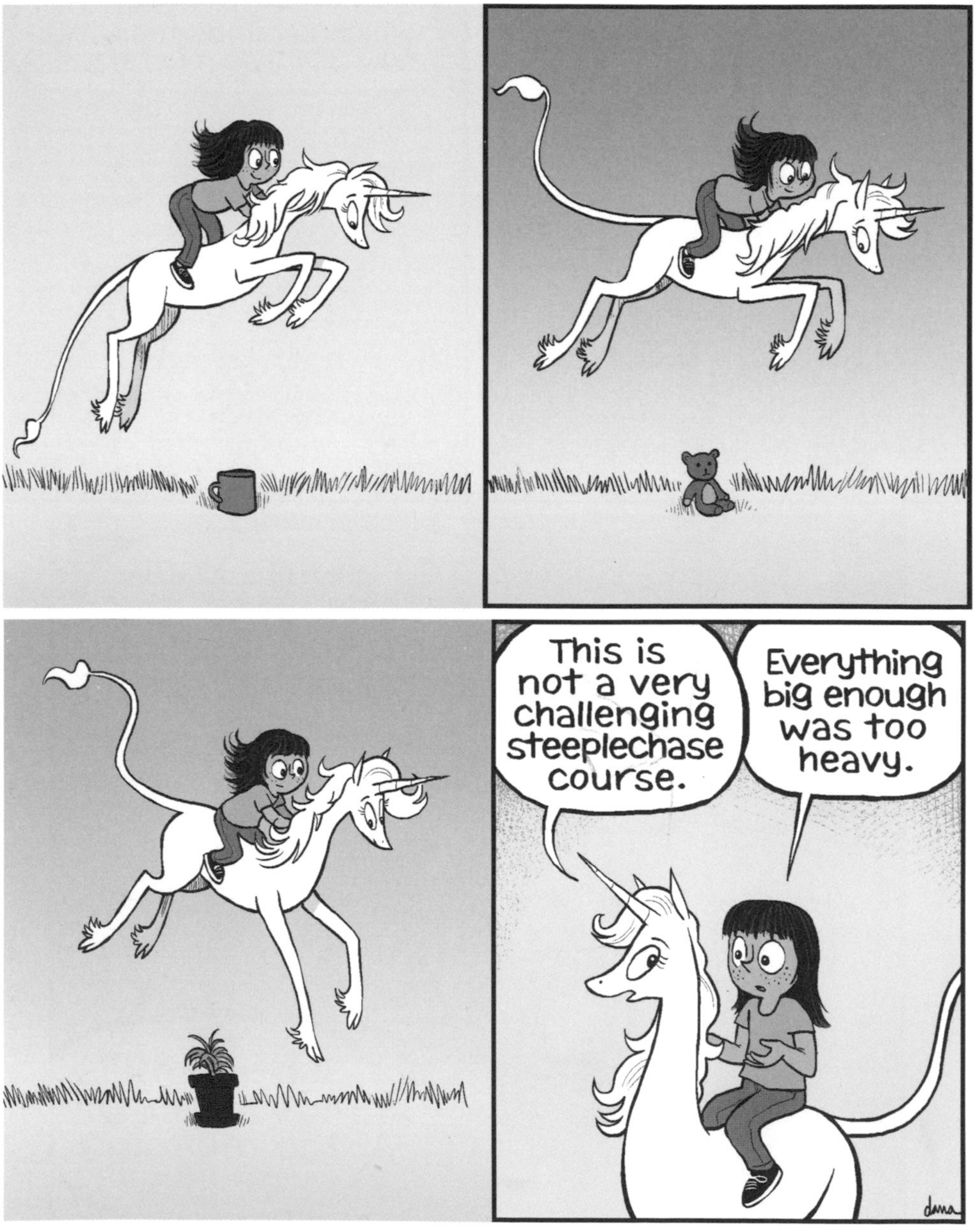
This is not a very challenging steeplechase course.
Everything big enough was too heavy.
dana

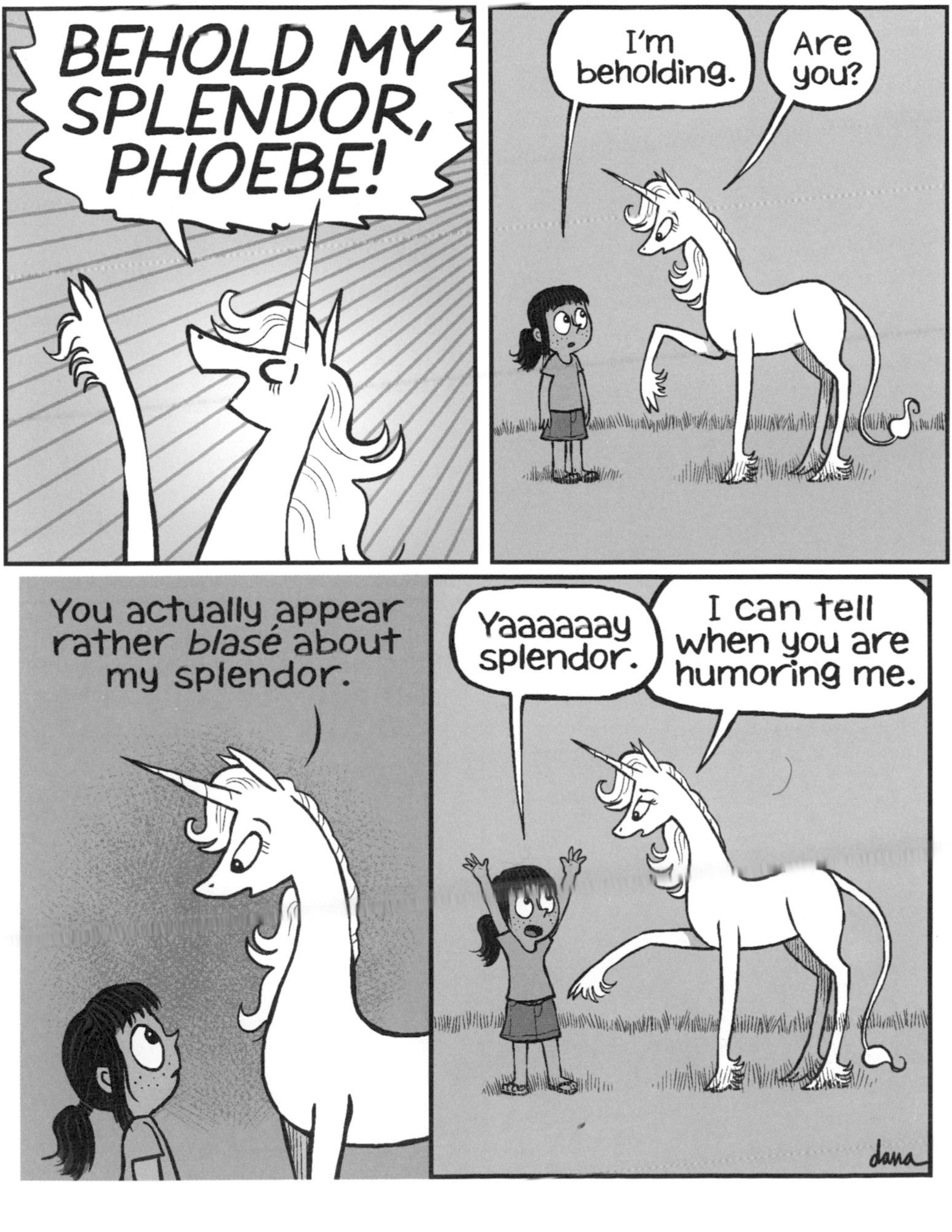
BEHOLD MY SPLENDOR, PHOEBE!
I'm beholding.
Are you?
You actually appear rather *blasé* about my splendor.
Yaaaaaay splendor.
I can tell when you are humoring me.
dana

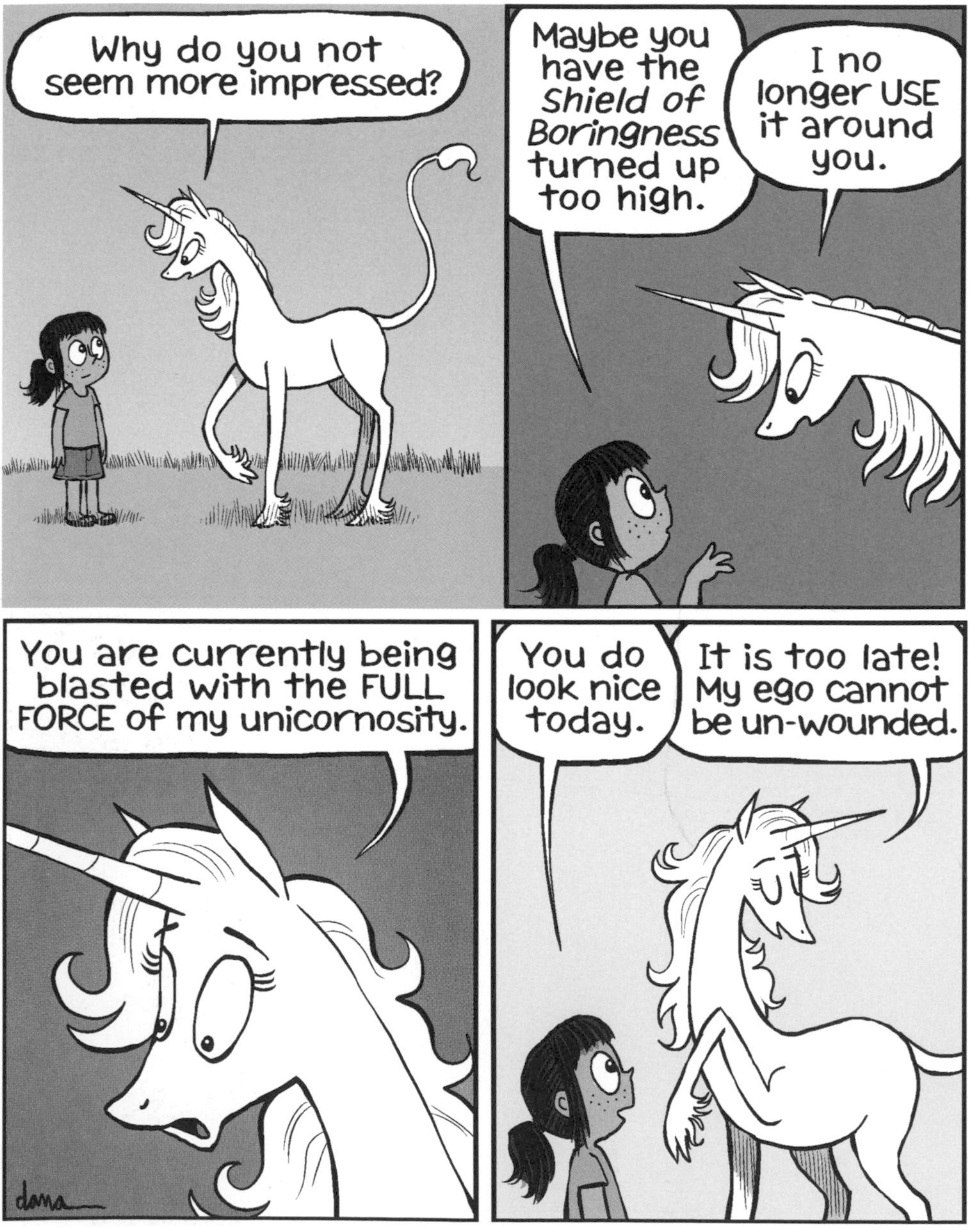

Why do you not seem more impressed?
Maybe you have the *Shield of Boringness* turned up too high.
I no longer USE it around you.
You are currently being blasted with the FULL FORCE of my unicornosity.
dana
You do look nice today.
It is too late! My ego cannot be un-wounded.

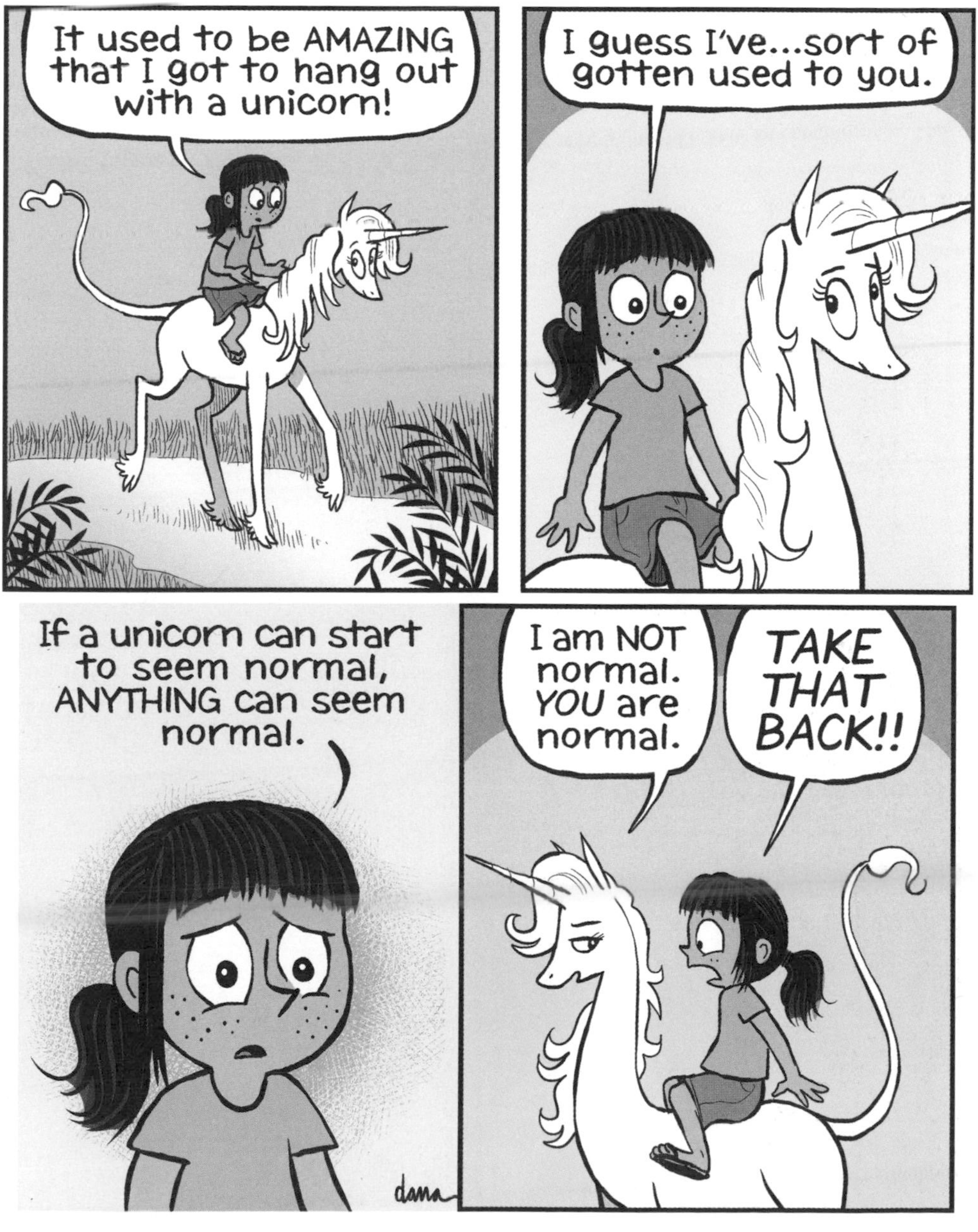
It used to be AMAZING that I got to hang out with a unicorn!
I guess I've...sort of gotten used to you.
If a unicorn can start to seem normal, ANYTHING can seem normal.
I am NOT normal. YOU are normal.
TAKE THAT BACK!!
dana

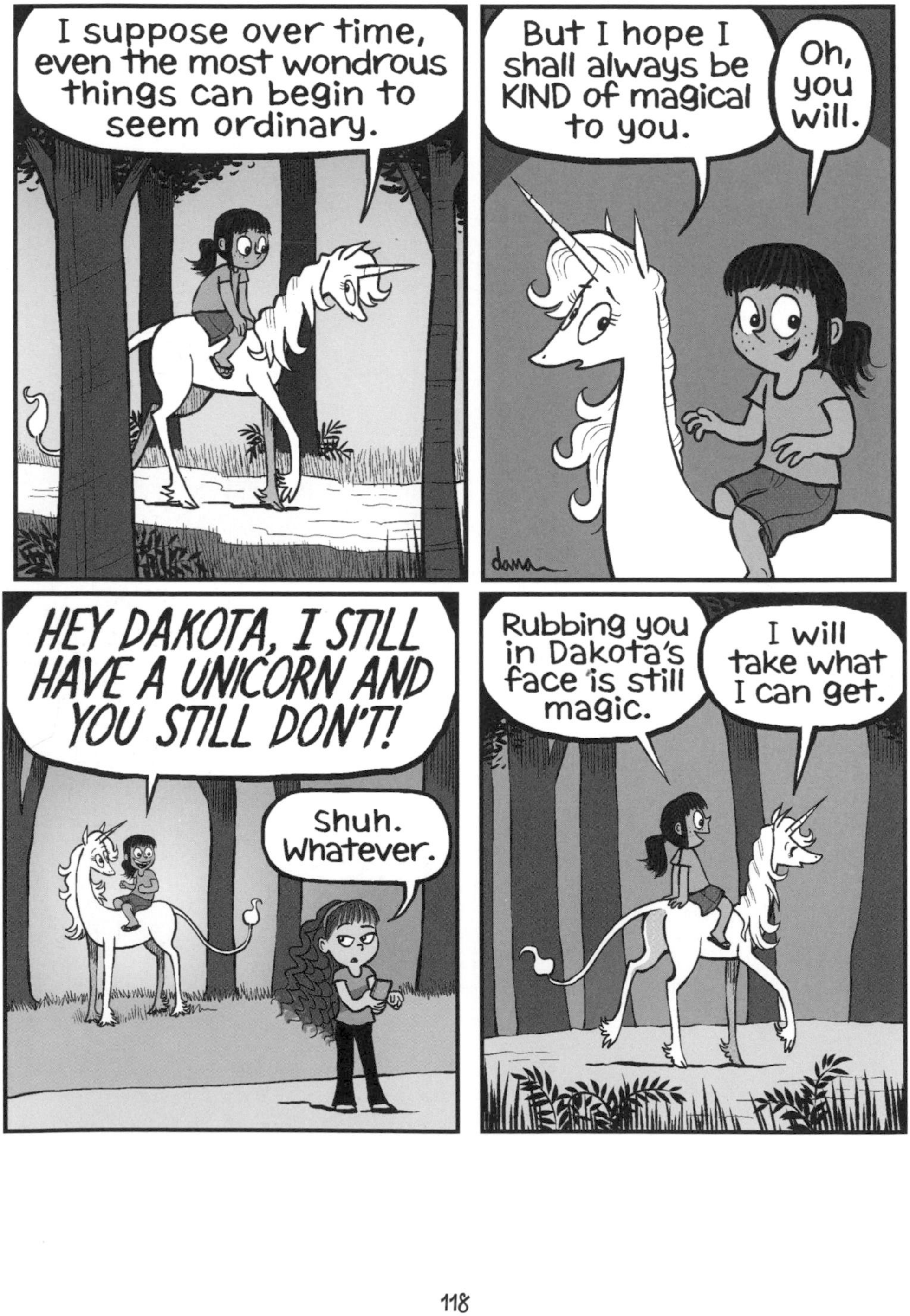
I suppose over time, even the most wondrous things can begin to seem ordinary.
But I hope I shall always be KIND of magical to you.
Oh, you will.
dana
HEY DAKOTA, I STILL HAVE A UNICORN AND YOU STILL DON'T!
Shuh. Whatever.
Rubbing you in Dakota's face is still magic.
I will take what I can get.

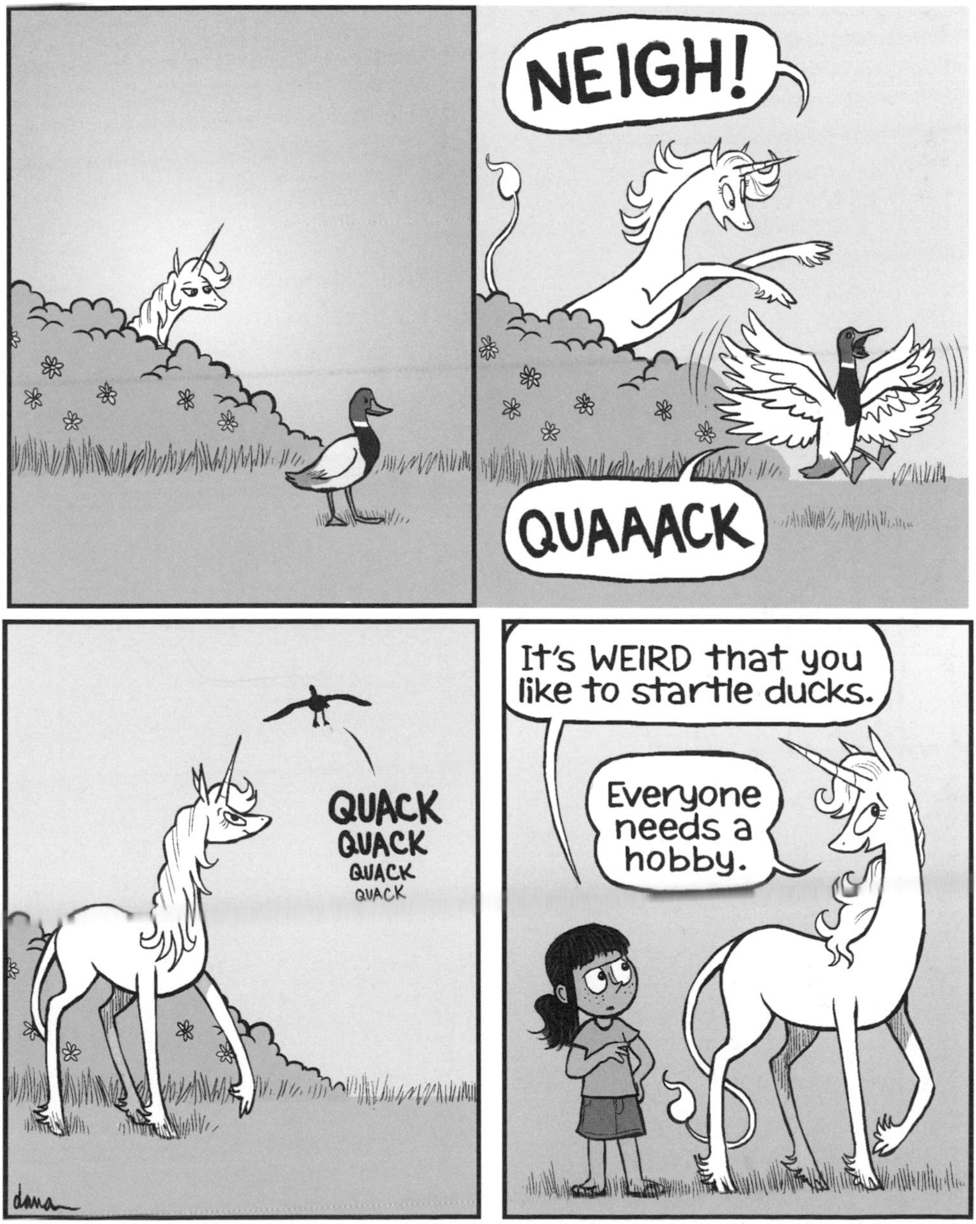
NEIGH!
QUAAACK
QUACK
QUACK
QUACK
QUACK
It's WEIRD that you like to startle ducks.
Everyone needs a hobby.
dana

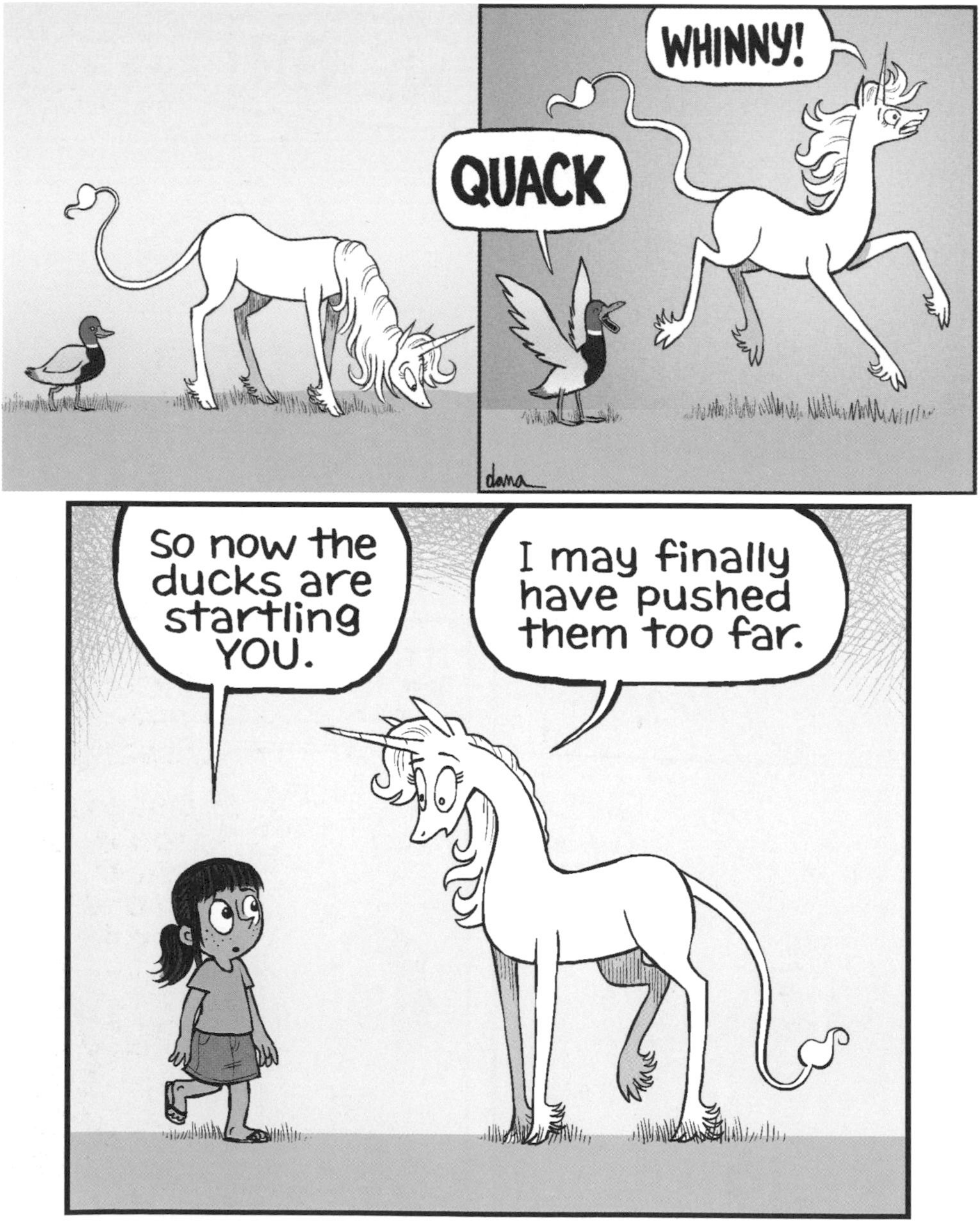
WHINNY!
QUACK
dana
So now the ducks are startling YOU.
I may finally have pushed them too far.

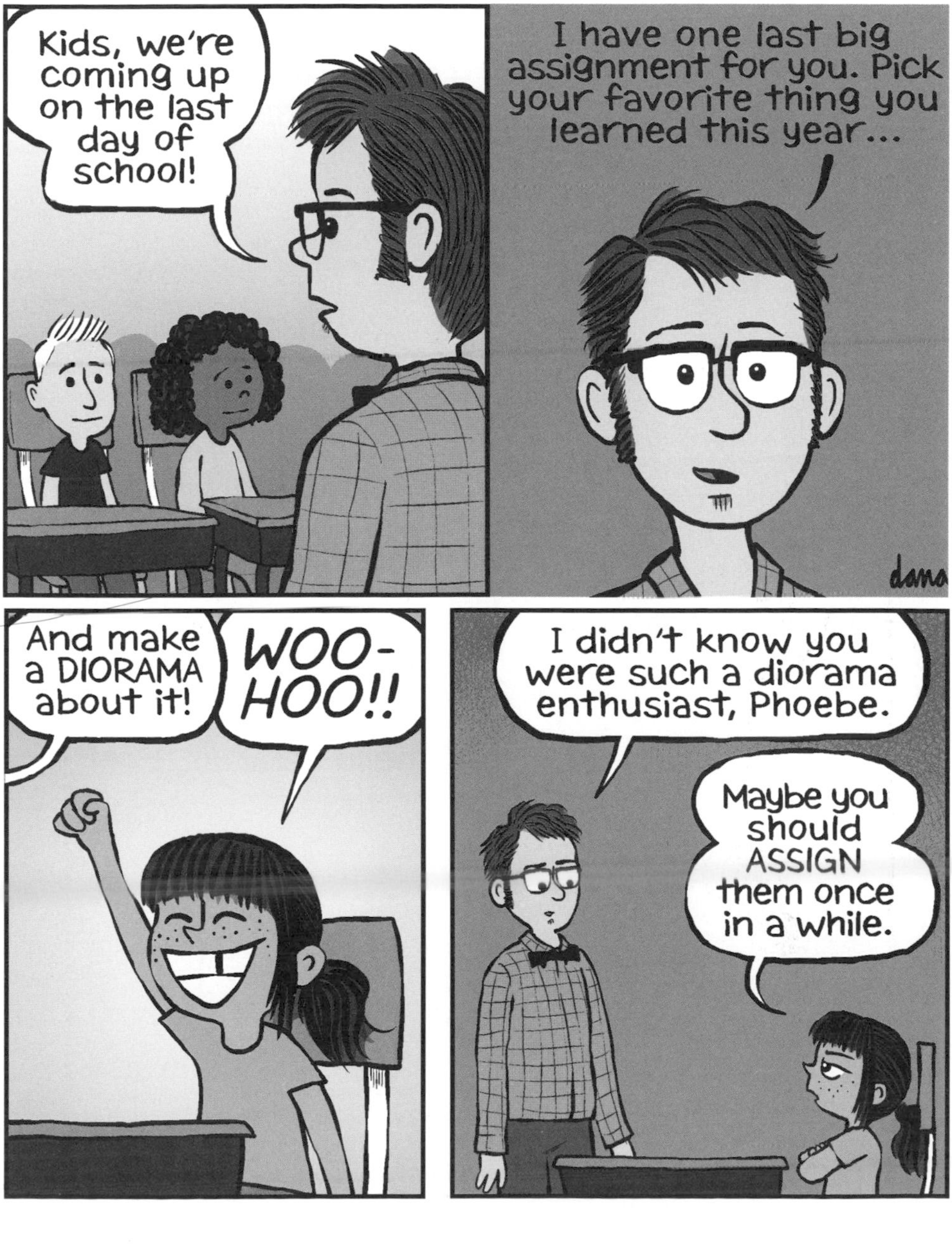

Kids, we're coming up on the last day of school!
I have one last big assignment for you. Pick your favorite thing you learned this year...
dana
And make a DIORAMA about it!
WOO-HOO!!
I didn't know you were such a diorama enthusiast, Phoebe.
Maybe you should ASSIGN them once in a while.

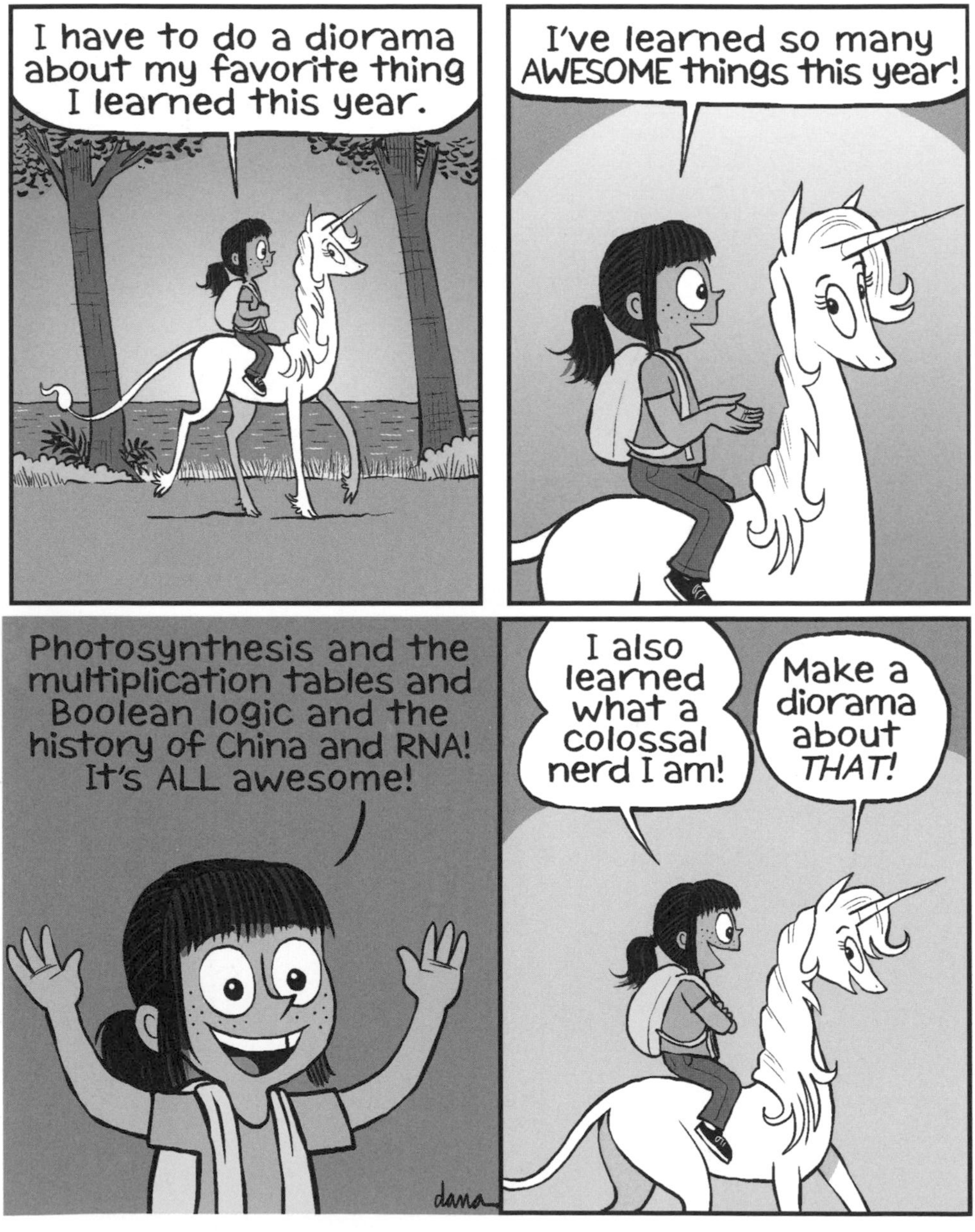
I have to do a diorama about my favorite thing I learned this year.
I've learned so many AWESOME things this year!
Photosynthesis and the multiplication tables and Boolean logic and the history of China and RNA! It's ALL awesome!
dana
I also learned what a colossal nerd I am!
Make a diorama about THAT!

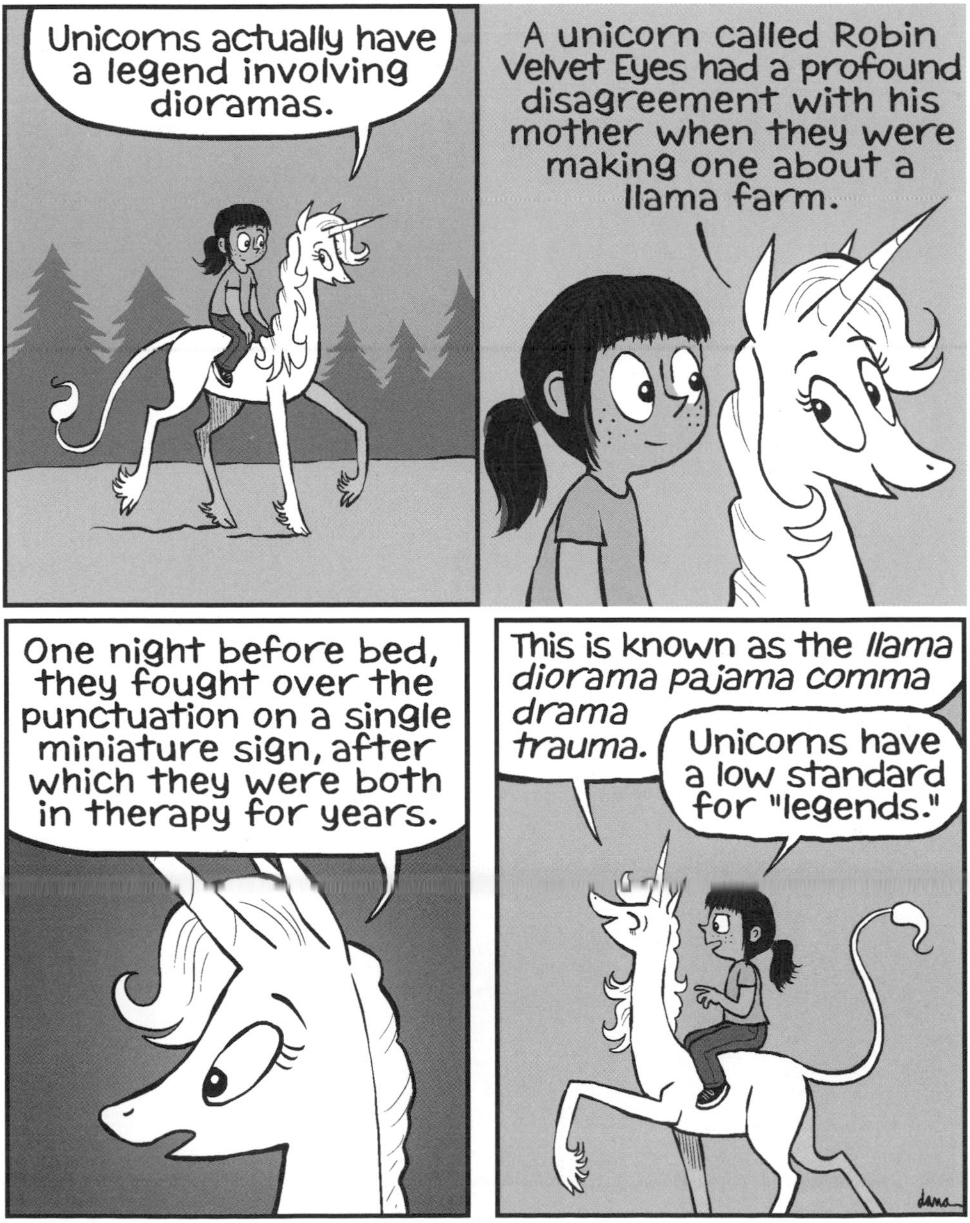
Unicorns actually have a legend involving dioramas.
A unicorn called Robin Velvet Eyes had a profound disagreement with his mother when they were making one about a llama farm.
One night before bed, they fought over the punctuation on a single miniature sign, after which they were both in therapy for years.
This is known as the *llama diorama pajama comma drama trauma.*
Unicorns have a low standard for "legends."
dana

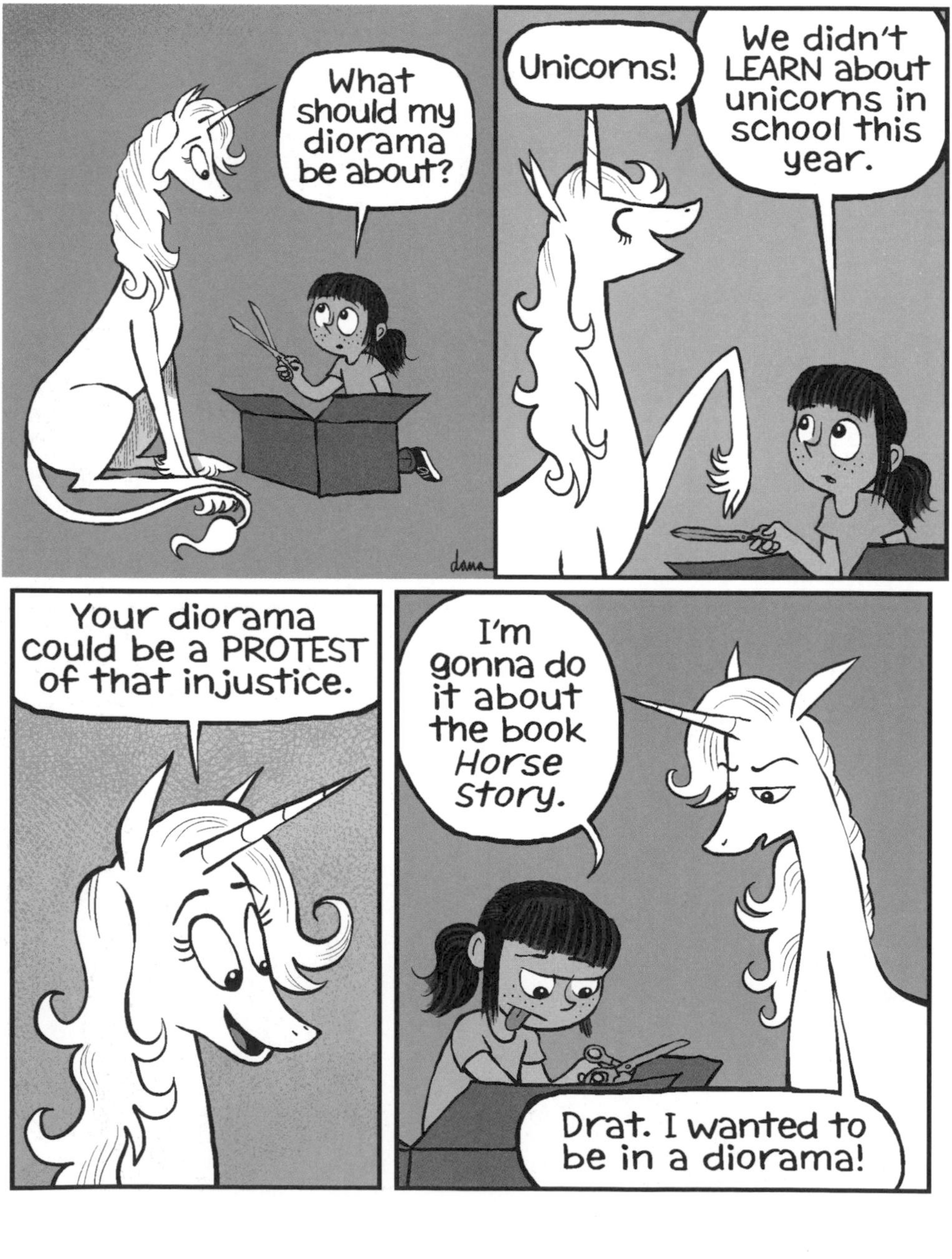
What should my diorama be about?
Unicorns!
We didn't LEARN about unicorns in school this year.
Your diorama could be a PROTEST of that injustice.
I'm gonna do it about the book *Horse Story*.
Drat. I wanted to be in a diorama!
dana

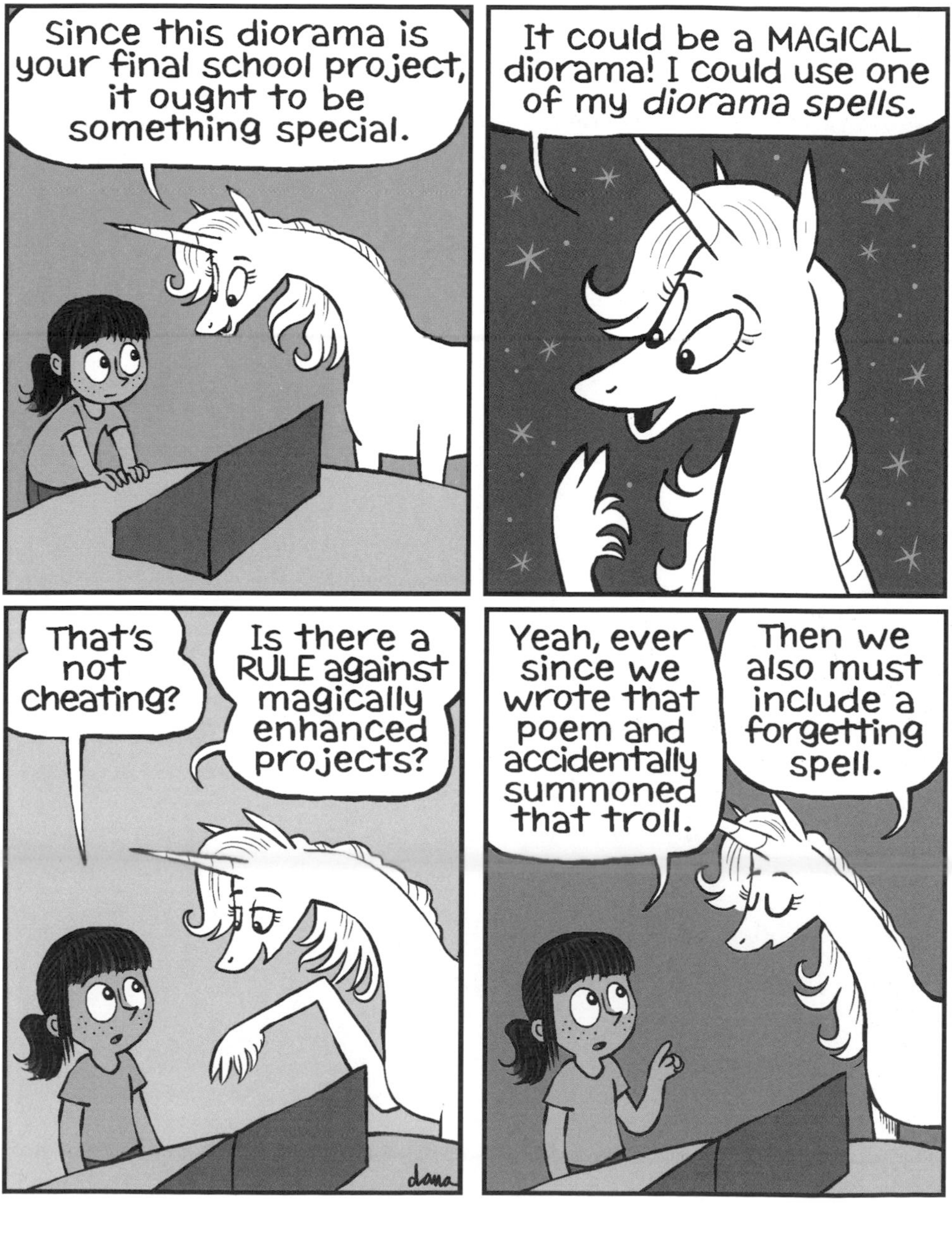
Since this diorama is your final school project, it ought to be something special.
It could be a MAGICAL diorama! I could use one of my *diorama spells.*
That's not cheating?
Is there a RULE against magically enhanced projects?
Yeah, ever since we wrote that poem and accidentally summoned that troll.
Then we also must include a forgetting spell.
dana

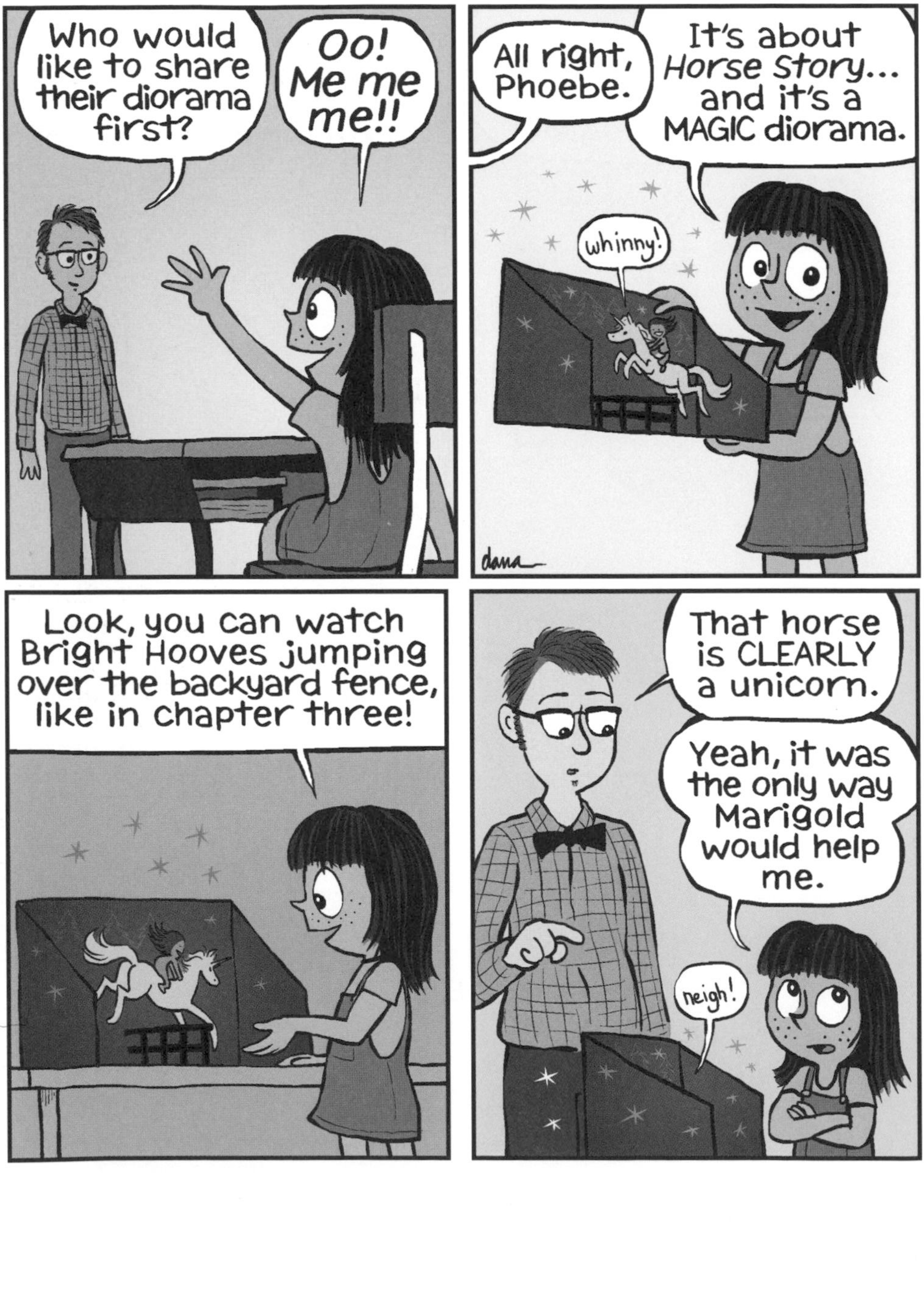

Who would like to share their diorama first?
Oo! Me me me!!
All right, Phoebe.
It's about *Horse Story*... and it's a MAGIC diorama.
whinny!
dana
Look, you can watch Bright Hooves jumping over the backyard fence, like in chapter three!
That horse is CLEARLY a unicorn.
Yeah, it was the only way Marigold would help me.
neigh!

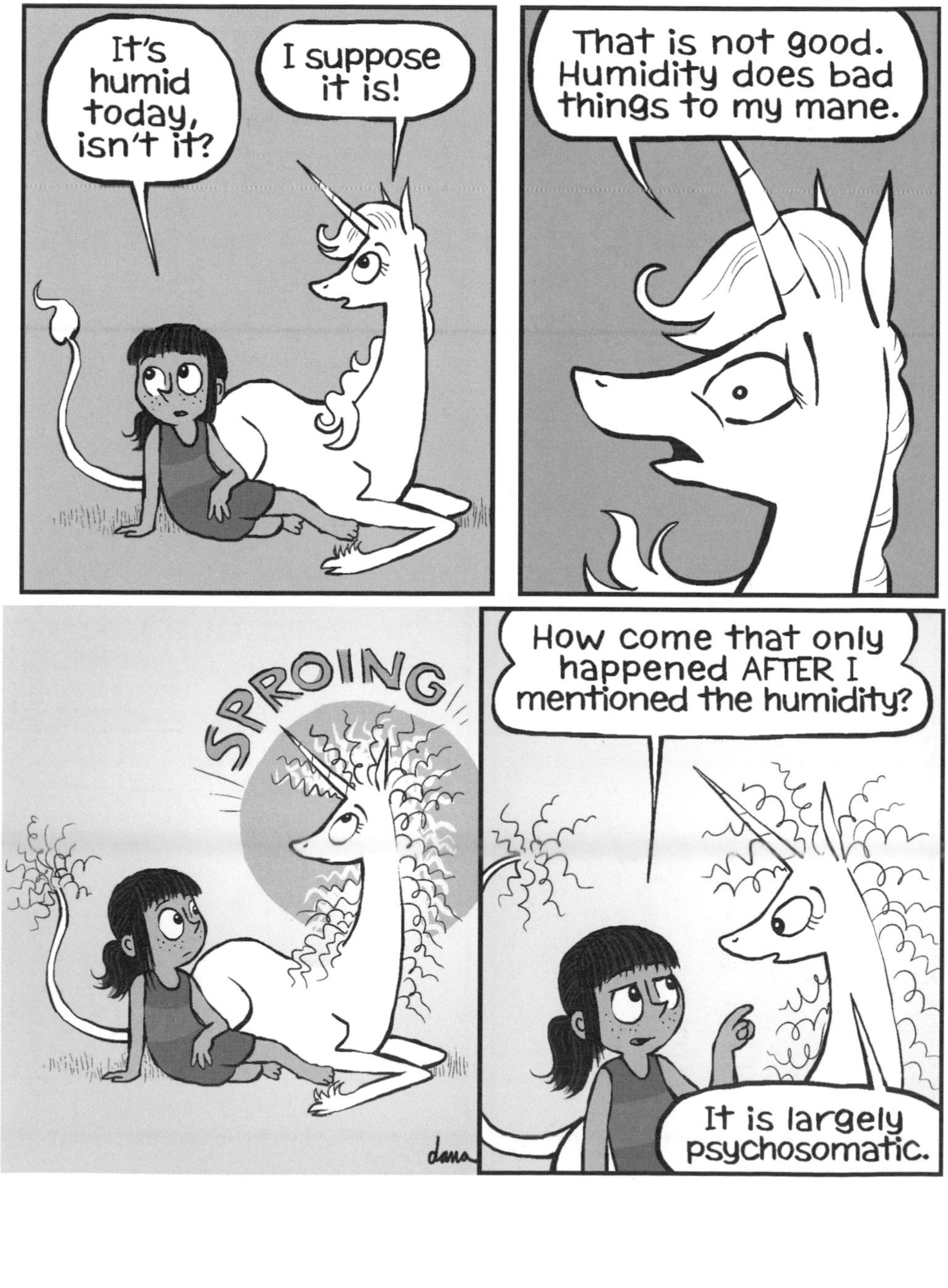
It's humid today, isn't it?
I suppose it is!
That is not good. Humidity does bad things to my mane.
SPROING
How come that only happened AFTER I mentioned the humidity?
It is largely psychosomatic.
dana

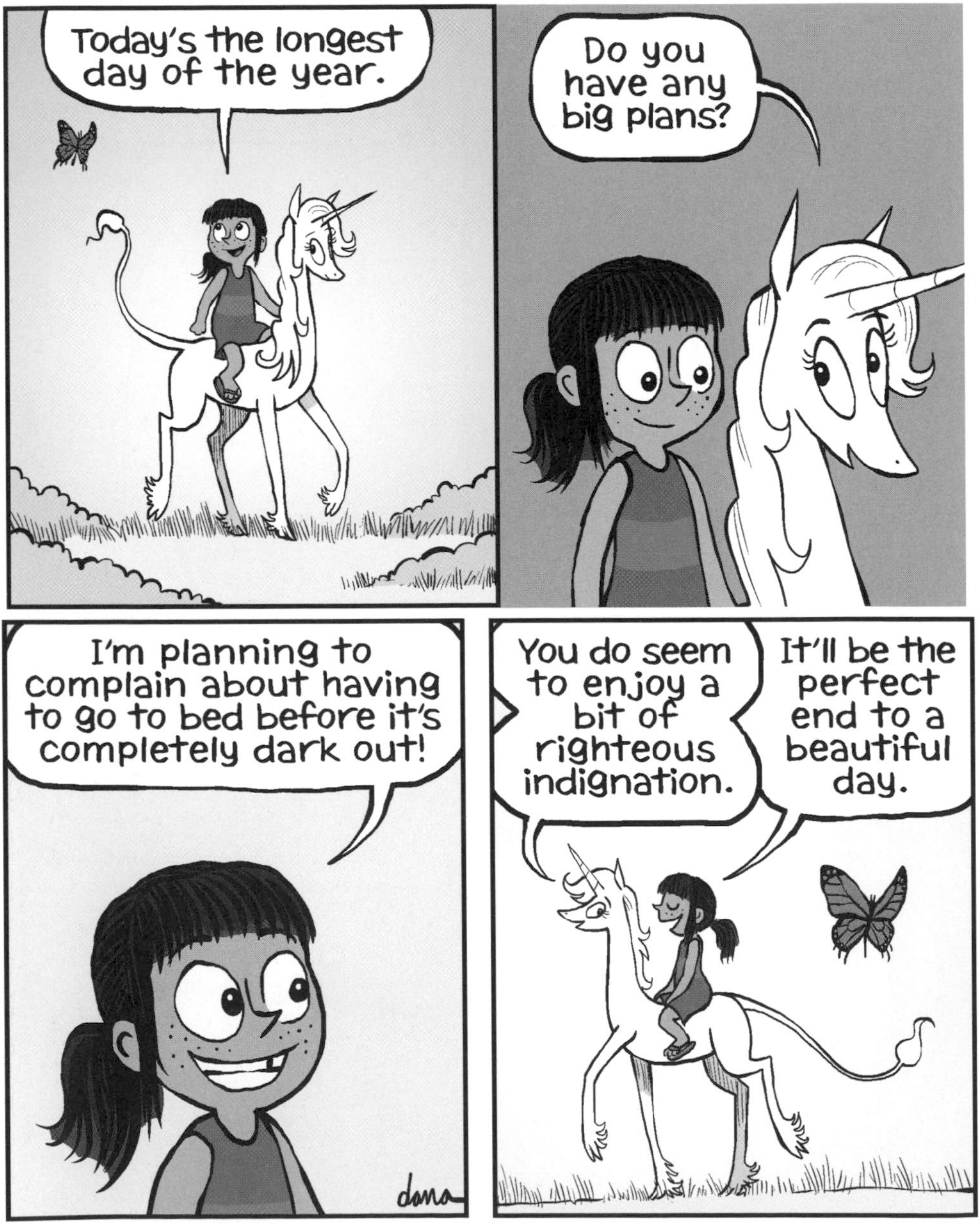
Today's the longest day of the year.
Do you have any big plans?
I'm planning to complain about having to go to bed before it's completely dark out!
You do seem to enjoy a bit of righteous indignation.
It'll be the perfect end to a beautiful day.
dana

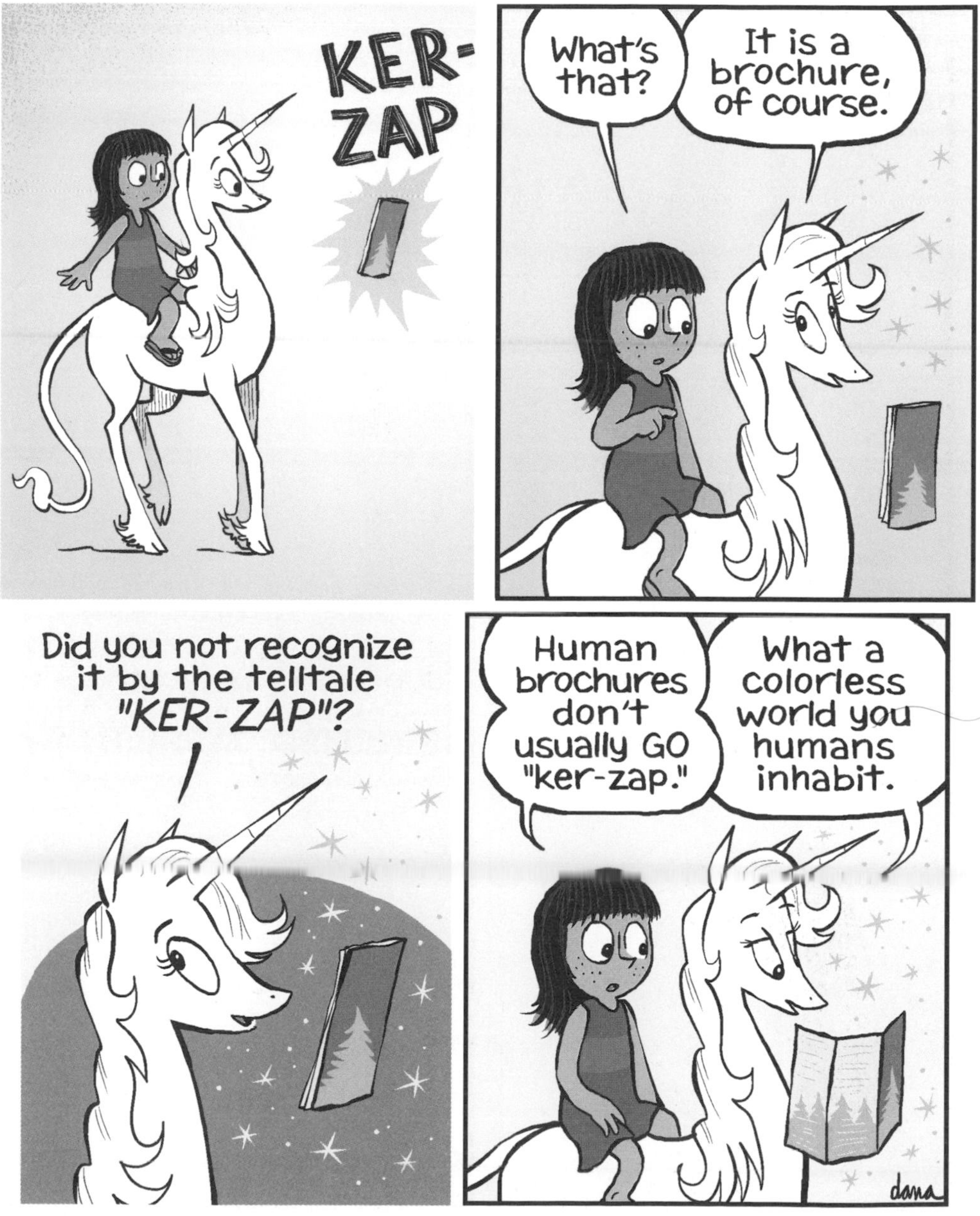
KER-ZAP
What's that?
It is a brochure, of course.
Did you not recognize it by the telltale "KER-ZAP"?
Human brochures don't usually GO "ker-zap."
What a colorless world you humans inhabit.
dana

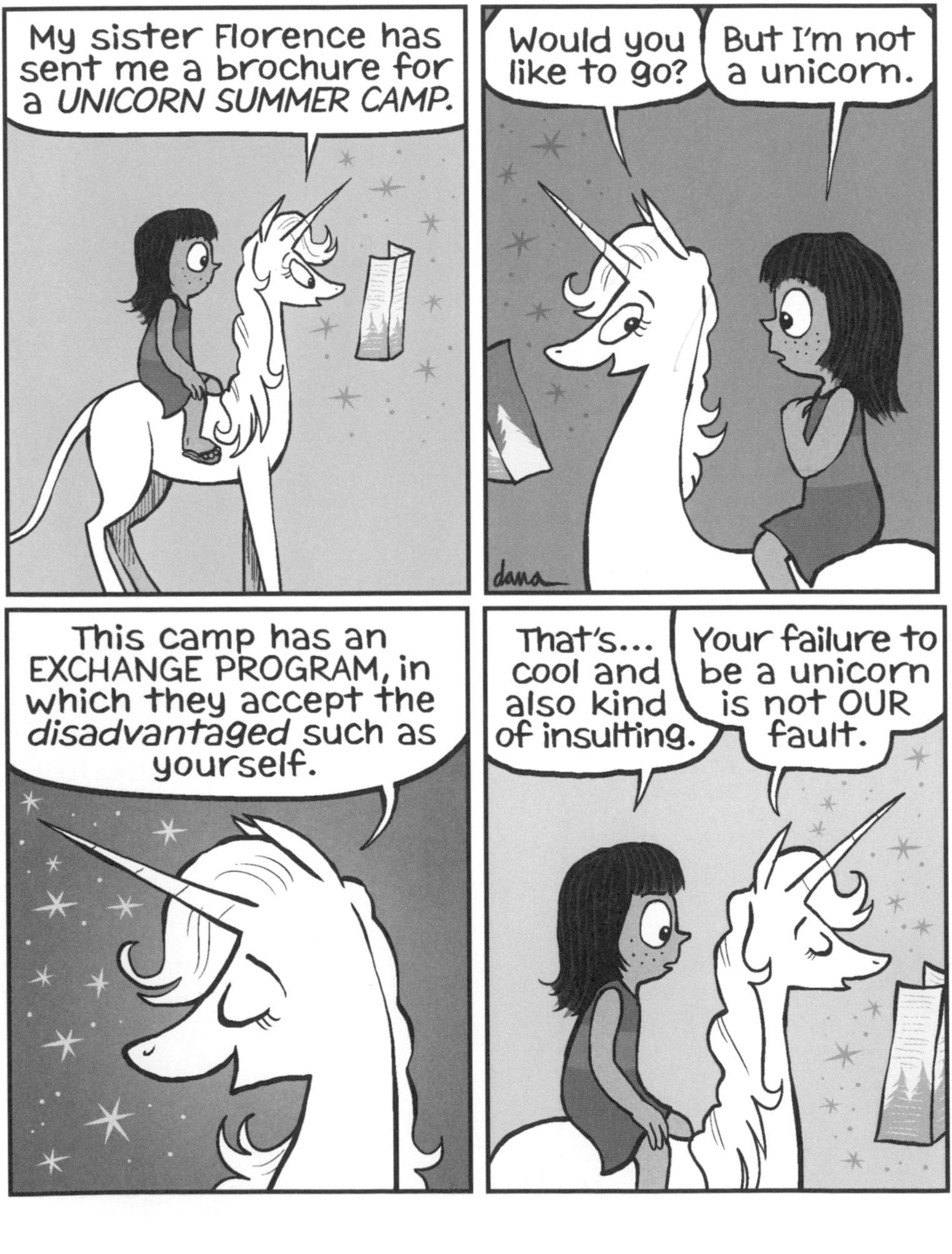
My sister Florence has sent me a brochure for a *UNICORN SUMMER CAMP.*
Would you like to go?
But I'm not a unicorn.
dana
This camp has an EXCHANGE PROGRAM, in which they accept the *disadvantaged* such as yourself.
That's... cool and also kind of insulting.
Your failure to be a unicorn is not OUR fault.

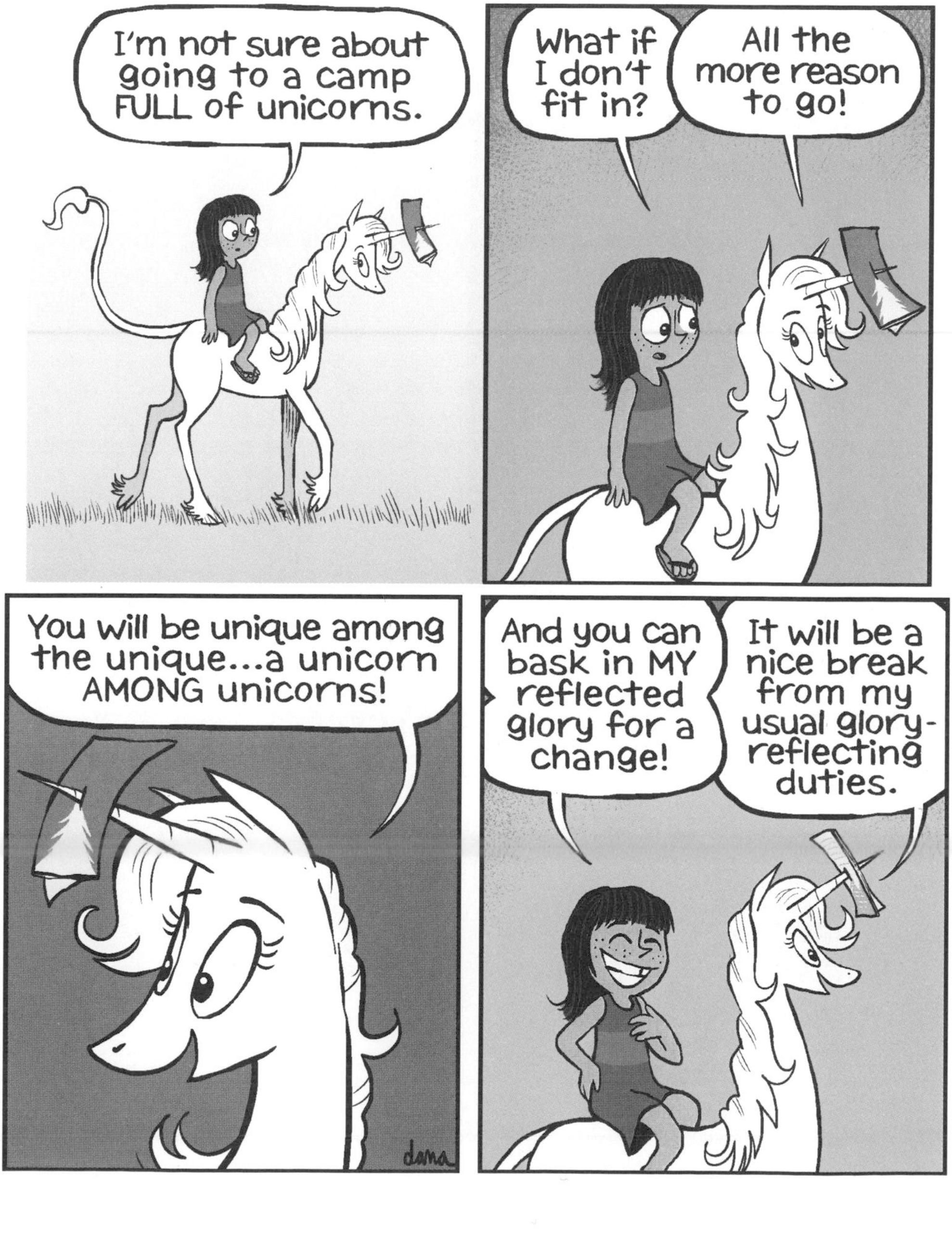
I'm not sure about going to a camp FULL of unicorns.
What if I don't fit in?
All the more reason to go!
You will be unique among the unique...a unicorn AMONG unicorns!
dana
And you can bask in MY reflected glory for a change!
It will be a nice break from my usual glory-reflecting duties.

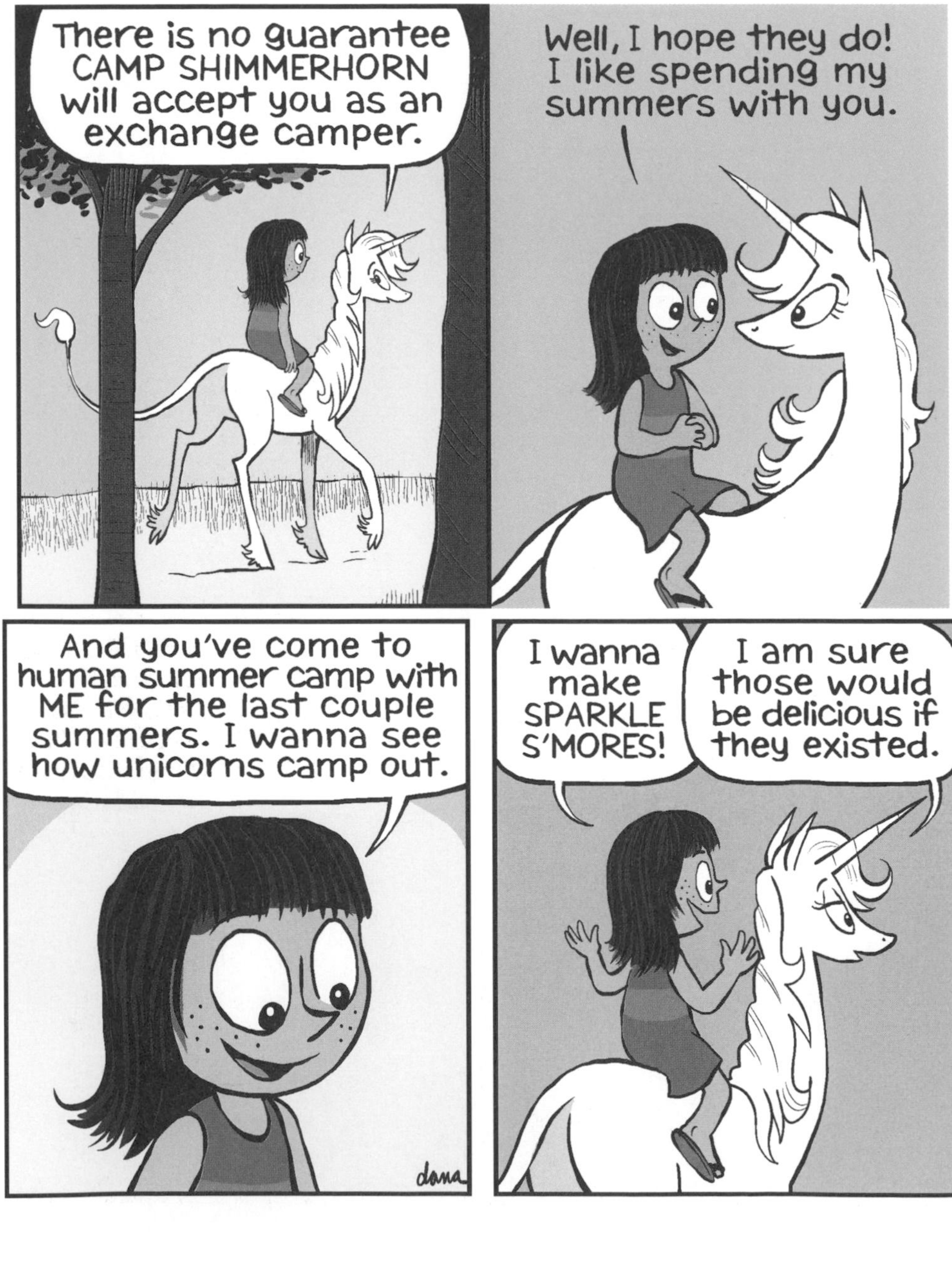
There is no guarantee CAMP SHIMMERHORN will accept you as an exchange camper.
Well, I hope they do! I like spending my summers with you.
And you've come to human summer camp with ME for the last couple summers. I wanna see how unicorns camp out.
dana
I wanna make SPARKLE S'MORES!
I am sure those would be delicious if they existed.

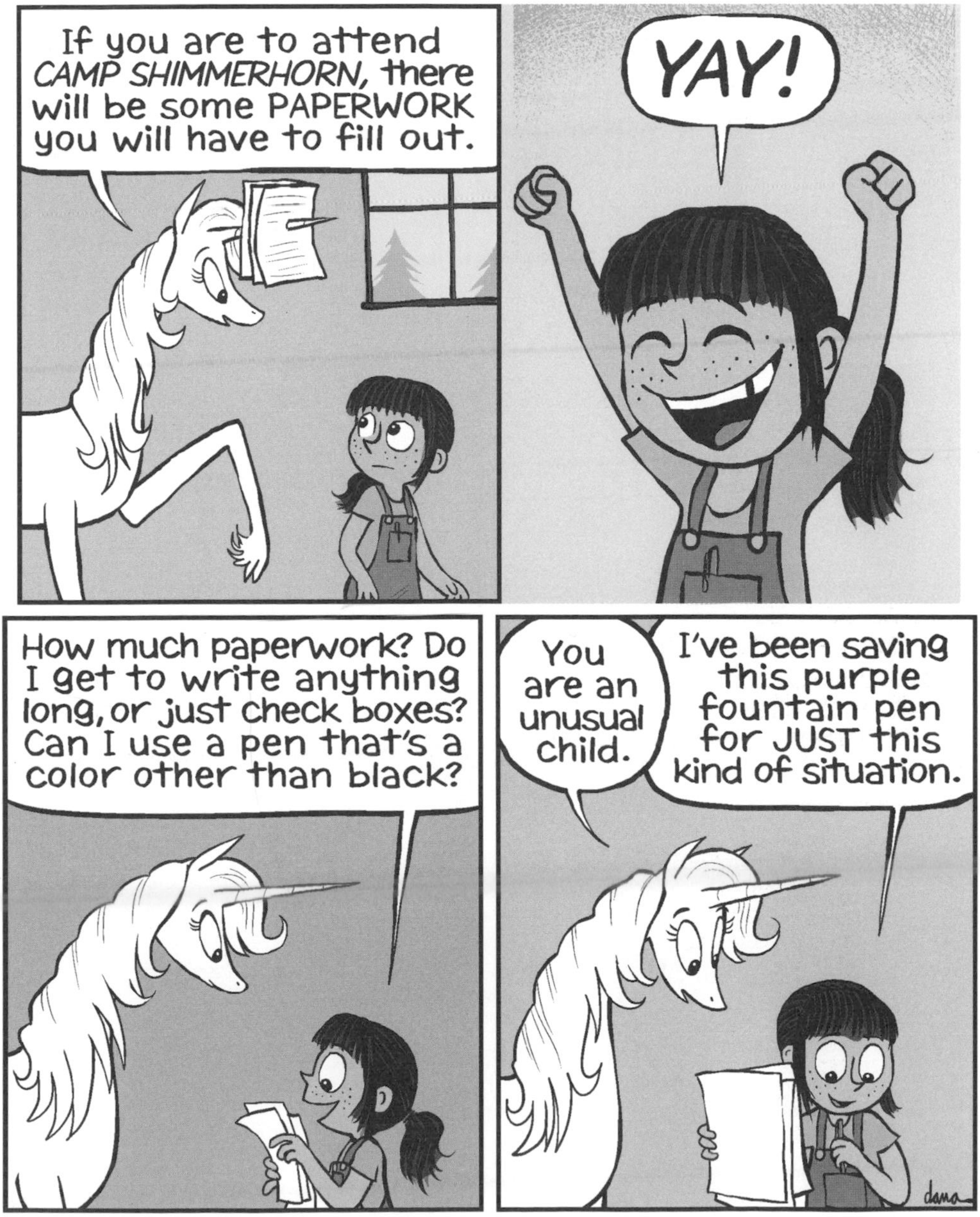
If you are to attend *CAMP SHIMMERHORN*, there will be some PAPERWORK you will have to fill out.
YAY!
How much paperwork? Do I get to write anything long, or just check boxes? Can I use a pen that's a color other than black?
You are an unusual child.
I've been saving this purple fountain pen for JUST this kind of situation.
dana

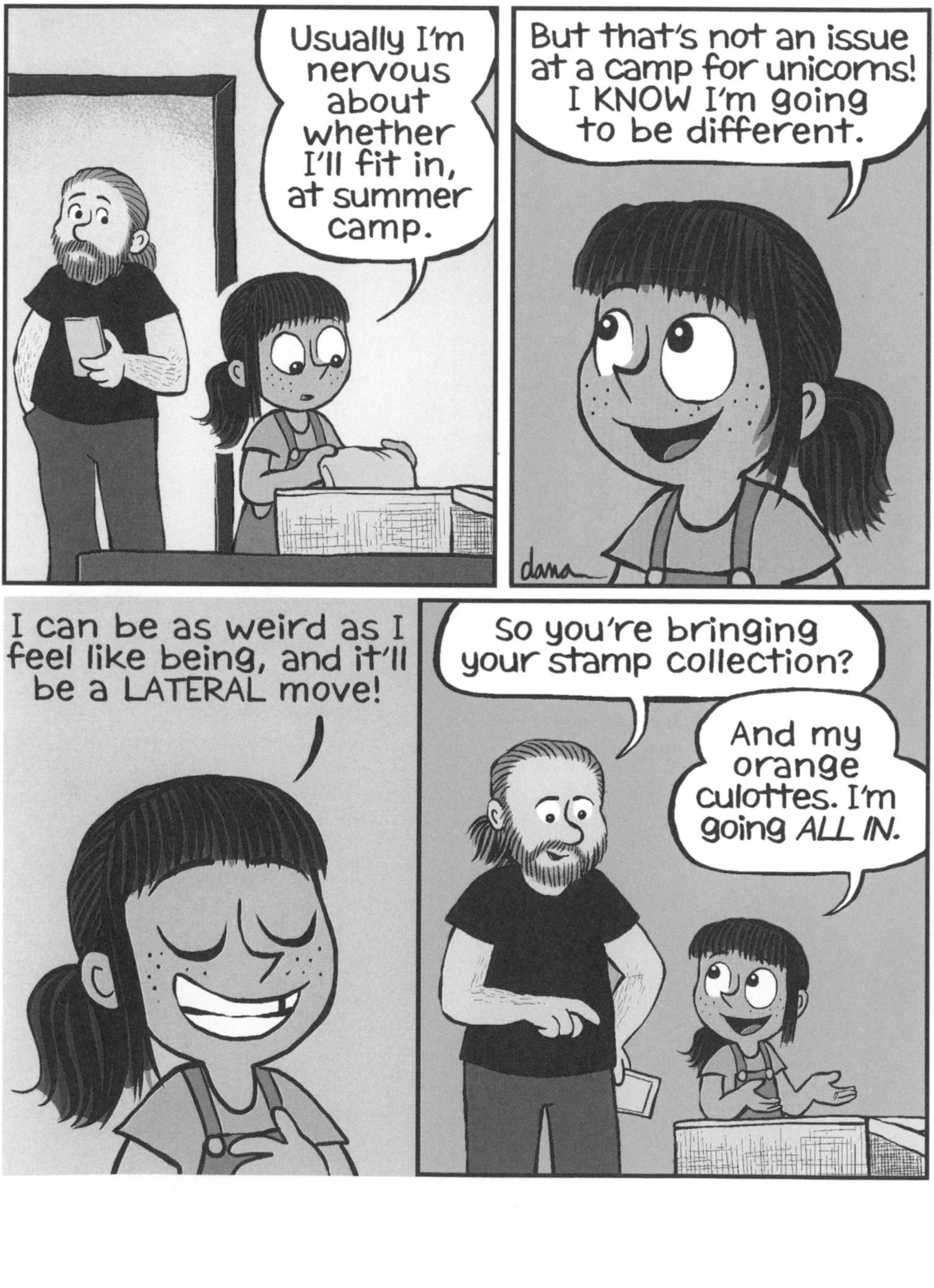
Usually I'm nervous about whether I'll fit in, at summer camp.
But that's not an issue at a camp for unicorns! I KNOW I'm going to be different.
dana
I can be as weird as I feel like being, and it'll be a LATERAL move!
So you're bringing your stamp collection?
And my orange culottes. I'm going *ALL IN*.

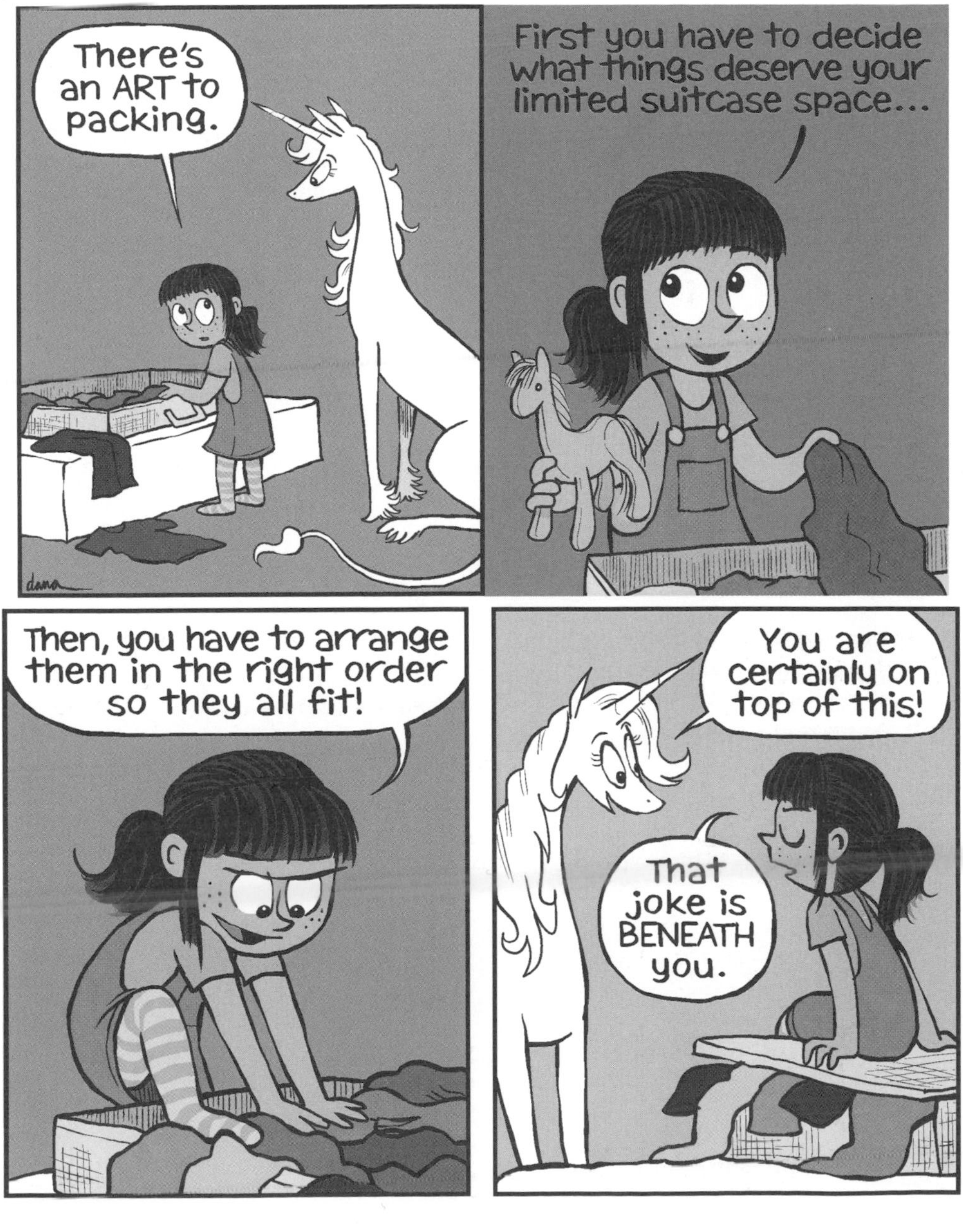
There's an ART to packing.
First you have to decide what things deserve your limited suitcase space...
Then, you have to arrange them in the right order so they all fit!
You are certainly on top of this!
That joke is BENEATH you.

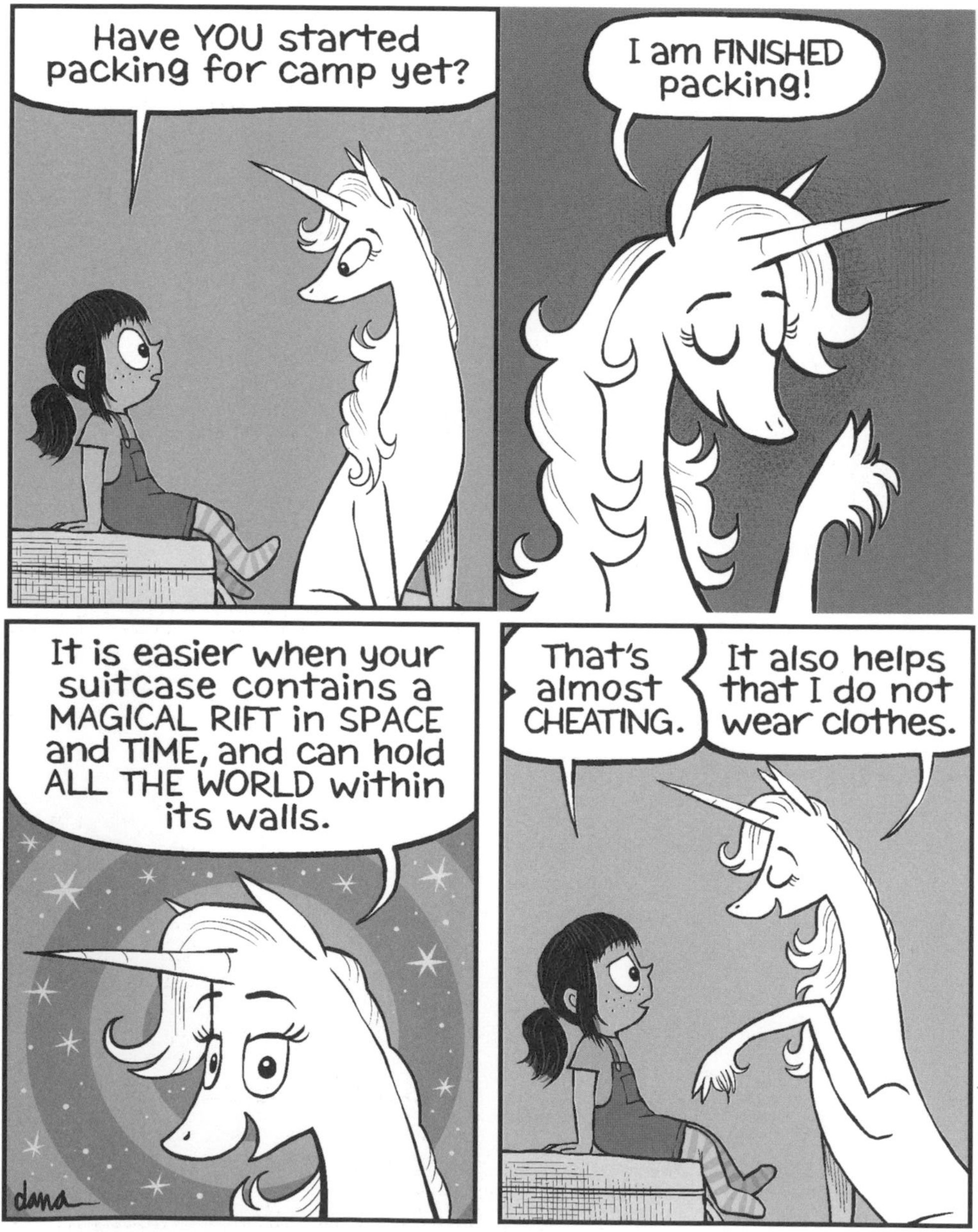
Have YOU started packing for camp yet?
I am FINISHED packing!
It is easier when your suitcase contains a MAGICAL RIFT in SPACE and TIME, and can hold ALL THE WORLD within its walls.
dana
That's almost CHEATING.
It also helps that I do not wear clothes.

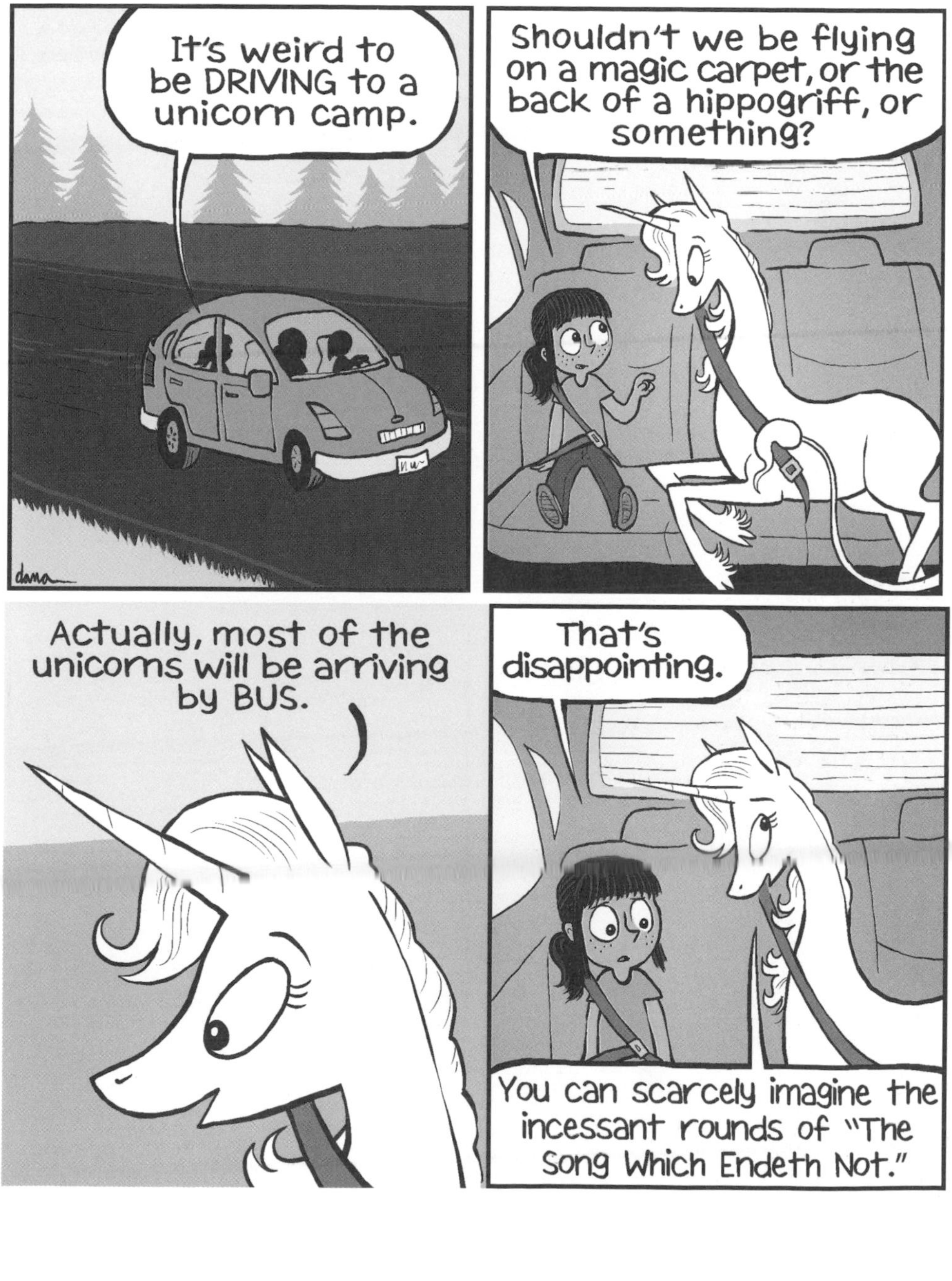
It's weird to be DRIVING to a unicorn camp.
Shouldn't we be flying on a magic carpet, or the back of a hippogriff, or something?
Actually, most of the unicorns will be arriving by BUS.
That's disappointing.
You can scarcely imagine the incessant rounds of "The Song Which Endeth Not."

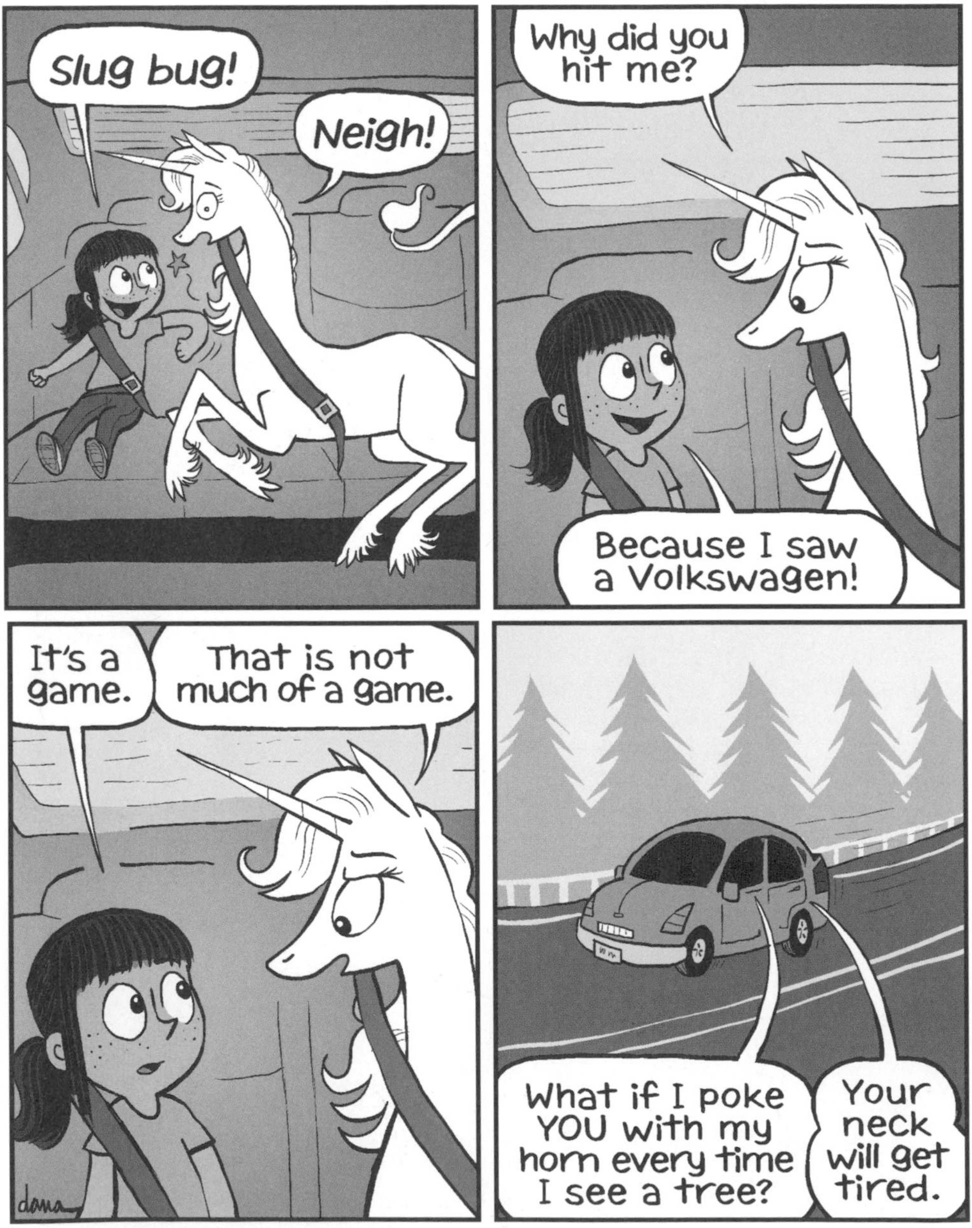
Slug bug!
Neigh!
Why did you hit me?
Because I saw a Volkswagen!
It's a game.
That is not much of a game.
What if I poke YOU with my horn every time I see a tree?
Your neck will get tired.

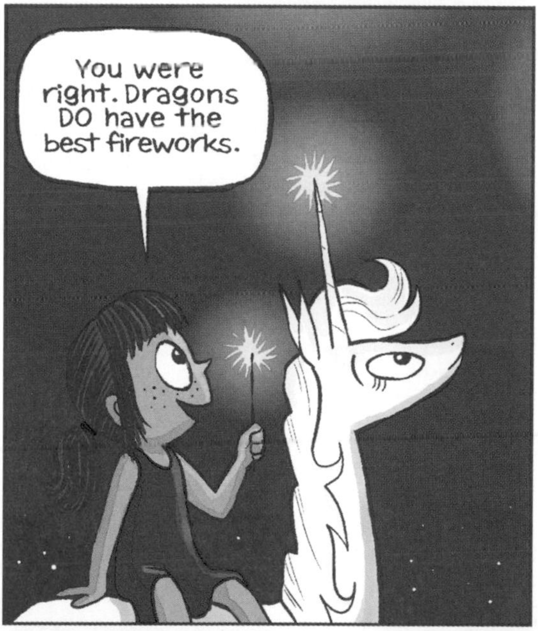
You were right. Dragons DO have the best fireworks.

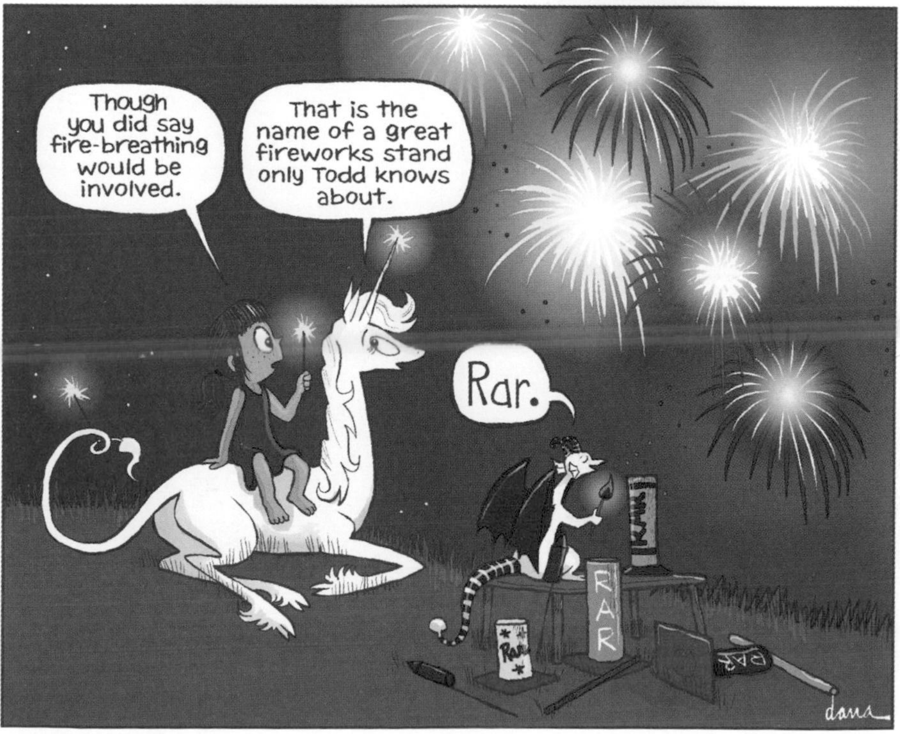
Though you did say fire-breathing would be involved.
That is the name of a great fireworks stand only Todd knows about.
Rar.
RAR
dana

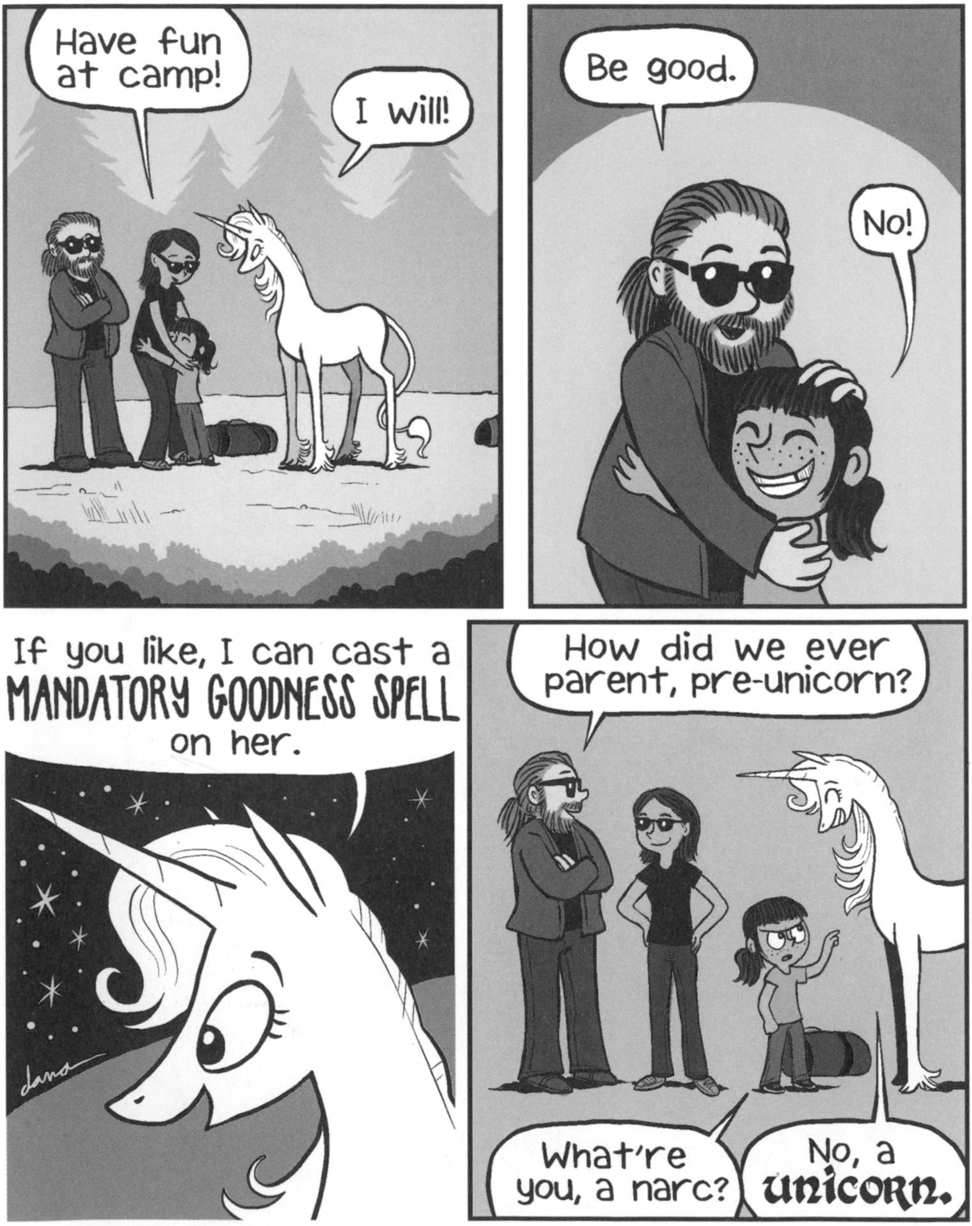
Have fun at camp!
I will!
Be good.
No!
If you like, I can cast a MANDATORY GOODNESS SPELL on her.
How did we ever parent, pre-unicorn?
What're you, a narc?
No, a UNICORN.

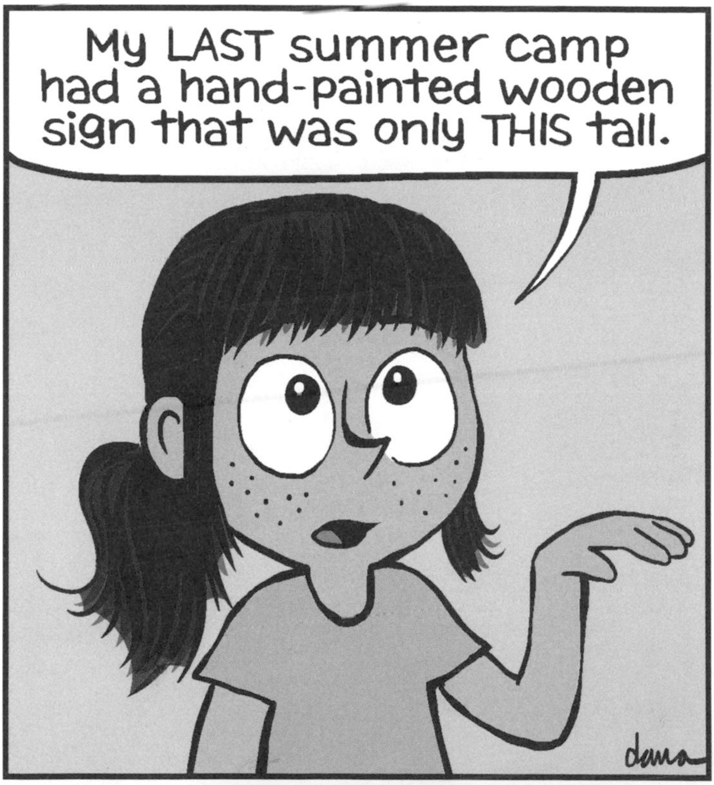
My LAST summer camp had a hand-painted wooden sign that was only THIS tall.
dana

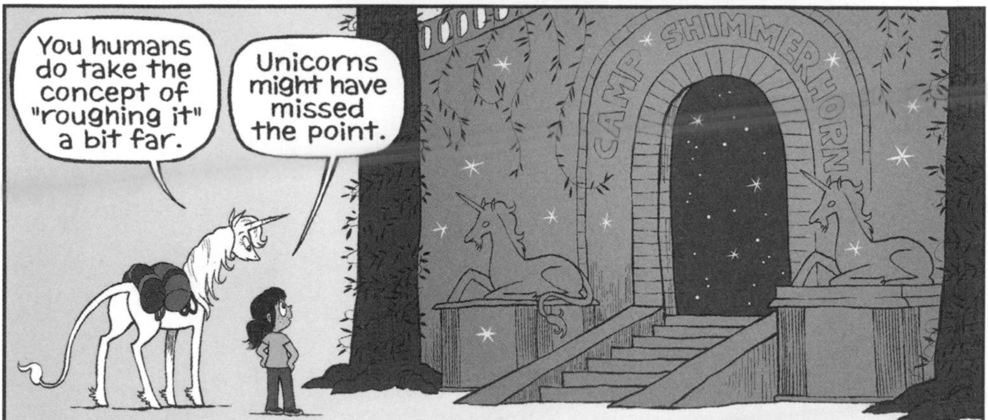
You humans do take the concept of "roughing it" a bit far.
Unicorns might have missed the point.
CAMP SHIMMERHORN

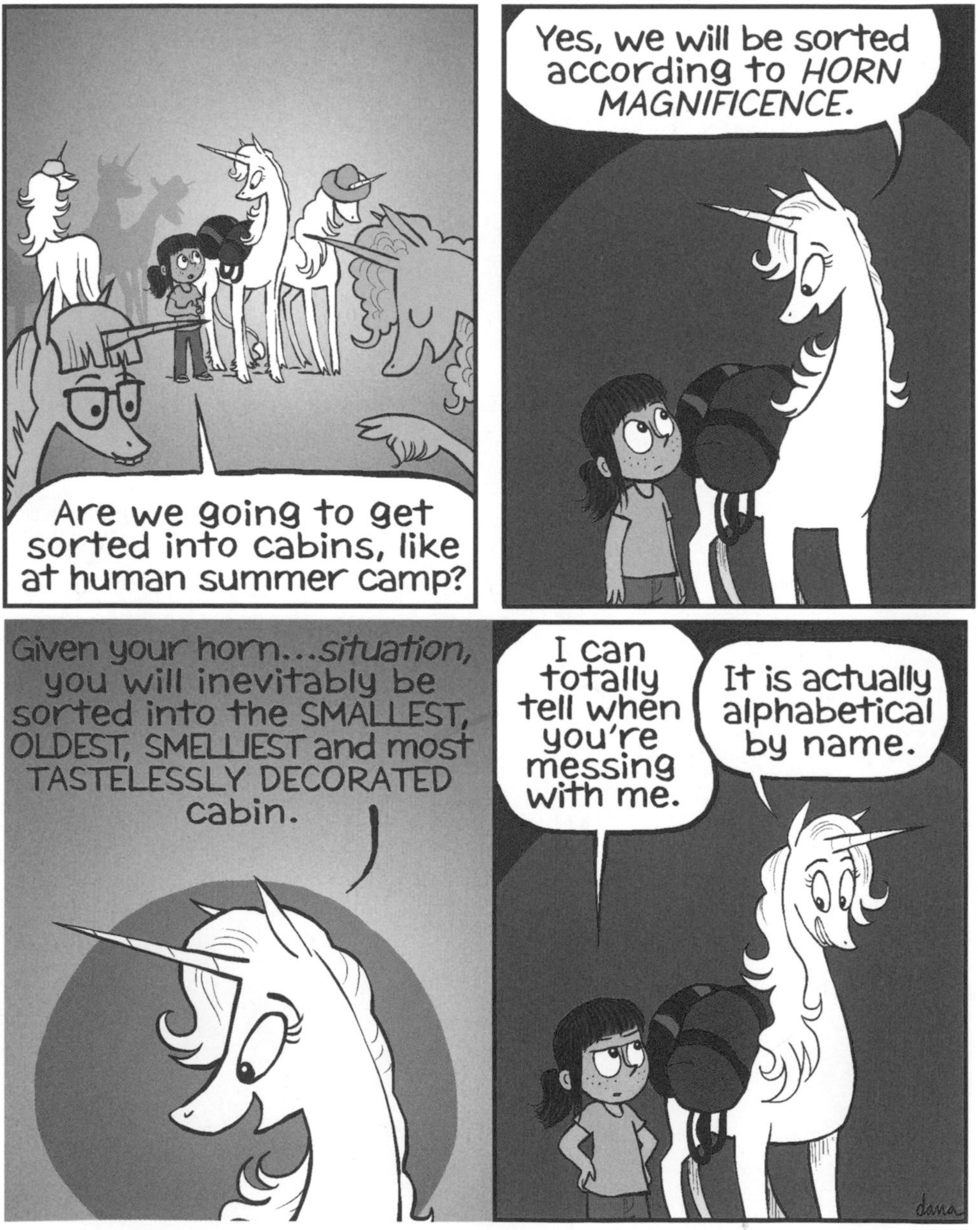
Are we going to get sorted into cabins, like at human summer camp?
Yes, we will be sorted according to *HORN MAGNIFICENCE.*
Given your horn...*situation,* you will inevitably be sorted into the SMALLEST, OLDEST, SMELLIEST and most TASTELESSLY DECORATED cabin.
I can totally tell when you're messing with me.
It is actually alphabetical by name.
dana

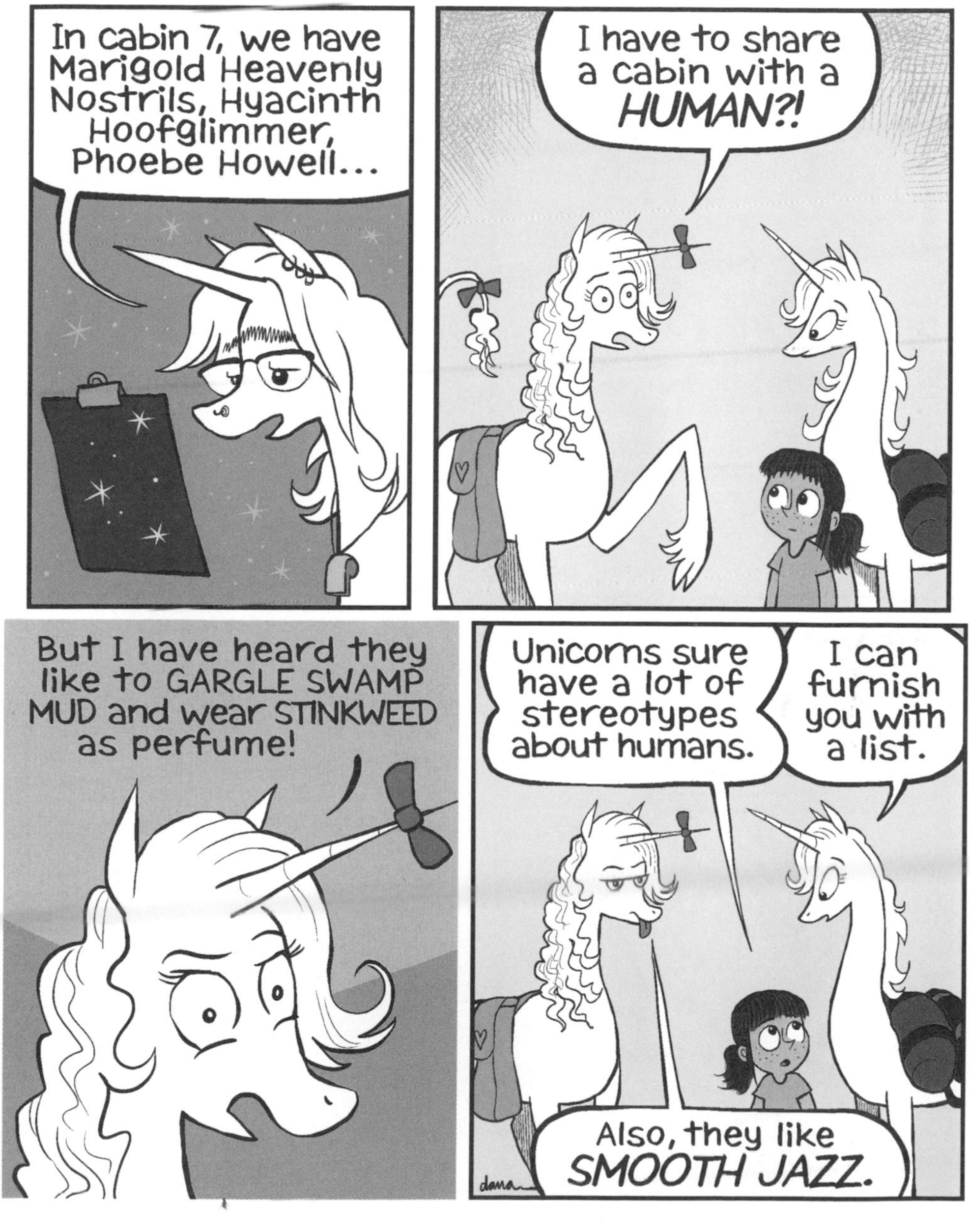
In cabin 7, we have Marigold Heavenly Nostrils, Hyacinth Hoofglimmer, Phoebe Howell...
I have to share a cabin with a HUMAN?!
But I have heard they like to GARGLE SWAMP MUD and wear STINKWEED as perfume!
Unicorns sure have a lot of stereotypes about humans.
I can furnish you with a list.
Also, they like SMOOTH JAZZ.
dana

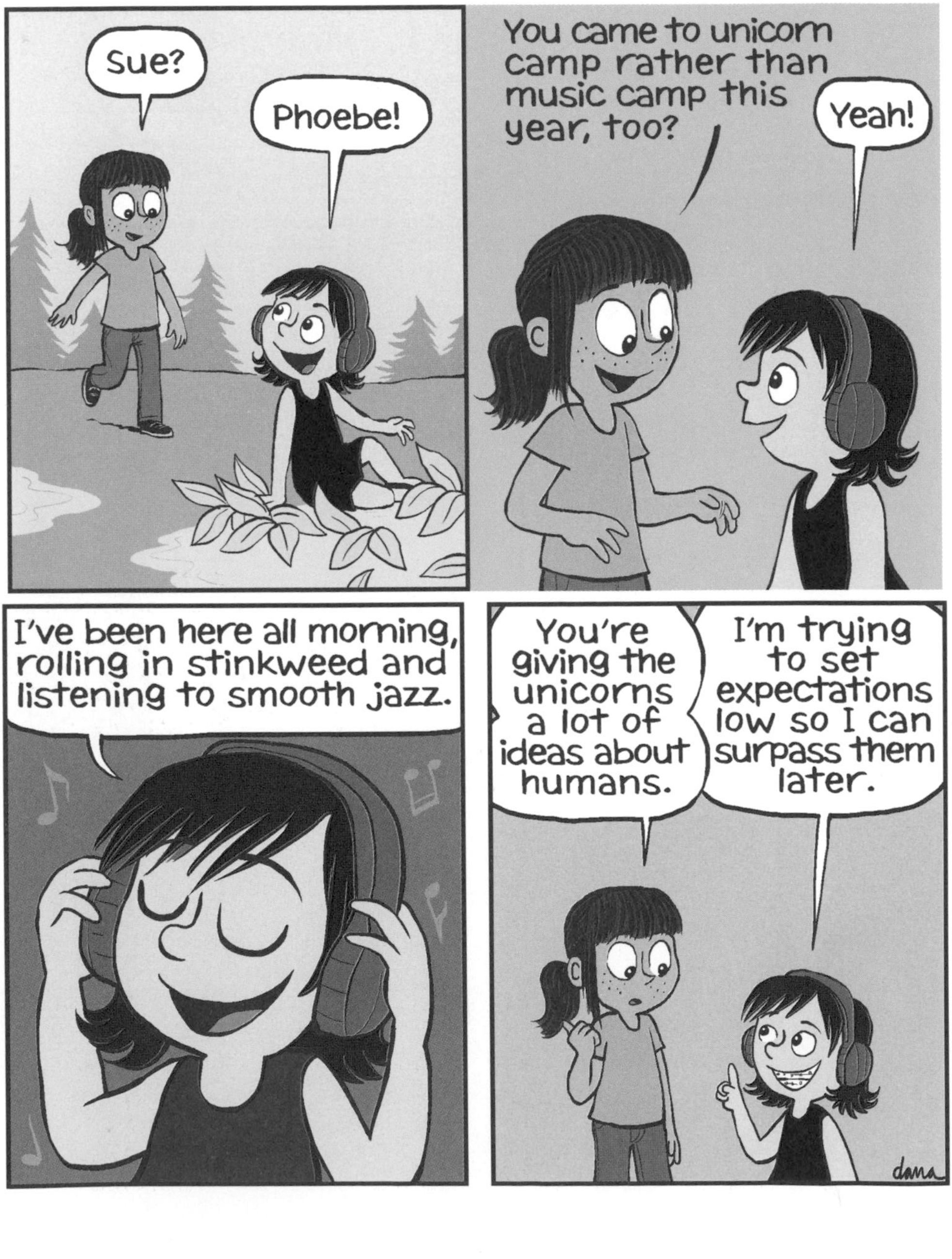

Sue?
Phoebe!
You came to unicorn camp rather than music camp this year, too?
Yeah!
I've been here all morning, rolling in stinkweed and listening to smooth jazz.
You're giving the unicorns a lot of ideas about humans.
I'm trying to set expectations low so I can surpass them later.
dana

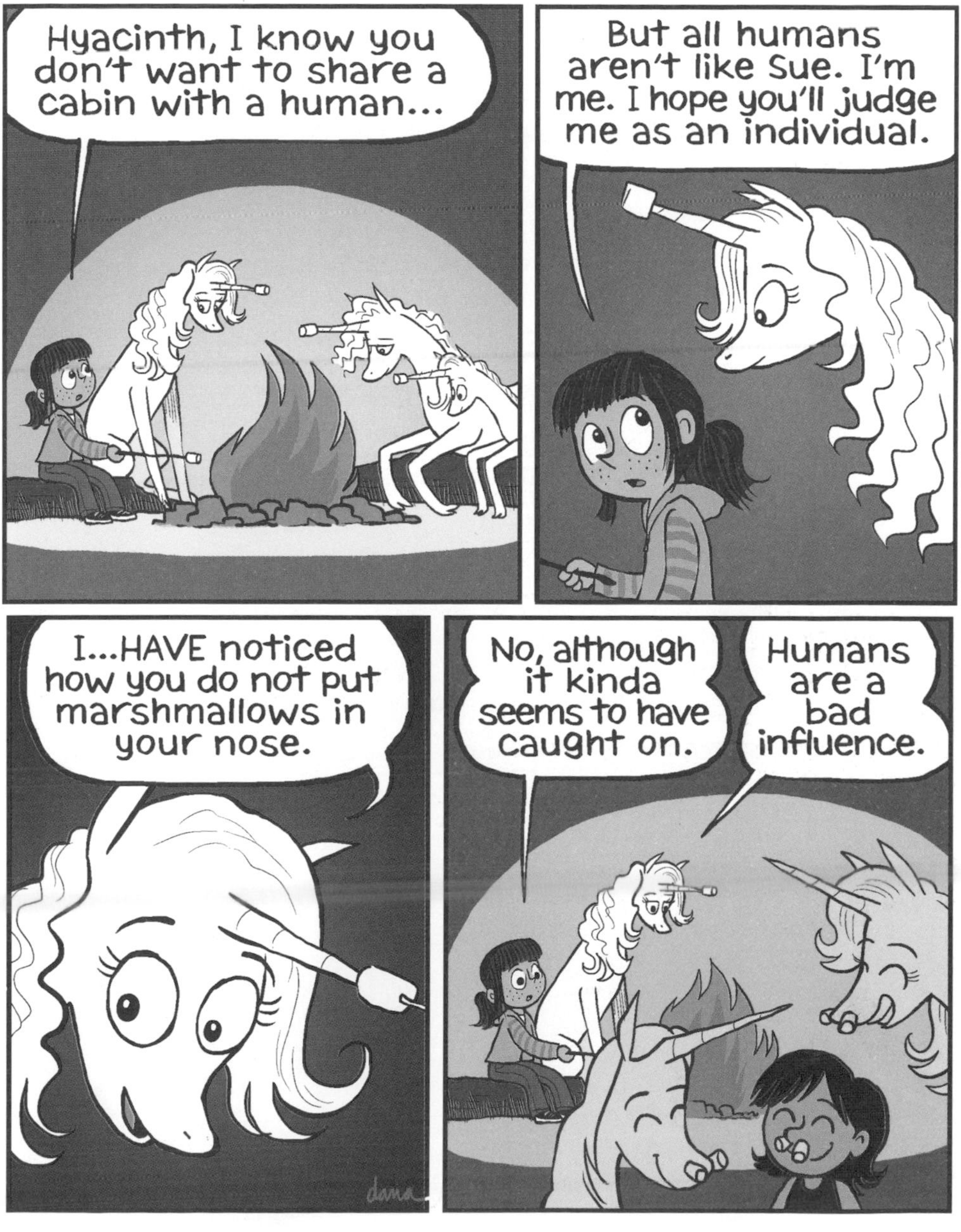
Hyacinth, I know you don't want to share a cabin with a human...
But all humans aren't like Sue. I'm me. I hope you'll judge me as an individual.
I...HAVE noticed how you do not put marshmallows in your nose.
No, although it kinda seems to have caught on.
Humans are a bad influence.
dana

Does it ever seem unfair that I ride you places?
Should it?
Well, it means you do all the work.
I have never minded.
Still, I want to be fair.

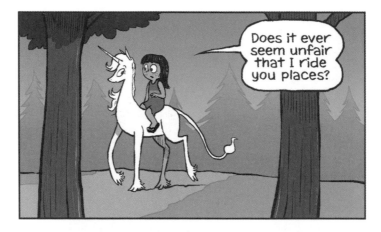

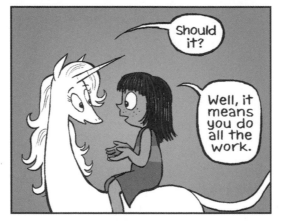

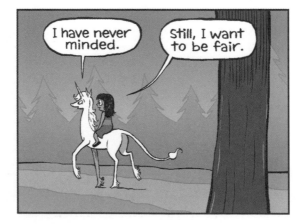

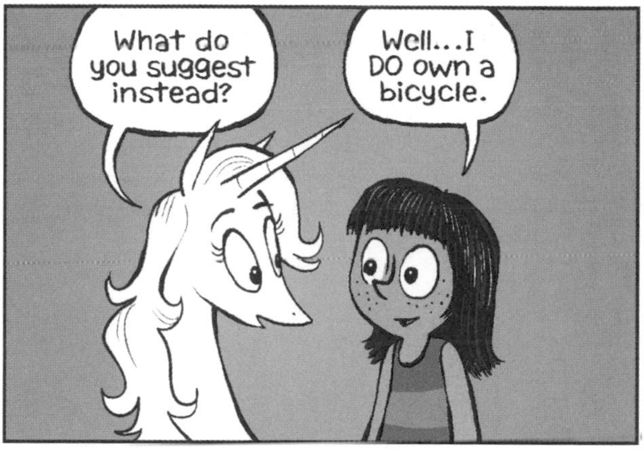
What do you suggest instead?
Well...I DO own a bicycle.

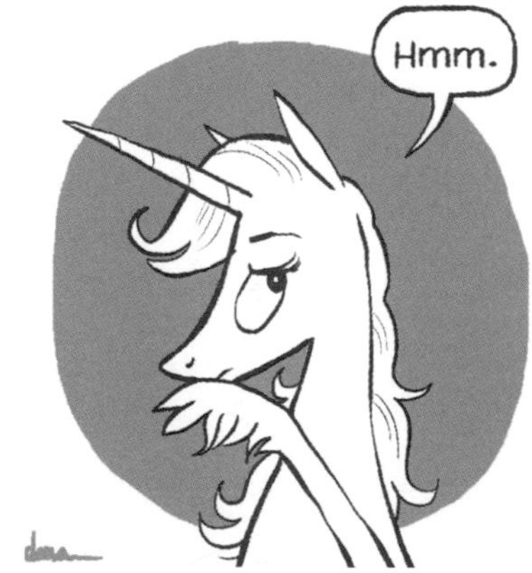
Hmm.

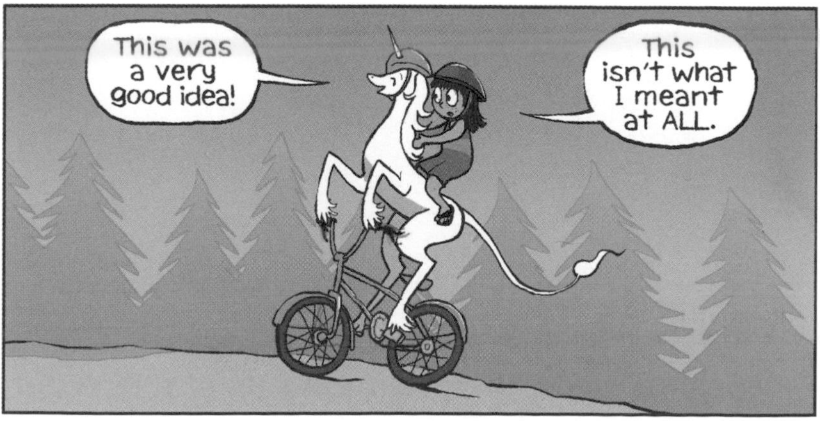
This was a very good idea!
This isn't what I meant at ALL.

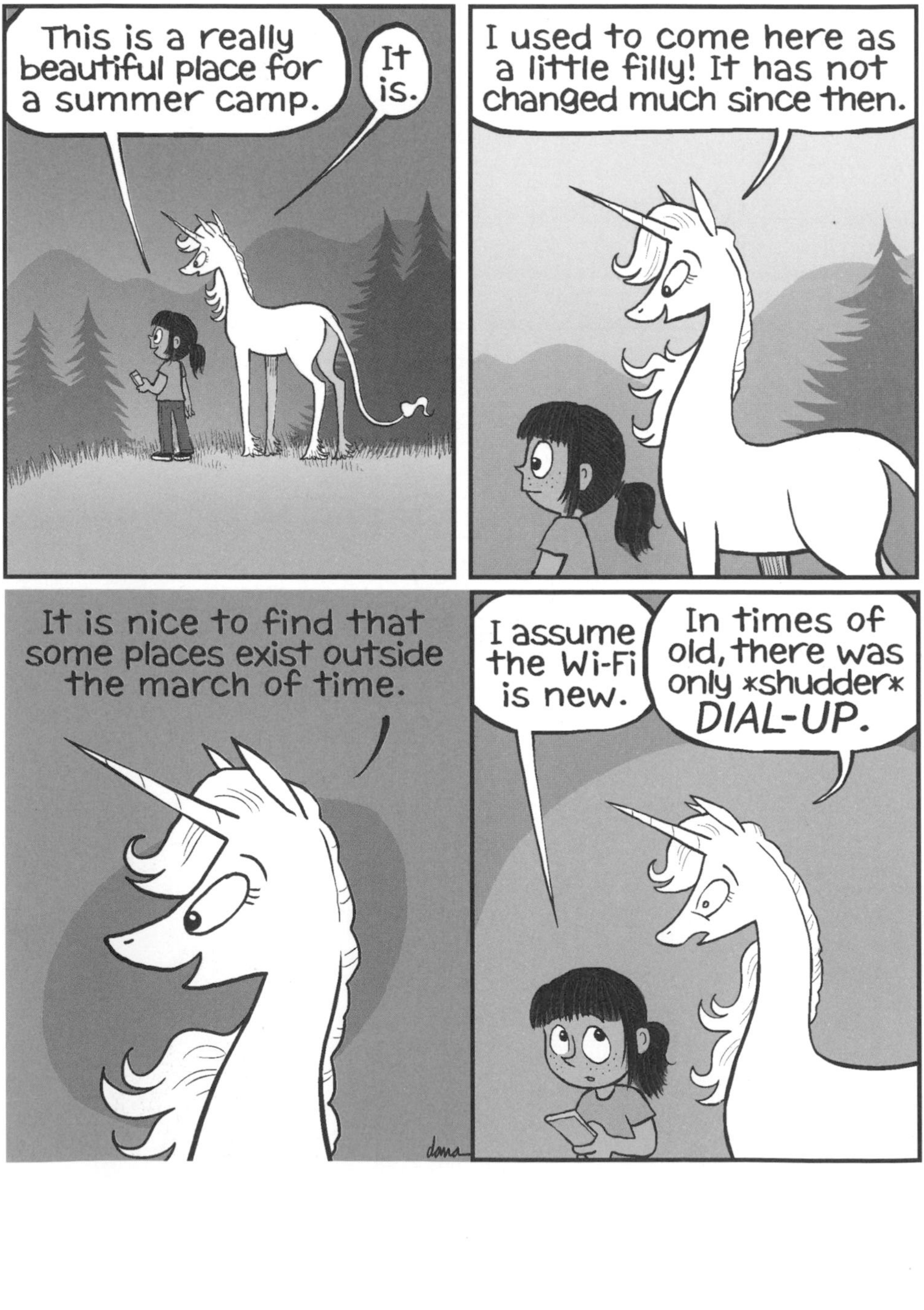
This is a really beautiful place for a summer camp.
It is.
I used to come here as a little filly! It has not changed much since then.
It is nice to find that some places exist outside the march of time.
I assume the Wi-Fi is new.
In times of old, there was only *shudder* DIAL-UP.
dana

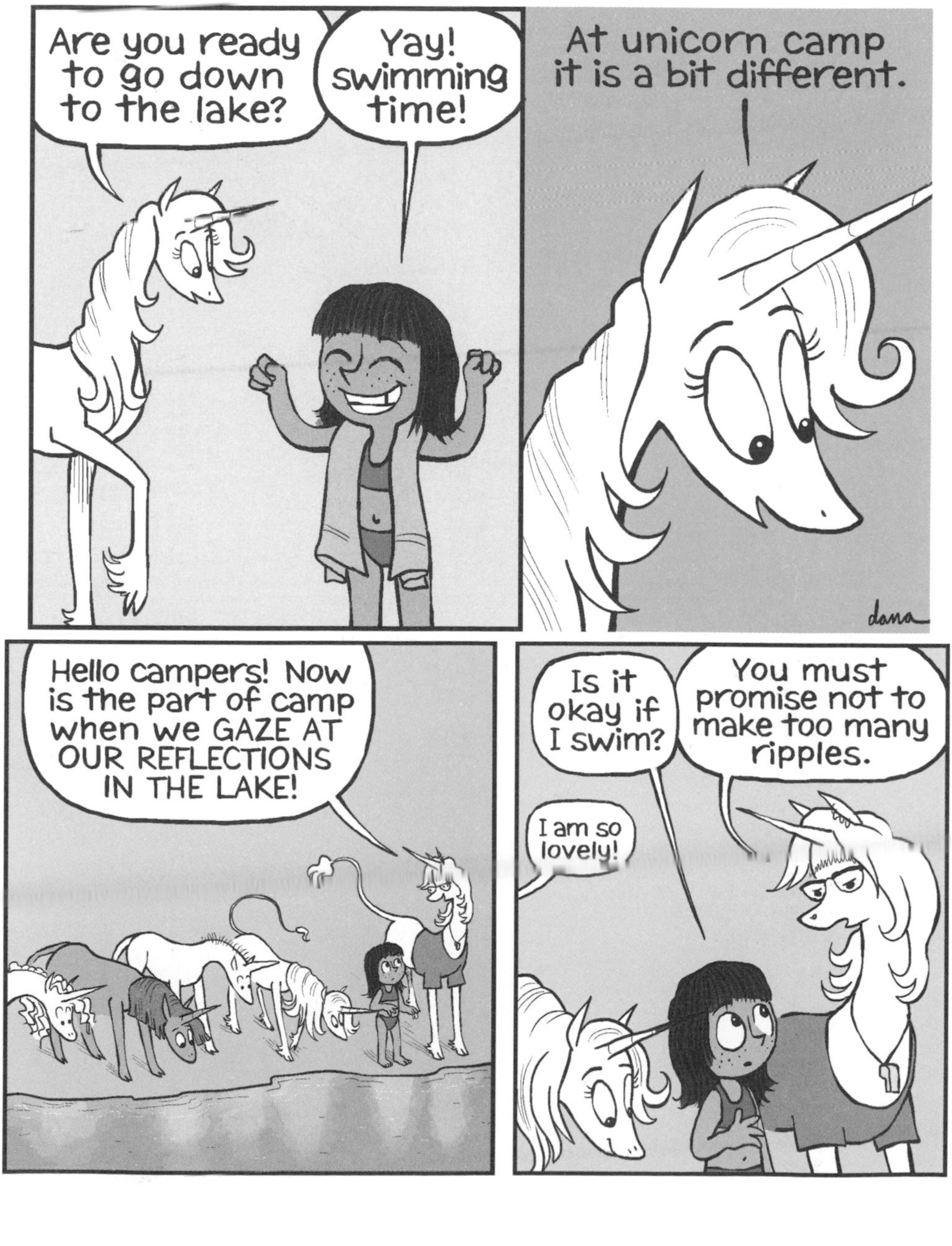
Are you ready to go down to the lake?
Yay! swimming time!
At unicorn camp it is a bit different.
dana
Hello campers! Now is the part of camp when we GAZE AT OUR REFLECTIONS IN THE LAKE!
Is it okay if I swim?
You must promise not to make too many ripples.
I am so lovely!

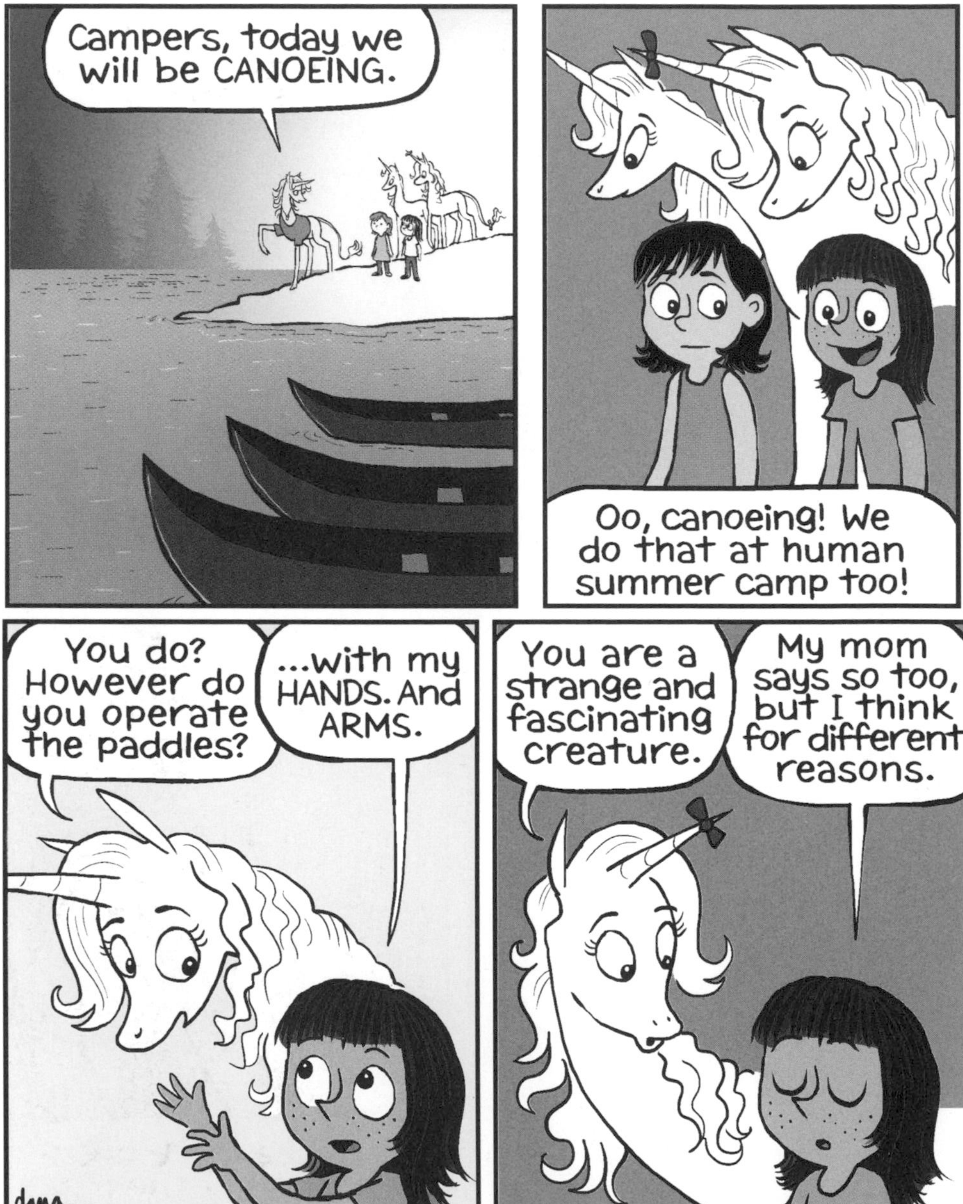
Campers, today we will be CANOEING.
Oo, canoeing! We do that at human summer camp too!
You do? However do you operate the paddles?
...with my HANDS. And ARMS.
You are a strange and fascinating creature.
My mom says so too, but I think for different reasons.
dana

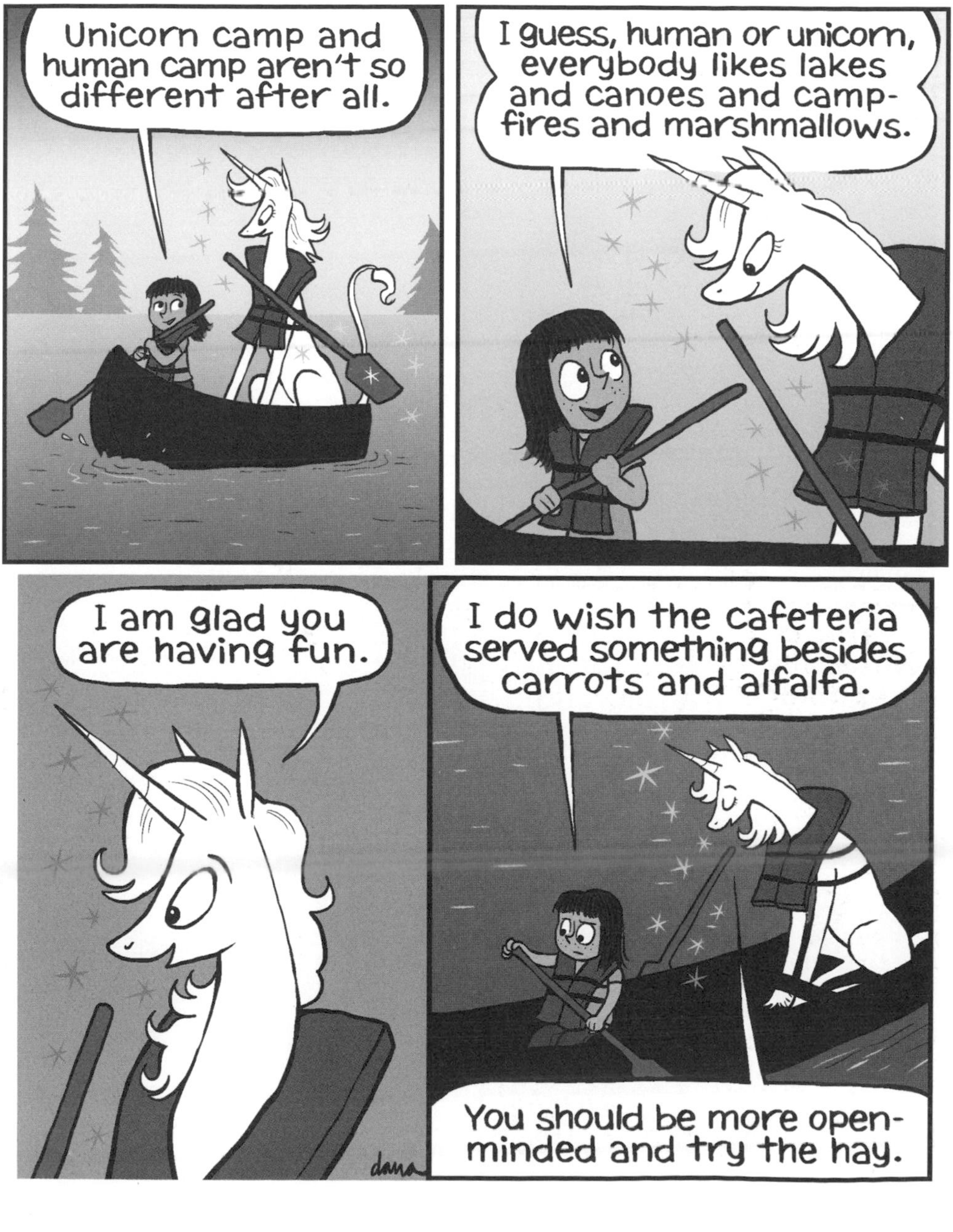
Unicorn camp and human camp aren't so different after all.
I guess, human or unicorn, everybody likes lakes and canoes and camp-fires and marshmallows.
I am glad you are having fun.
I do wish the cafeteria served something besides carrots and alfalfa.
You should be more open-minded and try the hay.
dana

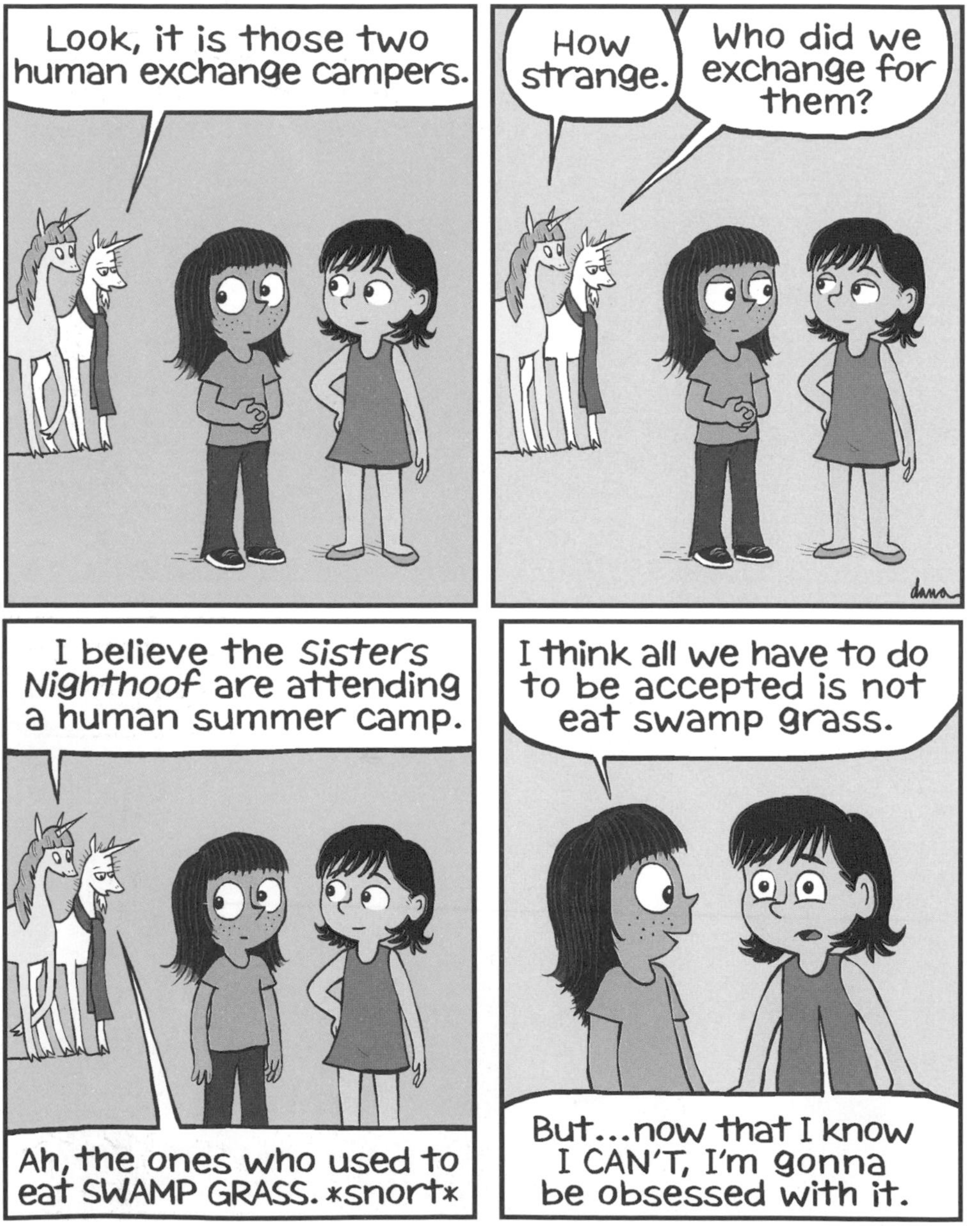
Look, it is those two human exchange campers.
How strange.
Who did we exchange for them?
dana
I believe the *Sisters Nighthoof* are attending a human summer camp.
Ah, the ones who used to eat SWAMP GRASS. *snort*
I think all we have to do to be accepted is not eat swamp grass.
But...now that I know I CAN'T, I'm gonna be obsessed with it.

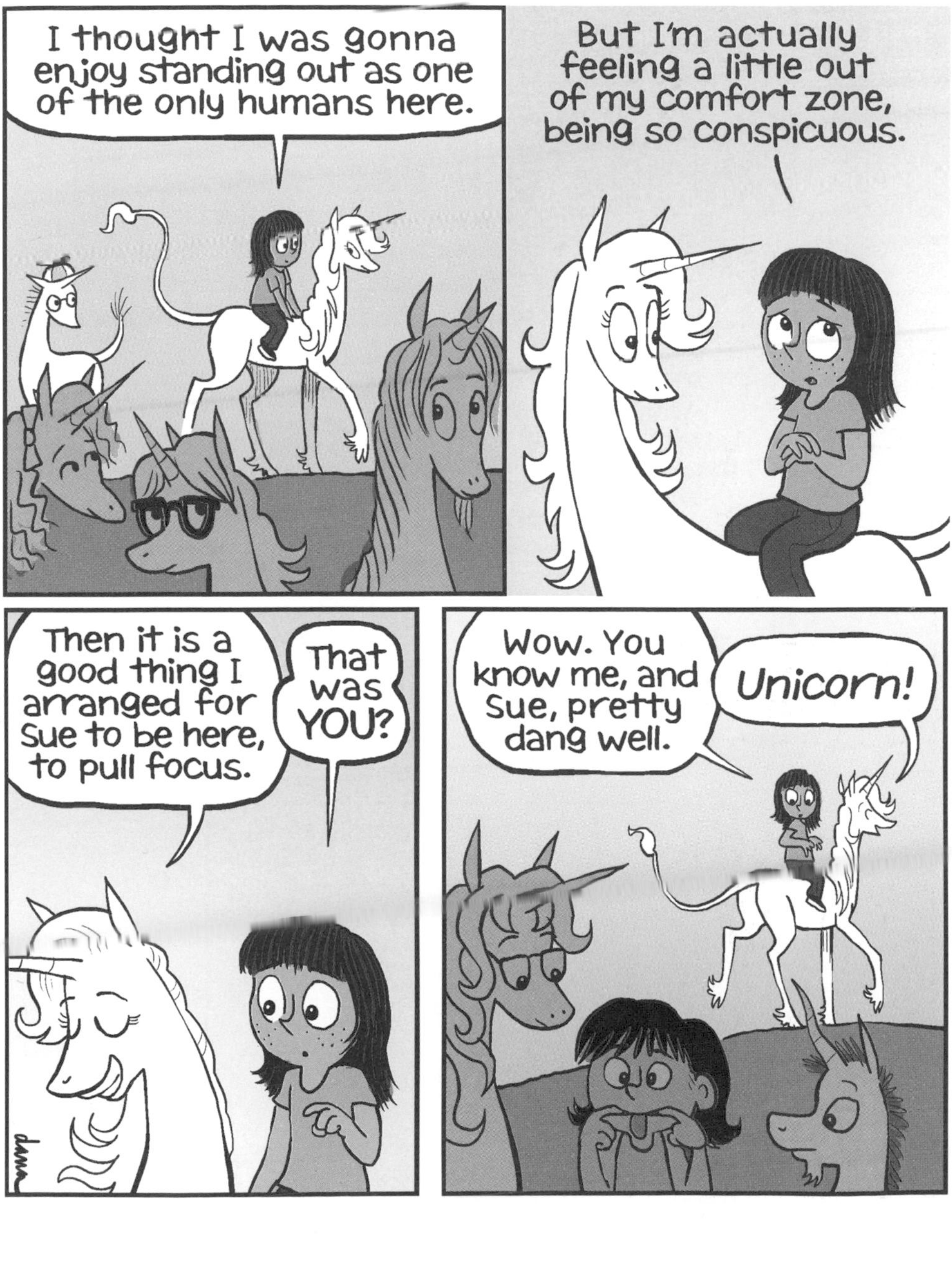
I thought I was gonna enjoy standing out as one of the only humans here.
But I'm actually feeling a little out of my comfort zone, being so conspicuous.
Then it is a good thing I arranged for Sue to be here, to pull focus.
That was YOU?
Wow. You know me, and Sue, pretty dang well.
Unicorn!
dana

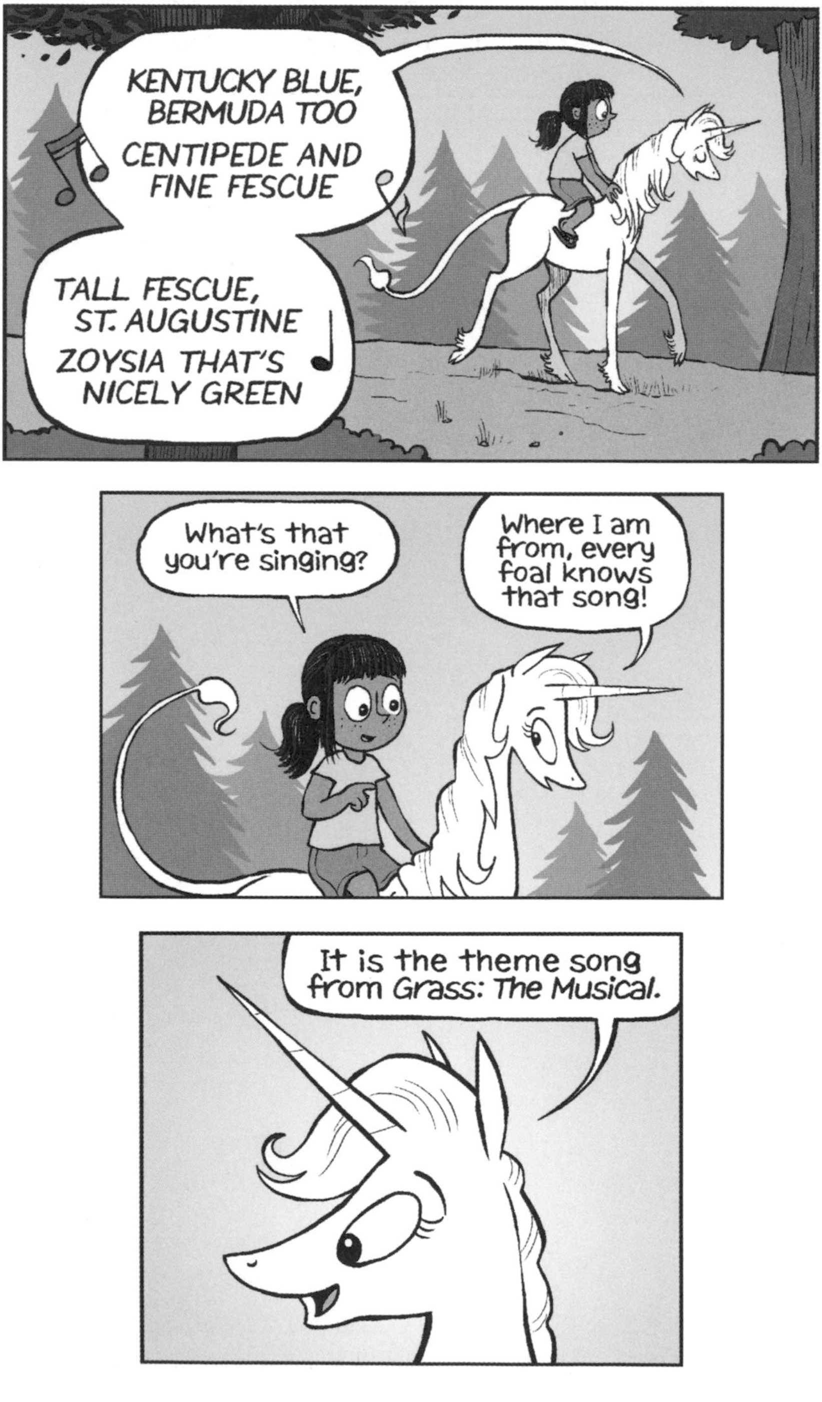
KENTUCKY BLUE, BERMUDA TOO
CENTIPEDE AND FINE FESCUE
TALL FESCUE, ST. AUGUSTINE
ZOYSIA THAT'S NICELY GREEN
What's that you're singing?
Where I am from, every foal knows that song!
It is the theme song from *Grass: The Musical.*

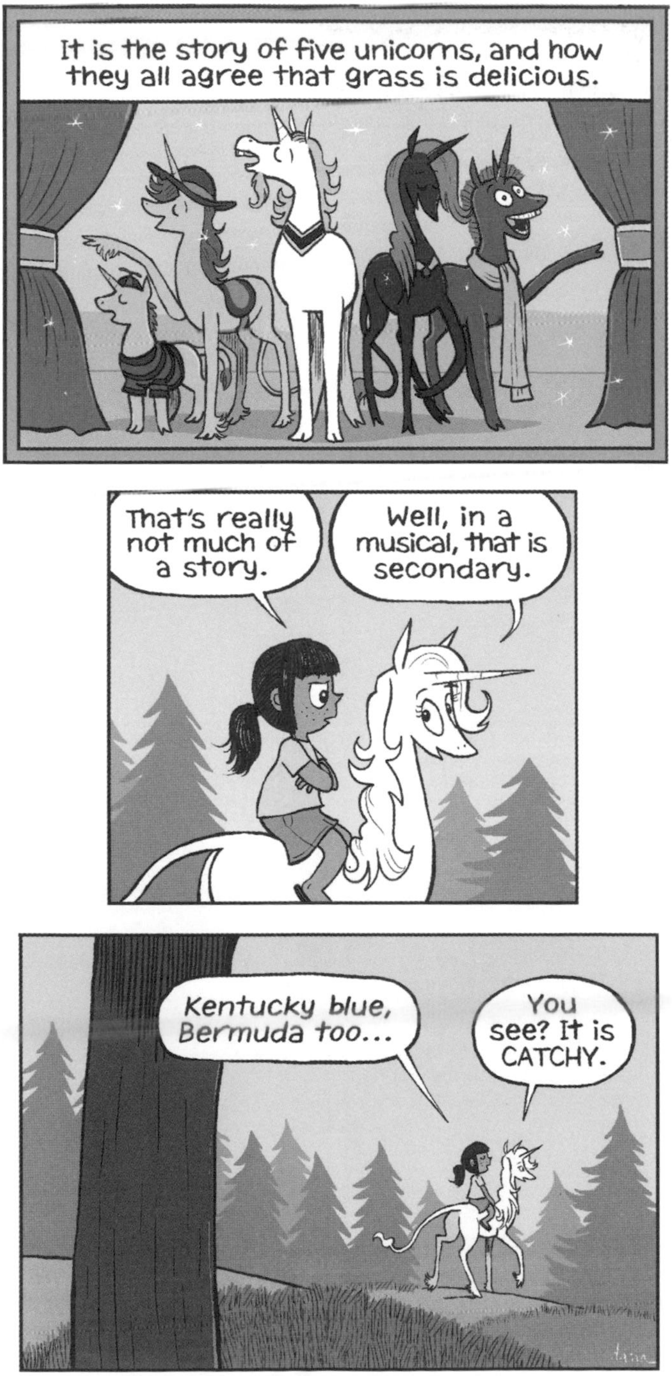
It is the story of five unicorns, and how they all agree that grass is delicious.
That's really not much of a story.
Well, in a musical, that is secondary.
Kentucky blue, Bermuda too...
You see? It is CATCHY.

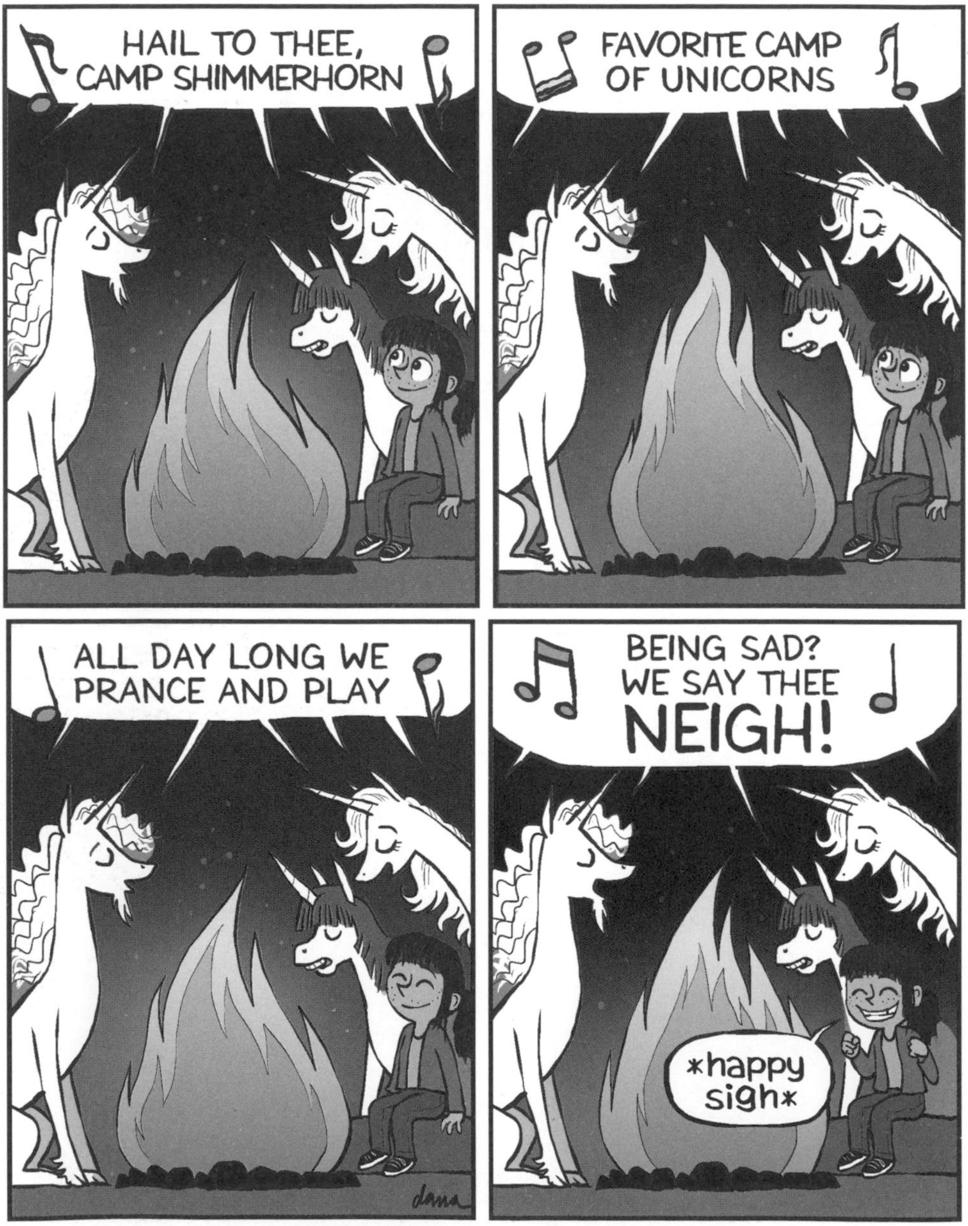
HAIL TO THEE, CAMP SHIMMERHORN
FAVORITE CAMP OF UNICORNS
ALL DAY LONG WE PRANCE AND PLAY
BEING SAD? WE SAY THEE NEIGH!
happy sigh
dana

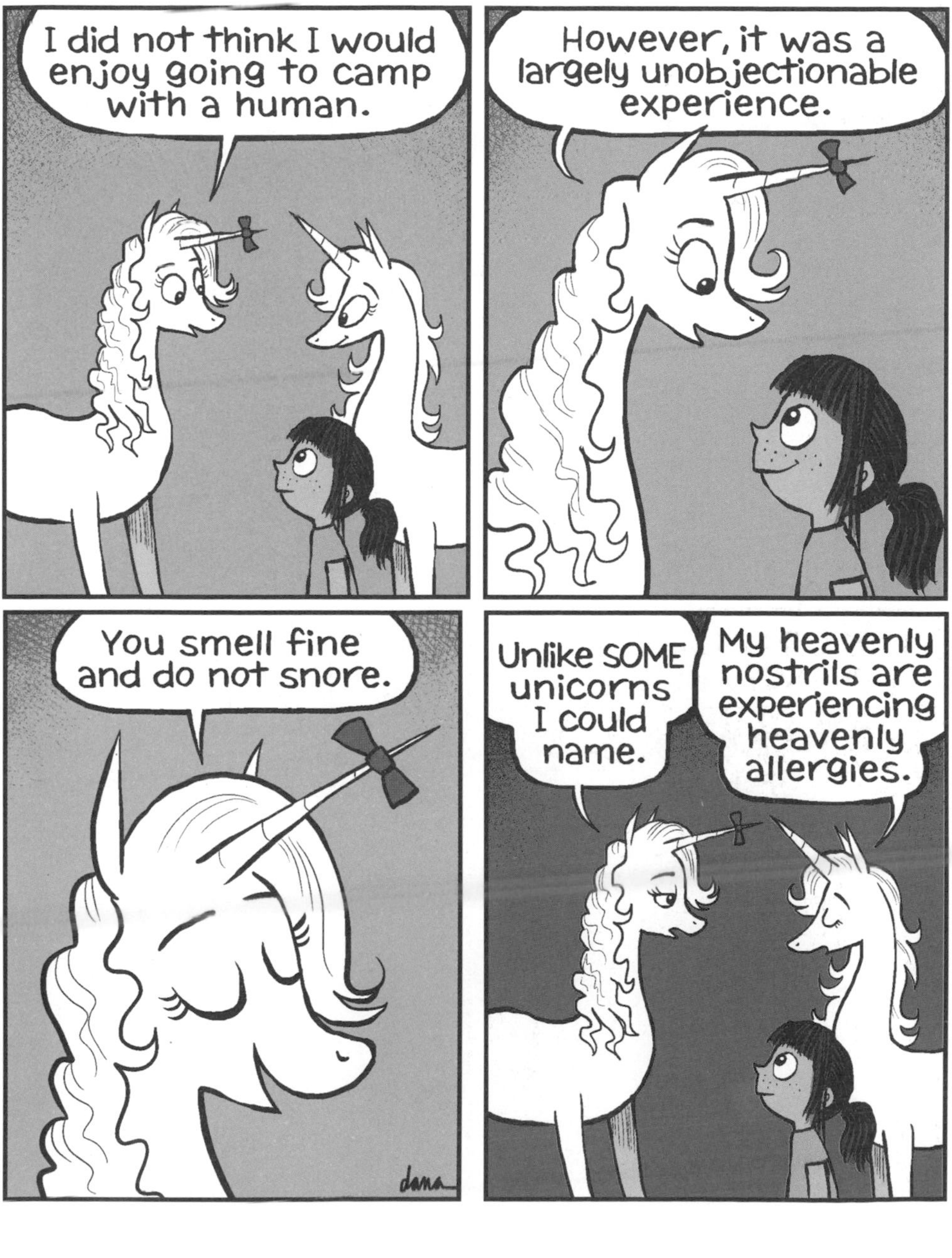
I did not think I would enjoy going to camp with a human.
However, it was a largely unobjectionable experience.
You smell fine and do not snore.
Unlike SOME unicorns I could name.
My heavenly nostrils are experiencing heavenly allergies.
dana

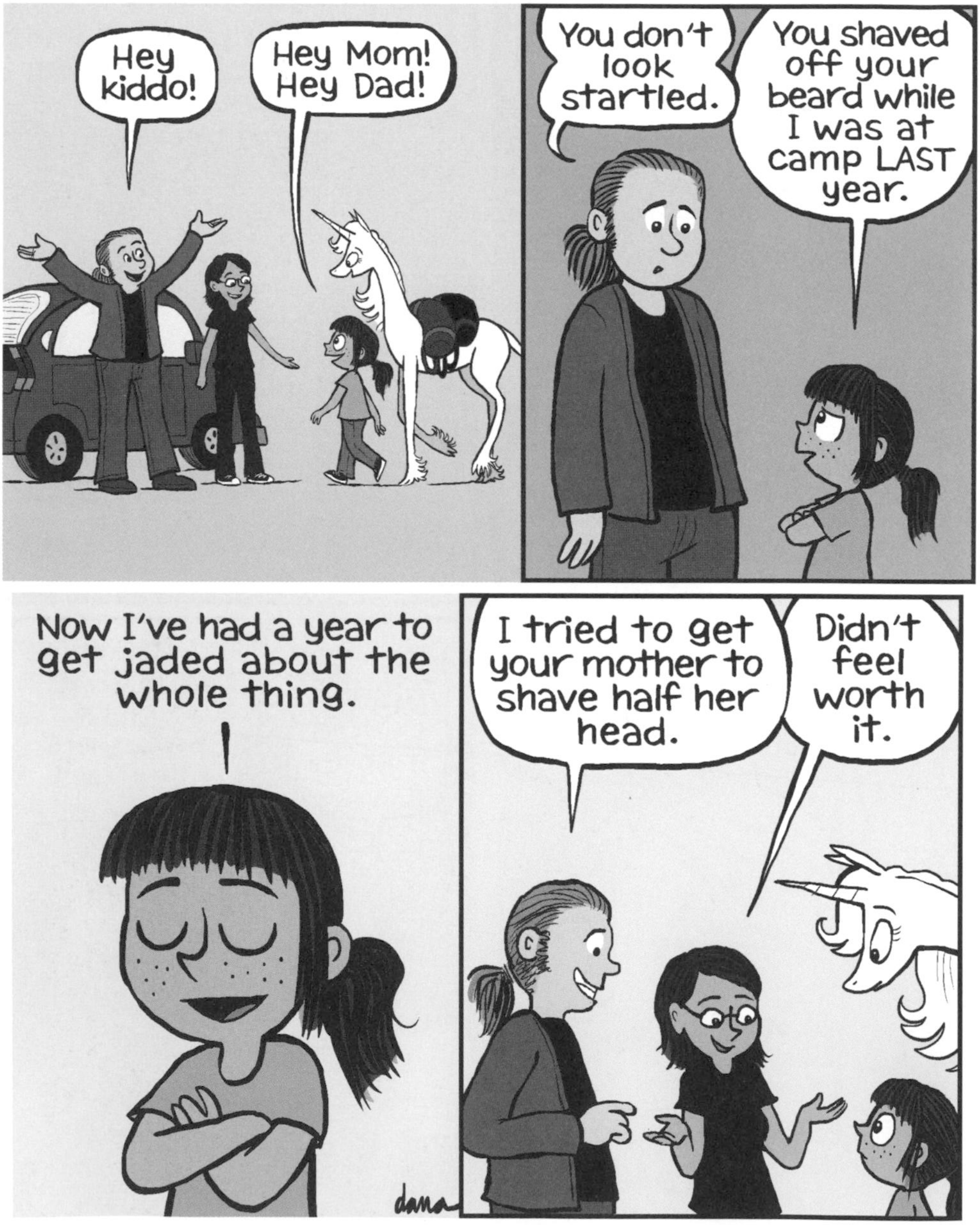
Hey kiddo!
Hey Mom! Hey Dad!
You don't look startled.
You shaved off your beard while I was at camp LAST year.
Now I've had a year to get jaded about the whole thing.
I tried to get your mother to shave half her head.
Didn't feel worth it.
dana

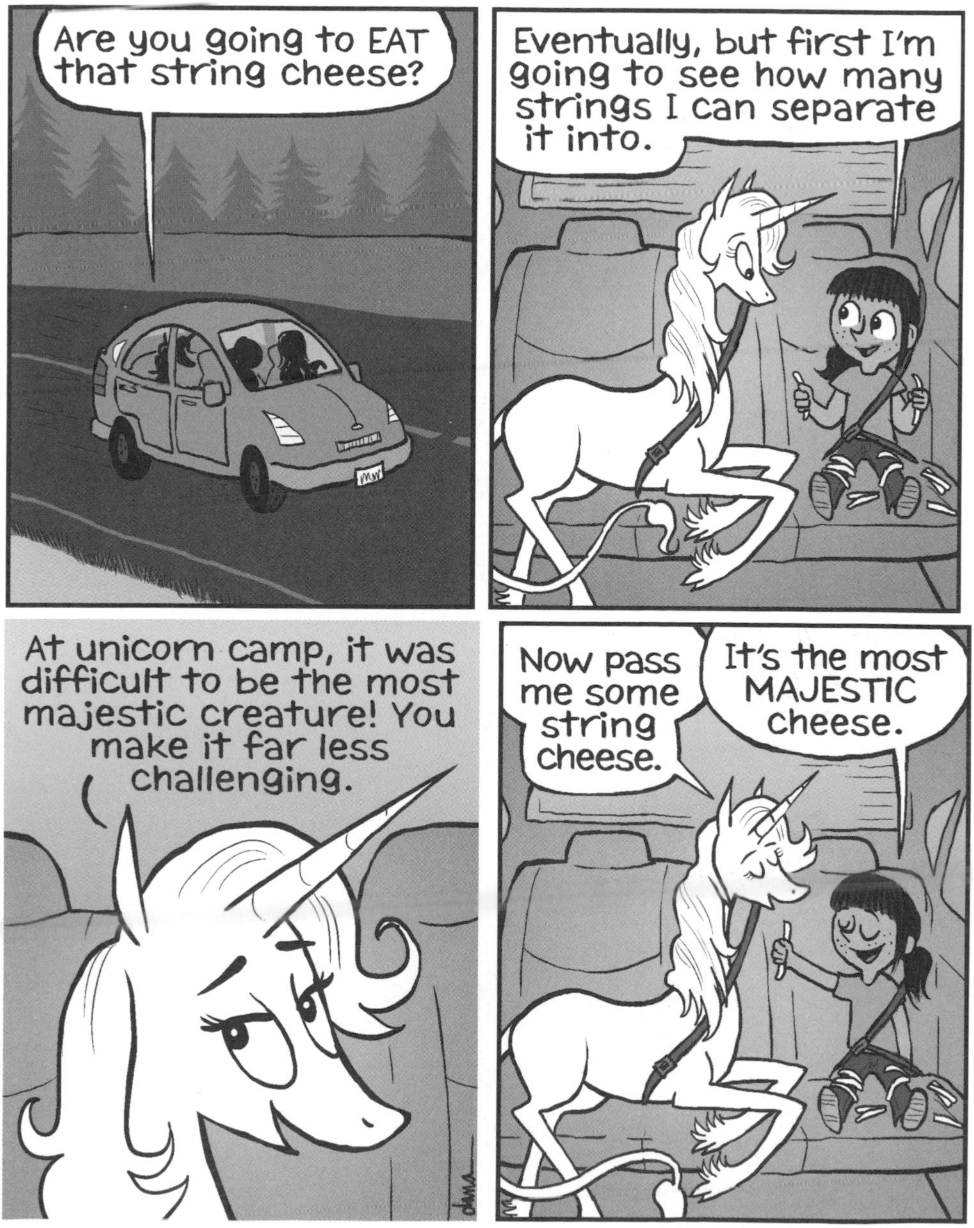
Are you going to EAT that string cheese?
Eventually, but first I'm going to see how many strings I can separate it into.
At unicorn camp, it was difficult to be the most majestic creature! You make it far less challenging.
Now pass me some string cheese.
It's the most MAJESTIC cheese.

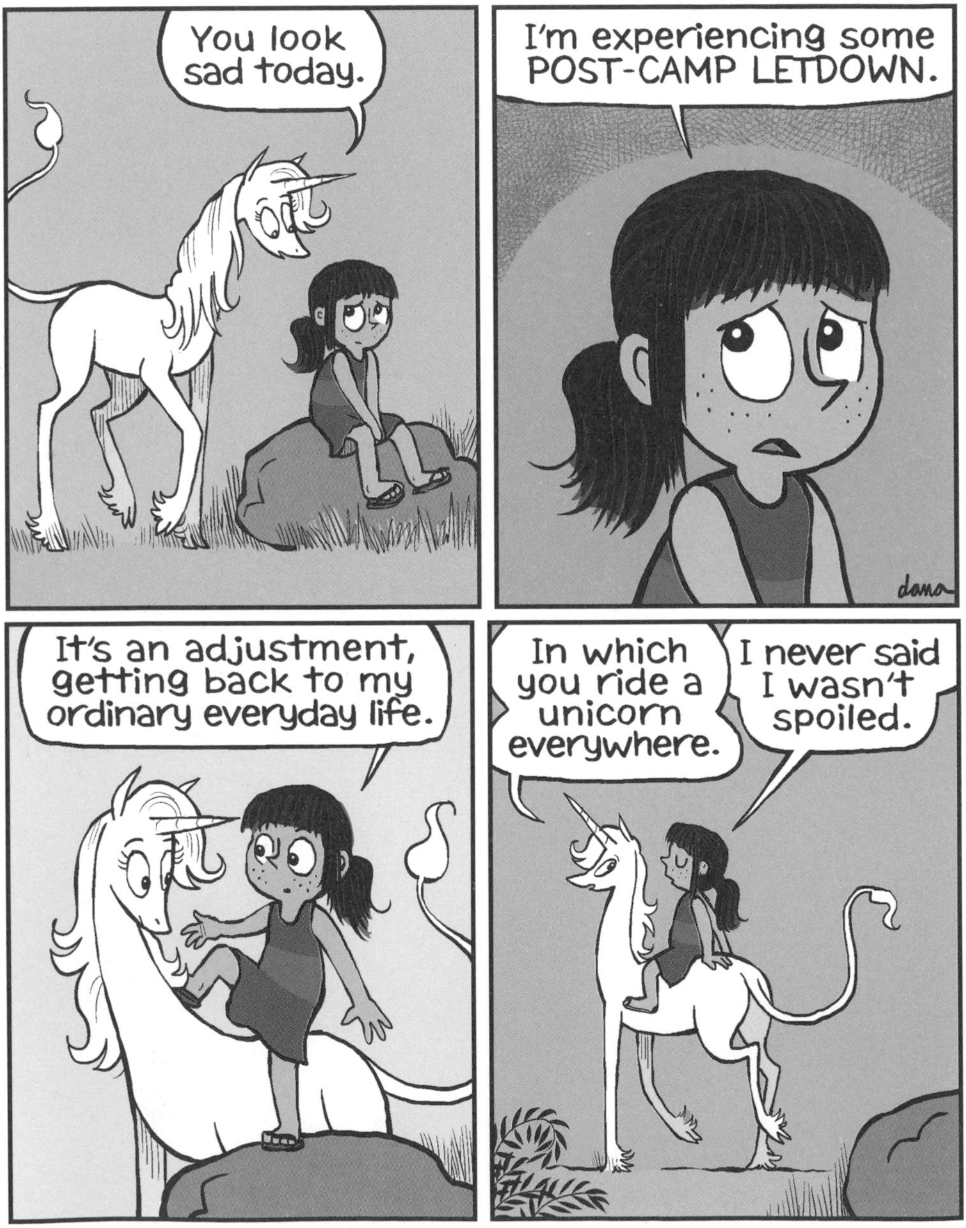
You look sad today.
I'm experiencing some POST-CAMP LETDOWN.
dana
It's an adjustment, getting back to my ordinary everyday life.
In which you ride a unicorn everywhere.
I never said I wasn't spoiled.

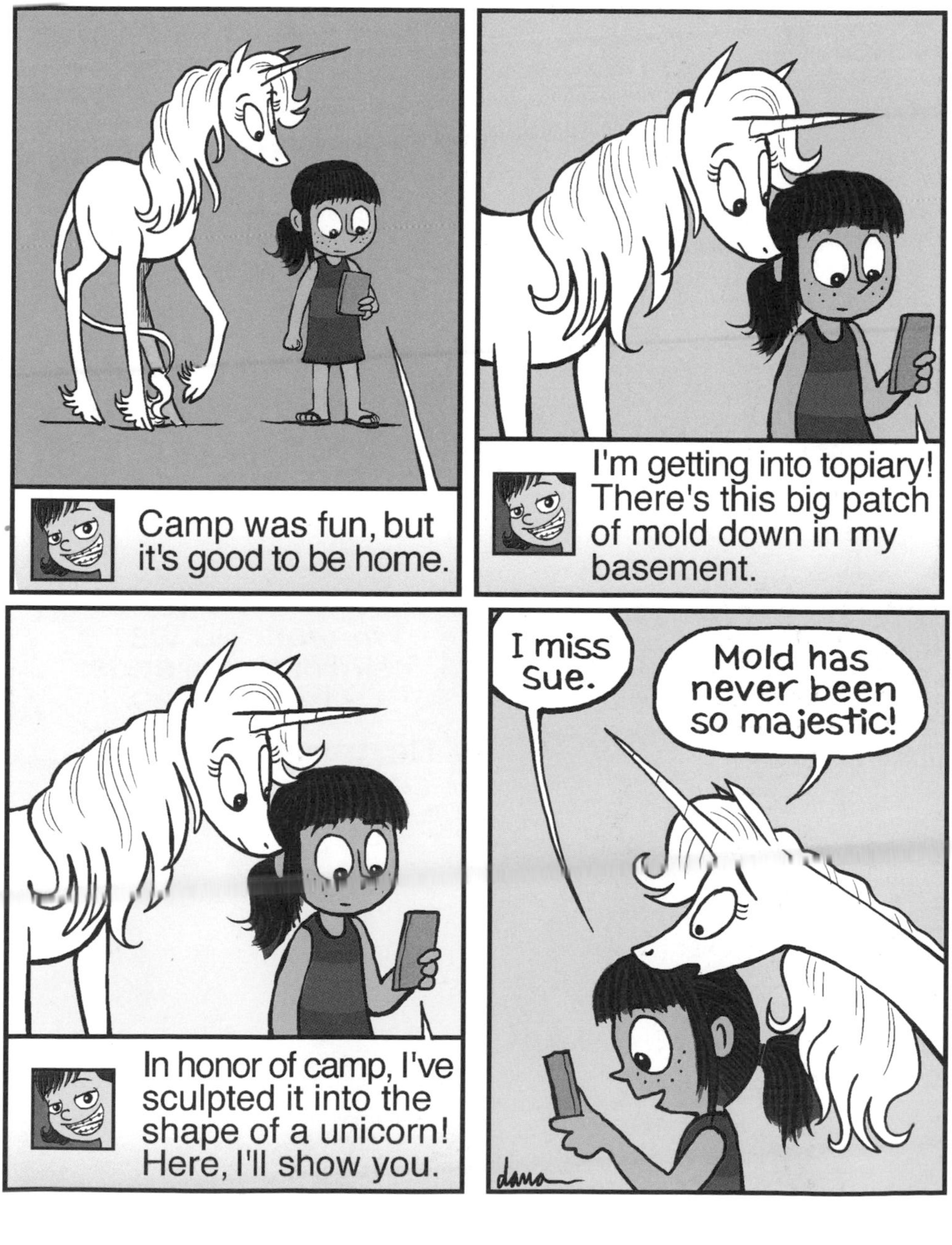
Camp was fun, but it's good to be home.
I'm getting into topiary! There's this big patch of mold down in my basement.
In honor of camp, I've sculpted it into the shape of a unicorn! Here, I'll show you.
I miss Sue.
Mold has never been so majestic!
dana

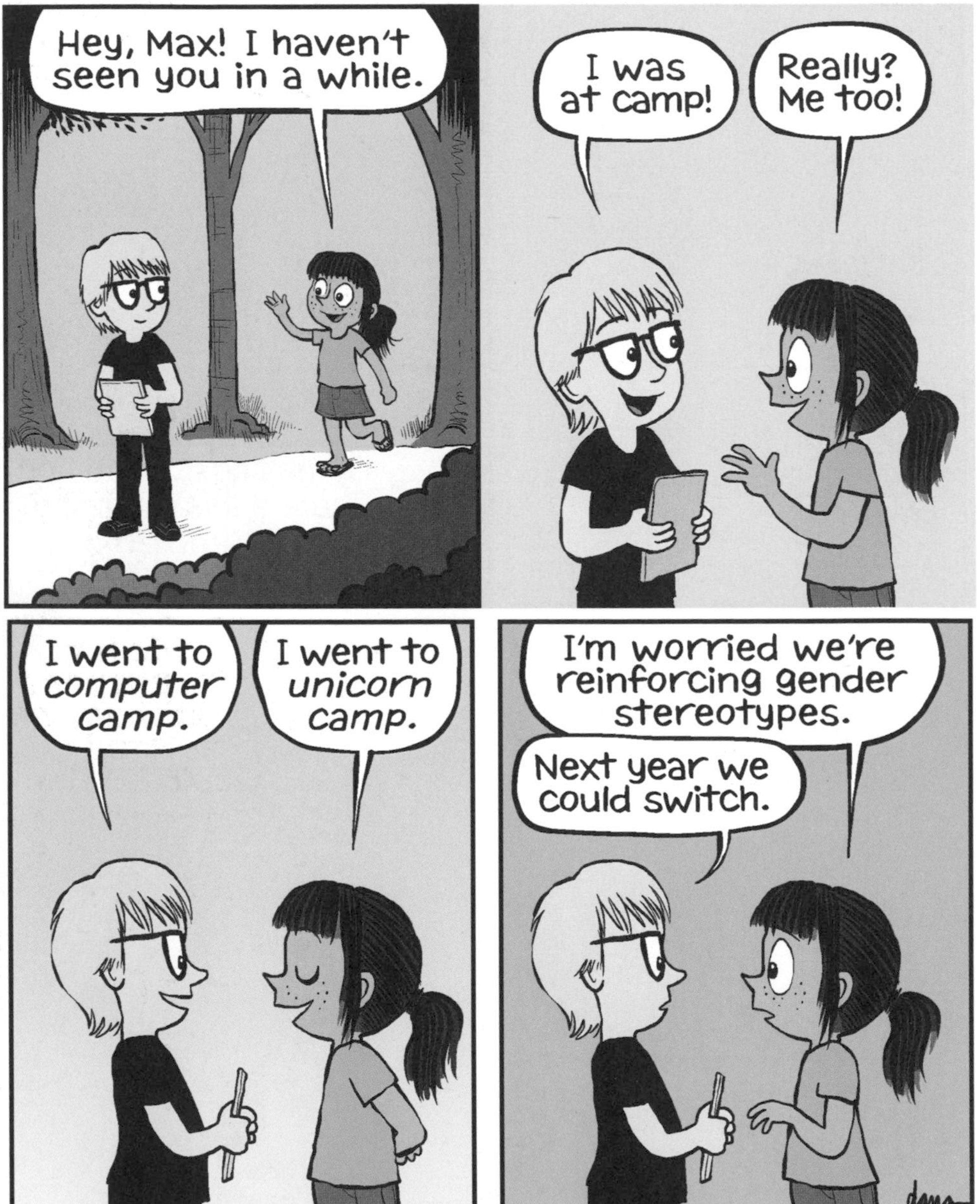
Hey, Max! I haven't seen you in a while.
I was at camp!
Really? Me too!
I went to computer camp.
I went to unicorn camp.
I'm worried we're reinforcing gender stereotypes.
Next year we could switch.
dana

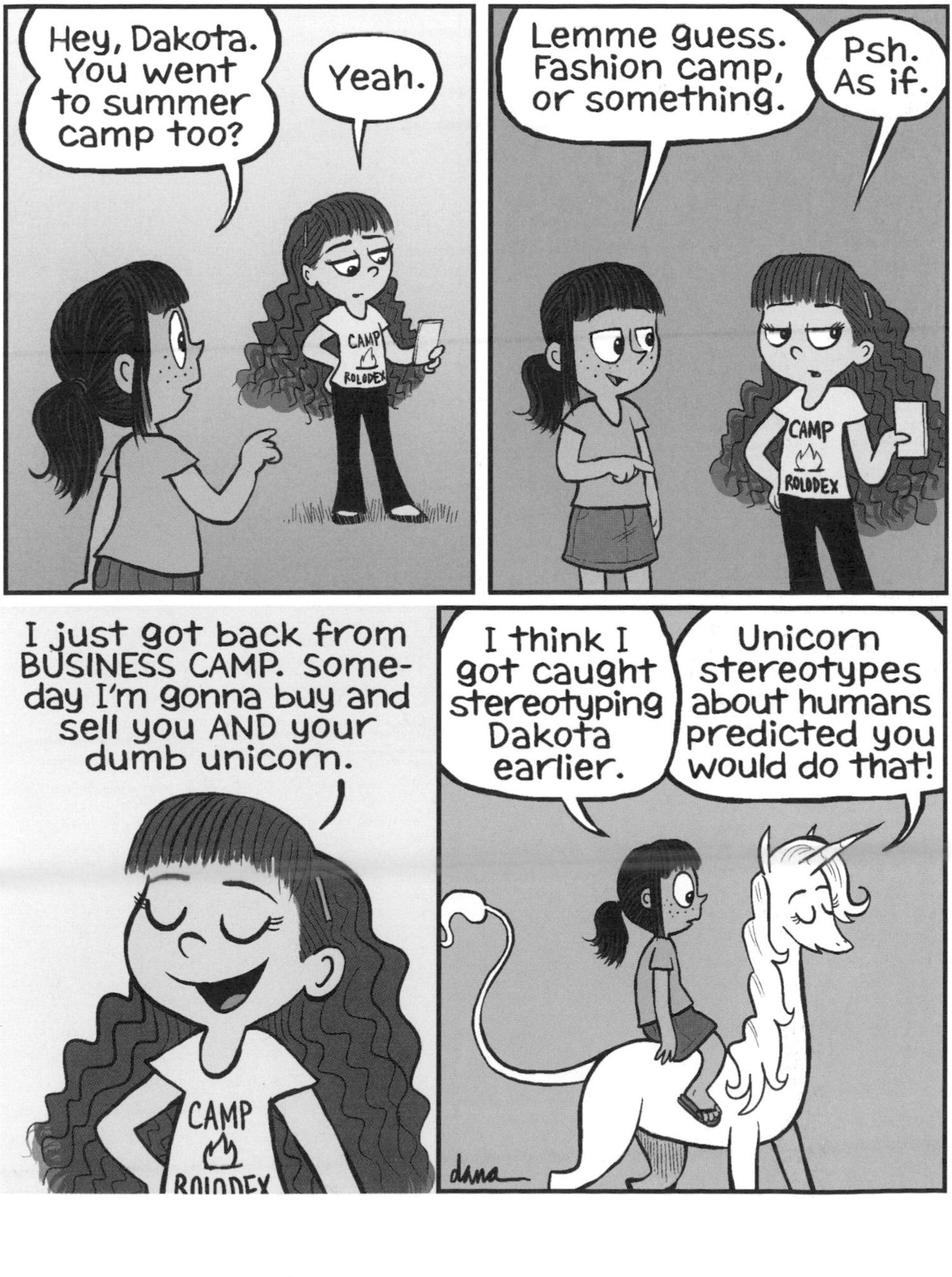
Hey, Dakota. You went to summer camp too?
Yeah.
CAMP ROLODEX
Lemme guess. Fashion camp, or something.
Psh. As if.
CAMP ROLODEX
I just got back from BUSINESS CAMP. Someday I'm gonna buy and sell you AND your dumb unicorn.
CAMP
I think I got caught stereotyping Dakota earlier.
Unicorn stereotypes about humans predicted you would do that!
dana

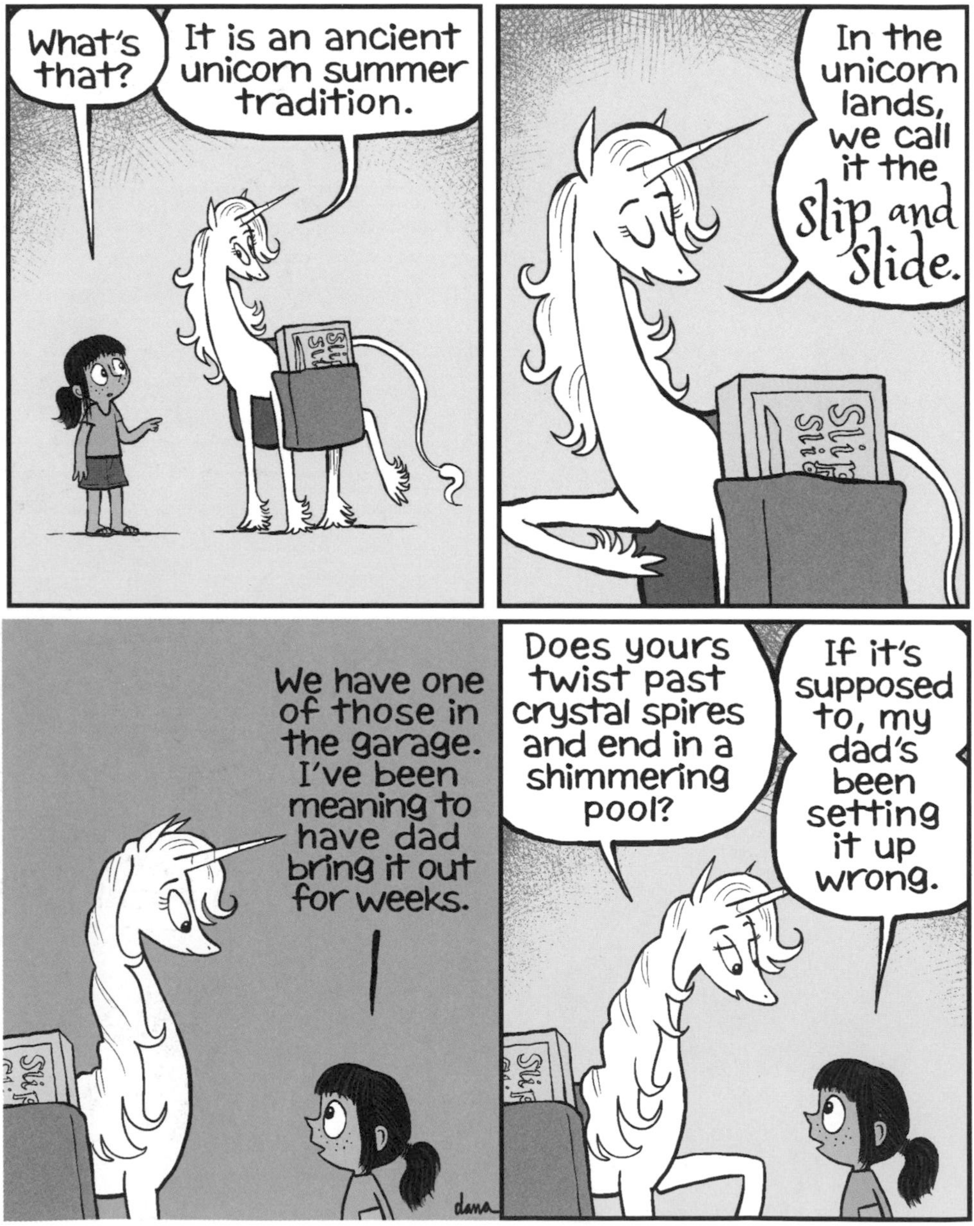
What's that?
It is an ancient unicorn summer tradition.
In the unicorn lands, we call it the slip and slide.
We have one of those in the garage. I've been meaning to have dad bring it out for weeks.
Does yours twist past crystal spires and end in a shimmering pool?
If it's supposed to, my dad's been setting it up wrong.
dana

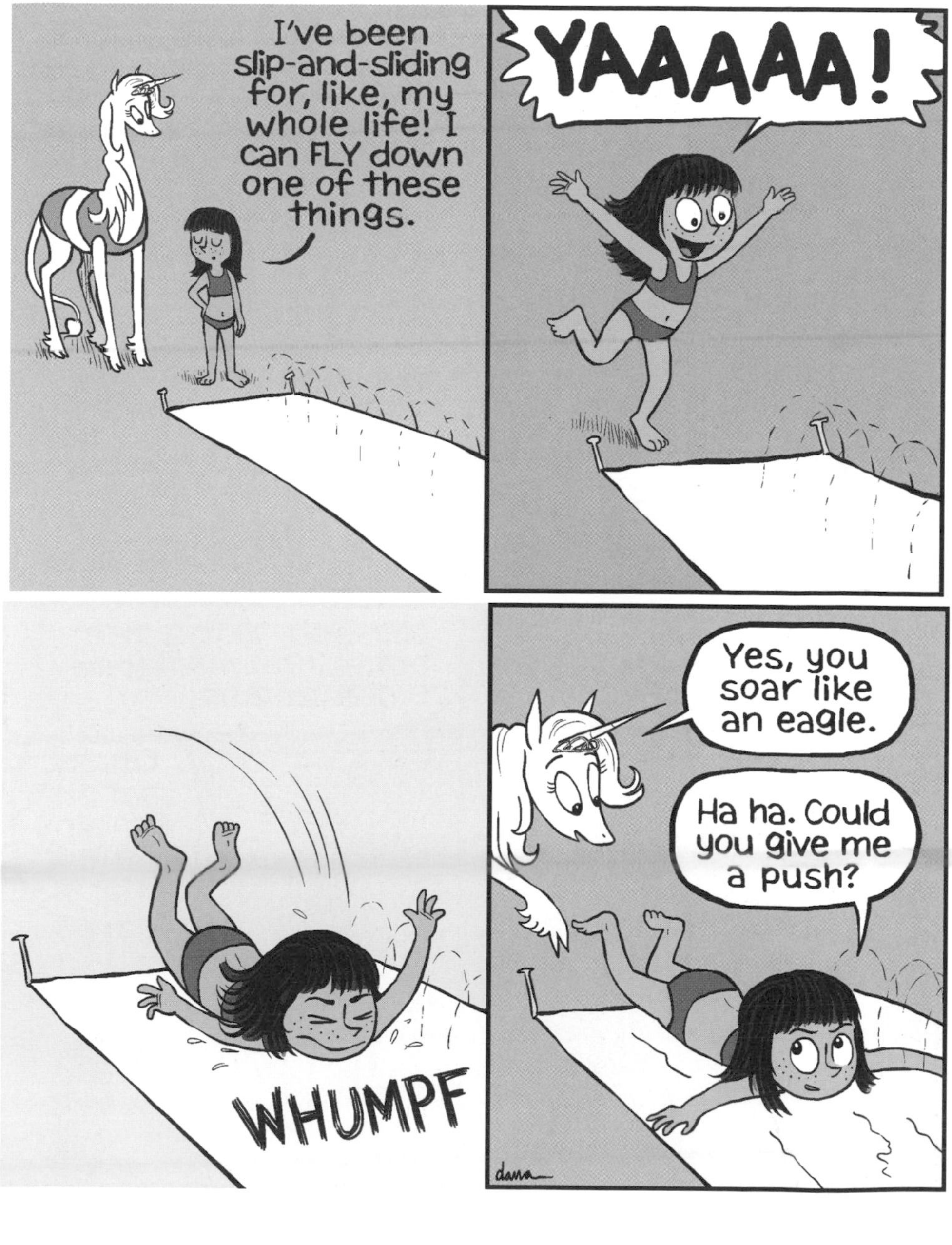

I've been slip-and-sliding for, like, my whole life! I can FLY down one of these things.
YAAAAA!
WHUMPF
Yes, you soar like an eagle.
Ha ha. Could you give me a push?
dana

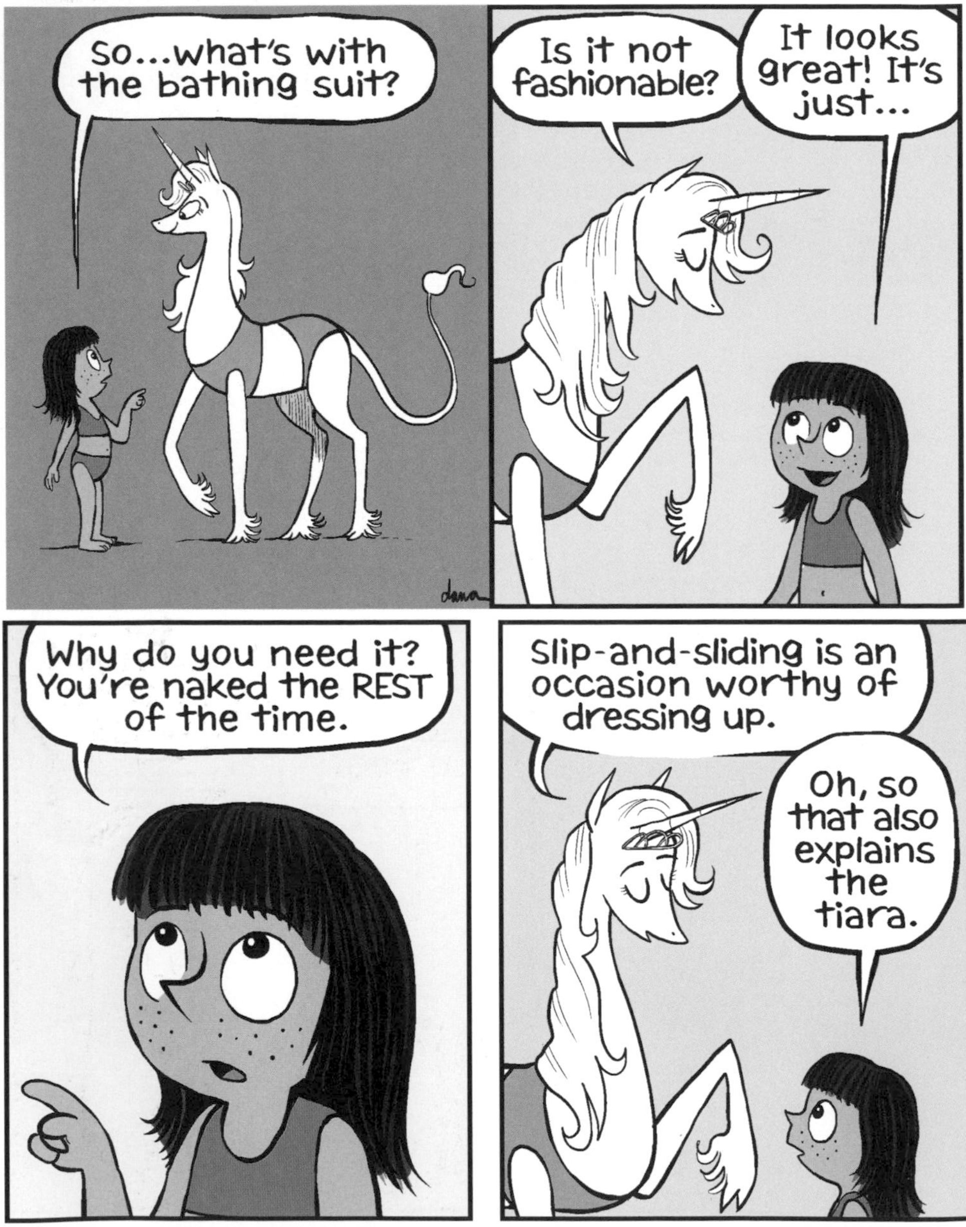
So...what's with the bathing suit?
Is it not fashionable?
It looks great! It's just...
Why do you need it? You're naked the REST of the time.
Slip-and-sliding is an occasion worthy of dressing up.
Oh, so that also explains the tiara.
dana

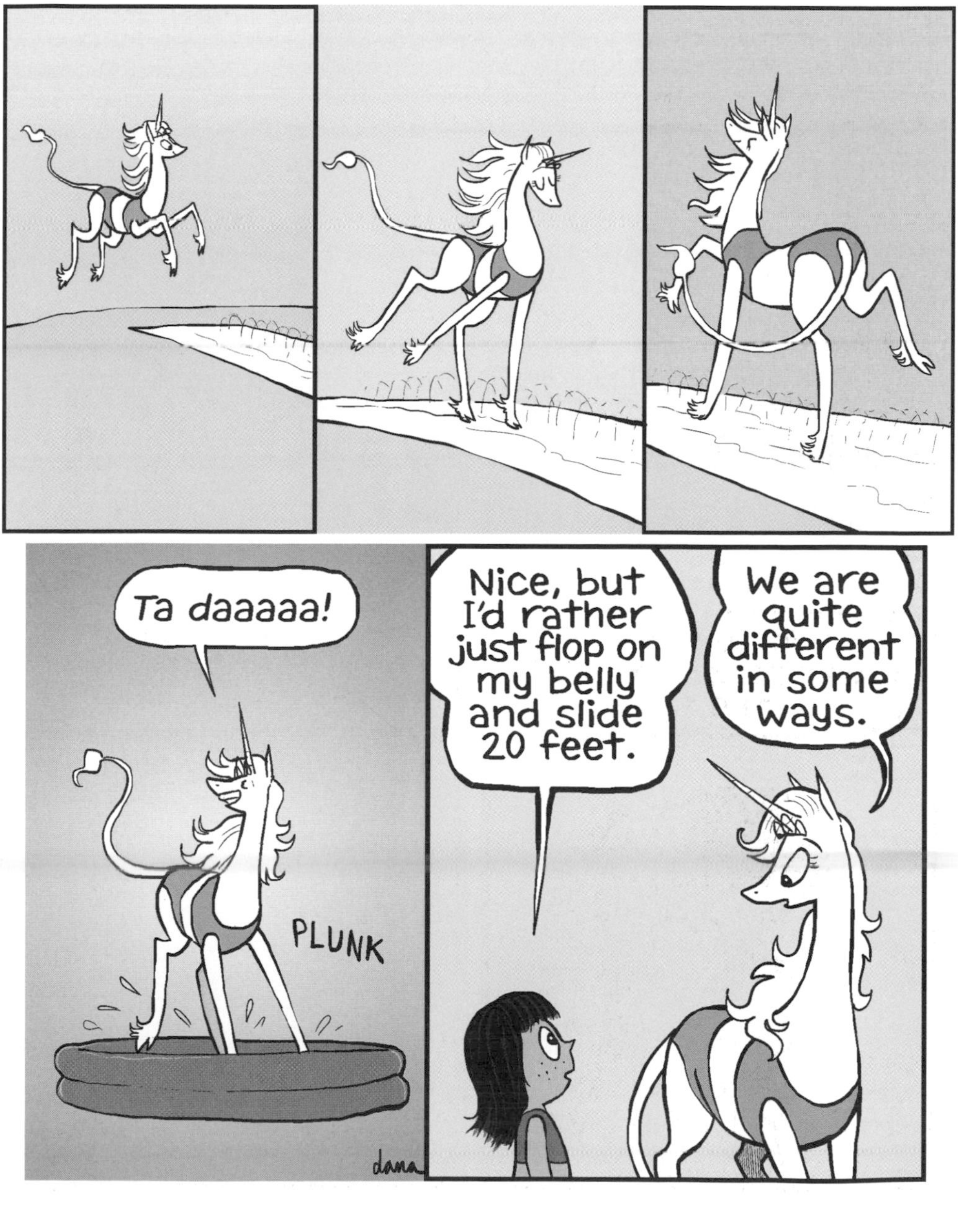
Ta daaaaa!
PLUNK
dana
Nice, but I'd rather just flop on my belly and slide 20 feet.
We are quite different in some ways.

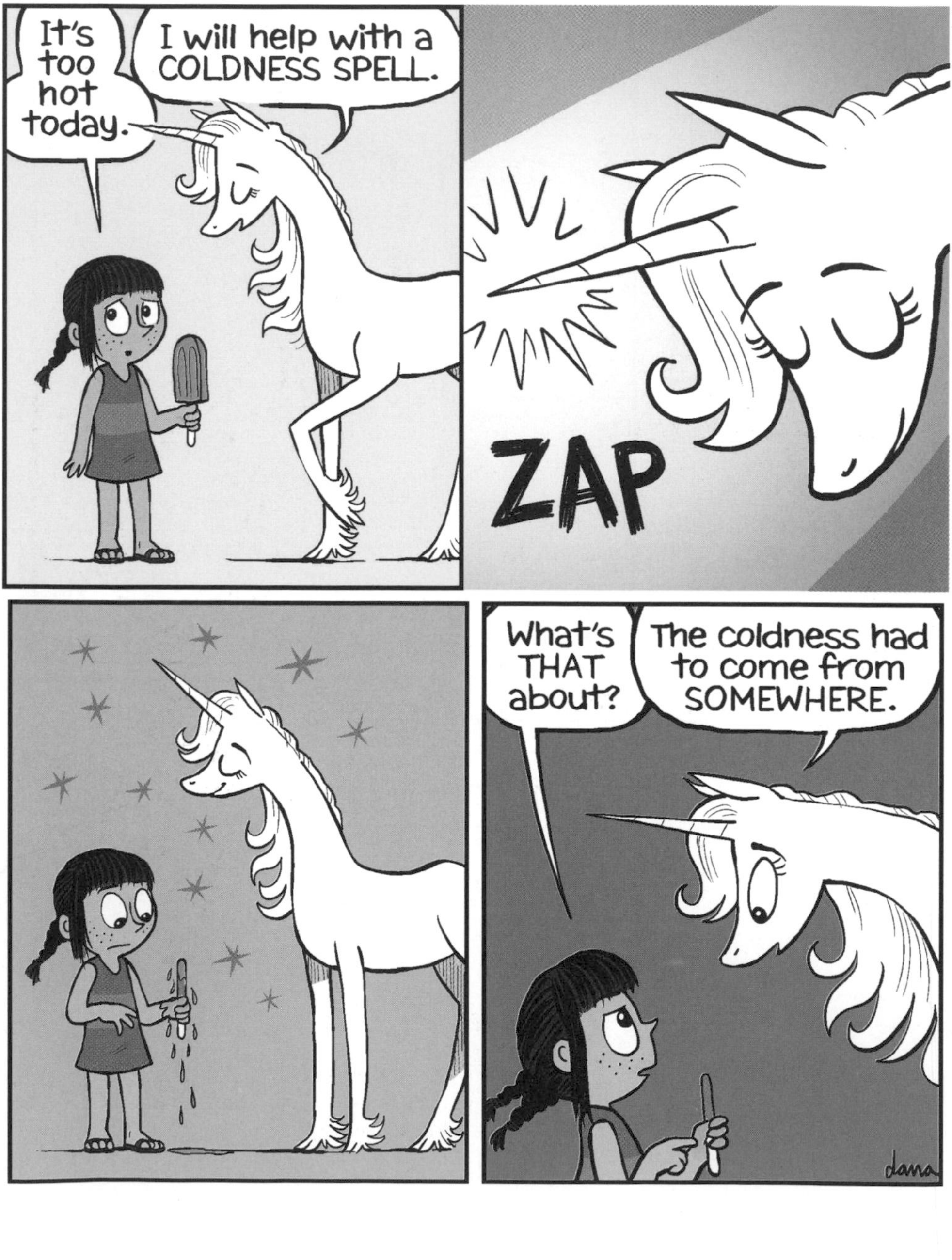
It's too hot today.
I will help with a COLDNESS SPELL.
ZAP
What's THAT about?
The coldness had to come from SOMEWHERE.
dana

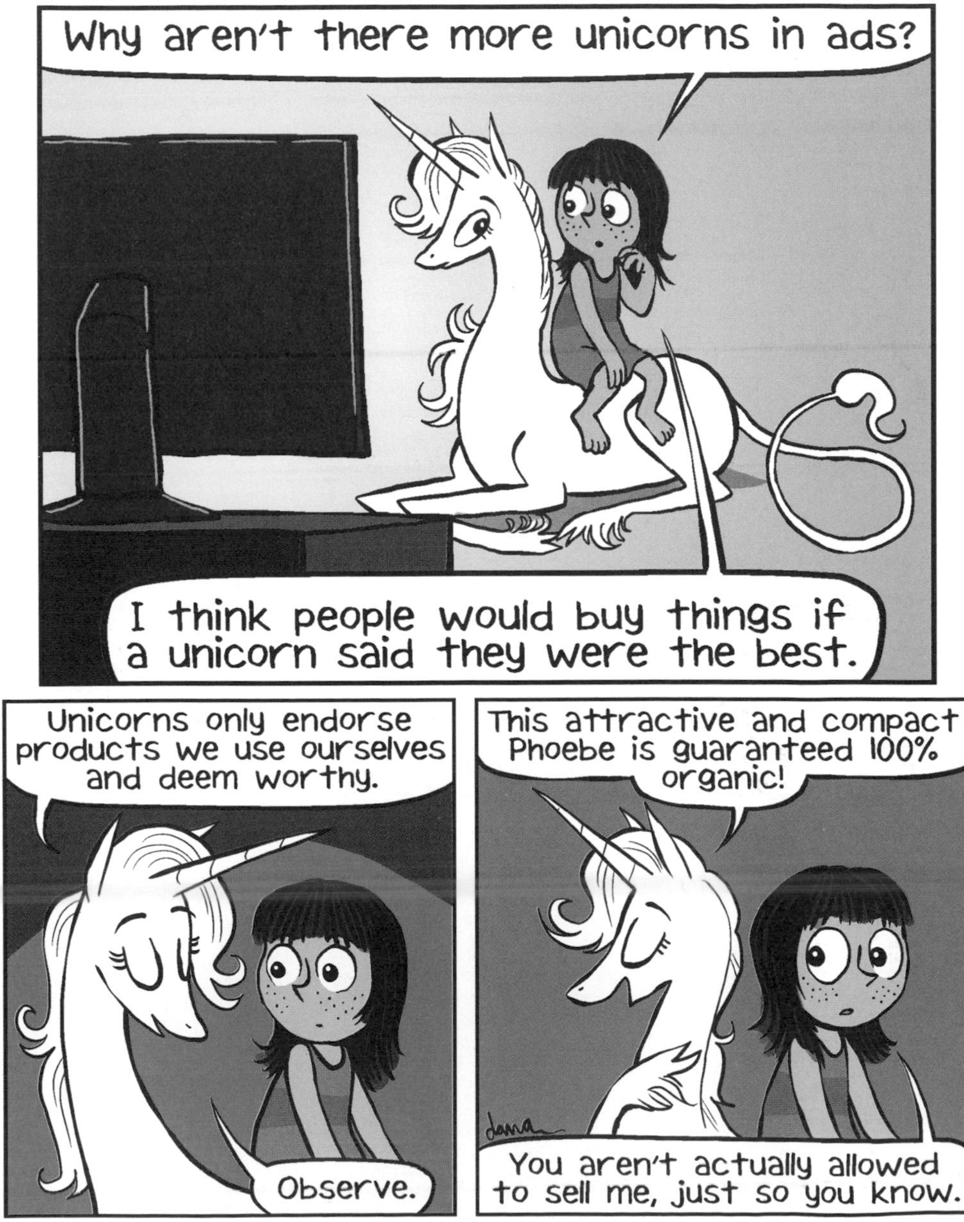
Why aren't there more unicorns in ads?
I think people would buy things if a unicorn said they were the best.
Unicorns only endorse products we use ourselves and deem worthy.
Observe.
This attractive and compact Phoebe is guaranteed 100% organic!
You aren't actually allowed to sell me, just so you know.
dana

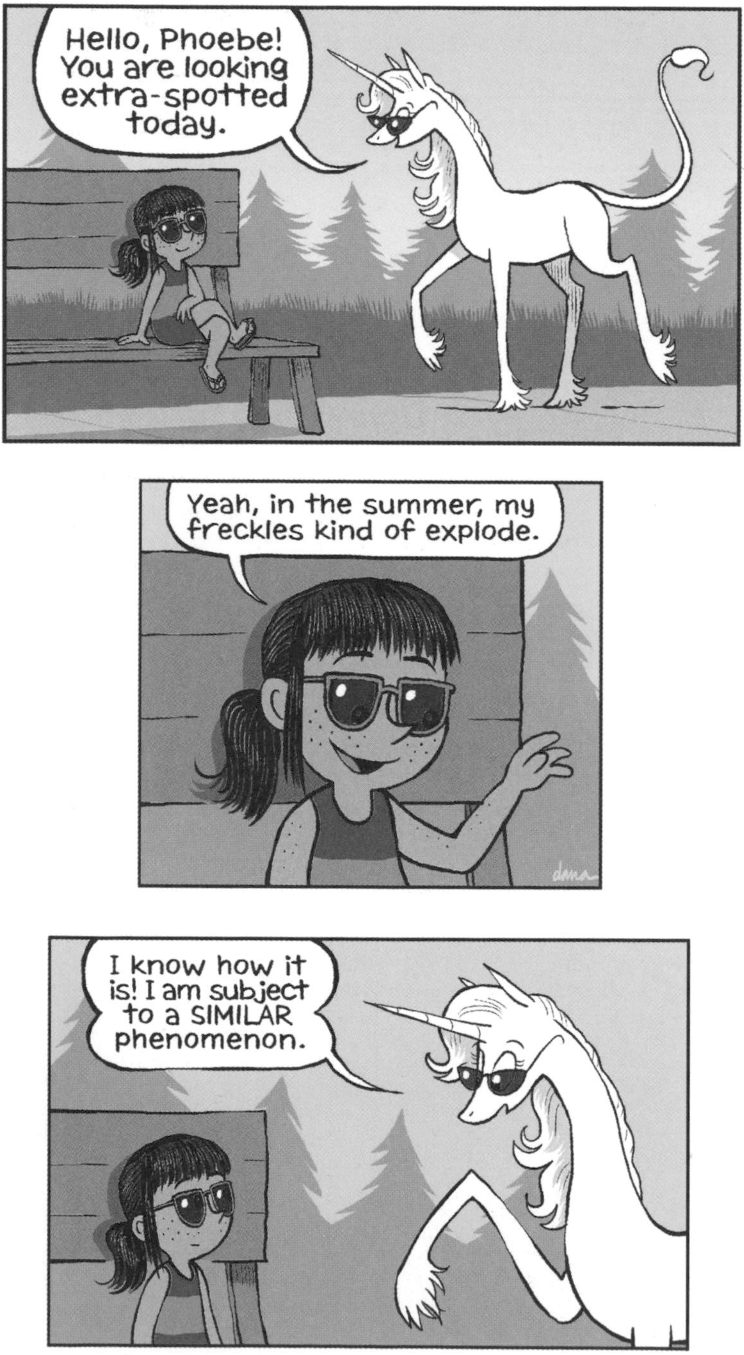
Hello, Phoebe! You are looking extra-spotted today.
Yeah, in the summer, my freckles kind of explode.
I know how it is! I am subject to a SIMILAR phenomenon.

My SPARKLES kind of explode.
So THAT's why you texted that I should wear sunscreen and sunglasses today.
That, and I wanted us to look cool.

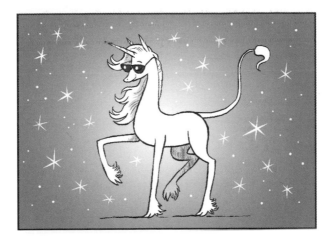

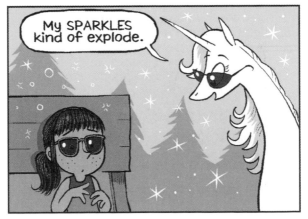

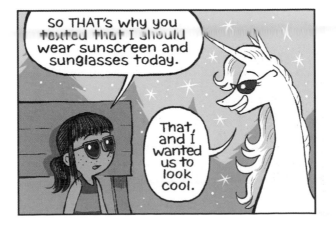

GLOSSARY

alternate dimension (ahl-ter-net di-men-shun): pg. 80 — noun / an entirely different universe or plane of existence than our own

brochure (broh-shur): pg. 129 — noun / a small booklet containing information about an issue, organization, or cause

camouflaged (kam-oh-flaj-d): pg. 107 — verb / to be disguised from view using a pattern that blends in with surroundings, such as tan clothes in the desert, or a chameleon changing its colors to avoid being seen

cataclysmic (kat-uh-kliz-mick): pg. 46 — adjective / violently destructive, such as a natural event like an earthquake or a flood

coda (koh-duh): pg. 97 — noun / a musical passage that appears at the end of the main section

conspicuous (con-spic-u-us): pg. 153 — adjective / highly noticeable and attracting of attention

credenza (kri-den-zuh): pg. 65 — noun / a piece of furniture that serves as a cabinet or storage space

culottes (koo-lats): pg. 134 — noun / a French word referring to pants or split skirts

defiant (di-fy-ant): pg. 46 — adjective / stubbornly resistant and willing to fight against an opposing force

enchant (in-chant): pg. 80 — verb / to bewitch or put under a spell

epic (eh-pick): pg. 57 — noun / a lengthy poem or story of heroes and adventure, often passed down from generations; also can be an adjective describing something long or monumental

hippogriff (hi-poh-griff): pg. 137 — noun / a legendary creature with the head and wings of an eagle and the body of a horse

hurtling (hur-tuh-ling): pg. 112 — verb / to move at fast speed, often on course to collide with something

inherent (in-hair-ent): pg. 112 — adjective / an essential or fixed part of something

initiative (in-ish-uh-tiv): pg. 107 — noun / the motivation, desire, or ability to begin doing something

lateral (la-ter-uhl): pg. 134 — adjective / to the side, rather than forward or backward

libel (lie-bull): pg. 95 — verb / to make a false statement about someone in a publication

paradigm shift (pair-uh-dime shift): pg. 54 — noun / an important change in the traditional way of thinking about something

photosynthesis (foe-toe-sin-thuh-sis): pg. 107 — noun / the process by which green plants use sunlight to create food, using carbon dioxide and water to produce oxygen

psychosomatic (sigh-koh-suh-ma-tick): pg. 127 — adjective / relating to a physical illness or condition that is caused by mental or emotional stress

righteous indignation (rhy-chess in-dig-nay-shun): pg. 74 — noun / anger over the mistreatment or insult of another

steeplechase (stee-puhl-chays): pg. 114 — noun / a type of horse race that requires jumping over obstacles

superficial (soo-per-fish-uhl): pg. 91 — adjective / refers only to the surface or what is apparent from the outside

validity (vuh-lid-di-tee): pg. 101 — noun / the quality of being logical and accurate

vanquishing (vayn-kwish-ing): pg. 46 — verb / able to defeat or conquer an enemy

waxing nostalgic (waks-ing nah-stahl-jick): pg. 18 — verb phrase / "to wax" is to grow bigger in size or intensity, and "nostalgia" is a longing for the past, so someone who is "waxing nostalgic" is becoming more nostalgic as they talk about or remember something

Phoebe and Her Unicorn is distributed internationally by Andrews McMeel Syndication.

Andrews McMeel Publishing
a division of Andrews McMeel Universal
1130 Walnut Street, Kansas City, Missouri 64106

www.andrewsmcmeel.com

19 20 21 22 23 SDB 10 9 8 7 6 5 4 3 2 1

ISBN: 978-1-4494-9938-9

Library of Congress Control Number: 2018953524

Made by:
Shenzhen Donnelley Printing Company Ltd.
Address and location of manufacturer:
No. 47, Wuhe Nan Road, Bantian Ind. Zone,
Shenzhen China, 518129
1st Printing—1/28/19

Check out more *Phoebe and Her Unicorn*

Unicorn on a Roll
Another Phoebe and Her Unicorn Adventure
Dana Simpson

Unicorn vs. Goblins
Another Phoebe and Her Unicorn Adventure
Dana Simpson

Razzle Dazzle Unicorn
Another Phoebe and Her Unicorn Adventure
Dana Simpson

Unicorn Crossing
Another Phoebe and Her Unicorn Adventure
Dana Simpson

Phoebe and Her Unicorn in
The Magic Storm
Dana Simpson

Phoebe and Her Unicorn in
Unicorn Theater
Dana Simpson

If you like Phoebe, look for these books!

Anne of Green Gables
a graphic novel

OZY AND MILLIE
Dana Simpson
AUTHOR OF PHOEBE AND HER UNICORN

WALLACE the BRAVE
Will Henry

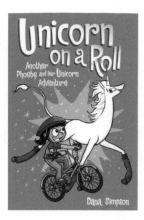

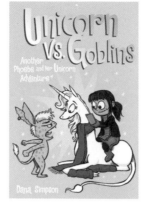

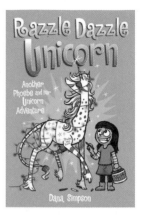

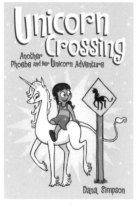

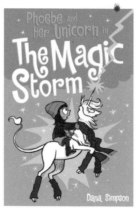

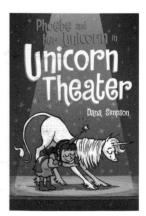

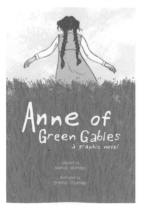

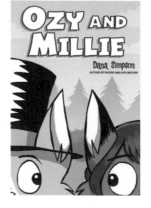

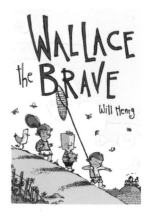